Nevertheless, She Preached

Margaret T. Kutz

Tracy-
Keep on
the journey.
Marg

Nevertheless, She Preached

Nevertheless, She Preached:
The Story of the Two Earliest Methodist Clergywomen in Virginia

Margaret T. Kutz

Nevertheless, She Preached

DEDICATION

**Dedicated to the Memory of
Reverend Rita Ann Callis
whose deep friendship informed this story.**

Nevertheless, She Preached

Table of Contents

Introduction

$\mathcal{L}$ike Joseph in Genesis and Joseph in the Gospel of Matthew, God often speaks to me in dreams. In October 2017, through a dream, I received an invitation to write the story of Lillian Russell and Mildred Long. I knew even as I dreamed that this invitation came from God. Lillian Russell and Mildred Long were names I first heard in 1976. But they were only names to me. A generation older, they preached in churches before I was even born.

I started research in the most obvious places: the Methodist archives, Google, Ancestory.com, and Newspapers.com. Over the next three years, I interviewed dozens of family members, former parishioners, clergy, and historians. I traveled to their places of birth, employment, and burial. I contacted their schools and climbed pull-down staircases into church attics. I followed every lead I could find.

Sometimes I talked to Mildred and Lillian, especially when I came to a dead end. "Lillian, if you want me to include this in the book, please provide the information. Guide me." I would then get very still and wait. Every time, a next step would appear, and the story continued.

In the institutional archives I learned the facts of their lives, such as names, dates, and places. In the local church records, I read Lillian and Mildred's pastor's reports, Bible studies, and prayers. But in the interviews of family and parishioners, I met them as real people.

Lillian and Mildred were vastly different from each other in personality, but were equally remarkable people. Before I typed one word of the book, I was in awe of them.

Organizing and putting their story into words has been one of the greatest privileges and challenges of my life. After talking to Connie Lapallo, author of several books on the women of Jamestown, I selected historical fiction as the preferred literary style to convey Mildred and Lillian as real people. Mainly through dialogue, fiction allows readers into the lives of people. I wanted readers to get to know them as I had grown to know them. Connie told me it is not unusual for people who write historical biographies, fiction or non-fiction, to feel called to do so, much as I had in that dream. Many authors also feel the presence of the characters in the process of their research and writing. It's as if there is a force that compels people to write the stories that will keep alive the Spirits of those who have gone before us.

Historical fiction is, by some standards, an oxymoron: history is factual; fiction is not. I looked for the facts, connected those dots as they made sense to me, and filled in the rest with imagination. Where I got it wrong, I apologize.

Often I questioned why God had asked me instead of some seasoned author. But when researching, I learned that my knowledge of and experience as a clergywoman in The United Methodist Church in Virginia was critical to putting the pieces together.

Writing a book is much harder than I ever imagined. Considering all the papers I had written for school and sermons for forty years of weekly preaching, I thought writing this book would be like riding a bike, natural. That was not the case. I had so much to learn. The peer editing groups helped me understand the need for character distinction and development and all the nitty-gritty of correct punctuation, grammar, formatting, and all the rest. Their patience with me and investment in this book has been a true gift. I thank Judith Howell, George Klein, Linda Lyons-Bailey, Cecilia Vaughan, Cathy Hill, and Joe Erhardt.

Many thanks to all the people who have helped with the research, to those who have dug into basement records or the recesses of their memories. Stephanie Davis, director of United Methodist archives for Virginia, bent over backward to research all my many questions in a timely way. Reverend Raymond Wrenn, retired United Methodist clergy in the Virginia Conference, was a tremendous help. Even as a centenarian, his unbelievable memory guided me on all things concerning Virginia Methodism.

Reverend Alvin J. Horton, a colleague and friend, served as a gifted story-development editor. During the 1980s, Al had also prepared the way for me to be appointed to St. Luke's United Methodist Church in Falls Church by inviting me to preach during his tenure there. When the district superintendent expressed concern as to what church might receive me as their pastor, he was puzzled when St. Luke's asked for me by name. They said, "We'll take a lady preacher if she's like Margaret Kutz." Thanks, Al!

My family and friends have served as patient support and encouragement. Special thanks to my long-suffering husband for the years I squirreled away in some corner of the house to write or packed up and drove to some corner of Virginia to do research, and for the many nights I spent with the peer-editors rather than him.

I pray this book accurately reflects the journey Mildred and Lillian traveled. May everyone who reads *Nevertheless, She Preached* be challenged and encouraged in their own journey to live the Gospel Lillian and Mildred so faithfully preached.

For more information, photos, and suggestions when using this book in a group discussion, check out the website: www.neverthelessshepreached.net

Nevertheless, She Preached

Chapter One
An Orchid

And why take ye thought for raiment?
Consider the lilies of the field, how they grow;
they toil not, neither do they spin.
Matthew 6:21 KJV

*L*illian looked out the streetcar window, her reflection in the glass as clear as the one in her mirror at home in the bedroom she shared with her sisters. The image confirmed the talent of her mother to braid hair perfectly. The light pink lipstick and blush gave color to her otherwise pale young face, blue eyes, and blond hair. She gave herself a brief smile as she smoothed her skirt on her lap, sat up straight, and repositioned her black lace-up shoes on the rumbling floor.

The warmth of the early spring sun drew her eyes upward past the second-story of the redbrick buildings along Broad Street. Even with the blue sky, Richmond felt dreary. Boarded-up storefronts displayed signs reading "closed." The sidewalks carried few shoppers.

Coming out of the corner grocery store, she spotted a mother with a child in one hand and a bag of groceries in the other. Child and mother wore black shoes, black skirts, white blouses, and gray sweaters. Neither appeared happy nor encouraged by the warm sun.

Lillian noted a black car parked along the curb with two flat tires. These terrible times had sucked the color, warmth, and air from everything and everyone.

Lillian heard the clang of the bell signifying the streetcar was about to make a stop. The brakes squealed, and the back-and-forth motion of the car ended with a pitched forward. Lillian looked down at the curb, surprised to see a flower growing out of the cracks. She turned so she could see the blossom better. Surely her eyes were deceiving her. It looked like an orchid—a small, perfect, white orchid. Lillian had seen pictures of them in books but had never seen a live one. *Those grow in the tropics, where it's warm and wet. How in the world could this possibly be?* She rubbed her eyes and lurched backward as the streetcar continued down the street. Lillian looked back, but the flower was gone.

An orchid. At lunch today, I have to walk back to that very spot and confirm what I think I saw. Maybe I should take somebody with me, just to be sure. Something as delicate as an orchid could not be in the cracks of the streets of Richmond, Virginia, in March. Impossible. But nothing is impossible for God. That's what the angel Gabriel said to Mary at the annunciation.

Lillian's thoughts were interrupted by the streetcar bell. "Next stop, Sixth Street," said the driver.

Lillian prepared to debark. In her left hand, she carried the sack lunch her mother had made her—likely a sandwich, pickles, and cookie. Her purse strap was over her shoulder. With her right hand, she grabbed the handle to help her navigate the steep steps down to the street. It was just a block to Miller and Rhoads. Lillian worked in the fabric department on the third floor of the five-story department store. She enjoyed the work and her co-workers. Every penny earned she gave to her mother to help with household expenses. When there was less than a yard of fabric at the end of a bolt and prices reduced, Lillian bought the remnant if she considered it practical for some use in her family.

I wouldn't have gotten this position if it weren't for my

grandmother. I remember we started with buttons when I was just five years old. I cried every time I stabbed myself with the needle. Grandmother told me to stick my finger in my mouth, and it would stop hurting. She was right. By the time she died, I had made skirts, blouses, dresses, and even lined suits. There aren't many questions customers have for me that I can't answer. Lillian looked up toward the sky. *Thanks, Nanna.*

As Lillian walked through the front door, she made a mental note to look for the flower on her lunch break. She had thirty minutes, plenty of time to eat, and walk down the street to the spot where she saw it. The whole image of an orchid growing in a city street roused impossible ideas in her head.

Is this a sign? The preacher has been talking about signs, mostly signs of hope. He's been encouraging us during these dismal times to look for them. He says they are everywhere for those who have eyes to see. Is this a sign for me? While I've never seen a real orchid, I sometimes feel like one. Mama and Daddy treat me like I'm fragile, delicate, like an orchid, and they love to dress me in white. But the rest of the world doesn't treat me that way. I'm just another girl with a useless high school diploma. They've thrown me to the street. Is this orchid a sign God has a plan for me? Maybe I am to bloom right here where I am planted.

Lillian walked to the back of the store to put her lunch in her cubby in the employee room. She climbed the stairs to the third floor and joined her co-worker, Betsy. They scanned the area to see what needed to be done and then organized fabric and notions scattered by customers the night before. By 10:00 A.M., customers began arriving, and the rest of the morning went as usual.

"Betsy, do you want to have lunch together?" Lillian asked.

"Of course. Don't we eat together every day?"

"Yes, we do. But today, I'd like to take a little walk down Broad Street to check on something. It's not far, and the weather is good."

"Sure, I'm always ready for something different," said Betsy. "Just as long as we have time to eat. I'm starved."

Betsy was twenty years old, three years older than Lillian. Miller and Rhoads encouraged the sewing department employees to wear clothing they had made from fabric purchased at the store. It was good for business, they said. Some days Betsy and Lillian wore identical dresses. On this particular day, they wore the same style skirt but made from different fabrics.

"So, what's down the street that you want to see? A handsome boy?" Betsy said with a smile.

"No, not a *boy* but a *flower*."

"A flower? You want us to walk down Broad Street to see a flower?"

"Yes. I saw it, or at least I think I saw it, from the streetcar. It was growing out of the crack in the curb," said Lillian.

"That's not so unusual. However, it's a little early in the season. What kind of flower was it?" asked Betsy.

"That's the thing," said Lillian. "I think it was an orchid."

"An orchid? Now, that's impossible."

"That's the same thing I thought," said Lillian, "But humor me and walk with me. We can stop at one of the benches and eat our lunch. Is that all right?"

"Sure, let's go."

Lillian and Betsy grabbed their lunches from the employee room and made their way out the front door to Sixth Street.

"Betsy, you never met my grandmother," Lillian said. "She died five years ago. But I've been thinking about her a lot today. When women got the right to vote just ten years ago, Nanna was so excited. She never marched in the streets or even wrote her representative, but she was very much in favor of women's suffrage. She never thought she would see it in her lifetime."

Lillian stepped behind Betsy, and they walked single-file long enough to allow a man in a business suit to pass them. Then they went back to walking in pairs.

"Your grandmother must have been a wonderful woman. You talk about her often," said Betsy.

"She was. I'm glad she didn't live long enough to see the steps backward for women since the stock market crash. I

4

wouldn't have this job if a man wanted it. So many women have lost their jobs so an unemployed man can have it. Nanna had grand plans for me. She wanted my dreams to be about more than a husband and children, although the family was the most critical part of her life. She just believed I could be a wife and mother *and* have an education and a career. Not just a *job*, but a *career*. She believed I could have it all, that I could be pretty *and* smart. When I was encouraged to advance a grade in school, my Nanna was all in favor of that. My Nanna believed in the impossible, like an orchid growing in the streets of Richmond in March."

"So where's that orchid?" asked Betsy. "I don't see anything."

"I don't either. This is the streetcar stop. I was sitting in the third seat back, so right about here." Lillian calculated the spot along the curb.

Both Betsy and Lillian looked down at the spot and then up and down the curb. "Maybe somebody picked it. I know I would," said Betsy.

"Or maybe it was meant only for me. A sign for me," whispered Lillian.

"Or maybe you're seeing things," responded Betsy. "Anyway, it's not here. Let's start back toward the store and stop at the bench to have lunch. Did I mention I'm starved?"

"You're starved every day," said Lillian and then chuckled.

The two of them walked to the bench, had lunch, and went back to work. Lillian couldn't get the image of the orchid out of her mind. She would wait as Mary did, wait for evidence that this was her sign of hope. She didn't have to wait long.

Chapter Two
Girl Evangelist

Then said I, Ah, Lord God! Behold, I cannot speak, for I am a child.
But the Lord said unto me, Say not, I am a child;
For thou shalt go to all that I shall send thee,
And whatsoever I command thee thou shalt speak.
Be not afraid of their faces;
for I am with thee to deliver thee, saith the Lord.
Jeremiah 1:6-8 KJV

Goldie Russell called to her daughter, her voice echoing down the hallway of the small white frame house in Richmond, Virginia. "Lila, you have a letter. I think it might be important. Do you want me to open it?"

"I'm coming right now, Mama," Lillian's voice came from the back of the house.

She ran down the hallway to the foyer, where her mother stood beside the mail slot with the afternoon-mail in her hand. The letter addressed "Miss Lillian Russell" was on top. Lillian took the letter from her mother, noting the postmark of July 30, 1931. She examined the return address before carefully opening the envelope. It was from the Reverend Ralph Yow. "I wonder why he is writing to me. Maybe he wants me to help with the young people at his church."

"Don't guess, Lila. Read the letter!" said Lillian's mother with an impatient smile.

Lillian unfolded the letter, took a deep breath, exhaled, and read.

> *Dear Miss Russell,*
>
> *I have heard a multitude of accolades concerning your sermon at Highland Park Methodist Church last Sunday. The congregation at Fairmount Avenue Methodist Church, where I have the privilege of serving as the pastor, has encouraged me to invite you to serve as our evangelist for a two-week revival series in October 1931. Indeed, it would be my honor to have you in my pulpit during this revival. You may select your theme and scriptures.*
>
> *Please respond at your earliest convenience.*
>
> *Sincerely,*
>
> *Rev. Ralph Yow*

Mother and daughter stared at each other with their jaws open. Lillian's mother broke the silence. "What an honor. I don't know what to say. You're so young, just seventeen. We had better speak with your daddy before we do anything else."

Lillian said, almost in a whisper. "My heart says, 'Yes!' but my Spirit says, 'Pray.' Yes, let's do talk to daddy. And let us both pray."

The Russell household was no stranger to spontaneous prayer. They were as likely to drop to their knees at the front door as they were at the side of their beds. Active members at Highland Park Methodist Church in Richmond, the entire family read the Bible daily and adhered to its teachings. This meant absolutely no dancing, cards, alcohol, or tobacco in the Russell household.

Both Lillian and her mother knelt in prayer. After a moment of silence, Goldie began, "Holy Father, a great invitation to serve has come to this house. Calm our hearts and let us be still and know that You are God. Contain our pride and lead us to Your perfect will."

After more silence, Lillian continued the prayer. "Precious Savior, You were just twelve years old when Your parents found You in the temple teaching. Help me not to fear anything except disobedience to You."

"Amen," said both mother and daughter and returned to their feet.

"Your daddy should be home in about four hours. We'll talk to him after dinner. Let's not speak of this to anyone until we talk to him."

"Yes, Mama," Lillian agreed and went upstairs to her bedroom.

The late hours of the afternoon crawled along as Lillian paced in the small bedroom she shared with her three sisters: twenty-two-year-old Virginia, ten-year-old Hazel, and seven-year-old Polly. She tried to pray and read scripture, but her head swirled with a thousand thoughts. *Two-week revival. I've been to many of those, and the speakers have been inspirational, anointed with the power of the Holy Spirit. Have I been anointed for this?*

Lillian decided to go outside. Maybe the fresh air would clear her head. She went downstairs, to the back of the house, and out the door. She sat in the swing her daddy had hung from a large tree limb years ago. As she sat there, her feet dangling, she took note of her black laced shoes. They're *so small, like the shoes of a child. I am so young. Am I too young? Can anybody be too young? David was young but fought for God against Goliath. Jeremiah was young when he became a prophet of God. The Bible is full of people who served God when young like me. Maybe graduating from high school at age fifteen is part of God's plan for me to preach at such a young age.*

Lillian so wanted to talk to her grandmother, Annie Shepherdson. She was her mother's mother and had lived with them, even shared a bedroom with Lillian for several years until her death five years earlier. Grandmother Shepherdson would know what to say. Lillian could almost imagine the scene in her mind.

Lillian's grandmother would walk out the back door to the tree where Lillian was sitting, staring down at her feet. She would know something was troubling Lillian and would ask in her gentle voice, "What seems to be the matter, my dear girl?"

Lillian would look up at her grandmother and share the news. "I got a letter today from Reverend Yow inviting me to be the speaker at a two-week revival at his church."

"My sweet child, that is quite an honor. What do you think?" her grandmother would ask.

"I don't know what to think. I've taught Sunday School in Daddy's class—the only female, young or old, to ever be invited. They seem to like what I have to share." Lillian would assure herself and remind her grandmother.

"And you've taught many times in your mother's class. They genuinely love having you—you're probably their favorite teacher, after your mother, of course. They know you to be a serious student of the Bible and a person who tries to live her faith."

"Thank you, Nanna. I always accept these invitations with great seriousness." Lillian would respond.

"Well, I'm going to go inside and help your mother with dinner. Will you check on the chickens and be sure we got all the eggs this morning?" Grandmother would ask, always concerned to get every dime they could from those chickens.

"Yes, Mam, I'll do that."

Lillian imagined her grandmother walking back through the yard and into the house. As the image disappeared from her mind, Lillian got up from the swing and walked to the chicken coop. She didn't spot any eggs.

It had been more than a year since the stock market crash of 1929. Times were increasingly difficult. Nearly every household had a garden and chickens. The chickens and the garden were her mother's projects. She had enough chickens to provide eggs daily and meat for Sunday dinner, plus extra to sell to the local grocery store. Reverend Yow did not mention anything about money for preaching. She knew that evangelists generally received something for their efforts. Indeed, any money she might earn in those two weeks would help her family. Her hours at the department store were not steady and provided minimal finances.

Then her mind reverted to its circles of self-doubt. *But I'm a girl. I've heard women evangelists, and they've been equally as good as men, equally anointed of God. But young and a girl, I don't know. Maybe I should wait until I'm older. Perhaps I should wait until I get married and serve under the authority of my husband.*

Her father had steady work as a typewriter machinist at American Typewriter Exchange, making typewriters, mimeographs, and adding machines. He had completed only the eighth grade but loved to read and was what he called "self-educated." He was also an entrepreneur. In addition to a job at the typewriter company, he had his own typewriter repair shop in their garage. By now, every member of the Russell household over the age of six knew something about repairing typewriters. He had taught all of them, and they helped him when needed.

Lillian walked to the garage, but her father had locked the door the night before. She was considering whether to get the key when her thoughts were interrupted by her friend Georgia. "Hey, Lillian! Glad to catch you outside. Did you hear the news about Elizabeth?" Georgia was about to burst with whatever she knew about Elizabeth, a girl in the neighborhood.

Friendships had been complicated for Lillian. By the age of twelve, she had already advanced two years in school ahead of other children her age. Two years later, she advanced a third year. She never knew where she belonged. The girls in her grade were three years older than she. It wasn't that they were more mature than Lillian; they were just interested in things, mostly boys, that she was not. But the girls who were her same age and three years behind her in school seemed so immature. Now, with her sister getting married, she was beginning to entertain the idea of a boyfriend, but the timing just seemed wrong. Maybe she'd missed her opportunity.

Lillian feigned her best smile and looked at Georgia. *Could two girls be any more different? Georgia was confident about her place in the world. Waltzing into our backyard, freely sharing information, and not afraid to pry for more. I'm so timid, so uncertain. I walk in the neighborhood because I have a purpose that provides me permission, like going to church, catching the trolley, or taking cookies to a neighbor. It's as if there's an invisible fence keeping me in. I can't imagine walking into Georgia's backyard and telling her all about the latest news, like my sister's wedding plans. Maybe I should be bolder.*

Lillian then spoke in a tone that was anything but bold. "Oh, hi, Georgia. I've been pretty busy today, so I haven't talked to anybody but family."

"Gee, Lillian, you're such a homebody. You need to get out more, have some fun. You're too serious. Now, about Elizabeth."

Lillian's mother's voice calling from the screen door saved her from the rest of the conversation. "Lila, your daddy is home. Come help get dinner on the table."

"Sorry, I have to run," said Lillian, and she hurried inside her house. The younger children were crowded around the kitchen sink, washing their hands.

During dinner, everyone took turns talking about their day. E.W. told about his work at the typewriter shop. "I'm not sure what was going on today, but the place was so busy. We had orders for every piece of equipment we make. I was so busy that I almost forgot to eat the delicious lunch your mother packed for me." He gave Goldie a warm smile and winked.

Then Lillian's siblings all had a turn. Virginia, whom everyone called Boots, started. At age twenty-two and recently engaged to be married, they daily heard the news about wedding preparations. Everyone learned every detail about her dress, the invitations, the flowers, everything, right down to the punch. Usually, Lillian enjoyed hearing her sister talk. Boots had just graduated from college and was the smartest woman Lillian knew. She counted on Boots' wisdom for guidance almost as much as her parents. But tonight, she just wanted dinner to be over. That was not to be as Virginia talked on about wedding flowers.

"I wish I could capture the magnolias in bloom, but that isn't possible. So, I guess by October, we'll have to rely on asters and maybe some early camellias. Flowers are a challenge in the fall. Well, it's too late now to change the date of the wedding."

Ernest, at age sixteen, was a large, muscular young man. As the oldest boy, he felt responsible for helping his family as much as possible. He had dropped out of the ninth grade to allow Boots to complete college. Work was not easy to come by, but Ernest worked wherever he could find it. Sometimes that was at the docks along the James River; other times, he delivered milk when one of the other men was out sick.

"I rode my bike down to the docks early this morning, but there wasn't much work. We heard there was a boat coming in mid-morning, so I hung around. Sure enough, around 9:30, a small barge docked, and we had some loading and unloading to do. But that was it for the day. I found a few friends, and we played some baseball in the lot at the corner. Mama, I put the little money from today's work in the jar in the kitchen." His mother nodded.

Lawrence was thirteen, tall for his age, and very athletic. He spent most of his summers helping around the house by feeding the chickens and cleaning out their coop. He also helped at their typewriter shop but tried to get away to be with his friends as often as he could.

Lawrence said, "I had a great time today. A group of us took off on our bikes. We went everywhere around Richmond. Did you know there was a fire over on Fifth Avenue last night? Burned the house to the ground. We looked through the rubble but didn't find a thing."

Goldie put her fork down and looked square at her son. "Lawrence, you should know better than to go through somebody's belongings, especially after a tragedy like a fire. What would you have done if you had found something? If you were to take anything, it would be stealing."

E.W. chimed in. "Your mama's right. What would you have done had you found anything?"

"Of course, I would've given it to the police. I know better than to steal."

With that, everybody relaxed, and the dinner conversation continued. Now it was Hazel's turn. She was ten years old and blonde, like most of her siblings. Her job was gathering the eggs every morning.

Then there were the twins, Pete and Polly, everybody's favorites. They were seven years old and full of life. For them, the economic difficulties were just a normal part of life.

"We had a great time today playing with the new kids down the block. They're from Washington, D.C. They talk so funny we could hardly understand them," said Polly, bobbing her blonde curls.

And so the chatter went on. Back and forth, around the table. Lillian thought, *Will this dinner ever end?*

Finally, everyone finished, the table cleared, and the dishes washed and put away. Goldie motioned to Lillian. It was time to go into the living room and speak with E.W. Lillian pulled the letter out of her pocket as they sat down on the sofa across from E.W.'s chair.

Goldie began, "E.W., Lila received a letter today. It's from Reverend Yow. Lila, show him the letter."

Lillian gave the envelope to her father. He opened it, unfolded the letter, read it, refolded it, and put it back in the envelope. His face took on a serious tone with lips pinched, brow furrowed, and eyes fixed on the letter and envelope. "This is quite an honor, Lila. What do you think?"

"I don't know what to think, Daddy."

"Have you prayed about it?"

"Yes, I've done nothing but pray since the letter arrived."

"Do you have an answer from God?"

"I believe I do."

"Before you say more, I want to share a story with you." E.W. repositioned himself in his chair, took a deep breath, and began his story.

"When you were a small child, you were very sick."

"Yes, I remember you telling me," said Lillian.

"Yes, but we have not told you everything. It's time now

for you to hear the whole story. You were so ill the doctor was uncertain you would survive. Your mother and I had already lost one child—our second child, to pneumonia. So I prayed to God that if you were allowed to live, I would make certain you would give your life to the service of God. Lila, do you think this is God's invitation?"

Lillian looked down at her hands, folded in her lap, then looked up at her father. "Yes, Daddy, I do believe this is of God. I'm terrified but also quite confident that I am to do this."

"Then I'll take you to visit Reverend Yow in the morning, and you'll give him your response." E.W. looked out the window then back at Lillian before continuing. "You have a couple of months to prepare but sharing a room with your sisters is insufficient for the uninterrupted time you'll need. I'll make space for you in my typewriter repair shop outback. You know the closet in the back of the garage. It will be your study. You already have your Bible, and we'll see to it that you have paper, pencils, and a typewriter. Bible commentaries, you can borrow. God heard my prayer when you were near death, and now God has extended His hand to you. We need to pray."

All three of them sank to their knees on the braided living room rug, and E.W. led them in prayer. Something in Lillian's Spirit changed. She felt she was no longer the same seventeen-year-old girl. God was preparing her to be an evangelist of the Gospel.

The next morning, E.W. put on his white shirt, blue tie, and gray suit. Lillian put on a dress her mother had made earlier that same summer, white with pink flowers and a lace collar. The sleeves cupped just below the shoulder, and the waist gathered with a white belt.

"Well, don't you two look mighty handsome this morning. It must be Sunday! Reverend Yow will know you took his invitation seriously," said Goldie to her husband and daughter.

Lillian fidgeted with her belt, not sure which notch to use. One seemed too tight and one too loose.

"Use the loose one, Lila. It's hot, and your waist will

appreciate the space," instructed Goldie.

"You're right; I'll do that. Is my hair all right? I braided it three times, trying to get it as tight as possible so no strand would come loose." Lillian fussed with her hair.

"You look beautiful, perfect. Now let's get going so we won't be late," said Lillian's father with a smile.

With that, Lillian and E.W. went out the front door, turned, and walked toward the church. Lillian knew her father was aware of her nervousness because he kept trying to make small talk. His attempts were futile. Lillian couldn't relax enough to utter a word. She just stared at the sidewalk. Finally, E.W. gave up, and they completed the trip in silence.

Reverend Yow had just arrived at church and was walking up the front steps to the church. He greeted them both with a handshake and warm smile and invited them into his office. After all three of them were seated, Reverend Yow said, "Let us pray. "Holy Father, we give you thanks for this morning. May we know your guidance in this conversation and may all we think and speak be pleasing to you. Amen."

Then Reverend Yow looked at Lillian and said, "I understand from your father that you have received my letter."

"Yes, we have," responded E.W., "and that is why we have come. Lila, tell the reverend what you are thinking."

Lillian looked down at her hands as they pressed the fabric of her white floral dress. She was wanting to dry the sweat to calm the nerves that were causing the perspiration.

"Reverend Yow, I'm honored, no humbled, by your invitation." Lillian had been rehearsing her part of this conversation most of the night. She hoped no one would interrupt her because she didn't want to forget anything. She wanted Reverend Yow and her father to understand how she had gotten to her decision.

"While I have some experience speaking to Methodist young people in Richmond, sometimes speaking to a small group and sometimes speaking to more than one hundred young people, this invitation is different. I'll be preaching to hundreds of people of all ages and denominations in the Richmond area, not one night, but ten nights. When speaking to youth, I often wrote plays, created Bible quizzes, or dressed as a Bible character. But this is quite different."

Reverend Yow was attentive to this young woman in his office, allowing her to speak as long as she wanted. He appeared mesmerized by her intensity.

Lillian continued. "I know that on my own, I'm not able to preach a two-week revival, but I also know that God is able and will provide. I know God has called me to do this and, with God as my helper, I will do the absolute best I can. God will do the rest. I can't believe I'm saying this, but I accept your invitation to serve as the revival speaker in October."

A big smile came over the faces of the pastor and the father. Reverend Yow clasped his hands in front of his face, a gesture somewhere between applause and prayer. E.W. leaned back in his chair and let out a long breath.

Still smiling, Reverend Yow put his hands down on the arms of his chair. "All right, Lillian, the matter is settled. Two weeks before the revival, I will need to know your scriptures and sermon titles. That is for the bulletins. I will also need your picture, revival theme, and some information about you. That is for the paper. On the last night of the revival, you will receive half of the offering as an honorarium. Will that be acceptable?"

Lillian responded, "I'll abide by your timeline. The honorarium is more than acceptable. Please continue to pray for me daily, and I'll pray for you and your church daily."

After a brief prayer offered by Reverend Yow, E.W. and Lillian left the church and returned home. While Lillian didn't utter a peep on the way to the church, on the way home, she talked nonstop, as if she were thinking out loud. "I have an idea for the theme. It needs to be something that both invites non-believers to faith in Christ and helps Christians grow in their faith. I was thinking about 'The Faith that Wins.' I could preach on a different Bible character each night and how faith in Christ helped them win in life. Do you think that will work?"

But before E.W. could even answer, Lillian went on. "What about the music? I should have asked Reverend Yow if we need to provide anything. Everybody in Richmond knows the Russell family can sing. And Mama plays the autoharp. In fact, everybody in the Russell family can sing except me."

E.W. interrupted his daughter. "That's not true, Lila. You have a lovely voice."

As if Lillian never heard her father, she just kept talking. She talked about what to wear, from dress to shoes, where to get a picture taken for the newspaper, what to include in her biographical information. At seventeen, there wasn't much to write.

When they arrived at home, E.W. went inside to change into his work uniform and then went to work. Lillian also changed her clothes but then stayed in her bedroom to begin her preparation for the revival.

Several days later, Virginia and Lillian were in the kitchen cleaning up from dinner. Virginia put down the dishtowel, got a sly grin on her face, and said, "Lila, Mama and Daddy asked me to take you out to the space they're preparing to be your study area. Can you keep your eyes closed, or do I need to blindfold you?"

"Please don't blindfold me. I promise to keep my eyes closed," answered Lillian.

Boots led her sister out the back door, carefully navigating the two steps into the back yard, then across the yard and into the garage. They zigzagged around the tables of typewriter parts until they got to the back of the garage. When they walked inside the small room, Virginia said, "All right, you can open your eyes now."

Lillian opened her eyes and saw the former closet cleaned and the walls of dark clapboards painted a pale pink. Then it was as if a family parade had been organized. First came her father carrying a table. Ernest followed adding a chair. Behind him came their mother with a lamp. She plugged it into an extension cord, and the bulb lit. After everything was put into place, Lawrence carried in a typewriter and set it on the table. Hazel followed with a tablet of paper. Finally, Pete and Polly came in with a cup of pencils and pens. Everyone was smiling from ear to ear.

Lillian started to cry. This was becoming far too real. For some years, the Russell home's backyard was the location of two family businesses: a typewriter repair shop and a chicken farm. Now the city lot would add a third business: evangelist office. Lillian wanted to run back into their house, up the stairs to her bedroom, and climb under the covers of her bed. But before she could bolt, Virginia said, "Daddy, I think we should all join hands and pray. We need to consecrate this space to the work of God."

After they all joined hands, E.W., with a firm grip on Lillian's hand, prayed, "Loving God, we come to You in humility, thanking You for what we know will happen in this room. May the words read and written here reflect Your Word. May Your Holy Spirit give wisdom until Lila knows Your perfect will. We give You thanks now for what we know You will do. In the powerful name of Jesus, we pray. Amen."

E.W. turned to Lillian, still holding her hand, said, "As you know, we have a small religious library in our living room, including several Bible commentaries. You're allowed to take those to your study as long as you return them to the house each evening. Other books, you will need to borrow from the church library, our pastor's library, or the public library."

"Thank you, Daddy. These commentaries are like gold to me. I can't wait to get started. How late can I stay here tonight?"

They all laughed. "You can stay for an hour; then you need to come into the house. We'll be waiting for you," E.W. tapped his wristwatch. Lillian noted the time on her pocket watch pinned to her blouse.

Everyone left and closed the doors behind them, leaving Lillian alone in her new space. She had never had her own room in all her life, and, though this room was small, it was hers. She would hang a cross on the wall and maybe a calendar. She spent her hour that evening praying. It would take more than furniture to make this former closet an evangelist's study. It would take the Holy Spirit, and that would take prayer.

Chapter Three
First Revival

Revive us again; fill each heart with Thy love;
May each soul be rekindled with fire from above.
Hallelujah! Thine the glory, Hallelujah! Amen!
Hallelujah! Thine the glory, revive us again.
William P. Mackay, 1863

$\mathcal{L}$illian stepped out of her study to get some fresh air. She had been in that tiny room all morning. The bright sun blinded her from identifying the figure walking toward her.

"Hi, Lillian. I'm so glad I caught you."

Even before Lillian's eyes adjusted to recognize the figure, she recognized the voice. It was her friend, Georgia. "Oh, hi, Georgia. What's up?"

"What's up? Haven't you seen today's paper?"

"No, I've been pretty busy with other things," said Lillian trying to be vague.

"Well, you're on the front page of section B, complete with a picture. 'Girl Evangelist to Preach at Fairmount Methodist Revival,'" said Georgia with grand gestures that pointed to an imaginary banner in the sky. "All the neighborhood is talking about it. We knew you're working as a salesclerk downtown and that you're really into church, but we didn't know you're a preacher."

"I'm not a real preacher. I'm just preaching a revival."

"Sounds the same to me. But I guess I don't know much about revivals. We don't do those in my church."

Lillian drew a long breath and offered up a brief prayer for patience. Everyone knew Georgia was the community gossip, and Lillian knew Georgia had stopped by only to get information to spread in their neighborhood. "Sit down, Georgia, and I'll tell you how all this works."

Georgia and Lillian sat in the two chairs under the lone tree in the yard. "Georgia, revivals are special religious services churches hold about once a year. They are supposed to strengthen the faithful for greater service and convert the unbelievers. A guest speaker preaches a sermon each night. Some revivals last a week, but most are two weeks. The one at Fairmount is two weeks. So, I'll be preaching ten nights there starting this Sunday night."

"I'd be so nervous, standing up there in front of all those people. Aren't you nervous?" asked Georgia.

"Sure, I'm nervous. Who wouldn't be? It's a big responsibility usually reserved for seasoned preachers, grown men."

"Then how did you get asked? I mean, you're not a preacher, or a man, or much grown."

"The pastor at Fairmount invited me." Lillian stopped right there. She didn't think Georgia would understand her call from God. She would just tell her the facts, not the faith behind it.

"I'm not trying to be mean, but do you think anybody will come?" asked Georgia.

"I've wondered the same thing. I guess I'll find out. But I've helped with revivals at my church, and I know the work that everybody puts into them. There are prayer vigils. People visit door to door throughout the neighborhood around the church. They invite members who have become inactive, people from other churches, and people who don't go to church. And, as you see, they advertise in the newspaper. Do you have that article with you?"

"No, sorry, I didn't think to bring it. But it is a good picture of you - love your hair."

"Thanks. We went downtown to get a professional to take that picture."

"So, what happens at a revival?"

"There's singing, lots of singing. People read scripture and pray. I'll preach for about thirty to forty minutes. Then-"

Georgia interrupted Lillian. "Wait, you preach how long?"

"Thirty to forty minutes. It's standard at a revival. Some preach an hour or more, but mine will be closer to thirty. I've been timing the sermons, so I know how long they are."

"I can't imagine talking in front of a group for one minute, but thirty? Alright, what else happens?" continued Georgia, licking her lips as if biting into something delicious.

"Well, at the end, there's an altar call. People who have been moved by the Holy Spirit come forward to dedicate their lives to Christ. It's the highlight of the whole evening."

"Then what? What do you do when people come forward?"

"I kneel with them and pray for them. There will be others also, like the pastor of the church, who will be praying with people."

Georgia was curious. "What happens if nobody comes forward? That would be awkward."

"That does happen sometimes. Usually, the speaker keeps inviting people until somebody comes. The hymn *Just as I Am* has five stanzas, so there is time," said Lillian with a smile.

"*Just As I Am*, What is that?" Georgia obviously had never been to a revival.

"Oh, that's the song we often sing at the end of a revival service. There are other songs, but that's a favorite. It moves people to respond," Lillian explained.

"My mom told me that sometimes people faint in these services. Is that true?" Georgia's eyes were open wide and she leaned forward.

"It's called 'slain in the Spirit,' and it doesn't happen very often. When it does happen, it's generally not just one person but many people, so there are catchers to be sure nobody gets hurt."

"Slain in the Spirit, huh? I just might have to come. What else can you tell me?"

Lillian decided that if Georgia was going to share this conversation with the neighbors, she might as well tell her something exciting. "Well, sometimes when the Spirit is really strong, people may speak in tongues."

"Wait, what? Speak in tongues?" Now Georgia's eyes were really wide and she was sitting at the edge of her chair.

"The technical term is *glossolalia*. It's a special language given to some people allowing them to pray words that are on their hearts but not in their heads. Am I making sense?"

"No, not really, but keep going."

"When people speak in tongues, there are supposed to be people to interpret so everybody can understand them. Frankly, I've never seen anybody interpret tongues, so I'm not sure how that works. I just read about it in my studies."

"Wow, Lillian, this whole thing is amazing. I can hardly wait to tell our friends. We'll all be there to cheer for you."

"People don't cheer for revival speakers. But you can say 'Amen,'" said Lillian with a smile. She wasn't sure she wanted her friends present to hear her, but she guessed it was better than nobody.

Georgia got up from the chair and made a beeline out of the yard. She had news to share. Lillian sat there for a moment, wondering about the revival. She had been so focused on her sermons that she hadn't given much thought to the revival itself. The next thing she knew, her mother was sitting next to her with a copy of the *Richmond Times-Dispatch*. Goldie had folded it so the article about the revival was on top. There was Lillian's picture, big as life.

"It captures both your innocence and your beauty, don't you think? It's a good picture and a good article. In these difficult economic times, I think people will come. I heard one woman at church Sunday say that revivals were the cheapest entertainment in town. That is a bit crass for me, but I do think she has a point."

"You're probably right, Mama, but I like to think they're the spiritual highlights of the year. Hopefully, people come for better reasons than cheap entertainment. But whatever reason brings them; God's got them."

They both smiled. Goldie asked, "How are the sermons coming?"

"I've written all of them. This morning I started to edit them by reading them over and over. I want the messages to be perfect."

Goldie tried to respond, but Lillian just kept talking.

"Each night, I am going to preach a Bible story where, through faith, people prevailed. This will encourage people to greater faith, but even more important, it will draw non-Christians to a first-time decision to become a follower of the Savior. Mama, it's amazing; the words just seem to tumble out of my brain and into my fingers. I can't type fast enough. That has got to be evidence that I'm in God's perfect will for me."

Goldie patted her daughter's hand. "Yes, it is. Indeed, it is. Now let's go inside for a bite to eat. The children are at school, everybody else is working, or looking for work, so it's just you and me for lunch. Is a sandwich alright?"

"That sounds perfect. But one more thing, Mama." Lillian paused and looked up to the clouds in the sky. Then she looked back to her mother. "I want to have an orchid pinned to my dress when I preach the first night. Do you think that is possible?"

"Oh, Lila, I don't know. They are expensive and hard to come by. I'll ask your father. But why in the world an orchid?"

"It is a sign for me, Mama, and I'm gonna need a sign from God to do this."

"Alright, Lila, I'll ask, but no promises," Goldie said and shook her head. They both stood and went inside.

#####

Sunday morning the Russell family went to Highland Park

Methodist Church like they always did. Polly, Pete, and Hazel went to their Sunday School classes. Goldie was prepared to teach her women's Bible study class and E.W. his men's Bible study class. Ernest, Lawrence, and Lillian attended their class for single young adults. Lillian often taught this class, but she had asked someone else to teach in the weeks leading up to the revival. She did not have time to prepare adequately.

The excitement at church that morning was evident—everybody was talking about the revival starting that night at Fairmont. The newspaper article and picture had placed a celebrity in their midst, but not everyone's excitement was a celebration.

E.W. began his class as he always did with announcements of church activities. He highlighted the revival at Fairmont, encouraging everyone to attend. Just as he gave his final appeal, one of the men in the class queried him. "E.W., don't you have some concern about your daughter preaching? The Bible is quite clear on this matter."

E.W. cleared his throat to give himself time to think about his response, but before he could say a word, another man spoke. "I have the same concern. My wife and I aren't sure we're going to attend. It's not the proper role of women to preach. They're to be silent in church."

"Gentlemen, gentlemen," said E.W. "The role of women is not our topic this morning, but we can make it our topic next week if you so desire. That will give all of us time to study. What do you want to do? Shall we take a vote?"

"Yes, let's take a vote," said the first man to raise the issue. "All in favor, say yea."

Three men raised their hands and said, "Yea."

"Alright, all opposed to studying the role of women say Nay," say E.W.

The rest of the fifty-two men raised their hands and said, "Nay."

To get control of his class again, E.W. said, "The nays have it by a wide majority. I hope to see you all tonight at the revival.

Now let's pray."

Goldie's class went much the same way. A group of three women was chatting in a tight circle in the back of the Susannah Wesley classroom as Goldie was trying to call the class to order. They, like the men, started their class with announcements. Goldie encouraged everybody to attend the revival. One of the women who had been part of the three-some in the corner raised her hand and spoke. "I don't want to create any hard feelings, but my husband and I don't plan to attend any of the revivals because it's not biblical to have a female preach. I don't mean anything against Lillian. You know I love her as much as you all do, and I know she probably feels called to this, but the Bible is clear. Women should have no authority over men. Preaching to a church full of women *and* men is not fitting."

"Ladies, ladies," interrupted Goldie, "we are doing our announcements, not having a debate. Now, if there are no more announcements, then let us bow in prayer."

Between Sunday School and worship, Goldie and E.W. went to the fellowship hall for their usual time of conversation with church friends. Standing in one corner of the room, E.W. motioned for Goldie to come to him. She checked to assure Pete and Polly were all right and then walked over to her husband.

"We have a problem," said E.W. "Today in Sunday School, some of the men were objecting to Lila preaching the revival. I wasn't sure what to say. I think it was just a few because the majority voted not to conduct a study on the role of women."

"Goodness, no, not you too," said Goldie. She looked around to be sure nobody could hear them. "I had the same thing happen in my class. What are we going to do? It would crush Lila's heart to know her own church was questioning her right to preach a revival."

"I agree. We won't breathe a word of this to Lillian. She's nervous enough about tonight. We have to protect her from this ignorance."

"All right, we agree. I'll go grab the twins and meet you in the sanctuary," said Goldie.

Sunday night finally arrived. Lillian was so wound up she spun like a top, going here and there to make sure she had everything, her hair was perfect, her dress wrinkle-free, and her shoes shining. Her family tried to be supportive, but she was driving them crazy.

"Lila, for goodness sake, stop your spinning. You're making me dizzy," said her mother.

"I'm sorry. I'm just so nervous. Let me go upstairs to my room and pray. Hopefully, that will calm my nerves." Everybody agreed that was the evening's best idea and relaxed as they watched Lillian go up the steps.

"I'll call you when it's time to go," said E.W.

"I have my pocket watch. I'll know when it's time. Thanks, anyway," Lillian shouted down the steps. E.W. looked at his wife, and they both shook their heads.

In about fifteen minutes, Lillian came downstairs, composed, Bible in hand, a smile on her face, and said, "It's time. Let's go."

The whole family packed into the car, the twins on the knees of their older brothers. No one could sit on Lillian's lap. It would wrinkle her dress and crush the orchid pinned to it. The trip to the church wasn't long. The boys could have ridden their bikes, but that was not a proper way for the evangelist's family to arrive at a revival.

It was six o'clock, and the revival started at seven. Members of Fairmont Avenue Methodist Church were already gathering to prepare the sanctuary for the anticipated crowd. Even though it was a cool autumn evening, the ushers had opened the windows a crack. As soon as the sanctuary filled, it would get warm, and worshipers would welcome the cool air.

Lillian left her family in the narthex to look for Reverend Yow. The rest of the Russell family went to the piano in the sanctuary. Goldie touched the middle C key on the piano, and her husband and children hummed that pitch. Then E.W., using his right hand, provided the 4-4 rhythm, and with a nod of his head, directed them to sing. Their voices filled the sanctuary singing

There Is a Fountain. This song was a favorite at revivals because it was a rousing song about the power of the blood of Jesus. And it was easy to sing because they sang it in unison.

The second hymn, *When I Survey the Wondrous Cross*, was more meditative. That song they sang in perfect four-part harmony. By then, a few people had gathered in the sanctuary. Several people responded with "Amen" and applauded. The Russell family noted their approval with a nod and smile.

The twins sang the last song, *Jesus Loves Me*, as a duet. Their sweet yet strong voices carried to the back of the sanctuary. Hazel directed them much the same way E.W. had directed the older Russell children. Even Lawrence and Ernest had to admit their youngest siblings were pretty cute.

Lillian found Reverend Yow in his office. He gave her a copy of the bulletin. "We will process together during the opening hymn. You will sit on the pulpit side and me on the lectern side. After the Epistle Reading, I will introduce you. You will then read the Gospel Lesson and preach. Are you comfortable with the altar call, or do you want me to do that?"

"I believe I can do that. I have worked it into my closing remarks. Do you want me to pray with people who come forward?"

"Yes, please do. I will join you. If more people come forward than we can pray for, I have asked leaders in our church to come and pray with people. We should be able to manage as many as thirty people. Frankly, we can't fit any more than that at our rail. Do you have any other questions?"

"Yes, do you want me to pronounce the benediction, or will you do that?"

"Why don't you do that, Lillian? I prefer the speaker do that. If there is nothing else, let's pray. Do you want to invite your family to join us?

"No, we prayed at home, many times—many, many times," said Lillian with a half smile.

With that, Reverend Yow and Lillian joined hands and prayed.

Reverend Yow left his office to check on last-minute revival details. Lillian stayed in his office because she did not want to greet people as they came. They might notice her hands shaking. Besides, what if nobody comes? She would just wait until Reverend Yow came to get her. Five minutes before seven o'clock, Reverend Yow returned to his office. "It's time, Lillian. Are you ready?"

"As ready as I'll ever be."

"I think you'll be amazed at the crowd tonight. The ushers are setting up chairs in the aisles. You and I will need to process single-file. I can feel the Spirit moving." Reverend Yow said as they stood in the vestibule.

"Me, too," responded Lillian.

The piano provided the introduction to the hymn, and the people stood to sing.

We praise Thee, O God! For the Son of Thy love,
for Jesus who died and is now gone above.
Hallelujah!
Thine the glory, Hallelujah! Amen;
Hallelujah! Thine the glory, revive us again.

The sound of their voices was glorious to Lillian's ears and spirit.

Reverend Yow motioned to Lillian to walk down the center aisle. She placed her feet, dressed in black patent-leather shoes, into the center aisle. With her hymnal in her hand, she sang with as much enthusiasm as her nerves would allow. Reverend Yow followed behind her. At the end of the aisle, she walked up the three steps to the chancel area, turned left toward the pulpit and the chair behind it designated as the "pulpit chair" or "preacher's chair." When she got to her chair, she looked out over the sanctuary. It was packed. Every pew was full, and people were sitting in chairs lined up and down the side and center aisles. The Spirit was here. She was going to be alright.

Reverend Yow invited everyone to be seated. That was when Lillian realized the furniture company did not design the tall pulpit chair for her. When she sat down, her feet did not touch the floor and her black patent-leather shoes fell off her feet. Clunk! Clunk! Thankfully, the rustling of this large crowd taking their seats drowned out the sound of her shoes hitting the wood floor. She immediately scooted out of the chair, placed her feet back in her shoes, and found a spot at the edge of the chair where she could be seated and still have her feet safely on the floor.

Worship opened with a welcome, prayers, and more hymns. Then came scriptures, testimonies of faith, special music by her family, and an offering.

Finally, Reverend Yow introduced Lillian. "Brothers and sisters, it is my honor to introduce our revival speaker, Miss Lillian Russell. She and her family are active members at Highland Park Methodist Church. Many of you know them from their work in the Richmond District. Some of you young people know Miss Russell from her work with the young people in the district. I have heard her speak. She is gifted and speaks with the power of God. You will not be disappointed." He then looked at Lillian. "Miss Russell, please bring the Good News of Jesus Christ to this hungry crowd. We are waiting."

Lillian stood to read the Gospel lesson. That's when she realized she couldn't see over the pulpit. So she stood on her toes. That seemed to help a little. She could see the people sitting in the back rows had furrowed brows as she began to read. They could not hear her. She projected more and their brows softened. There was so much to think about, standing on her toes, shouting. This was not how she imagined it. Nevertheless, she preached.

"Brothers and sisters, tonight we begin with *The Faith that Wins*. We live in difficult times. Many men are out of work. People cannot pay their bills. Children are hungry. But as believers in Jesus, we have a faith that wins. Peter fished all night but caught nothing. With faith in Jesus, he caught so many fish the net broke, and the boat nearly sank. He won the fishing contest that day. I proclaim to you this night that we have a faith that wins."

And with that introduction to her ten sermons, Miss Lillian Russell began the two-week revival. Her message moved the congregation to respond. More than thirty people came forward that first night. They were kneeling two-deep at the rail.

After the benediction, Lillian recessed to the sanctuary door and stood next to Reverend Yow, where they greeted people on their way out of the church. Some people were emotional; tears still wet on their cheeks. Everyone seemed more than politely appreciative; they seemed genuinely excited about what might be next, eager to return the following nights.

But what caught Lillian's attention, more than appreciation and anticipation was the curious way people greeted her. Their handshakes were strange, like touching something unfamiliar. She remembered going to the circus and being allowed to touch a snake, thinking it would be wet and slick, only to discover it was dry and scaly. She felt like that snake, only not dry and scaly. Lillian wondered if people would be telling their neighbors that they had touched a lady evangelist. It didn't make her feel special. It made her feel peculiar. Right then and there, Lillian determined that no one would ever treat her like a circus sideshow. She would be a preacher of the Gospel and give people no cause to criticize or ridicule her. She would be above reproach.

One handshake that stood out to Lillian that night was from a young man she recognized from the neighborhood. He held her hand a little too long, pulled her close to him, looked her square in the eyes, and said, "I would love to spend more time with you talking about your message of new life."

Lillian's body stiffened as her heart went from a normal rhythm to rapid. She felt both panic and outrage as she jerked back her hand, took a step back, changed her warm smile to a deep frown, and said, "Good night, sir."

Reverend Yow must have noticed the change in Lillian's voice. He asked her, "Is everything all right?"

"Yes, I'm fine." Lillian recovered quickly and continued to shake hands and greet worshippers.

It was after nine o'clock before the Russell family climbed into their car. The twins were sleeping, one in Ernest's arms and one in Lawrence's arms.

E.W. spoke first. "Lila, that was one of the best—no—the absolute best, revival first nights that I have ever witnessed. The Spirit was almost visible. You were on fire."

Goldie spoke next, "Yes, Lila, I was so proud of you. But more than proud. I hardly recognized you. God got hold of you tonight, that is for sure."

Lawrence and Ernest spoke in whispers as they did not want to wake the twins, "Yes, Lila, you were great."

"Thanks," said Lillian. "But we need to get a stool. My feet and legs hurt so bad from standing on my toes for so long!" Everybody laughed.

"It's not funny. Well, I guess it is a little bit. But can we get a stool? And I think I'll be able to project better if I'm on a stool. All my energy was in my feet!" The Russell's laughed again, and the twins stirred.

"What's so funny?" asked Pete.

"Oh, nothing. Go back to sleep, little guy," said Lawrence.

"So we have to do this again tomorrow night?" asked Hazel. "Do all of us have to go every night?"

E.W. and Goldie responded in unison, "Yes, every night."

E.W. went on, "And we'll sing every night too. This is a family affair."

"A family affair," agreed Goldie.

Suffering from over-exhaustion, Lillian had trouble going to sleep. She lay awake thinking about and walking through each part of the evening, giving God thanks, and scolding herself where she felt she could have done better. *In addition to the stool, I need to practice volume. If there had been people outside, they wouldn't have heard a word I said. I also need to slow down. I was preaching entirely too fast, talking like a youth instead of a preacher. I need to find a more dignified cadence.*

The next night, even more people came. By Friday night, the church had to set up folding chairs, covering the steps and sidewalk outside the church. The ushers opened the windows wide, and Lillian heard many people comment that her voice seemed to be carried on the wind. The stool helped, and her confidence increased each night. By the end of the ten nights, more than two hundred people had come forward to give their lives to Christ. People said it was one of the best revivals they had ever attended, that Miss Lillian Russell was one of the most gifted revival preachers they had ever heard.

The men in E.W.'s class and the women in Goldie's class who raised concerns about women and leadership came as a group to the revival on Tuesday the first week. That's when Goldie and E.W. realized it was three couples at their church who were stirring up trouble.

"E.W., we've got to keep a lid on this. Lila can't hear a peep about this," said Goldie.

"I've already spoken with Reverend Yow. It turns out he is well aware, and the problem is more significant than just the six from our church. He is facing resistance from his own people too. Have you noticed how close he stays with Lila, especially as they greet people after the service? He's protecting her from hurtful comments from the nay-sayers."

"I don't understand, E.W., how people can so clearly see the fruits of her preaching and still think she shouldn't be doing this."

"I think it's the fruits that scare them. I think there would be less criticism if Lila failed."

"Now, that's just ignorant," said Goldie with a snort.

"You know what Lila would tell us?"

"Pray for them," E.W. and Goldie said in unison.

"I've been doing that, but I can't say my heart is in it," sighed E.W.

"Me either," said Goldie.

The last night of the revival, a young man approached E.W. in Lillian's presence and said, "Mr. Russell and Miss Lillian, I'm Reverend Larry Johns. I believe we have met before, at a church meeting, perhaps. I'm the pastor of the Presbyterian Church two blocks from here. Mr. Russell, may I be so bold as to ask if I might stop by one Sunday afternoon to spend some time with your delightful daughter, Miss Lillian? She has certainly captured my attention."

"I'll need to speak with her mother. We have not permitted Lillian to court yet. She's still very young."

"Thank you, sir; I look forward to hearing from you. Be assured I'll not leave the front porch with your daughter."

Both E.W. and Lillian stared after him as Reverend Johns smiled at Lillian, turned, and then walked down the street toward his church and rectory. E.W. was looking at his neck. Lillian was looking at the confident way he walked with his suit coat hooked to his finger and hung over his shoulder.

Chapter Four
Renowned Evangelist

It pleased God, who separated me from my mother's womb,
and called me by his grace, to reveal his Son in me,
that I might preach him among the heathen.
Gal. 1:15-16a KJV

"**L**ila, there's a letter for you. It's from another church in the area. Oh, wait, there's a second one. It's from Elkton." Once again, Lillian's mother stood at the front door mail slot with letters addressed to Lillian in her hand.

"Bring them to the dining room table and let's see my calendar," responded Lillian from the back of the house.

Between meals, the dining room table had become "Revival Grand Central Station." Lillian had neatly organized the letters and newspaper articles. She used a large calendar to record all the times and locations for the revivals she had agreed to preach written in ink. She compared the new invitations to the calendar and then wrote the information on the calendar in pencil until confirmed. Any conflicts meant Lillian notified the pastor. Often the pastor quite willingly changed the proposed date to accommodate Lillian's schedule.

Fall and spring proved to be the fullest months when cooler weather allowed for more comfortable travel and better temperatures in non-air-conditioned sanctuaries in the South. Lillian had resigned from her two part-time paid positions: the youth worker at her church and a department store clerk. She earned little from those positions, and she needed more time for travel and sermon preparation. With these adjustments to her schedule, everything seemed to run smoothly.

One night at the dinner table, E.W. looked at his daughter and said, "Lila, it's time for you to learn to drive. With your schedule, it's becoming increasingly difficult for me to serve as your revival driver."

"Drive? Me? A girl? Drive? I know this is a hardship for you, Daddy, but me, drive? That's more terrifying than, than my first revival," Lillian sputtered. She couldn't believe what her father had just said.

"Well, let's give it a try." E.W. turned to his son. "Ernest, you're a good driver. Would you teach your sister how to drive?"

"Sure," Ernest said. "Lila, after supper, let's have you take the car around the block. Okay?"

Pete and Polly were nearly beside themselves with glee. "Lila, drive? Can we watch?"

"You can watch, but only from the front porch," their mother said. "Don't take a step off the porch, not even to be on the sidewalk. Your sister has never driven before."

Goldie went out the front door with her husband and the twins, while Ernest and Lillian went out the back door to get into the car. For the first time in her life, Lillian sat in the driver's seat. She had no idea what to do.

"Okay, Lila, put your left foot on the clutch and the key in the ignition," said Ernest patiently.

"What's the clutch?"

"The clutch pedal is on the left. The one in the middle is the brake. The one on the right is the gas pedal. Can you push the clutch all the way to the floor?"

That's when Lillian discovered she could barely reach the pedals, let alone push them down to the floor.

"Get out of the car, Lila, so I can adjust the seat," directed her brother.

Lillian got out, as did Ernest. He came around to the driver's side, lifted a handle beside the seat, and gave the seat a mighty push forward. "I hope that's enough. It won't go forward any more than that. Wait, I'll get a pillow."

Ernest ran into the house and grabbed a pillow off the sofa in the living room. He ran back outside and set the pillow against the back of the driver's seat. "Try that."

Once again, Lillian got into the driver's seat. She adjusted the pillow, then tried to push the clutch all the way to the floor. "If I sit at the edge of the seat, I think I can make it work."

"Okay, just this one time. After that, we'll have to think of something else to get you closer to the pedals. They don't make these cars for women," Ernest said, shaking his head.

"There's a lot of things they don't make for women," mumbled Lillian.

Ernest got back in the passenger's seat and continued his instructions. "Now, keep pushing the clutch all the way down, press the gas pedal just a little, and turn the key."

Lillian did as her brother told her. The engine started up. She looked at her feet, trying to remember which pedal did what. Both hands gripped the steering wheel. She was determined to get it right.

"I'm going to release the emergency brake and slide the gear into drive now." Ernest pushed the brake handle down and moved the gear shift on the steering column.

"Now put your right foot on the gas just a little, and very, very slowly ease up on the clutch."

Lillian tried to follow her brother's instructions, but the car lurched forward and stalled.

"Very slowly, Lila. Very slowly."

Lillian took a deep breath and, with a renewed sense of determination, tried a second time with the same result—stalled. Finally, on the fifth attempt, the car started to move forward.

"Lila, stop looking at your feet. Look where you're going. You're about to run into the house." Ernest yelled.

Lillian jerked the steering wheel in the other direction. "Stop yelling at me. I'm doing the best I can."

Ernest lowered his voice. "Okay, now when you get to the end of the driveway, put your foot on the clutch and the brake at the same time. That will stop the car without it stalling."

Lillian did as she was instructed. The car stopped, but so did the engine. Lillian released her grip from the steering wheel and said, "I can't do this. It's just too complicated."

"You can do this, Lila. It just takes practice. I didn't learn overnight either, although I have to say I did better than you."

Lillian scowled at her brother.

"Sorry," Ernest said. "Now, let's start again. Push the clutch down to the floor using your left foot and turn the key. Then let up on the clutch very slowly as you gently push the gas pedal with your right foot. As the car moves, you will need to turn the wheel to the right to get out into the street." Ernest was gesturing his hands as if they were feet on the pedals.

Lillian pushed the clutch to the floor, turned the key, put her right foot on the gas pedal very gently, then started to ease up on the clutch. She was excited when the car didn't stall. But her sense of accomplishment abruptly stopped when her brother yelled at her. "Lila, turn the wheel, turn the wheel!"

Lillian looked up to see a tree immediately in front of the car. She froze in fear, her short life passing in front of her. This death would not be as a result of an automobile accident but shame and humiliation.

Ernest grabbed the wheel and gave it a hard jerk to the right, but it was too late. They hit the big oak tree on the opposite side of the street. The sound of metal hitting bark cut through Lillian's ears. She bumped her head on the steering wheel. Ernest put out his hands to stop himself from hitting his head on the dash.

"Lila, when you're driving, you have to look where you're going, not at your feet! Now, get out of the car so we can assess the damage. Daddy's going to be furious."

Ernest pulled on the emergency brake. They both got out of the car. Her father was already off the porch and standing in front of the car, accessing the damage. Lillian couldn't tell if the steam was coming from the radiator or her father or both.

The damage didn't seem significant to Lillian, but she didn't think her father felt the same way. He shook his head and mumbled something to Ernest about the bumper, grill, radiator, hood, and chassis.

"I'm sorry, Dad," Ernest said. "I tried, but Lila just couldn't coordinate the pedals and the steering wheel at the same time."

"Well, the twins and Mama are waiting for us. Let's go tell them about your first driving lesson," Ernest said to Lillian.

Lillian started to cry. "There isn't much to tell them that they didn't already see." She looked at the water drain in the street and wished herself into it, like a snake slithering out of sight.

Ernest stayed with the car. E.W. stomped to the porch shaking his head. Lillian dragged two steps behind, head hung. Goldie came down the steps toward them. The twins were draped over the porch railing, pointing at the car and laughing to each other. Several neighbors left their front porches, the men walking toward the car and the women toward the Russell's house.

"Was anybody hurt?" asked Goldie.

"No, they're fine, but the car isn't. No more driving lessons for a while," said E.W. through gritted teeth.

"No more driving lessons *ever*," said Lillian through her tears. She rushed into the house and ran upstairs to her room, slamming the doors behind her. Once in her room she walked to the open window that overlooked the front of the house. She heard her father ask some of the neighbor men standing around the car to help Ernest push it back into their driveway. Most of these men didn't own a car—it was too expensive during these challenging economic times—and they knew the value and sacrifice of this car to the Russell family. E.W. pushed the driver's seat back so he could get in and steer the car while his neighbors and Ernest pushed. As Lillian watched, she sniffled and thought, *this is like a funeral procession, with pallbearers moving a dead car, and I'm the one who killed it.*

The next morning at breakfast, Lillian said to her father, "Daddy, I'm so sorry about the car. If you need money to help pay for the repairs, I can give you the entire honorarium from my next revival. That should help a little."

"I might need you to do that, Lila. I plan to take it to the repair shop today and get an estimate. Let's see how all this works out."

"I really am sorry." Lillian's voice quivered.

"No need to apologize." E.W. sighed. "Accidents happen. Ernest is going to try to get some extra work to help with the expenses. After all, it's mostly his fault, not yours, or maybe my fault for thinking up this crazy idea."

#   #   #

One night, Goldie went to the garage typewriter repair shop to have a conversation with her husband. Lillian was in her study with the door closed, working on a sermon. She quietly got up from her desk, tip-toed to the door, and pressed her ear against it so she could overhear her parents' conversation.

"E.W., it's probably just as well that Lila doesn't want to drive. Some of the women at church talked about a revival in the city that got out of control. Men and women demonstrated very inappropriate intimate behavior with each other. The evangelist was even part of it. It was a tent revival, and the sins were committed in the field behind the tent. How awful! I'd never want our little Lila to have such a thing happen at one of her revivals."

"You're right, Goldie. It's best for me or some other trusted man to travel with Lila."

Lillian realized she was young and naive, but she knew more than her parents thought she knew. She knew what happened at some revivals, and the possibility of it happening at one of her revivals terrified her. Lillian often prayed for protection. Sometimes she hated being that orchid and resisted her parents' protection, but tonight she appreciated it. She waited a few minutes for both her parents to return to the house, and then she went inside too.

#   #   #

In 1935, when Lillian was twenty-one years old, she received another invitation from Reverend Yow, now the Moseley Memorial Church pastor in Danville, Virginia. She sat on the front porch swing, trying to find a breeze in the hot Virginia August heat. As she read the invitation, her friend Georgia climbed up the porch steps and sat with her on the swing. A bucket of freshly picked green beans waiting for somebody to snap sat between them.

"Hi, Lillian. How are you? I haven't seen you in a long time. Every time I come over, your mom tells me that you're traveling, preaching revivals."

"Yeah, this has been a hectic year for me. I have an invitation nearly every month, sometimes more. This is an invitation right here." Lillian showed Georgia the letter from Reverend Yow. "He invited me to travel to his church in Danville to lead a revival."

"Danville? That's three hours from here. No wonder you're never home! Where do you stay when you travel? A nice hotel, I hope." Georgia returned the letter, picked up a bean, snapped the head and tail off, and then broke it in half, throwing the head and tail over the porch railing and putting the bean halves back in the bucket.

"No, I generally stay with the pastor's family in the parsonage or with one of the church leaders. My father or brother go with me. This invitation is a little different, though. Usually, I preach at Methodist revivals, but this one includes a Baptist Church. Now, that will be different. I've never preached at a Baptist church before. They often baptize lots of people on their last night. But this is just a one-night event, so I'm not sure what they have in mind. I guess Reverend Yow will tell me." Lillian folded up the letter, put it back in the envelope, and picked up a bean, joining Georgia in the rhythm of snapping beans.

"I never thought about all of those differences. So, do you think you'll do it, that is preach at the Baptist Church?"

"I think so. Reverend Yow has said positive things about me to the pastor at Calvary Baptist Church. According to this letter, Reverend Yow told the Baptist minister, and I quote, 'Lillian is well-prepared and a gifted conveyer of the Gospel.'" Lillian pushed her chest out a little.

"Wow, that's pretty impressive. Will you be nervous preaching at a Baptist church?"

"No more than I am at my home church. Preaching at Highland Park is where I recognize a lot of faces. I see my family, friends, and neighbors. You're there, so you know what I mean. At other churches, the congregation is a sea of strangers. I don't mind greeting people at the church door after the service, but people want me to go to their homes for dessert or something at Highland. By that time, I just want to go home and be alone. Besides, I wonder what all these people I have known since birth think of me and my preaching. I often get the feeling they are more polite than sincere in their praise and support of me."

"I guess that makes sense. Well, I'll see you later. Hope your revival in Danville goes great." With that, Georgia hopped down the porch steps, walked down the sidewalk, around the corner, and out of sight. *Sometimes I wonder about that girl,* Lillian thought. *She seems to lack a rudder. She just gets information from one friend and shares it with her other friends, like a telephone. More faith in Jesus will help her. I'll pray for Georgia every day.*

On Sunday, the first day of the Danville revival, Lillian spoke at Moseley Methodist in the morning and Calvary Baptist in the evening. Then she spoke every evening at Moseley for two weeks. She discovered that preaching to Baptists wasn't much different from preaching to Methodists. They sang many of the same hymns with piano and organ to accompany the music. The smell of fresh oil on the pews and floors mixed with the scent of burning wax candles was also familiar. But what was most apparent to Lillian was the people's response to the Gospel. Baptist or Methodist, the good news of salvation called people to repent.

What Lillian didn't know was how much resistance there was in Danville to having a female evangelist. Reverend Yow heard it in the local restaurants and his own pews. The Baptist minister called him to ask for further assurance that Miss Russell was worth the criticism he was getting from some of his people. Even Reverend Yow's district superintendent called him and suggested he either cancel the revival or get a different speaker. Reverend Yow reminded him that in the Methodist Church, the pastor has authority over who gets to be in his pulpit and that he has asked Miss Lillian Russell to be in his pulpit, and that was it.

"Mr. Russell," Reverend Yow greeted E.W., "good afternoon. It's good to see you again." It was Sunday afternoon, and the revival was to start that evening. E.W. and Lillian had just arrived in Danville. Lillian was in the parsonage unpacking her suitcase in the guest room. E.W. was checking the oil level in his car. "I want to let you know that I hear more criticism about this revival than I did when in Richmond," Reverend Yow continued. "Danville can be a bit backward. I will try to protect your daughter, but I'm not sure I can fully insolate her from this."

"I'm sorry to hear that but understand," said E.W. "She has so much more experience now than she did those years ago at Fairmont. She has heard it all. I think she'll be alright."

"So glad to hear that, but nonetheless, I will do my best to protect her. Just one word of advice: keep her away from the restaurant near my church. That seems to be a hotbed of negative chatter."

"I'll do that, and thank you, Reverend Yow, for all your support of our Lila. You have been such a pioneer in this matter. She would not be where she is today, and so many souls saved if it were not for you taking a chance."

"No need to thank me. I thank Lillian for her courage and faith," said Reverend Yow.

One week into the revival, the *Danville Bee* newspaper reported:

> *The large church auditorium's capacity was over-taxed Sunday night, and chairs had to be placed in the aisles to take care of the congregation. Miss Russell's subject was "Coming Home." Much interest is being manifested in these services, as is attested by the increasing crowds each night. Miss Russell is a gifted speaker and has held successful revivals in various parts of the state.*

Many local newspapers interviewed Lillian. Their questions were so predictable that she developed pat answers. In one of those interviews, the reporter asked her, as most reporters did, to describe the differences she experienced as a woman evangelist.

"Well, being short in stature, I have to carry a stool with me to all the revivals, just to be sure I can see over the pulpit. Sometimes my legs dangle from the large pulpit chairs, and if I'm not careful, my shoes fall off. I've learned always to wear shoes with straps."

"That's pretty funny. I would never have thought of that," said the reporter. "What about your voice? Is it loud enough?"

"People tell me that my voice carries well yet is very pleasing to the ear," Lillian repeated what she had heard many times from others.

The reporter had done his homework by interviewing people from the church community, and his next question went off the standard reporter script. "The people I talked to commented that listening to you preach is like listening to Jesus, that you have a presence about you, gentle yet powerful. They tell me that when the light is just right, your long hair, braided and wrapped around your head, provides a halo effect. 'Petite, powerful, beautiful, holy,' that's what they tell me."

Lillian shook her head. She couldn't let this reporter, nor the readers of his article, ever think of her as powerful or holy. *Only God is holy. God has all the power.* Lillian leaned into the reporter to make her point. "It's not me, but God working through me. To Him goes all the glory. I'm just His servant."

Lillian sat back in her chair. The reporter made a few notes, and then with a smile, asked, "I also heard that you have had more than one marriage proposal but have turned them all down without even a thought of consideration."

"That's true. I'm completely devoted to my call to preach the love and grace of Jesus. Husband and family would only detract from my divine purpose."

Lillian thought back to the one proposal she had seriously considered—from the Presbyterian pastor. They had seen each other several times on Sunday afternoons. He had even taken her to the movies. She blushed as she recalled liking the feel of his hand wrapped around hers. After the movie, as they were saying good night on her front porch, he had asked for a kiss, and she had obliged. She could still taste the sweetness of his breath. *Could the reporter see her blush?* But when the pastor asked for her hand in marriage, she said no. He was a good, decent man and would be a faithful husband, but she knew God did not intend for her to marry and have a family. The pastor had since married a member of his church, and both seemed to be happy. Lillian tried to convince herself she had no regrets about turning down his proposal. Most of the time, she was content with her decision, but there were other times she regretted what she had done or had failed to do and wanted to kick herself for being so foolish.

The reporter made a few more notes. Lillian sensed his disappointment at not getting a front-page story, but she reminded herself that she was not front-page material. He thanked her and returned to his car.

Newspaper headlines continued around Richmond and across the state:

"Girl Evangelist to End Services at Sandston" — 1936, *Richmond Times Dispatch*

"Miss Russell to Begin Series of Revival Services" — 1940, *The News Leader*, Staunton, VA

"Woman Evangelist Speaks in Hilton – Miss Lillian Russell Opens Revival at Methodist Church" — 1936, *Daily Press*, Newport News, VA

Often newspapers wrote about Lillian, but in the Daily Press article, they wrote about her message. She was delighted to know that the reporter had attended and paid attention. This article about the Hilton revival described her messages.

Miss Russell testified that Jesus was all to her – that she could see Him in the sunshine, in the water she drank, with reminders whenever she opened a door of the significance of the Kingdom of God and in the sheep of the pasture where He reigned as the Good Shepherd. Speaking of Jesus as the best friend humanity has, she declared that a true friend is one "who knows all about us and yet loves us just the same." She declared that Jesus' birth, life, and death attested His great love for humanity.

His birth was a lowly manner, his life amidst criticism and hardships, His death upon the cross – all of these were not easy, she asserted, but love opened the way. The evangelist declared that seldom do people really understand their closest friends, even, but Jesus understands all people. She declared that He is a friend in need, stronger than man and more gentle than woman. "We do not have to walk the paths of life alone if Jesus takes us by the hand," she declared. "Jesus has the highway marked and guides us today just as the prophets of old were guided."

This article omitted the most significant reason for Lillian's popularity and effectiveness. It wasn't so much what she said as it was her. Lillian carried within her the powerful presence of God. For anyone seeking God, they found Him in her. Reporters struggled to communicate the reason for her spell-binding preaching. To repeat what she said was empty, but to put her words in her was life-changing. You simply had to be there.

#   #   #

Boots, Lillian's sister, and her husband, Fenner, who lived in Falls Church, Virginia, often visited Boot's family in Richmond on Sunday afternoons. It was 1936, and the young couple had a daughter and son born less than two years apart. On this particular Sunday afternoon visit, Boots had put both of her children down for a nap and come out to the porch to talk to Lillian.

"Hi, Lila, can I sit with you for a spell?" Lillian had her nose in a Bible commentary on the book of Romans.

"Sure, have a seat. My eyes were starting to blur anyway. Romans can be hard to understand."

"I would guess that's true. So, how are you? I mean, you're so busy with so many revivals. I can't keep up with them. Are you still enjoying them?"

"Yes, even more than when I started five years ago. I've worked through the biggest challenges and have found a rhythm to my life. I've never been happier."

"But what about a family, husband, and children? Don't you ever think you'd like to do all of those things? Life would be so lonely without a husband and so unfulfilled without children, don't you think?"

"Seeing you with Fenn and the children does cause me to consider what my life could have been or, I guess, could still be. You do seem happy."

"Oh, yes, even as crazy as my life is with a toddler and an infant, I wouldn't trade it for anything. Lila, you know it's not too late. You're still young enough to marry and have a family."

"I guess I'm still young enough. Believe it or not, I've had several men court me. Two have spoken of marriage. But I told them no."

"Why is that? Did you not like them?"

"Daddy is strict about who is allowed to see me. As I recall, he was that way with you too, right?"

"Yes, he was strict, but I would guess, not as strict as he is with you. He has always watched over you like a hawk." They both laughed.

"So, with Daddy's hawk eye," said Lillian with a smile, "my suitors have been well-groomed, handsome, educated, employed, well-spoken, and definitely Christian. So it isn't the quality or character of the suitors; it's me. I'm just not interested. It's as if God has taken the desire for marriage and a family from me. I look at you and your family and am so happy for you, but I don't want that for myself. I wish only to serve God through preaching His Word."

"Don't you think you'll regret that decision? Perhaps when you're fifty and too old to have a family, will you regret the decision you're making now?"

"I don't know for sure. I don't think so. I hope not. All I can do is what I know now. And for right now, marriage and family aren't what God has planned for me."

"Then, please feel free to babysit my children any time you want," said Boots with a smile. "They can be a handful, and that may be enough to remove any doubt you have."

That night Lillian stood on the front porch, looking up at the quarter moon. She thought about Boots and Fenner and their two little ones. She could hear her parents at the kitchen table listening to the radio. She imagined the Presbyterian pastor and his wife in their rectory discussing church life. Then she thought about the room she shared with her sisters Hazel and Polly. *They're still children, but soon they too will be gone, married with children most likely. Will my life feel empty without a husband to hold me, or a child for me to hold? I'll never be called "wife" or "mother." Is being "Miss Lillian Russell" enough? Will it always be enough? What happens when the invitations to preach stop coming? What will become of me then?*

Chapter Five
The Dan River Mills

For I know the thoughts that I think toward you, saith the LORD,
thoughts of peace, and not of evil,
to give you an expected end.
Jeremiah 29:11 KJV

One hundred fifty miles away, a twenty-one-year-old Mildred sat quietly in the passenger seat of the car her brother was driving.

"Look at that sky. It looks like it might rain any minute." Theodore's voice seemed to drone on like the tires against the pavement. He had been talking nearly non-stop since they had left their home in Biscoe, North Carolina. Mildred knew her older brother was just trying to calm her nerves and, while she appreciated the effort, it was more annoying than helpful.

Theodore drove the car north on Route 29. The sign indicated they were crossing the Virginia state line. Within minutes of the warning clouds, the skies opened, and rain poured down on the hot blacktop. They both rolled up their windows. Theodore turned on the wipers and slowed the car. The rain was the only sound in the car for a few miles, but once it let up, the one-way conversation continued.

"Look at that rainbow! From horizon to horizon, perfectly arched across the sky." Theodore said.

Mildred saw the rainbow and smiled. She knew this rainbow was God's promise to her. Great things lay ahead for her in Danville. She felt apprehensive yet confident that this was her best course of action.

Their father had died six years before, in 1929, the same year the stock market crashed. Mildred was fifteen years old then, the year their whole family was thrown into economic turmoil. Mildred and Theodore came from a large family of seven brothers and four sisters. The oldest brother, Edward, had died in 1907 in a car accident when he was just seven years old. Mildred had heard from a neighbor that a car owned by a businessman in town hit and then ran over the boy. Mildred was born seven years after little Eddie's death. Seldom did anyone speak of him or the accident. It made her mother too sad.

With so few cars in 1907, Mildred wondered what the odds were of being killed by a car in a small place like Biscoe. Lately, Mildred had been thinking a lot about *the odds*. Her father's death, the stock market crash, her brother's death, so many things. She didn't want her life determined by *the odds*. She didn't want just to sit back and watch her life play itself out. She wanted to seize her life and control *the odds*.

This decision to work at Dan River Mills was Mildred's big move to take control of her life. Three of her older siblings had gotten married and were raising families of their own. Mildred's mother, Manerva Victoria, still had children at home and worked as the Biscoe Postmaster. At twenty-one, Mildred was now the oldest sibling living in the family home, and she held primary responsibility to assist her mother with the many household tasks. She was also trying to find work to help her mother with the household expenses, but employment wasn't easy to find. Aileen Plant, a yarn mill in Biscoe, had gone bankrupt in 1928, a victim of the economy.

The Biscoe Coca Cola Bottling Company was hiring only married men with children. Mildred had a high school education, an accomplishment that didn't seem to make much difference when securing employment.

But the event that catapulted Mildred from her home in Biscoe into this whole new life in Danville was her sister Edith's death. Edith had been thirty-two years old, single, and living at home when she died of pneumonia. Mildred's scenario was all too similar, and it frightened her. She did not want her obituary to read like her sister's—so tragically short. She wanted more, much more.

Mildred believed Dan River Mills was the move she was seeking. She had heard that many individuals and families with no future had gone there and found a new life. Men found work. Women found a future for their children. The Mill provided education and health care as well as electricity, water, and heat for their homes. It was like the pot of gold at the end of the rainbow. People from the Piedmont region of Virginia flocked there in large numbers and found a life better than they ever dreamed possible. She knew many people, even from Biscoe, who had gone to work at Dan River Mills. A few had returned to Biscoe, but most had stayed, weaving a good life for themselves and their families.

But what particularly attracted Mildred to Dan River Mills was the promise of a new life for single people. The textile company had partnered with the YMCA to house single men, plus they had built a large dormitory for single women, a dormitory famous for the swimming pool in its basement.

Mildred knew all about the women's dormitory. She had read the little booklet, so many times it was tattered. Six months ago, she had written to Dan River Mills about employment. They mailed a whole packet of material with the application, including this booklet, entitled *A Pleasant Story of an Unusual Enterprise – Hylton Hall*. Mildred opened it and read a section to her brother.

"Listen to this:

Every convenience afforded in the modern hotel is combined with the many features that go to make up a happy home-life atmosphere. The very spirit of the house itself is one of joy, of good cheer, good fellowship, and freedom; a freedom that delights itself in thoughtful consideration of others. It gives to young women between the ages of 16 and 35, at a moderate cost, comfortable rooms, good food, every facility for recreation and self-improvement, and the opportunity for the cultivation of a delightful social life, all under the protecting and refining influence of charming women of high Christian ideals and character. These young women, employees of the Dan River Cotton Mills, are earnest, intelligent workers who command the respect of all who are privileged to know them."

Mildred looked up from the booklet and sighed. "Does it seem too good to be true?" Mildred asked her brother.

"Maybe. We'll soon find out," answered Theodore.

All her future seemed to hang on the words in this little booklet. They were promising words for Mildred, who had lived her whole life in a town so small it barely deserved a spot on the map. For her mother, they were words that promised her daughter a future.

Mildred and her mother had had long talks about this potential move. Victoria saw it as an opportunity for her daughter to find a husband. But if that didn't work out, she would at least have a means of supporting herself as a single woman. Even so, Theodore's mother sent him with strict orders to be sure everything was as the brochure described. He was to bring his sister straight home if anything wasn't proper.

They drove into the city limits of Danville. The rainbow disappeared, but on the horizon appeared a four-story colonial building of red brick, with white trimmings and a silver-gray roof. It had a huge front porch, with a second layer of porches above them. Large windows covered all sides of the building.

Young women sat on rocking chairs and porch railings. The sign above the front door read "Hylton Hall."

This must be the pot of gold everyone believes is at the end of the rainbow, Mildred thought.

Theodore parked the car in front of Hylton Hall. As they got out and started up the steps, a tall, slender woman, appearing to be in her fifties, dressed in a silk dress, stockings, and sturdy shoes, greeted them.

"Good morning. I'm Miss Hylton. And you must be the Longs. I've been expecting you." She extended her hand first to Mildred, then to Theodore.

"I'm the superintendent of this residence hall. You may have noticed that the building carries my name. Let's go inside. You can freshen up a bit, and then I'll give you the grand tour." Miss Hylton opened the screened door and held it for Theodore and Mildred.

"The men's room is on the left, and the ladies' room is on the right. I'll wait for you here," said Miss Hylton as she pointed first to the left and then to the right. Mildred was grateful to get off the front porch. The gaggle of girls gathered there watched her every move, listening to every word, and it made her uncomfortable to be the center of attention.

As Mildred stood at the sink to wash her hands, she caught a glimpse of herself in the mirror. The trip in the car had not been kind to her appearance. Her white blouse looked as if she had never ironed it. Her brown skirt had a crease across her lap. At least her shoes still shone. She tried to run her fingers through her hair to give it some life, but her fingers got stuck in the tight curls. She splashed some water on her face and dried it with the towel on the rack. Then she dug in her purse and found her lipstick. The red lips gave color to her face. It was the best she could do.

Mildred joined Theodore and Miss Hylton in the entryway. "Now, let's begin the tour," said Miss Hylton. "First, I'll show you the dining room, kitchen, and serving rooms," she said. "They're on this level."

As they entered the dining room, Miss Hylton said, "We provide all the meals. It's part of the $7.50 per week fee. As we continue down this hall, you'll see the assembly room where we hold socials with the young men living at the YMCA." She looked at Theodore as she added, "All these socials are diligently chaperoned by me personally. There is no alcohol or tobacco of any kind allowed on the premises. The Dan River Mills is dry. Of course, tobacco is much harder to control due to Danville being a tobacco town. It's an industry that employs many people and creates significant income for the entire community," Miss Hylton shook her head with clear disapproval.

They turned down a wide hallway, and Miss Hylton escorted them into a classroom. "Here are the classrooms where the women learn to sew, cook, and even get their high school diploma. These are free opportunities you may want to consider, Mildred."

Mildred looked around the room crowded with tables, chairs, sewing machines, and ironing boards. A small kitchen with sink, stove, and oven occupied one corner. A blackboard spanned most of one wall. Windows on the outside wall provided light for the entire room and intensive light for the sewing area. Mildred wasn't sure her participation in these activities would be necessary. After all, she knew how to sew and cook, and she had her high school diploma. But she would consider it.

"Let's go upstairs to the living quarters. Theodore, I've notified the women that there will be a man on their floor this morning, so you'll find all the bedroom doors closed," said Miss Hylton as she led them out of the room.

The three of them went up the back steps and started down the second-floor hall. Miss Hylton continued, "The bedrooms are designed for two people, but with the stock market crash and the loss of business, thus loss of employees, many rooms have only one woman per room. I hope you don't mind not having a roommate," said Miss Hylton to Mildred.

Mildred was thrilled. For the first time in her life, she would have her own room. "That will be quite adequate. I'll rather enjoy having a room to myself."

Miss Hylton escorted them to what would be Mildred's room. Mildred walked into the room. Theodore stood just outside the room behind Miss Hylton, who stood in the doorway. "As you can see, the furnishings include two single iron beds; the best grade felt mattress, princess dresser, table and chair, washable rugs on the floor, and dainty curtains at the windows."

Mildred made her way around the room, sitting on the bed with a little bounce, touching the curtains, and taking a moment to look out the window. Her excitement was building. The room felt like an oasis to her, safe and comfortable. This room could be her home with no effort at all.

Miss Hylton added, "There are bathrooms on every floor with toilets, sinks, tubs, and showers. Mildred, you can peek in the bathroom on this hall."

Mildred walked to the bathroom, opened the door, and looked inside. The bathroom was large and spotless; the smell of bleach caught the attention of her nose. *I'm used to sharing the bathroom at home with everybody, so this will be easy,* thought Mildred.

Miss Hylton continued the tour, showing the infirmary, the sun parlor, the roof gardens, the large public parlor plus ten small parlors, and the reading and writing rooms lined with books.

"This single building seems to house an entire city," said Mildred in a whisper to her brother.

Finally, Miss Hylton took them both to the basement, where they saw the swimming pool. It was long, with five swimming lanes marked by lines of black tile on the bottom of the otherwise blue-tiled pool. At one end of the pool, a girl dove into the pool. At the other end, a young woman stood shoulder deep. Several other women were swimming laps. Mildred glanced at Theodore and noticed his eyes bulged as big as saucers. He cleared his throat and quickly regained his composure by furrowing his forehead and narrowing his eyes. Mildred, however, could not contain her excitement. She hugged Theodore long and hard and considered hugging Miss Hylton but thought better of that. Instead, she jumped up and down, clasping her hands to her chest.

"So, what do you think, Mildred?" asked Miss Hylton. "Do you have any questions?"

"I think I love it and have a million questions," replied Mildred.

"You'll have lots of time to get your questions answered. Right now, let's get your things up to your room so you can get settled in."

Theodore carried Mildred's one suitcase and one box of personal belongings into Hylton Hall and up the stairs to Mildred's bedroom. He looked at her sternly, "Mildred, the family is counting on you."

"Teddy, I'm not a child, so stop treating me like one. I can manage all of this. After all, I am a Long," said Mildred as she looked at him and straightened her shoulders.

Theodore smiled. "We do come from a long line on both sides of the family of stubborn, hardheaded, determined people. Just do your very best, and if you need anything or need to come home, just write to Mother. I'll come back up here and pick you up."

Theodore hugged her, then left. From the window in her room, Mildred watched her brother get into the car. She offered up a short prayer for him. He had a three-hour drive ahead of him, but she had a whole new life ahead of her. At long last, she was on her own.

She knelt beside her bed to thank God and ask for His guidance and protection. It was Saturday, and she would start her new job on Monday. She had so much to learn, so many people to meet. And she realized she was hungry. *What time is dinner?*

Chapter Six
The Challenge to Make History

Then I saw a new heaven and a new earth.
Revelation 21:1 KJV

*M*ildred was by herself just a few minutes when she heard a knock on her door, which she had left ajar. She looked up and saw two smiling faces peeking in the doorway.

"May we come in?" said one girl.

"Of course," said Mildred.

Both girls stepped into the room. They appeared to be about her age.

"We're on our way to the dining hall. Want to come with us?" the shorter one asked.

"I'm Betty," said the taller girl. "I'm from the mountains. Ellen here is from Christiansburg. A country girl and a city girl. How about you? What's your name? Are you from the country or the city?"

Mildred took a deep breath and mentally itemized the questions fired at her. "I'm Mildred. I'm—well, let me see, I would say a country girl from a little town in North Carolina called Biscoe. And, yes, I'd very much like to go to dinner with you."

"Then, let's go!" exclaimed Betty as she clapped her hands on the word go.

The three young women made their way down the hall and then down the steps. Mildred had so many questions and so many things she wanted to know. But there was no time. Betty, clearly the one in charge, moved fast and talked even faster, giving a running commentary of everything, from Hylton Hall's decorations to the weather in Danville.

Does this girl ever stop talking? thought Mildred.

Betty led them to a table in the dining hall. As they stood behind their chairs, a young woman stepped up to a microphone and asked everyone to bow their heads for prayer. "Be present at our table, Lord. Be here and everywhere adored. These creatures bless and grant that we may feast in paradise with Thee. Amen."

"Amen," said everyone in unison. The room immediately filled with the screech of chair legs on the floor and the chatter of hungry female voices mixed with the clatter of dishes, silverware, and glasses.

"Pass the meat, please," said Mildred.

"Just the meat? What about the potatoes, gravy, greens, and rolls?" asked Betty.

"Oh, go ahead. Pass everything!" said Mildred with a smile. "This is just like Biscoe and my mother's great southern cooking. I think I could get used to this."

"Wait," Ellen said. "The best part is yet to come—pie!"

"No," Betty said, "that's not the best part. The best part is we don't have to do the dishes."

The three of them laughed. Once they scraped their pie plates clean, they waited to be dismissed by Miss Hylton. After dinner, Betty and Ellen took Mildred for a tour of the town. First, they walked up the street to see the Methodist church.

Ellen informed Mildred, "Dan River Mills gave property for all the churches, money to build the churches, and money to build the pastors' homes. The Mill maintains these buildings. The pastors live in their homes rent-free."

Mildred said, "I know I'll be attending the Methodist Church because that's the church I've been attending in Biscoe. My family and I have been members of Page Memorial Methodist Church my whole life."

"Fine with us," said Betty. "We've been to Methodist, Baptist, Presbyterian, and you name it, we've been there. They're all good."

"Do you mind if we stop at the Methodist Church so I can get a peek?"

"Sure, we're in no big hurry," said Betty.

They walked up the steps to the front door of the church, Mildred leading the way. She grabbed the handle to the large wooden door and pulled hard. It opened, and she looked into the dark space.

"Let my eyes adjust a minute," said Mildred. "I'd like to see the sanctuary and see if the pastor might be in."

"The pastor?" asked Ellen. "Why do you want to see the pastor?"

"I'd just like to meet him and ask some questions about his church."

"All right, but don't expect us to join in that conversation. Pastors make us nervous. When they look at you, it's like they know all your sins—terrifying." Betty rolled her eyes.

"Pastors are no different from us. They put their trousers on one leg at a time," said Mildred with a smile, and stepped into the church with Betty and Ellen immediately behind, their shoes clicking on the wooden floor. They walked through the narthex into the sanctuary.

Mildred stopped and looked up at the high ceiling. "This is beautiful," she said. "The Mill was very generous, even providing stained glass windows." Mildred took a deep breath. "I can feel the Holy Spirit here." She closed her eyes, took another deep breath, and then opened her eyes. "Now, let's go see if the pastor is here. We'll try that door." Mildred pointed to a door beside the pulpit.

Betty and Ellen followed Mildred down the center aisle to the right of the pulpit. Mildred opened the door into a hallway. She looked both ways and said, "Let's go down this way."

Again, Betty and Ellen followed Mildred until they came to a door with a sign that read *Pastor's Study*. Mildred knocked on the door. From inside, they heard shoes on the floor and then saw the door open. A man in his thirties, dressed in a white shirt with an opened collar, greeted them with a warm smile. "What a pleasant surprise this Saturday evening. I'm Reverend Johnson. How can I help you?"

"I'm Mildred Long, and these are my friends Betty and Ellen. I know you're probably busy getting ready for tomorrow, but can I ask you just a couple of questions?"

"Why certainly, come right in."

The three young women walked into the small office. The pastor pulled his chair from behind his desk and offered it to Mildred. "Betty and Ellen, please have a seat in one of these chairs. This study is pretty small, but if I sit on the corner of my desk, we can make it work."

"Thank you," said Mildred, "but we won't be here long enough to rearrange your furniture. I just want to know if this church is Methodist Episcopal South or Methodist Protestant?"

"Ah, I see you're a student of the never-ending schisms and mergers," said Reverend Johnson. We are technically MEC South, but everyone is welcome."

"Thank you," said Mildred. "Just one other question. Do you favor the ordination of women? You know MEC South does not, but the Protestants do. Where do you stand on this issue?" Mildred was looking intently at the pastor's green eyes and dark, perfectly shaped eyebrows.

"My personal opinion is to favor full rights for women in the ordained ministry of the church. Some people at the church agree with me, and some do not. Again all are welcome. Why do you ask? Are you interested in ordination?"

"Of course not, but I am interested in becoming involved to the fullest extent of my abilities," said Mildred.

"You will be most welcome to do that. I'll enjoy working with you. What kind of things are you interested in?"

"I am particularly drawn to missions. Do you have opportunities here in that area?"

"We have many, many opportunities. There are people in need around the world and right here in this community."

"I believe I am going to like it here, Reverend. Thank you so much for your time. We'll be going now and allow you to get back to your work. I'll see you tomorrow morning."

"Well, thank you so much for stopping by. Will I see all of you tomorrow or just Mildred?" asked Reverend Johnson looking at Betty and Ellen.

Betty answered for both of them. "We'll both be here with Mildred. She's new here, from North Carolina, so she'll need us to show her around."

"I have a feeling Mildred can find her way around by herself," said the pastor with a chuckle.

The three girls left and continued their walking tour past the primary and secondary schools and then on to Alcorn Park, a 100-acre park with a lake. The Mill had built and maintained everything they saw. Betty then led them back to the entrance to Hylton Hall. There they walked down a path and into a tunnel that went under the railroad tracks. As they walked out of the tunnel, the entrance to Dan River Mills appeared before them. There were acres and acres of red brick buildings, some of them five stories tall. Large windows wrapped symmetrically around every floor. The uniformity from building to building conveyed strict control and high expectations.

"It's unbelievable," gasped Mildred. "Biscoe had a textile mill, but it can't compare to this. I could get lost here and never find my way out." Mildred scanned the brick buildings back and forth and up and down.

"It's amazing and intimidating. We've all gotten lost here at least once," said Ellen.

"But don't worry," said Betty. "You'll have a guide the first several weeks. By then, you'll know the place like the back of your hand."

Betty reminded Mildred of her big sister, and she felt an ache for her. Even though Edith had been fourteen years older than Mildred, she filled the role of a sister, mother, and best friend. Life just wasn't the same without her.

"Tomorrow, we'll get on the train and go into town. We can spend some time at the YMCA where the *boys* live," Betty said, rolling her eyes as she said, *boys.* "We can't go in the Y, but the boys can come out to us. Sunday is the best day for visiting. You just wait. But I can see you're getting tired. People say I talk too much. Do you think I talk too much?"

Thankfully, before Mildred could respond, Betty went on, "Let's get you back to your room. We'll stop by tomorrow at eight A.M. sharp to go to breakfast and then on to church."

Mildred nodded in agreement. They turned around, walking back through the tunnel to Hylton Hall, everyone going to their respective rooms.

Mildred showered, organized a few things, and knelt next to her bed to pray. Every feeling from ecstasy to terror mixed together, tumbling around in her head. She tried to make sense of them.

This is a test I will pass. I need to stop second-guessing myself, get rid of self-doubt, and strengthen my resolve. Our preacher instructs us to starve our doubt and feed our faith. My family is counting on me. I am counting on me. With God's help, I will be a weaver at the Mill and maybe even a leader in the community. I believe I have the potential. Perhaps I will even make history! After all, my father was the local postmaster and was elected a state senator. My mother's ancestors came from Scotland in 1769, and with nothing but hard work, started a whole community. I feel their determination in my very spirit. I have it in my blood to make history and to make the world a better place.

"I can do all things through Christ, who strengthens me," Mildred said out loud. And with that, she got off her knees and into bed.

Chapter Seven
Mildred in Training

And a certain woman named Lydia, a seller of purple,
of the city of Thyatira,
which worshipped God, heard us: whose heart the Lord opened,
that she attended unto the things which were spoken of Paul.
Acts 16:14 KJV

*a*s planned, at eight o'clock sharp, Mildred heard a knock on her door. Betty and Ellen stepped into Mildred's room, dressed in their Sunday best—cotton dresses, straw hats, and white shoes and gloves. Mildred had two Sunday dresses, one for winter and one for summer. The summer dress she had on was blue with tiny birds printed on the skirt. The white belt showed off her slender waist. Hat and white shoes and gloves completed her wardrobe.

"Don't we look like the three musketeers?" said Ellen.

Mildred and Betty smiled in agreement. After a breakfast of biscuits and gravy, they walked to the Methodist Church.

The hymns and liturgy rang familiar to Mildred and made her long for home. *Surely I'm not homesick already,* she thought. She couldn't stop thinking about her mother and siblings at Page Memorial in Biscoe. *Mom is probably busy getting the children ready for church, missing my help. Maybe they're singing the same hymns.*

Clearly, the liturgy is the same: The Apostles' Creed, the Lord's Prayer, the Doxology, and the Gloria Patri. Thinking about this gave Mildred both an ache in her heart and comfort in her soul. *God is the same yesterday, and today,* she reminded herself, *the same in Biscoe and Danville.*

Back at Hylton Hall after the service, the three of them joined the other young women for a lunch of fried chicken, mashed potatoes, gravy, greens, rolls, and pecan pie.

"I'm going to gain 50 pounds!" Mildred exclaimed to Betty and Ellen.

"We've all gained weight, for sure," said Betty. "But don't worry, the walking at the mill Monday through Friday helps us keep our girlish figures."

After lunch, the trio changed out of their Sunday clothes and into flowered cotton dresses and then headed for the train that took them into town, the YMCA, and *the boys.* Mildred had never been one to flirt or act silly around boys, like so many of her friends had done in Biscoe and, apparently, how Betty and Ellen planned to do very soon. Based on their giggles, they were using the time on the train to warm up for the encounter at the Y. Mildred could feel her anxiety and the circles of perspiration under her arms expanding.

The train felt familiar to Mildred, as she used to take one to school in Biscoe. In some ways, Biscoe and Danville were strikingly similar. Dan River Mills dwarfed the Biscoe's closed Ailene Plant, but both industries provided their communities many amenities, including schools, rails, employment, health care, stores, churches, and more. Her transition would be easier because of these similarities, Mildred assured herself.

The YMCA was a large three-story building. Like nearly everything built by the Mill, it was red brick. A sweeping brick staircase, bordered by thick concrete railings, led up to the large front porch. Young men were everywhere. Long legs hung over the porch railing and open windowsills and dangled from the lower limbs of the large trees in the front yard, though "yard" was a gracious description of the dirt and weeds between the street and the front porch. Cigarette butts were scattered like confetti after a ticker-tape parade. Nearly every young man had a cigarette hanging from his mouth.

Mildred noticed they weren't the first girls to arrive. She saw dozens of young men paired with a young woman. Looking at them gave her hope for a pleasant afternoon.

As the three of them approached the Y's front yard, five boys subtly nodded at each other, jumped down off the porch railing, and walked toward the girls. All of them narrowed their path to Betty. She brightened up, and so did they. As if choreographed for theater, two boys spun off toward Ellen, leaving the other three determined to win Betty's attention.

Mildred looked around, wondering what she should do when a young man jumped down from a tree and made his way to her. He was tall and lanky, with brown hair neatly parted down the middle. He had on worn but clean brown pants and a blue shirt. He bent over and quickly brushed his pant legs and the top of his black shoes. His nose was long, his lips thin, and his neck outlined with muscle. He smiled at Mildred, revealing white teeth, with a gap on the bottom front from a missing tooth.

Mildred smiled back, but this was not easy for her. She had always been awkward around boys. She had overheard people say, "Mildred is a pretty girl, but she's just too serious. Boys want a lighthearted girl."

That whole thing with the eyes rolling and hips swaying back and forth, giggling, and being coy — Mildred had never gotten the hang of it. And when she tried it, she didn't like herself, and it didn't seem to attract boys any more than her standard, more direct approach — the approach where she extended her hand and introduced herself. Mildred liked sports and was no stranger to politics, agriculture, lumber, mechanics, and other "manly" things. So, she could easily talk to boys about many topics, but they didn't seem to want to talk about those things, at least not with a girl. At least, not with her.

As the young man got close to Mildred, she extended her hand. "Good afternoon."

"Good afternoon. My name is Willie. What's yours?" he said with a warm smile.

"I'm Mildred, Mildred Long."

"Nice to meet you, Mildred Long." He pumped her hand and then motioned for her to sit on a bench under the tree.

As Mildred sat down on the bench, she quickly glanced around and noticed that the vetting was complete. All three girls now had one boy engaged in conversation. Clearly, Betty was having a wonderful time. She laughed and talked non-stop. Ellen too could hold her own, just not as loud and fast as Betty. Mildred and her new friend talked intermittently; each attempt to have a conversation stalled before it got out of the station.

"So, where did you go to church this morning?" asked Mildred.

"I slept in, didn't go. What about you? Did you go to church?" Willie asked.

"Oh, I went to the Methodist Church. I'm Methodist."

"I'm Catholic, I guess. At least that's what my mama told me."

Both Mildred and Willie looked up into the tree above them to spot a bluebird calling to its mate. Their eyes returned to gaze at their hands in their laps.

"Where are you from?" he asked, daring to glance up at Mildred.

"Biscoe, North Carolina."

"Never heard of it."

"How about you—where are you from?" asked Mildred.

"Galax, Virginia."

"I've never heard of that," said Mildred.

Another long pause, then Willie tried again.

"I've worked at the Mill for three years. What about you? Are you new? I've never seen you before."

"Yes, I start tomorrow. Frankly, I'm a bit nervous. Can you tell me what to expect?"

"Not really. It seems like a long time ago, and things have changed so much since then. Not much I can tell ya."

〝   "What about the strike last year? How were things during that time?"

"I don't get involved in politics. I guess you could say I don't talk about religion or politics."

Mildred uncrossed her legs at the knees, crossed them at the ankles, and used her hands to press the skirt of her dress. *The time is crawling. Can't we just call this a day and go back home?*

She looked from Betty to Ellen, but they were too engaged in conversation to notice. Finally, she looked at Willie and said, "Excuse me for a minute. I need to talk to my friend."

"Sure, no problem," he said.

Mildred walked over to Ellen. "Excuse me, Ellen." She waited for a lull in the conversation and for Ellen to look at her. "I'm ready to go back to Hylton Hall. Do you want to go with me?"

"I guess that would be all right," she said to Mildred, then turned to face her male friend. "Do you mind if I go with my friend back to Hylton Hall?"

"No, go ahead. But I'd like to see you again sometime," he said with a smile.

"That would be nice. Maybe next Sunday?"

"Yes, next Sunday would be nice."

Mildred and Ellen walked together to where Betty was engaged with her new friend. "Excuse us," Ellen said. "Mildred and I are going back to Hylton Hall. Do you want to go with us?"

"No, I think I'll stay a bit longer. Joe, here, will walk me to the train station. I'll see you at dinner."

Ellen gave Mildred a shoulder shrug. Ellen and Mildred's male friends walked over and stood next to them. Ellen said to them both, "We have to get back to Hylton Hall. We enjoyed meeting you. Thank you for a lovely afternoon."

"Yes, I enjoyed meeting you," Mildred said to Willie. "Maybe we can talk more sometime, that is, if you want."

"Sure," said Willie.

Ellen and Mildred walked around town for a while, recalling their brief time at the Y and wondering what might be happening with Betty. The stores were all closed—with the blue laws, nothing open on Sundays but churches—but the display windows showcased beautiful clothes and housewares. Mildred imagined a time when she would have enough money to purchase the dresses in the windows, and a life where all those household items would surround her, and possibly a husband and children, too. She would certainly need to hone her dating skills before a husband and children became a possibility.

They walked to the train station, arriving just in time for the next train to Hylton Hall. Mildred took a brief nap before dinner, which was a lighter fare that evening, only sandwiches and fruit. Mildred knew her waistline would appreciate the change in diet.

That night, as Mildred lay in bed, she thought about the world buzzing around her. It was a most challenging time. The economy was the worst anybody could remember and showed little sign of improving. The Dust Bowl had devasted the Midwest and impacted the entire country. The President had just announced the New Deal, as he called it, but she guessed that few southern states would vote to participate. With a state senator for a father, Mildred knew her politics. She sighed as she thought about all the unemployed people, including some people in her own family. She felt blessed to have this position.

Mildred picked up the information she had gotten from the Mill when she was still living in Briscoe and considering this employment. She read some of the most recent statistics again. There were more than 6,000 employees at the Dan River Mills, some as young as fourteen. The men were paid an average of 36 cents per hour and women 21 cents to 25 cents per hour. But weavers made 34 cents per hour. *That is the job I want. If I were to become a weaver, I would make enough money to help my family significantly. It might take me several weeks to be accepted into the apprentice program and several months to be trained, but I am committed to making this happen. I might not make history, but I will make textiles.*

Then her mind went to boys. *Is courting supposed to be this hard? It seems so easy for most of the girls I know. Why is it so awkward for me? Honestly, it's more like an obligation than a desire. I like the idea of having a family. I just don't like the process of getting there. Maybe those cultures with arranged marriages are a good idea, at least for girls like me. Just pick somebody for me. Perhaps we would fall in love or maybe just become friends. It sure would be so much easier than this whole courting thing.*

Although if Daddy had picked Willie, I'm not sure how happy I would be. I need somebody with a strong mind who likes to talk about religion and politics and somebody who respects my mind and dreams, somebody who wouldn't laugh at me for wanting to make history.

Chapter Eight
A Time of Rapid Change

To everything, there is a season and a time to every purpose under the heaven:
Ecclesiastes 3:1 KJV

*M*ildred jumped out of bed at the sound of the alarm ringing down the corridors of Hylton Hall. It was six A.M., and everybody had to get up. After a breakfast of eggs, ham, rolls, and juice, she joined Hylton Hall residents as they lined up to walk under the railroad tracks and Dan River Mills' gate. Mildred couldn't help but notice what people were wearing. Clothes were clean but worn, patched, and stained. The recruits stood out because their clothes were not nearly so ragged.

"The work at the mill must be hard on clothes," she said to Ellen.

"Yes, indeed. You'll find that the sewing machines in Hylton Hall are busy. If you didn't know how to mend when you came, you will before you leave. You'll see. That dress you have on now will look like mine in no time."

After dinner the previous night, Miss Hylton had talked to the new employees, answered their questions, and explained what to expect on Monday. Mildred learned what building number and room number to report to. She was entering a whole new universe. Anticipation filled her chest. She turned to Betty and Ellen and said, "Wish me luck."

The girls smiled, and Betty said, "Good luck! Orientation is like school. Urgh!"

And with that, they went their separate ways. Mildred had always enjoyed school, so she was excited about the next two weeks.

On the first day of orientation, about a dozen new employees, mostly female, filed into the classroom and took a seat. The orientation included a history of Dan River Mills, the importance of the work done there, an explanation and map of the Mill's campus, and a walking tour of the campus. She was sure she walked five miles that morning.

The Mill provided lunch, just as promised in the brochure. During lunch, she saw Betty and Ellen and several other girls she had already met, but she couldn't speak to them because she had to stay with the recruits during the week of orientation. She couldn't pick out Willie or the other boys she had met the day before because there were too many people. *Just as well*, she thought. The afternoon continued with more information about the Mill and their work.

Tuesday's orientation included information about the Schoolfield community. Mildred's tour the first day with Betty and Ellen had included some of that community. They saw streets of houses built and owned by the Mill. Some homes had two bedrooms, others as many as four. All homes included running water. The Mill provided wood for the stoves; large backyards allowed for family gardens; front porches encouraged neighborly conversations. Because of the depressed economy, not everyone had employment every day, but the Mill allowed families to stay for a short time without paying rent. The Mill encouraged families to buy their homes, and many who were able did just that.

Outside the classroom in one of the reading rooms at Hylton Hall, Mildred read through some old newspapers and discovered information about the Industrial Democracy. She was intrigued. Industrial Democracy was brought to Dan River Mills by Harrison R. Fitzgerald when he was President of Riverside and Dan River Cotton Mills from 1918 to 1931. Mr. Fitzgerald got the idea from John Leitch, who started this concept in the Chicago stockyards. This "democracy" modeled itself after the United States federal government with a House of Representatives elected by the workers based on one representative for every forty employees. Management appointed the Senate, made up of supervisors and department heads. The Cabinet was akin to the executive branch and included all the officers of the company. Initially, Mildred was impressed with this system. Still, after more observation and conversations with some of the long-time employees, she recognized the system had been heavy on industry heads and light on workers.

The end of the great Industrial Democracy happened on September 29, 1930, when 4,000 Riverside and Dan River Mill workers left their jobs due to a United Textile Workers strike. The two primary issues were a ten-percent wage cut and the "stretch-out" system whereby the company gave additional work to the mill hands. The Mill implemented both of these over the objections of the Industrial Democracy organization. The Schoolfield community fractured between strike supporters and opponents. Violence erupted. Unhappy employees bombed houses, overturned cars, and harassed residents in Schoolfield. It was a time of fear and division, causing an enduring break in the community. The strike lasted fifteen months, ending on January 20, 1931, with none of the strikers' goals accomplished.

Although the strike happened five years prior, Mildred felt the tension still present in the community. She noticed people huddled in groups talking in whispers, turning regularly to see who might be watching them. Mildred also witnessed people crossing the street to avoid someone coming the other way. That was a common practice when a Negro crossed the street to avoid sharing the sidewalk with a white, but what she saw in Schoolfield was among whites.

Learning about the recent political history of the Mill fascinated Mildred, yet she felt relieved that she had arrived after everything had settled a bit. The orientation included nothing about the Industrial Democracy. When one of the students asked about it, the instructor said, "That is not part of our curriculum," and then abruptly moved on to the next topic.

The second week of orientation took a new direction: they were to spend time learning about various work types at the Mill. This activity allowed each of them an opportunity to consider what job best matched their interests. Mildred enjoyed learning more, but she already knew what position she wanted: weaver.

By the end of that second week, the Mill offered Mildred a position as a weaver in training. This training normally required six months. The person who led the training was the world-famous Mr. George Robertson. Even the people in Abilene Textiles in Biscoe had heard of him. He was from England, and Mildred was fascinated by his British accent. The people at the Mill seemed to ignore his fame and affectionately called him "Uncle George." Mildred was humbled to be selected to train under him – "the best in the world," she heard repeatedly.

The weeks flew by. Mildred met more girls at Hylton Hall and more boys at the YMCA. Willie moved back home to Galax, and Mildred never heard from him again. She got involved in various clubs and organizations at church and the Mill. Because the Mill owned the church and everybody who attended the church worked for the Mill, there wasn't much difference between the Mill's activities and the church's activities. She offered to help with the young people's activities at church and soon found herself in charge. Mildred knew a lot about cooking and sewing but took the classes at Hylton Hall anyway and was surprised to learn new recipes and techniques. People in her own family had trouble with alcohol, so she joined the temperance union. She also joined the softball team, a sport she had learned from her brothers.

Mildred enjoyed being in organizations, especially those whose purpose was to serve. And she often found herself in leadership. The community newspaper, called *Contact*, provided information Mildred needed in order to get involved. The Employees' Benefits Association required weekly dues from the workers and covered a whole host of services and activities for the Mill's employees. Mildred's evenings and weekends filled up with many community activities and causes. Her time and interest in going to the YMCA dissipated. Her attempts to find a suitable young man did not meet with success, and the duty of helping her family and country called to her daily. It looked more and more like she was not going to marry. Some days that suited her just fine, and other days she felt almost a sense of panic—living my whole life by myself—I can't do that. She attended a few socials, mostly because she was in charge of them, but never met anybody she liked who wasn't already taken.

The Young Women's Club at the Mill had the high purpose of fighting tuberculosis, sometimes called consumption or the white plague. Even with the anti-spitting laws, T.B. was ubiquitous in Virginia, necessitating several sanatoriums across the state. Mildred joined her club members in selling Christmas Seals to raise funds.

But community involvement did not stop Mildred from missing home and her family. She wrote regularly, and her mother wrote to her as she had an opportunity. As a way to encourage family visits, Hylton Hall allowed families to stay one week a year for free. Mildred was thrilled when she learned that her mother and younger siblings would be taking the train from Biscoe to Danville to visit her. Mildred had described everything to her mother in letters, but nothing compared to seeing it firsthand.

She met them at the train station and showed them to their quarters. Then she led them on a grand tour of Hylton Hall, the Schoolfield Methodist Church, Schoolfield houses, the Mill, and "her loom." The tour intentionally ended at the swimming pool so her younger siblings could take a dip—their first time in a swimming pool. Oh, the squeals!

Nevertheless, She Preached

#   #   #

The days and even the years passed quickly. The years of 1932 to 1940 came to be known as the "lean years" at Dan River Mills because the need for textiles dropped considerably during the depression. Many families left Schoolfield; young men left the YMCA; young women left Hylton Hall. Mildred experienced the loss of good friends, but she chose to stay. She was a valuable employee, and the Mill needed her. Her hours were dependable, and she did not want to return home a perceived failure.

Things at the Mill were not all gold and glitter as advertised and as she had first thought. Mildred was very disturbed to learn that unjust practices hid behind the Mill's massiveness and the values they advertised. Laborers, including spinners, weavers, carders, and maintenance workers, occupied most of the Front Street houses. None of the better-educated, better-dressed mill office workers lived in these small, basic houses. Negroes were segregated to specific jobs, the lowest paying jobs, even less than women. Their housing was separate, inferior, and a distance from the Mill.

Mildred wasn't sure why, but the injustices burned in her like a fire. Most employees just accepted it, but Mildred did not. She tried talking about it at her meetings and Bible studies, but people said it wasn't safe to talk about such things. So she went to her pastor. He was in his office at the church.

"Reverend, do you have a minute?" asked Mildred.

"Certainly. Come right in and sit down," said Reverend Johnson.

Mildred sat down, and Reverend Johnson came out from behind his desk to sit in a chair across from Mildred. "What's on your mind?" inquired Reverend Johnson.

"Things here are so unfair to so many people. The unfairness of everything keeps me up at night."

"Yes, Mildred, they are. Just be careful. Many people lost their jobs when they raised the issues of unfair treatment."

"Why don't you preach about this?" asked Mildred.

"Certainly, the prophets in the Bible provide lots of scripture to preach about the injustices to the poor, widows, and children," said Reverend Johnson.

"And the injustices against the negroes. How do you sleep at night?" asked Mildred. She was incredulous, and her tone conveyed it.

"Mildred, God gives some people the prophet's spirit of justice. It burns in them, just like it burns in you. My advice is to find avenues where you can make a difference. The mills are massive, and you are only one. So pick your battles carefully. God will honor even one small thing you make happen. Think of it like your small lunch that feeds thousands."

"It's hard to keep the fire contained," said Mildred.

"Pray about it, Mildred. God will lead you into opportunities for change. You just have to trust God to do this and not think it all rests on you."

Both were silent for a minute as Mildred absorbed what her pastor had just told her.

"You're right," said Mildred. "Thank you so much. Your advice is just what I needed. And will you pray for me?"

"I already have been," chuckled Reverend Johnson. "On more than one occasion, I've observed the prophet's gift in you. Remember it's a gift that comes with a burden, but the world needs people like you. So don't ever snuff out your fire. Just use it wisely."

#   #   #

The textile industry was in fast transition even during these lean years with new fabrics and techniques. A textile school opened in 1935, the year Mildred arrived. She spent much time there, mostly as a student, but sometimes as an instructor. If she was to lead, she knew she had to learn new skills continually. Mildred was a fast learner, smart, dedicated, disciplined.

God opened an opportunity for Mildred at the YMCA to shake up the status quo. She was one of five women who led a new women's initiative at the Y, allowing the Y to serve both men and women. She opened doors long closed to women.

Mildred wrote home to her mother. *"I am discovering skills and abilities I never knew I had. Nearly every day, I receive praise from my supervisors. They are constantly presenting new challenges to me. I can feel my confidence growing, and I am so grateful for this opportunity."*

Wages during this period also changed. In 1937, skilled men received 53 cents per hour at the Dan River Mill, compared to 49 cents in other southern mills. In that same year, the women earned 46 cents per hour for skilled jobs, compared to 42 cents at other southern mills, a considerable increase from the year before when Mildred started. In 1939, the average workweek was less than thirty-four hours, but by 1941 those hours increased to nearly forty-one per week. The cause of those increased work hours: World War II and the desperate need for all kinds of fabrics. Just before the war, in 1939, Virginia passed a law limiting women's maximum workweek from seventy to forty-eight hours per week. By 1943, Dan River Mills signed the first union contract. With all these advances, Mildred was confident of a fair and bright future at the Mill.

By 1940, the Mill had already introduced wool, worsted yarn, and synthetic fibers like rayon. But the war effort required almost entirely cotton. It appeared cotton was king once again. Drills and twills for uniforms, special combed yarn, wind-resistant oxfords, sateens, and chambray for Navy work uniforms, plus sheets and pillowcases for the armed forces, yarns for machine gun cartridge belts, and parachute harnesses represented the Mill's primary war-time business. The government assisted with both the research and production, but it was not enough to produce everything needed for the war effort. The Mill secured patents for new ideas, but the demand for new fabrics just kept coming: Prince Oxford, Spunray, Skytop, Scotspun, and more.

Every change in fabric and machines necessitated additional training. Mildred became known for her skill and ability to teach others. The Ladies Loom-Fixing School started in

1942. The Mill generally assigned repairs to the men, but with the shortage of male employees, they had no choice but to train the women to do a "man's job." The Mill relied on Mildred during those years, and Mildred felt it her duty to support the war efforts in this way. Many of her family were in the military, including her brothers Elwood, Auley, Herbert, and Raymond. Eventually, she was promoted to work in the personnel department. In this position, Mildred secured a better platform to influence women's upward mobility.

But even as busy as Mildred was, she found it challenging to be away from home for so long. She visited as often as she could, making a special effort to attend funerals, weddings, and baptisms. With a family as large as Mildred's, these family events happened often. Mildred's father had only two brothers and one sister, but Mildred's mother was from a family of fifteen children. And, of course, Mildred was from a family of 12 children. There was always somebody getting married, having babies, or, unfortunately, dying.

Mildred mourned the tragic loss of her Uncle Barnie McCaskill, who was crushed in a mining accident. Uncle Barnie had seven children by his first wife, who had died in childbirth. He had then remarried. His second wife, and their many children, relied upon his income. His extended family struggled to respond with adequate assistance. Mildred worked extra hours and was frugal with her income to send as much money as possible to her family.

In 1938, Mildred's Uncle Mial Colonel Long (her father's brother) and her grandmother on her mother's side died. She had shared a bedroom with her grandmother, so they were unusually close. One of her greatest heartaches came in 1942, when her brother, William Vance, died in a bridge construction accident. It was so hard not to be home for these significant events. Traveling only for the funeral was not nearly enough time.

On Sunday evening, the day after William's funeral, Mildred was dreading the return to Danville. The refrigerator was still full of casseroles brought by neighbors. Her brother, Auley, waited in the car to drive her back to Hylton Hall. Mildred, with arms wrapped tightly around her mother, said through tears, "I don't want to leave, but they need me back at the Mill. My heart tells me to stay right here, but my head says I must return to help the war effort and our family. Help me, Mama."

Victoria released her daughter's embrace just enough to look into her eyes. "You'll be all right. I'll be all right. God will provide, and we'll see each other again. Let's make a promise to write every week until this season of grief passes. Can we do that?"

"Yes, Mama. We'll do that. But promise me that if you change your mind and need me to come home that you'll tell me. I'll be on the next train."

"I promise, Mildred. Now go with your brother, Auley. He's waiting."

And with that, Mildred again left her family in Biscoe and returned to her life at the Mill.

Chapter Nine
A Six Week Revival

And Jesus went about all the cities and villages,
teaching in their synagogues,
and preaching the gospel of the kingdom, and healing every sickness
and every disease among the people. But when he saw the multitudes,
he was moved with compassion on them because they fainted,
and were scattered abroad, as sheep having no shepherd.
Then saith he unto his disciples, "The harvest truly is plenteous,
but the labourers are few; Pray ye, therefore, the Lord of the harvest,
that he will send forth labourers into his harvest."
Matthew 25:35-38 KJV

$\mathcal{B}$ack in Richmond, Lillian, now in her late twenties, was contemplating a journey of her own.

"Mama, listen to this letter. It's from Reverend Baughman in Cumberland, Maryland. Remember, he is the pastor of First Church where I preached last year," Lillian said. She was standing at the door to the kitchen where her mother was peeling potatoes for supper.

"Yes, I remember that revival. But Lillian, that's so far away. What was it, over two hundred miles? It was a hardship for all of us. Surely he's not asking you to come back," said Goldie.

Nevertheless, She Preached

"Reverend Baughman thought we might have that response. Listen to what he wrote."

> *Dear Miss Russell,*
>
> *Greetings to you in the name of our Lord Jesus Christ. The hills and valleys of Cumberland haven't been the same since your revival here last year. They are calling out for you to return. Now, knowing you might object to coming so far so soon, the area churches have put together a plan we would like you to consider.*
>
> *First Methodist Church would like you to come on Palm Sunday and preach for two weeks, including Easter Sunday. Then Trinity Methodist Church and their pastor, Reverend Neel, plus Davis Memorial Methodist Church, both here in Cumberland, would like you to preach the two weeks after that. We are already considering how to increase space to accommodate the expected large crowds. The local radio station has agreed to broadcast the services.*
>
> *Also, churches in Bedford, Pennsylvania, would like you to preach a two-week revival up there following your time at Trinity. We hope that with this combined effort, we could persuade you to travel the extended distance from Richmond for a six-week revival.*
>
> *May I be so bold as to say that God desires to have you come? The harvest is plentiful, but the harvesters are few. We believe you are the one God has chosen to harvest these souls for Christ.*
>
> *Of course, you are welcome to stay with my wife and our family the entire time you are in Cumberland. I look forward to hearing from you.*
>
> *Sincerely,*
> *Reverend George E. Baughman*

"Six weeks," exclaimed Goldie. "I just don't think that is possible for so many reasons. It's so far away. Nobody could travel and stay with you that long, and it's just not safe for you to be by yourself even if you're staying with the Baughman's. Six weeks? I've never heard of such a thing." By this time, Goldie was talking so fast that she was gasping for air, so she sat down at the kitchen table.

"Six weeks?" Lillian said. "Even if I preach only five times a week, that's thirty sermons. How in the world would I ever prepare so many sermons?" Lillian sat down at the table with her mother.

"It's just so outrageous. Do we even tell your father?" Goldie questioned.

There was a pause in the conversation as both women took deep breaths and collected their thoughts. Finally, Lillian said, "We will put this to prayer, just like we do every revival invitation. And we will talk to Daddy. His understanding of this is important. Don't you agree, Mama?"

"Yes, I suppose we should at least let him know you got this ridiculous invitation," Goldie said with a sigh. "He should be home in about thirty minutes. Will you stay and help me get supper?"

As Lillian and Goldie continued to prepare supper, they were silent, each one considering the pros and cons of a six-week revival in Cumberland, Maryland. Lillian found her mind and spirit opening to the possibility. She was eager to hear what her father had to say.

After everyone had eaten and washed the dishes, Lillian sat in the living room with her parents. E.W. was reading the paper, and Goldie was mending a pair of his socks. She looked up at Lillian and nodded her head just slightly.

"Daddy, Mama and I want to talk to you about something," Lillian said.

E.W. put down the paper. "Certainly, what is it?"

"Do you remember last year when I did the revival up in Cumberland, Maryland?"

"Yes, of course, I remember that. Pete went with you. As I recall, it was quite successful with more than one hundred people committing to Christ."

"Well, I got a letter today from Reverend Baughman. The churches in that community have organized and invited me to preach a four-week revival," Lillian said.

"Four weeks? That's a long time," E.W. said.

"But there's more. Just north of them, in Bedford, Pennsylvania, the churches have asked me to follow up the four-week revival in Cumberland with a two-week revival in Bedford," Lillian handed the letter to her father.

"That's six weeks, Lillian. Six weeks. I've never heard of a six-week revival." E.W. took the letter and read it. "They really want you to come, don't they? Very persuasive, that Reverend Baughman." E.W. read the letter a second time. "Very persuasive. You can think of it as three two week revivals. That's a lot of pressure on you, but you have done revivals back to back before. Goldie, what do you think?"

Goldie was almost in tears. "I think this is a ridiculous invitation to a young, single woman, and any responsible parent would say absolutely not."

"But Mama, I'm a grown woman. While I appreciate your concern, this is not a decision for you to make but is mine to decide. Help me understand why you are so opposed to this. Tell me what frightens you the most."

"Your safety. There are so many things that could happen. Your father and I have always managed to be sure some other adult travels with you. But none of us can do that for six weeks."

"What if I found somebody who could go with me and stay with me the entire time?" asked Lillian.

"That would certainly help. But who could do that?" asked Goldie.

"I don't have anybody in mind but let me pray about it. Do you have other concerns?"

"Not really. Your wellbeing is my big concern. Of course, I'll miss you terribly, but that is something I have to deal with, not you," Goldie said.

E.W. said, "Why don't we all pray about it. And Lillian, you start thinking about who could go with you. We probably have several weeks before you have to respond to Reverend Baughman. Is that all right with both of you?"

Both women nodded their heads in agreement.

The next morning Goldie greeted Lillian in the kitchen with a cup of hot tea and a bright smile.

Goldie said, "I prayed much of the night, and I think I might know the perfect person to accompany you to Cumberland. She lives just a couple of blocks over. Maybe you've met her and her mother at our church. Her name is Mary Gills. Her mother is Alice Mae, but they call her Mae. She's a widow of some years. They share a home. Mary works as a switchboard operator. Do you know them?"

"I think I met Mary at church one time. She's a little older than I am, right?"

Goldie nodded as she wiped the soap bubbles out of the sink.

"Seems like a nice lady. Maybe I'll talk to her about this," Lillian said. "Do you have their address? I could arrange a visit to their home. But frankly, Mama, I'm surprised you're suggesting this. I thought you opposed my going to Cumberland for six weeks."

"I am opposed, but I agreed to pray about it, and this is where prayer led me. I cannot hide this answer to prayer from you. I've written the names and address down for you." Goldie slid a piece of paper across the kitchen table to Lillian. "The Gills don't have a phone, so you'll need to write to them."

Lillian wrote Mary a letter and put it in the mail slot of the Gills' home's front door. Mary wrote back that she was interested and suggested a time to meet at her home.

A week later, Lillian appeared on the Gills' doorstep.

"Good evening, Miss Russell. It's an honor to have you in our home." Mary greeted Lillian. "Please, come in."

Lillian walked in. The modest living room had a two-cushion sofa and a dining room chair that, based on the indentations in the linoleum floor, had been taken from the small dining room table. A rocking chair was rocking slightly after Mae rose from it and moved to the door. White doilies covered the sofa's worn arms, sheer curtains hung over the windows, an area rug covered a section of the floor, and a tray with a teapot, three teacups and spoons, and a sugar bowl sat on the coffee table.

"Please, sit here on the sofa and allow me to pour you some tea," said Mae.

"That would be lovely." Lillian said.

Mary poured tea, and the three women stirred sugar into their tea. Mae spoke over the clatter of spoons against cups. "I'm Mae Gills, and this is my daughter, Mary. We understand from your letter that you want to talk to Mary about accompanying you for six weeks in Maryland and Pennsylvania."

"Yes, I do. Thank you for allowing me this time." Lillian pressed her skirt with her hands, a nervous habit she was unsuccessfully trying to stop. She noticed both Mae and Mary were dressed modestly in white blouses and long skirts. Mae's skirt was navy blue; Mary's had pink and yellow flowers. A sewing machine sat under the window, and Lillian suspected one or both of them had made their skirts since she had seen the flowered fabric at the store in Highland Park. Their shoes were worn but recently polished. Both wore their long hair braided and in a bun, just like Lillian's. Mae's hair was salt and pepper; Mary's was black as coal. Both had fair complexions with deep blue eyes.

"I've got a rather unusual situation. As you likely know, I'm a revival speaker and have recently received an invitation to speak next spring in Cumberland, Maryland, and Bedford, Pennsylvania, for a total of six weeks. While the pastor has graciously invited me to stay with him and his wife for four of those weeks, it's just not appropriate for me to travel alone. Usually, a family member travels with me, but no family can be gone that long. So I'm seeking a woman to travel with me."

Lillian turned to face Mary. "Mary, if I may be so bold before we talk about this potential trip, would you mind telling me about yourself?"

"Certainly, Miss Russell. I'm honored you are even considering me."

Mary looked at her mother, who nodded for her to continue. "In 1919, when I was just thirteen years old, our father died in a mining accident, leaving my mother a widow and my younger brother Robert and me without a father. We couldn't survive on our own, so we moved to Lynchburg, where my father had extended family. They offered to help us. My brother and I completed high school there. He got married and moved away."

Lillian nodded, and Mary continued.

"I'd hoped to get married and raise a family, but the possibilities in Lynchburg were limited, so I begged mother to move to Richmond where there would be more men to court. She agreed." Mary looked at her mother and then down at her ringless hands in her lap.

Mae picked up where her daughter left off, a painful place in this story. "But it was too late. Mary was too old. Men her age were already married."

Everyone was silent for a few moments before Mary continued, a conviction in her voice.

"Yes, but I want my life to count. I want it to matter. I want to be more than a telephone operator."

Mae interrupted. "While I greatly appreciate her taking care of me all these years, I want more for her too. I want her to have her own life, to travel and see more of the world. I understand this is just six weeks and only in the next state, but it's a beginning."

"Thank you for telling me all of this. As a single woman myself, I know some of this was not easy to share. Can you tell me about your faith? I assume you are a Christian."

"Oh, yes, I've been a Christian all my life. I don't remember a moment when I haven't relied upon God as my Provider and Christ as my Savior. Mind you, I'm not perfect, but I'm totally devoted to serving my Lord. Traveling with you would allow me to do that in ways I couldn't before. I should also mention that I play the piano, self-taught. I play for the children's Sunday School at Highland Park Methodist Church."

Mary uncrossed her legs and leaned forward, putting her elbows on her knees. "Miss Russell, can I tell you something?"

"Certainly."

"I knew about you when I lived in Lynchburg. You did several revivals there. I attended many of them and heard you preach. You're very gifted. Everybody in Lynchburg knows about you. You're famous in those parts." Mary's voice grew earnest. "Helping you in any way at all would bring me so much happiness. While I don't make much as a switchboard operator, it would be a hardship for me not to work those six weeks. Is there any way you could pay me something?"

"Yes, I can do that. Let me know the amount your employer would usually pay you, and I will tell the churches they will need to compensate at least that amount. I don't want this to be a hardship for you or your mother. Would that be all right?"

Mary gave her a wide smile. "That would be more than all right."

"Mary, I understand that you drive. I'm curious if you have a car?"

"Yes, I do drive. Mother and I brought a car with us from Lynchburg. When my brother left, my father's family said it was essential for us to have a car and a driver. So they taught me how to drive and bought us a car."

"That's good to know, but I don't think it would be proper for us to travel that far alone," Lillian said. "I will see if one of my brothers or even my father can take us there. Once in Cumberland, the people there will provide whatever transportation we need. Would you be comfortable with that arrangement?"

"Yes, I know your family from church. That will be fine," Mary said.

"I do have a few more questions." Lillian leaned forward in her chair.

"Okay, go ahead and ask anything you want."

"Do you smoke?"

"Absolutely not. Never have. Never will."

"That's good to hear. What about alcohol? Do you drink?"

"Oh, Miss Russell, alcohol has never touched my lips. I consider it the work of the devil."

"Thank you for answering me so directly, Mary. I think we have an agreement. I will write to the pastor in Cumberland and let him know our plans. And I will get back to you with more details. Right now, my big task is to write thirty sermons.." Lillian leaned back in her chair and smiled.

"Can I pour you some more tea?" asked Mae.

"No, thank you, I need to be going. But I'll be back in touch."

All the women stood, and Lillian walked to the front door, shook hands with Mary and Mae, and left. She whistled as she walked back to her home.

# # #

"I'm going to miss you, Lillian. Six weeks is a long time to be gone." Polly and Lillian were both in their bedroom packing Lillian's suitcase. "I wish I could come with you, but I can't be gone from work that long."

"I wish you could come too. Pete's driving me up and staying a few days to provide music for the revival opening and to be sure my accommodations are in order. Daddy and Mama are also driving up for a few days about two weeks later. Everybody's nervous about this six-week revival except me. Maybe you could ride up with them when they come."

"If my softball schedule allows, I'll go with them," said Polly. "Lillian, it's too bad you don't have a robe. It would save packing so many suits." Polly compared the pile of clothes lying on the bed to the size of the suitcase.

"You know, because I'm not a reverend, I don't wear a robe. I'm taking two black suits and will wear those. If one gets soiled, I can take it to the cleaners and still have one to wear. Those suits are as close to a robe as I'll likely ever have."

"So, why aren't you a reverend? You preach more often than most pastors of local churches."

"I've thought about that too. Our *Book of Discipline* states that no church member shall be at liberty to preach without a license, yet I do that every time I preach a revival. Maybe I'll check into it with our pastor when I get back from Cumberland. Now sit on this suitcase, so I can get it closed."

Polly climbed up onto the bed and sat on the suitcase. Lillian secured the latches. "That should do it," said Lillian.

Early the next morning Pete, Mary, and Lillian left Richmond and drove to Boots and Fenner's home in Falls Church, Virginia. They spent the night there and then went the next day to Cumberland, Maryland. Around 6:00 P.M., they pulled into the parking lot of the Methodist Church. The church door was open, so they went in. People were busy in the sanctuary setting up chairs in the aisles and putting new candles on the altar. After inquiring, they learned Reverend Baughman was in his study.

Lillian recognized him immediately from having been with him the year before. Reverend Baughman was a tall man with broad shoulders and an infectious smile. He had a good speaking and singing voice. Lillian remembered him as nervous; something was always moving. Sometimes he was tapping his foot, and other times his fingers. He ran his fingers through his light brown hair so often that it looked like he had forgotten to comb it. But the members of his church loved him. Lillian noted he was a good listener, a trait so essential to pastoral care.

Reverend Baughman welcomed Lillian, Mary, and Pete. "Good evening, Reverend Russell. It's such a privilege to greet you. And Pete, it's good—"

Lillian interrupted Reverend Baughman. "Oh, I'm not *Reverend* Russell. I'm *Miss* Russell. I've no official status in the Methodist Church. I thought you knew that from when I was here last year."

"I'm sorry. I guess I forgot. But it's not a problem, other than our publicity has listed you as Reverend Russell. The bulletin for tonight also lists your title as a reverend. What do you want me to do?"

"Please introduce me as Miss Russell. Maybe the bulletins for the following nights can be corrected before you print them."

"I do have one other concern about the reverend title," Reverend Baughman said. "Here in the Baltimore Conference, we require evangelists to have a license to preach. Have you received that in your conference in Virginia?"

"I haven't. No one has ever asked me about that."

"I don't mean to create a problem if there is none. Can you tell me why after all these years of revival preaching, you aren't licensed?"

"I would guess it has to do with being female. The Virginia Conference has never licensed a woman. We're rather traditional down there, even though it's 1941."

"I understand. There is quite a movement afoot spearheaded by the Women's Society to petition the General Conference for full clergy rights for women. They are hoping for that to happen in 1944. After witnessing you preach, I'm one of their biggest supporters. We need to stop wasting the gifts of our women."

Lillian nodded her head in agreement. Pete said, "I couldn't agree more." Mary didn't respond.

"Anyway," said Reverend Baughman, "all the churches in this area are ready and excited about your six weeks here. There's no stopping us now." He smiled that infectious grin.

Pete straightened his shoulders and interrupted, "I would hope so. My sister has been preaching revivals for more than a decade. Let me tell you; there is no issue here."

"Pete, it's all right. We're all in agreement," Lillian said. "Thank you, Reverend Baughman, for understanding. Just introduce me as 'Miss Russell', not Reverend Russell. Although, I do like the sound of the reverend." Lillian smiled.

Lillian was so popular in Cumberland that she preached three times Easter Sunday: 11 A.M., 3:00 P.M., and 7:30 P.M. She was scheduled to conclude her time at Trinity on Saturday night but agreed to one more, a farewell sermon Sunday morning. Word of Miss Russell's popularity and the success of these revivals spread throughout the panhandle of Maryland. Even the newspaper in Richmond carried the story.

Chapter Ten
License to Preach

And Jabez called on the God of Israel, saying,
Oh that thou wouldest bless me indeed,
and enlarge my coast, and that thine hand might be with me,
and that thou wouldest keep me from evil, that it may not grieve me!
And God granted him that which he requested.
I Chronicles 4:10 (Prayer of Jabez) KJV

*W*hen Lillian returned to Richmond after the six-week revival in Cumberland, she investigated the process and possibility of receiving a license to preach. She started with her home church, Highland Park Methodist Church. Reverend Engle, their pastor, supported Lillian in every way. She was a celebrity in Richmond, and her celebrity status also gave Highland Park Methodist Church status. So securing their approval was relatively easy. However, the recommendation by the Richmond District presented a challenge.

Reverend Thomas F. Carroll, superintendent of the Richmond District in 1941, was well-educated, having attended Randolph-Macon College, the University of Virginia, Princeton, and American University, where he received his Ph.D. He was both the son and the brother of clergy in the Virginia Conference. Before coming to Richmond, he had served as the District Superintendent of the Norfolk District. He had accomplished all of this by supporting the traditions of the church. Bishops knew they could send Reverend Carroll into most any church situation where the traditional ways of Methodism were challenged, and he would restore Methodist orthodoxy. Nothing in his background opened his mind or spirit to be the first superintendent in the Virginia Conference to consider a woman for a license to preach.

Lillian wrote Reverend Carroll and asked to meet with the District Committee on Ministry. A week later, Lillian gathered the mail at her home and found a letter from the Richmond District office addressed to her. She opened the envelope, read the letter, and then went into the kitchen where both of her parents sat at the table listening to the radio. Lillian was crying.

"Mama and Daddy, I just received this letter from our District Superintendent. He has refused to meet with me about obtaining a license to preach. I'm so angry and so," she paused, "so devasted. How can this happen? After all I have done. My record merits at least an interview. I'm going to march right into his office and give him a piece of my mind." By this time, Lillian was sobbing with indignation.

Goldie got up from the table and hugged Lillian. "Now, now, Lila, everything's going to be all right. God didn't bring you this far to stop now."

E.W. turned off the radio and pulled out a chair for Lillian. "Your mother is right, Lila. Let's talk this through."

"What's there to talk about? It sounds like Reverend Doctor Carroll has already made his decision, and the door is closed," cried Lillian.

"Ah, yes, but where man closes a door, God opens a window. Let's see if we can see God's open window," said E.W.

There was some silence. E.W. gave Lillian the handkerchief from his pocket. She dabbed her eyes and wiped her nose with it, and sniffled. "All right, a window."

"I've heard excellent things about our Bishop, and I've had the opportunity to speak with him on several occasions. He seems progressive, one less about maintaining tradition and more about making progress. Sometimes you have to work around the obstacle, even go to the top. If you're willing, you can make an appointment with Bishop Peele, and I'll take you to see him."

"I like that idea,' Goldie said.

"Lila, didn't Bishop Peele attend one of your revivals here in Richmond?"

"Yes, he did. I had forgotten that. I actually met him afterward. He seemed very nice. Yes, Daddy, I'll contact him."

"Let's see if this is our window," said E.W.

Lillian wrote Bishop Peele and sought his advice. He wrote back and said an in-person visit was unnecessary and suggested she contact the superintendent of the neighboring Rappahannock District. He had already discussed the idea with him and would not be surprised by her contact.

Lillian followed his suggestion and called Reverend Charles Fredrick Williams. He was amenable to having Lillian come through his district to apply for a license to preach.

Before she could be approved, Lillian had to complete one year in the Conference Course of Study. This study included reading several books: *The Bible Speaks in Our Generation* by Frank Lankard; A *Manual of Christian Beliefs* by Edwin Lewis; and *The Art of Preaching* by Charles Brown. Lillian purchased and read these books thoroughly, taking detailed notes, preparing to be interviewed by the district licensing committee.

On the day of the interview, Lillian dressed in a white suit, pinned her watch to her suit jacket, and secured the latch on her pearl necklace. Her father drove her to the Rappahannock District office.

"Daddy, I think I'm as nervous as I was going to my first revival. I prepared as much as I knew how through study and prayer. Do you think I'm ready for this?"

"Lila, I've never met anybody who prepares as thoroughly as you do. I can't imagine you will have any problems today. None at all."

"It's strange that for all those years of preaching revivals, the idea of having a license to preach was never important to me. But today, nothing is more important. I want this, Daddy."

"If it's God's will, it will happen. Just trust," said E.W.

"I do fully trust God in this and in all things," said Lillian.

"Deep breath, Lila. Take a couple of deep breaths of the Holy Spirit. You'll be fine."

Lillian took some deep breaths through her nose and relaxed her shoulders. In a few miles, they pulled into the church parking lot.

"Good morning, Miss Russell," Reverend Williams said as he extended his hand to Lillian and then E.W.

"I assume this is your father."

"Yes, this is my father, E.W. Russell," Lillian said.

"Mr. Russell, I hope you will join us for this meeting," said the District Superintendent.

"Of course, I will be glad to accompany my daughter, if it's all right with her."

"Yes, that's fine with me," Lillian said.

Reverend Williams escorted E.W. and Lillian into the front door of the church. They walked through the sanctuary to a classroom behind the sanctuary. The walls of the classroom were painted a pale green. Dainty curtains covered the windows. The sun coming through the curtains overpowered the dim ceiling lights. At one end of the room stood a large blackboard. In the center of the room sat a large wooden table with wooden chairs all around. The men seated around the table stood when Lillian entered the room.

Reverend Williams gestured to his guests and said, "Please, Miss Russell, have a seat at the head of the table. Mr. Russell, please be seated next to her."

Reverend Williams sat at the opposite end of the table. Lillian noted that the eight men sitting around the table were all dressed in black suits and white shirts. Only their ties distinguished them. The most common color was red. *It is Pentecost season, so a red tie on a preacher is liturgically appropriate,* Lillian thought. Some of the ties were fashionably four inches wide, others narrower. One man donned a narrow, black tie. *It suits his downcast countenance,* thought Lillian. They leaned over the table to shake E.W. and Lillian's hands. As they sat down, to a one, Lillian noted, they pulled their ties down while keeping their gaze on her. She suddenly realized she felt half-dressed without a tie. She gently pulled on the string of pearls around her neck.

After introductions and prayer, the questions began.

"Miss Russell," said Reverend William, "may I state the obvious. This is a historic meeting. No woman in the 158-year history of the Virginia Conference of Methodism has ever been granted a license to preach. Some speculate no Methodist Conference south of the Mason-Dixon line has ever given a license to preach to a woman. Also, it is highly unusual that we are doing this across district lines. It is only with permission from Bishop Peele that we hold this meeting."

Then Reverend Williams took his focus off Lillian, expanding it to the entire group. "For all of us around this table, we must follow the *Book of Discipline* strictly."

They began with the questions outlined in the *Book of Discipline*.

"Do you know God as a pardoning God?" asked Reverend Williams.

"Yes, I do know God as a pardoning God. My sins are many, and I go to God every day in prayer, pleading for forgiveness."

Another member of the committee asked, "Have you the love of God abiding in you?"

Lillian lowered her head, then looked up at the minister asking the question. "Yes, I asked the love of God to abide in my heart when I was just a child. That love has never left. It's only grown."

They continued around the table. "Do you desire nothing but God?"

Lillian remembered her first invitation to preach a revival and her automatic obedience to the will of God. "Yes, I desire nothing but God."

The same clergyman asked, "Are you holy in all manner of conversation?"

Lillian didn't hesitate. "That is my goal, but not as yet my accomplishment."

Nevertheless, She Preached

The questions moved toward queries about gifts and graces for the work of preaching as well as the fruits of her preaching. As they got to this subject, Lillian noticed some of the men were relaxing their shoulders, sitting back in their chairs instead of on the edge of their seats. A few smiled at her. She recognized all but one of the men at the table because she had preached at their churches. The one she didn't know was the lone man in the black tie. She knew the other men had witnessed the power of her sermons to convict sinners of their sin and convert them to God's saving grace. They could testify to seeing believers edified and transformed by her preaching.

All the questions spelled out in the *Book of Discipline* had been asked, suggesting the end of the interview. Lillian felt a sense of relief.

However, the black-tie-clergyman, cleared his throat, straightened his collar, and said to Lillian, "You know that no woman in the history of Virginia Methodism has ever received a license to preach. Why do you think that is, and why do you think we should vote to change history today?"

The other men leaned in as they waited for Lillian's response. So many thoughts came to her mind. *That question is not in the Discipline. I wonder if they are even allowed to ask me that. What I would like to say would probably disqualify me. God, help me speak the truth without disqualifying myself.*

Lillian sat up straight in her chair. "I cannot speak to the reasons for the omissions of our history, as I am only twenty-seven years old, and have never served in district or conference leadership. All I know is that the *Methodist Book of Discipline* requires all those who preach regularly in Methodist pulpits to have a license. I have preached hundreds of times in Methodist pulpits in multiple conferences without a license. It's time for me to comply with our polity."

E.W. exhaled and leaned back in his chair with a smile on his face. The other men looked at each other and nodded.

Reverend Williams said, "That pretty much sums up why we are here. Are there any other questions?" When no one responded, he asked E.W. "Is there anything you would to add?"

E.W. responded, "Yes." He cleared his throat before continuing. "I have accompanied my daughter Lila to many revivals and witnessed the power of Christ in her. She is as called by God as any of you around this table. Since she was a small child she has taken her faith seriously. She's devoted to Bible study, prayer, and service. I've no reason to doubt her qualifications for a license to preach."

"Thank you, Mr. Russell and Miss Russell," said Reverend Williams. "Would you be so kind as to step out of the room for a few minutes while we discuss our decision?"

Lillian and her father went into another classroom and waited. Neither of them spoke a word to each other. Lillian had no idea what the room even looked like because she kept her gaze on her hands folded in her lap with the plan to pray. However, prayers were impossible for her. She could not calm her mind to formulate a coherent sentence. She hoped her father was able to pray. If she isn't approved, will anybody invite her to preach another revival? Maybe she should have left this whole endeavor alone.

In fifteen minutes, Reverend Williams came into their classroom and invited Lillian and E.W. back to the meeting. Once everyone was seated, he spoke. "Lillian, it is with great joy that we tell you that we have recommended you receive a license as a local preacher. Because of the historic nature of this decision it should have been most difficult, full of much debate, but you've made our task easy. You are a serious student of the faith and a gifted conveyor of the Gospel. Your father is very proud of you, as well he should be. With the approval of the District Conference and clergy session of the Annual Conference, you may continue your ministry of evangelism as a licensed preacher."

Lillian wanted to give this district superintendent a big hug around his neck, but he was too tall, and she thought better of that idea. Instead, she pulled her ear-to-ear-smile to a more controlled grin and thanked him. She moved around the table, thanking all the men and shaking their hands.

She walked with her father to the parking lot. When they got to the car, she turned to him, released the big smile she had been holding back, squealed, "I passed!" and gave him the hug.

Following her approval by the Rappahannock District Conference, the Richmond newspaper captured the story this way:

> Miss Lillian Russell was yesterday granted a license as a local Methodist preacher by the Rappahannock District Conference of the Virginia Methodist Conference meeting at Tappahannock. Miss Russell is the first woman ever to be granted such a license in Virginia.
>
> Miss Russell, a member of Highland Park Methodist Church, was described by her pastor, Dr. J. A. Engle, as a capable and fine young woman and an experienced lay evangelist. She has been in demand as a preacher since girlhood and has held revival meetings over a large part of Virginia. Last April she conducted a six-week meeting at Cumberland, MD.
>
> Miss Russell's father, E.W. Russell, is teacher of the Russell Bible Class at Highland Park Methodist Church, and her mother conducts the Suzanna Wesley class there.
>
> The license granted Miss Russell means that she may take over a pulpit for a minister, or conduct revival services, but does not mean that she is admitted to the Methodist conference as a traveling pastor subject to appointment.

[1]Within months Lillian was approved by the Rappahannock District and the Annual Conference. The Richmond District listed Miss Lillian Russell under the category of "License to Preach."

---

[1] It is unclear why a candidate for a license to preach from the Richmond District was approved by the Rappahannock District. Decades later, a retired bishop who knew the district superintendents involved commented that "while the Discipline at that time did not prevent a woman from receiving a license to preach, there may have been some other impediments," suggesting Reverend Carroll may have been the impediment.

Miss Lillian Russell was now *Reverend* Lillian Russell. Superintendent T.F. Carroll was reassigned by Bishop Peele from Richmond to a different assignment in 1944. The magazine for Methodists in Virginia called the *Advocate* made no mention of history being made with Lillian's approval for a license to preach.

Each year, all licensed preachers, including Lillian, were required to return to the Licensing Committee to have their license status continued. The concerns explored at those annual interviews were mostly those of abstinence from tobacco and alcohol. She also was required to continue the Course of Study. Abstinence and study had been essential elements of Lillian's life for as long as she could remember. She had no problems maintaining her license to preach.

Chapter Eleven
Evangelist to Pastor

"Are ye able," still the Master whispers down eternity.
And heroic spirits answer, now, as then in Galilee.
"Lord, we are able, our spirits are Thine,
Remold them, make us like Thee, divine.
Thy guiding radiance above us shall be
A beacon to God, to love and loyalty."
Author, Earl Marlatt (1926)

$\mathcal{I}$n the 1940s there were many stained glass ceilings for women to break. Depending upon the church and the pastor, women could teach children, youth, and women. They could lead worship on Sunday morning, and serve in certain leadership positions. But women seldom, if ever, worked as the pastor of a local church. However, Pearl Harbor and the United States' involvement in World War II changed that. If necessity is the mother of invention, then the invention of female pastors was necessitated by the shortage of men due to the war.

In nearly every *Annual Journal* and weekly *Advocate* the Methodists in Virginia were decrying the desperate need for clergy. The educational goals of clergy demanded high school, college, and seminary. But the need for clergy outweighed the need for educated clergy. This meant men were taken from fields, factories, and forests with little more than a promise they would work toward a high school diploma. Eventually even this strategy of lowering the standards proved inadequate to produce enough pastors. Pews were full, but pulpits empty.

Now that Lillian was a licensed local preacher, she attended the Annual Conferences. She could not help but be aware of the critical need for more pastors. The last day of the conference the appointments were "fixed" by the bishop. Lillian listened as the churches on every district across the Virginia Conference were read with the name of the man appointed to serve as their pastor. She knew many of these men because of her travels as an evangelist. Some of them she greatly respected. Others she knew to be unqualified and ill-prepared.

I know I could do a better job than some of those so-called preachers. They hardly know a Gospel from an Epistle. Too bad women can't be a pastor. That sure would solve a lot of problems in our church.

The Book of Discipline contained the official doctrine and polity of the Methodist Church. It did not prohibit women from being appointed to serve as local pastors. The Bishops of Virginia and their District Superintendents had always been free to appoint women as pastors. This had been true for the church's entire 160-year history. They simply had never taken the leap of courage to exercise this option. That was about to change. History was about to be made, again.

In October 1944, the Methodists of the Virginia Conference met in Lynchburg at the City Auditorium with Bishop W.W. Peele presiding. World War II and Crusade for Christ were the big emphases that year. Lillian attended Annual Conference as a licensed local preacher.

Reverend Dr. Roscoe Jones, District Superintendent of the Petersburg District, sought Lillian out. He was sixty-seven-years-old, and close to retirement. His daughter was the Dean of Women at Madison College in Harrisonburg, Virginia. Over the years he had learned much through his daughter about the many abilities of women.

"Rosie is more than a riveter," she said to her father more than once. "You're in a position to make a difference, Father. Seize the day before it's too late."

Reverend Jones spoke directly to Lillian. "Miss Russell, I'm in a bit of a fix. There's a small church in my district in need of a pastor. I know that you've preached there before as part of a revival at their church. I've already spoken with the Bishop and the local church leaders. All are amenable to having you as their pastor."

Lillian's head spun. *Women don't drive cars and women aren't pastors. Which church is he speaking of? I've preached revivals at several churches in his district. Really, it doesn't matter which church. I bragged to myself that I could do this. So, can I?*

Dr. Jones interrupted Lillian's thoughts. "I'm asking you to go to Blandford Methodist Church in Petersburg to serve as their pastor. They've less than two-hundred members, and a little less than one hundred in Sunday School. There's no parsonage. Their music program is poor and could benefit from your singing voice. The salary is more than enough for you. May I tell the Bishop and the people of Blandford that you will serve?"

Before Lillian could stop herself, she responded. "Yes, I'd be honored to serve. I remember them from the revival there. They're a good congregation."

A strange sensation gripped her, that she was not in control of her mouth, as if she were outside herself listening to her own voice. But she knew that this was of God. God had taken control of her mind and her voice. She was speaking now in the same Spirit she preached.

Here she was again, feeling the same emotions she had when she was invited to preach her first revival: frightened yet confident. *I can do all things through Christ, who strengthens me*, she assured herself.

Dr. Jones walked back to the platform of the Annual Conference, whispered in the ear of the Bishop, and sat in the chair reserved for him. Lillian's eyes followed him, and as he sat down, her own knees buckled.

Get a hold of yourself. Is this really happening? Preaching is one thing but serving as a pastor is so much more. There's pastoral care, Sacraments, administration, stewardship, teaching, and attending meetings. The list goes on and on. My family is active enough at Highland Park for me to know there's much I don't know. I'm going to need the strength of Christ more than ever.

Suddenly it occurred to her: *I still have revivals scheduled. What do I do with those commitments? One of them is next week, the same week I'm to start as the pastor at Blandford. Mercy me, what was I thinking?*

On the last day of the 1944 Virginia Annual Conference, the same year the General Conference rejected the petition from the Women's Society for Christian Service for full clergy rights for women, Bishop Peele read the pastoral appointments. Lillian heard her name, *Miss Lillian Russell,* read as the pastor of Blandford. The gasps in the auditorium at this historic announcement were like a whisper compared to the pounding of her own heart. It was official. After the closing hymn and the benediction, several clergymen sought her out to congratulate her. She felt the genuineness of their support and recognized her need for their affirmation. But those congratulatory handshakes were few. She knew this would not be easy.

E.W., a lay delegate to Annual Conference, could not contain his pride for Lillian. He drove like a wild man from Lynchburg to Richmond. As soon as he parked the car in their driveway, he ran into the house shouting, "Goldie, Goldie, where are you?"

"I'm in the kitchen. What in the world is wrong? Is Lila okay?"

"Yes, she is more than okay. She is going to be a pastor."

"What? Slow down. Tell me everything."

By this time Lillian had caught up to her father.

"Lila, tell me what's going on. Wait, Pete and Polly are here. Let's get them," said Goldie. Then she raised her voice and said, "Pete, Polly, come to the kitchen, right now. Right now."

The sound of feet running down the stairs and through the living room, filled the small house like thunder. "We're coming," yelled Polly. "What's going on?"

They ran into the kitchen and stopped. "Oh, hello Daddy and Lila. We didn't know you were home from conference. Anything exciting to report?" asked Pete.

"Exciting? I can hardly wait to tell you," E.W. was panting as he spoke and leaned on the kitchen counter. "Lila has been appointed to a church. She is the pastor of Blandford in the Petersburg District."

"What? How can that be? She's a woman," said Goldie.

"Yeah, a woman," said Polly.

"Well, Reverend Jones asked me to serve as the pastor of Blandford Church, and I said yes," said Lillian.

"And Bishop Peele announced it, so it's official," added E.W.

"Now, all I have to do is conduct a revival next week and learn how to be a pastor," said Lillian with a wry smile.

"You'll be great, Lila," said Polly.

"You'll be okay, I guess," said Pete with a wink.

"You'll be amazing. You were created for such a time as this," said Goldie.

"Amen," said E.W.

The *Virginia Advocate* made no mention of this historical appointment. The Richmond newspaper included her picture and told the story this way:

Woman Pastor Takes Church in Petersburg

Miss Lillian Russell, first woman to be named Supply Pastor in the history of the Methodist Conference of Virginia, will assume her new post at Blandford Church in Petersburg the first Sunday in November.

Taking over a pastorate, a duty heretofore sacred to men in Virginia, will be to Miss Russell a continuation of the pleasant experiences of twelve years of evangelistic work conducted particularly in Virginia as well as throughout the East.

As a Supply Pastor, her duties will correspond exactly as those of Methodist ministers, although because women are not ordained by the church, she is not an ordained minister.

The new appointment is the second of Miss Russel's "firsts." Two years ago she was the first woman to be licensed to preach by the Methodist Church in Virginia.

A graduate of John Marshall High School, Miss Russell left a job with a local department store to begin preaching at the age of eighteen. Her training has been that of practical experience during the twelve-year period of evangelistic work, Miss Russell reports.

She has lived all her life in Highland Park, and her residence is at 3101 Sixth Avenue but to put it more accurately, she says, "I've lived the last twelve years in a suitcase."

She is looking forward to her pastoral duties and said yesterday that already she has been welcomed to the Blandford Church by several members of the congregation. The situation will not be entirely strange to her, she says, because she has conducted meetings there as an evangelist.

A small woman, only five feet two inches tall, and weighing less than 120 pounds, Miss Russell has a pleasant, resonant voice, and says that public speaking has been an easy task for her since she was fifteen years old.

Although she is scheduled to go to her new pastorate on the fifth Sunday in October, she must postpone this until the first Sunday in November, because she already had arranged to conduct a meeting at Branch Memorial Methodist Church, October 22 to November 3.

Lillian completed the scheduled revival at Branch Memorial. Maintaining focus on the messages those two weeks was a challenge because her head and her heart were already at Blandford. She began to write her first sermon and sketched out a schedule to visit the entire congregation, starting with the sick and homebound. She estimated that with a membership of two hundred, she could visit everyone within the first six months. Without a driver's license, she would need to depend on buses. She wondered if her family and church members would assist with transportation as well.

Hopefully, some of the members live near the church and I can walk to visit them. I'll establish regular office hours so my people—"my people," dear God, I love the sound of that—will know where to find me.

Chapter Twelve
Learning the Ropes

Blest be the ties that bind our hearts in Christian love;
The fellowship of kindred minds is like to that above.
--Lyrics by John Fawcett, 1782

$\mathcal{T}$ he first Sunday, Lillian was a nervous wreck. She woke up at five o'clock, put on her navy blue suit, braided her hair, and wrapped it in a perfect circle on the crown of her head. After a quick breakfast of toast and juice she was ready to go by six o'clock. She and her father had decided that leaving by eight would provide them ample time to arrive for both Sunday School and worship. The entire family insisted on being present for the debut, so the whole house buzzed with activity. Lillian paced in her tiny bedroom, with periodic stops at her bed to kneel and pray.

Finally, her sister Polly said, "Lila, I can't look in the mirror long enough to fix my hair without you walking in front of me. Please, go outside and pace so the rest of us can get ready."

Lillian went outside and walked up and down the sidewalk in front of the house stopping about every five minutes to check her watch pinned to her suit jacket. Lillian always wore a watch pinned upside down to her blouse or jacket so she could easily read it. She believed she was too magnetic to wear a wind-up watch on her wrist. Every time she tried wearing a wristwatch, the hands would either stop or move quickly around the face of the clock in double-time. By 7:30 A.M., Lillian couldn't take the suspense any longer. She went back into the house and found her father at the kitchen table drinking a cup of coffee.

"I think we should leave now. What if there's traffic? I can't be late my first Sunday."

"Lila, we timed this trip and allowed an extra thirty minutes for traffic. If we go now, the church isn't likely to even be unlocked. We'll leave at eight, the time we agreed to."

Lillian gave her father an exasperated look, stomped back outside, and paraded up and down the driveway. At 7:55, E.W. stepped out the back door with his Bible in one hand and his car key in the other. Lillian climbed in beside him with her Bible and sermon manuscript under her arm. She assumed the seat her mother would normally sit in because she didn't want her suit skirt to wrinkle. The rest of the family climbed in the car, each one of them carrying a Bible. They arrived at 8:45, just as a church trustee pulled into the church parking lot to unlock the sanctuary doors.

Lillian was thrilled with how well everything went on that first Sunday. The district superintendent was present, adding a sense of importance to the whole event. It looked as if all the members of Blandford had come, plus many curious folks from the community. Add Lillian's large family to the pews, and the place was packed. Lillian felt the power of the Holy Spirit in her and in the church. She preached with boldness and confidence. She also preached a bit faster than normal because she was so nervous, but no one complained when church was over five minutes early.

Following worship there was a covered dish lunch in the fellowship hall of the church. There weren't enough tables and chairs to accommodate the large crowd, so some people had to sit outside. But in typical Methodist fashion, there was plenty of food. Lillian had thought maybe she would spend the entire day at the church, but by two o'clock, she was exhausted. She returned home with her family and went to bed as soon as the evening dishes were washed.

Lillian had worried because the church had no parsonage, and she didn't drive. But the leaders of the church, Lillian, and her district superintendent agreed upon a schedule. Miss Russell would work from home three or four days a week. She had her evangelist office in the family garage that she could now use as her pastor's study. She could write sermons and prepare Bible studies there. When she needed to be at church for meetings, worship, or visitation, a family member would provide transportation, or she would take the bus.

Lillian's mother was an accomplished seamstress, and Lillian was a perfectionist. All the preaching robes at the Cokesbury store in Richmond were designed for tall, broad-shouldered, long-armed men. She tried on robe after robe, but none fit her the way she wanted. So her mother tailored two robes for Lillian, a white one for summer and weddings, and a black one for winter and funerals.

Getting the rhythm of ministry was perplexing for Lillian. She had to plan time for sermon preparation, visitation, meetings, and administering the affairs of the church. Even as she worked to find her stride in that rhythm, she noticed areas that needed extra help. The district superintendent had mentioned the small, poor choir. He was right about that. But other areas needed attention as well—children and youth, for certain. Lillian immediately set to work organizing the children for a pageant on Christmas Eve. This meant songs to learn and costumes to make. Lillian's mother helped her with the costumes. While Lillian also knew how to sew, making that many costumes required help. The music Lillian could manage on her own, but her brother Pete would add an element of fun with his showy performance on the piano and spirt-filled singing.

Lillian's family continued to support her ministry at

Blandford, especially through music. Her brothers Pete and Lawrence sang in the Blandford choir. Pete also preached on occasion. He was talented, and gregarious, and the congregation loved him in the pulpit and at the piano.

# # #

It was January,1945, and Lillian had been at Blandford for two months.

"Lila, do you have everything you need? Have you completed all the reports?" Lillian's mother cleared breakfast from the table as she fussed at her daughter. "Are you absolutely sure you're ready? Quarterly conferences are important, and this is your first. Your district superintendent will be there."

"Yes, Mama, I'm ready. I've completed all the reports and reviewed them a hundred times. Like I told you, I called the district superintendent to clarify his expectations. Then I created a list and checked it a thousand times. Now, stop fussing at me. You're making me nervous," said Lillian.

"Maybe you should stay home today and double check everything," said Goldie, ignoring Lillian's words.

"Mama, I told you, I'm fine. Daddy's ready to take me to church now. I'll see all of you tonight at church at the conference."

With that, Lillian gave her mother a kiss on the cheek and went out the side door to get in the car with her father. She had several folders holding meeting reports in her hands. She had reviewed them so many times, she had them memorized.

"Lila," Lillian's father greeted her as she climbed in the car, "do you have all you need for tonight's meeting? This is your first quarterly conference and everything is so critically important."

Have my parents been rehearsing their lines? Do they not realize I'm thirty years old? I'm not a child.

Her father continued. "I've attended more of these over the years than I care to count. Lack of preparation makes the pastor look bad. I've seen it too many times. Preparation makes the pastor look good. You need to look good in the eyes of your supervisor and the congregation. Do you understand, Lila?" Her father turned and looked at her just before he pulled out of the alleyway. He had arranged to be late for work this day so he could take his daughter to Blandford. He had told her he didn't want her riding the bus today.

"Yes, I get it. You know if I'm doing this, everything will be perfect. Surely, you know me better than that." Lillian appreciated her parents' interest in all of this, but not their lack of confidence in her.

"You're right. I do know you better than that." Her father nodded. "You're always well prepared. I know you'll do fine. All of us will be there to support you. We'll come early to have some dinner before the meeting. Your mother is going to cook some chicken and bring it with us. Is there anything else you would like to have? Pie, maybe?"

"Mama is so good to fry chicken for us, especially when she herself never eats it—raising all those chickens but has never eaten a one of them." Lillian smiled and shook her head. "But I love her fried chicken. It will be perfect before this big meeting, if I'm not too nervous to eat. No pie for me but do bring a large napkin. I don't want to soil my dress."

Lillian had made a list of all the expectations she had been told by her district superintendent. Evangelism and stewardship were at the top. Baptizing and receiving new members was the goal of Christian ministry. Stewardship was the visible sign of faith. Plus, stewardship paid the bills and allowed the church to meet its financial obligations to the Conference. She knew she had to report on those two top concerns.

Other essential reports included Sunday School and youth ministries. The report needed to include how many were on the Sunday School roll and what percentage of that roll actually attended. Those two numbers were important. She had to report how many pastoral calls she had made and how many weddings and funerals she had officiated. So far she had had no weddings or funerals, but there were several people critically ill, so she knew funerals were in her near future.

The quarterly conference addressed the women's group and local and global missions. In addition, Lillian felt the need to report on the choirs. After all, the district superintendent had mentioned those when he asked her to go to Blandford. The agenda also included reports on lay leadership, changes in membership, pastor's salary, and maintenance of church property. She had made her list and checked off each item as she prepared.

Riding south on Route 1, she mentally reviewed her plan for the day. *Once Daddy drops me off at the church, I'll review the reports one more time, work on my sermons for Sunday morning and evening services, review the reports again, have dinner with my family, and finally attend the meeting. Thank goodness the district superintendent will preside, but I'll participate, along with my key leaders. Maybe I should call each of them to be sure they have everything they need. No, I just called all of them yesterday, and they're more than ready. After all, this is not their first quarterly conference. Now I'm starting to act toward my leaders like my parents are acting toward me!*

The day went as planned, and everything was ready. Lillian set up a table and three chairs in the front of the sanctuary. She had prepared three folders, labeled "District Superintendent," "Pastor," and "Secretary." At 6:45 P.M., Reverend Doctor Roscoe Jones, the district superintendent, arrived. Lillian greeted him at the door and escorted him to the front of the sanctuary.

"Everything looks in order," said the superintendent as he leafed through his folder. "I look forward to our time together. You know the conference leaders believe Blandford church will be closed within two years. That's one of the reasons I was able to appoint you here. So don't get discouraged. Just give it your best."

Lillian was taken aback. She knew Blandford was small, but there were many small Methodist churches in Virginia.

"Pardon me for being so bold. I know I haven't been here long, but I think Blandford has a long, bright future ahead. They are committed to Christ and love each other."

"Maybe you're right, Miss Russell. Time will tell."

At this point, Lillian's family walked into the sanctuary. "Reverend, this is my family. E.W. Russell, my father; Goldie, my mother; and my siblings Lawrence, Hazel, Pete, and Polly."

"Yes, I've met your parents before. Nice to see you again, and nice to meet the rest of the family," said Reverend Jones as everyone shook hands.

"Oh, this isn't everybody. I have two other brothers and one other sister who could not be here," said Lillian.

"Large families are good. It helps our churches grow." The district superintendent chuckled.

Members of the Blandford Church began to arrive. Lillian greeted each one by name and thanked them for coming. At 7 P.M., Reverend Jones asked if anyone could play the piano and lead in singing a hymn. "I want to start us in unison, maybe even harmony," he said with a smile.

Pete raised his hand and offered to help. "What hymn do you want to sing?"

"How about 'Come, Thou Fount?'"

Pete sat down at the piano like he owned it. His hands moved up and down the keyboard with ease, adding base lines that stirred the soul. Everyone stood and sang with great spirit.

Closed in two years. I don't think so. Lillian thought as she sang the words "streams of mercy, never ceasing."

After all the reports were given, Reverend Jones asked if there was anything anybody would like to add. One older gentleman in the back pew stood up.

"Yes, sir, I'd like to say something. I heard the conference is thinking about closing Blandford. Is that why you sent us a lady preacher, to close us?"

Lillian was sitting at the table facing the congregation. She tried to conceal her shocked expression by putting her hands up to her mouth and looking down at the table.

"Good evening, Mr. Bailey. It's good to see you. What makes you say that?" said Reverend Jones.

"Well, I've been a Methodist all my life and I get around. I know how things work in Richmond. So is it true? Are there plans to close Blandford? Is that why you sent us a woman?"

"Mr. Bailey, viability is always an issue for churches as small as Blandford. Currently, there are no definite plans to close Blandford. My advice to you and the rest of this church is to work with Miss Russell to strengthen and grow your church. Now, Pete, would you come back up and close us in song? 'Revive Us Again' seems like an appropriate song for tonight."

Pete came forward to the piano and led the music. Lillian had never heard him play with so much enthusiasm. It was as if he was saying to the superintendent, "I'll show you."

Following the benediction, people exited the sanctuary, taking up the meeting after the meeting in the more informal setting of the church parking lot. Lillian's family helped her put away the table and chairs, turn off the lights and secure the building. By the time they were done, just a few people lingered in the parking lot. The Russell family got into their car and headed north toward Richmond. E.W. spoke first.

"The meeting went well. You were very well prepared, Lila, just as you told us you would be. But what was all that about at the end? Closing Blandford? Why they appointed a woman? Where did that come from? I thought I might go back and punch that ol' guy."

"E.W., calm down," said Goldie.

"Daddy, there's more. Before the meeting, before you 'al came into the sanctuary, the superintendent told me the same thing, that the conference sent me to Blandford because they think it'll close in two years. I was so hurt and mad too."

"We'll show 'em," said E.W.

"We sure will," said Pete. "Revive us again!"

The entire car of Russell's broke into song. It got so loud; Goldie rolled down her window.

Revive us again;
Fill each heart with Thy love;
May each soul be rekindled with fire from above.
Hallelujah! Thine the glory. Hallelujah! Amen.
Hallelujah! Thine the glory. Revive us again.

Lillian was exhausted but had trouble sleeping that night. The events of the day, the shocking revelation from her superintendent, the remark from Mr. Bailey, all of this kept turning over in her mind, ruminating like a cow with her cud. It left a sour taste in her mouth that would not go away. *Do they think women aren't gifted enough to revitalize a church, that all we can do is bury a church? I'll prove the conference wrong. I'll prove them all wrong. Mr. Bailey will change his opinion of me. I'll do that through working harder than any pastor has ever worked. I'll do everything possible and do it all perfectly.*

Chapter Thirteen
High Expectations

Women are especially vulnerable to the perfection trap.
From "How Women Rise" by Sally Helgesen and Marshall Goldsmith

"Goldie, what's that noise? Has someone broken into our house to use the bathroom?" It was 11:00 P.M. E.W. and Goldie were in bed and had been asleep for two hours.

"E.W., don't be silly. That's just Lila washing her hair."

"Washing her hair at this hour? What in the world."

"You know our daughter. She wants to always be available to her parishioners. She told me today she decided to start washing her hair Friday nights at 11:00, allowing her to be available for emergency calls to the hospital or somebody's home. Now go back to sleep."

Lillian did everything for Blandford, much like a big sister would do for younger siblings or a mother for her children. She was determined to be available to them anytime she was needed and provide for all their needs. If she worked hard enough, Blandford would grow, and the Conference would not close it.

At least one day a week, Goldie and Lillian rode the local Richmond streetcar to the central station. There they boarded the

Trailways bus that took them to the central station in
Petersburg. From there, they rode various local buses to get to
Blandford Methodist Church, Petersburg Hospital, or to members'
homes. These days were hard on their feet and their appearance.
Between heat in the summer, rain in the spring, and cold in the
winter, visitation days were challenging.

"Lila, slow down. It's hot as blazes out here, and I'm not as
young as you," said Goldie.

"Sorry, Mama. It's hot, but I know the next place we're
going always has a cold glass of lemonade for us. Just two more
blocks," Lillian slowed her pace a bit.

She looked down the street. The homes around her church
were small, white-frame houses in need of repair and painting,
most front stoops cluttered with shoes, toys, and garden tools.
Front yards had tomatoes and cucumbers growing in victory
gardens. Lillian could hear children playing in the back yards
under the shade of tall oak trees. Young families occupied most of
the houses, struggling to survive with husbands gone to war.

At the end of the sidewalk, Lillian stopped and asked,
"Mama, how does my hair look?"

Goldie pulled a bobby pin out and used it to reattach a
blonde strand that had gotten loose from Lillian's braid. "There,
that's better. You look lovely, as always."

"Just one more visit after this one. My goal is to visit all my
members in this block. Then we can get back on the bus and make
our way home. You know you don't always have to escort me,
Mama. I know the bus route by heart."

"We've talked about this before. With Camp Lee so close,
it's not safe for you to be traveling alone. I respect our soldiers
fighting in this war, but sometimes they've had too much to drink.
The bar's close to the bus station. It isn't safe for you. Besides,
these are lovely people, and I enjoy being with you. It's only this
heat that bothers me. Just one more visit." Goldie put on an
encouraging smile. "We can do this."

Even with the challenges of weather, Goldie and Lillian
enjoyed their days of visitation. They planned them out ahead of

time, deciding whom to see and the order that made sense with the bus routes. Sometimes they baked cookies and took them to people. When a new baby was born, they gave them handmade booties. War had been hard on the families. If the Russell's had extra produce from their garden or an outgrown winter coat, they gave them away. Knitting hats, scarves, and gloves was a regular evening activity at the Russell home. In addition to tending to physical needs, Lillian tended to people's spiritual needs, always reading Scripture and praying with people, often on her knees. Doors and hearts opened wide to receive mother and daughter.

Lillian accomplished her goal of visiting all the members. She loved being with her people, listening to their stories, and sharing the Gospel story. Lillian carried the Spirit of Jesus with her, and it helped her people—that was obvious. She made sure every member had all the necessities, including food and clothing. It wasn't unusual for her to bring coats and boots to a family just before a winter storm or a meal to a family when the mother was recovering after another child's birth. Lillian knew and loved her church family. She loved being their pastor.

The *Book of Discipline* stated: "Women are included in the foregoing provisions except in so far as they apply to candidates for the traveling ministry." The traveling ministry referred to the itineracy and guaranteed employment. Women were eligible to be ordained a deacon and an elder but were not eligible for full clergy rights. The understanding was a preacher in every pulpit and a pulpit for every preacher. The preacher's willingness to itinerate or go where sent and the church's willingness to accept any preacher appointed to them were the two essentials in making this process work. Bishops and district superintendents assumed that few churches would accept a female preacher, so the issue was this: how can women be in the traveling ministry or guaranteed an appointment when the local churches refuse them?

Lillian was aware of all the biases expressed in *The Discipline* against women, but her mind and hours were so full of doing her very best at Blandford that she gave it little intentional thought. However, she was aware of an underlying desire for more equality, a status that was due to her. First, she must prove Mr. Bailey and her district superintendent wrong. Then she could concern herself with the next steps.

Chapter Fourteen
Ordained Deacon

Have Thine own way, Lord! Have Thine own way!
Thou art the potter, I am the clay.
Mold me and make me after thy will,
While I am waiting, yielded and still.
—lyrics, Adelaide A. Pollard, 1902

𝓕or Lillian, receiving a License to Preach was just the first step in a long Methodist ordination process. She had to maintain an episcopal assignment and report to the ministerial committee quarterly. These quarterly reports included a description of her "labors," such as the number of sermons preached, the number of funerals conducted, the number of marriages performed with the names of persons married, and the number of baptisms administered, with the names and ages of the persons baptized, as well as progress made in the prescribed course of study.

The *Methodist Book of Discipline* of 1944 stated: "Accepted supply pastors who are giving their full time to pastoral work under the district superintendents shall be required to take the conference course of study." These courses were available by correspondence, residential-full-semester pastor's school, or summer school. Not having a driver's license, Lillian chose the Correspondence School of Emory University, Atlanta, Georgia. The *Book of Discipline* included a list of books for admission into a probationary or trial period and studies for the first, second, third, and fourth years. Each level included "collateral studies" for those equipped for more rigorous academic challenges. Lillian believed herself to be academically ready and participated in the collateral studies.

By 1947, after three years in the course, Lillian had completed the equivalent of two years of the Course of Study at Emory. This put her in a position to apply for ordination as a deacon. As a local preacher, accepted supply pastor, and member on trial/probation in the course of study, she was more than eligible. Any one of those categories would have qualified her. A deacon had the authority to preach, conduct divine worship, perform the marriage ceremony, administer baptism, and assist an elder in administering the Lord's Supper. The reality was Lillian had already been doing all of these as an accepted supply pastor.

A further reality was that since the inception of the Methodist Church in America held in Baltimore, Maryland, in 1784, no woman in Virginia had ever been ordained a deacon. Lillian believed she was the woman called by God to change that reality.

"Lila, you really should pursue deacon orders," her father said one night at Sunday dinner.

"Yes, I agree," said Lillian's mother.

"We all think you should," said Polly.

"I'm thinking about preaching myself," added Pete. "I've been feeling the call. It would be a great combination with my singing. And I know how to drive a car so that I wouldn't be limited that way." He winked at Lillian as he pretended to be steering a car and made the sound of a roaring car engine at high speed, pushing his foot into the dining room floor.

"Pete, we'll talk about your ordination future another time," said E.W. "Right now, let's see what Lila has to say."

It was clear to Lillian that her family had discussed this earlier when she was not present. Her forehead wrinkled and fists tightened in annoyance, but she then checked those feelings. Maybe this was the Holy Spirit confirming the recent desires of her own heart.

"Honestly, I've been feeling a nudge by the Holy Spirit to consider this," said Lillian. "I'm firmly established at Blandford, and the church is thriving. Daddy, do you think they'll want you to go with me when I'm interviewed this time? There'll be two interviews."

"Probably. But whatever it takes, we're with you."

Lillian and her father met with the Petersburg District Committee. The committee of clergymen met in a classroom at Washington Street Methodist Church. Once again, black suits and dark ties circled the table. Lillian had chosen her dark suit that day with a white blouse and red scarf. Reverend Jones, the District Superintendent, invited Lillian to sit at the head of the table and her father next to her. She knew every man at the table as they all served in the same district, and she saw them every month at the ministers and wives' meetings.

Reverend Jones opened in prayer and then instructed the group. "The Bishop and I have spoken about this situation. We are all well aware that Miss Russell is the first female in Virginia Methodism to seek ordination as a deacon. However, her being female is not our concern this morning. Our only responsibility today is to determine her fitness for a deacon in the Methodist Church. We would be wise to adhere to the questions outlined in our *Book of Discipline*. The bishop has asked me to hold us accountable to that focus. Are we all clear in this matter?"

The men looked around the table at each other and nodded their heads. All of them opened their copy of *The Discipline* to the questions for ordination as a deacon.

"All right, let's begin," said Reverend Jones.

The questions were similar to the questions asked when she received her License to Preach. She had written the required papers, studied, and prayed. She was ready, and the committee stayed with the questions in *The Book of Discipline*.

The District Committee recommended her to the District Conference for consideration. Without fanfare, the district gave their approval, and then a month later appeared before the Conference Committee. All candidates were required to write papers on various topics of theology and practice of ministry. The committee members had read her essays and asked many of the same questions the Petersburg District Committee had already posed. Again, the interview committee had their *Discipline* opened to the questions listed there and stayed within those questions. It seemed clear to Lillian and her father that Bishop Peele, although not present, had provided strict directions for the conduct of these interviews. Lillian was grateful for that. She grew weary defending her gender and call to every insecure man and woman who felt justified challenging her. *Sometimes I feel like a pear tree in an orchard of apple trees. My limbs are heavy with pears, while other trees have very few apples. And yet, I'm the one questioned if I'm genuinely a fruit tree. Jesus said that we are known by our fruit. Look at my fruit, brothers!*

After their recommendation, she appeared before the Annual Conference's clergy session, the final hoop in this long process. This step required Lillian to go to Annual Conference held in Roanoke, Virginia, October 16-21, 1947, with Bishop W.W. Peele presiding. The business sessions convened in the City Armory, but the ordination service gathered at Green Memorial Methodist Church.

Lillian stepped out of her father's car and looked up at the towering steeple of the church. There was a bell tower, a clock tower, and then the steeple holding up a large cross. It had to be the tallest building in the city. The light stone building was huge compared to her small church in Petersburg. She had worshiped at this church before, but it took on a new meaning for her that night. She would make history here. The setting sun shining through the stained glass windows created a water-color scene on the courtyard leading to the church. Once inside, her family sat as close to the front as they could. Lillian went to the fellowship hall where all those awaiting ordination that night were to line up in alphabetical order for the procession. Her black robe hung over her arm. All the male voices created a low hum like car engines waiting at a traffic light. She suspected her voice would sound like a honking horn at that same traffic light, but no one spoke to her, and she spoke to no one.

Soon the sound of the powerful pipe organ filled the sanctuary and echoed down the hall into the fellowship hall. Lillian's heart was pounding in her chest, beats of excitement. She processed with the others down the center aisle of the church while the congregation sang, "O God, Our Help in Ages Past." Lillian took her place in the front pews reserved for the ordinands. The service proceeded with prayers, Scripture reading, preaching, and more hymns. Then it was time for the ordination.

Lillian walked up the steps to the chancel, the only woman in a long line of men. With her short stature, she was almost invisible. From this viewpoint, she saw the church sanctuary filled to capacity with Methodists from across Virginia. Every time the congregation was asked to be seated, the pews groaned under their weight. Lillian had been part of the Conference long enough to know most of the women in attendance were accompanying their husbands. Most of the men in the room were either clergy or elected lay delegates. Lillian knew her entire family, and many of the members of Blandford were present and spotted them when several of them raised their hands to wave at her.

The strong voice of Bishop Peele echoed through the sanctuary. His eyes gazed at the ordination candidates, "Do you trust that you are inwardly moved by the Holy Spirit to take upon you the office of the ministry in the Church of Christ, to serve God for the promoting of his glory and the edifying of his people?"

Many bass voices responded in unison, drowning out the lone treble voice, "I trust so."

But the deep voices did not dampen Lillian's Spirit. All she heard was her voice in faithful response to God's clarion call.

It was Lillian's turn. She heard the bishop call her name, "Lillian Phyllis Russell."

She walked to the altar rail, knelt, and bowed her head. The bishop placed one hand on her head. Then a second bishop put his hand on her head. Her district superintendent and the chairman of the Conference Committee laid their hands on her shoulders. Lillian began to tremble, uncertain if the trembling was due to the weight of the hands on her head and shoulders or to the sheer significance of what was happening.

Lillian tried to take a deep breath to calm her nerves, but with the bodies pressed so tightly around her, even a shallow breath was a struggle. She opened her eyes, hoping to gain perspective, but the black morning dress coats of the bishops and district superintendents blocked out the dim lights of the sanctuary, allowing her to see only black. All she smelled was wool and men's cologne. She thought *this must be how the Israelite felt going into the Promised Land only to encounter the Anakites. I'm finally here but surrounded by giants!*

So she closed her eyes and prayed. "I am yours. Use me." A fresh breath of air filled her Spirit, and a light, deep in her soul, permeated her whole being.

The bishop proclaimed, "Lillian Phyllis Russell, take thou authority to read the Holy Scriptures in the Church of God, and to preach the Word. Amen."

Just twenty-two words, but they made history. Reverend Lillian Phyllis Russell was now a deacon in the Virginia Conference of the Methodist Church.

The Petersburg District was one of the most historic districts in all of Methodism. The first Methodist circuit riders, including Francis Asbury, Thomas Coke, Jesse Lee, Freeborn Garrettson, and Edward Dromgoole, had preached in the Petersburg District. But the history of Petersburg is broader than Methodism. Before the Civil War, the city of Petersburg was a center for female education. During the Civil War, Petersburg's women maintained the city through a nine-month siege. Blandford Methodist Church was in a city known for strong, well-educated women. Miss Lillian Russell joined their ranks the day the bishop appointed her to Blandford Methodist Church, and again the day she was ordained a deacon in the Methodist Church.

# # #

After that first Quarterly Conference, when Lillian learned of the planned closing of Blandford, she was meticulous about her reports to the district superintendent. She wanted him to know every sign of life at her church. In the first Quarterly Conference of 1948, feeling empowered by her recent ordination, she made a plan to share a comprehensive report of all the wonderful ministries at Blandford.

After Reverend Jones led a time of devotion, he called on Lillian to give her pastor's report.

Lillian stood to speak. "While I have worked for years with my home church youth in Richmond, and while I was sought by many as a resource in this ministry, I know my responsibility now as the pastor is to recruit, train, and equip adult volunteers."

Lillian smiled as she looked around the small sanctuary of Blandford Methodist Church. Nearly seventy members of her church were seated in the pews, listening intently to their pastor.

"I am pleased to report that this strategy is working, and the young people's program is growing in numbers, faith, and service. Of course, I continue to lead the membership class for confirmation and lead their choir called the Glee Club. With this vibrant young people ministry, Blandford has a strong future for many years to come."

"I want to thank all those who sing in our choirs and for their willingness to sing every Sunday. I especially thank my brothers, Pete and Lawrence, for singing with us. Music has increased our attendance Sunday morning, Sunday evening, and Wednesday evening. People are growing in their faith. Reverend Jones, the adult choir and Glee Club are both here tonight and would like to sing a special anthem for you. I hope you don't mind."

"Miss Russell, that would be lovely. We can never hear too much good music."

"Pete, please come to the piano. Choirs, please come to the choir loft," directed Lillian.

After all thirty-five of the adults and young people had squeezed into the choir loft. Pete sat at the piano and opened his hymnal to "How Firm A Foundation." Lillian stood in front of the choirs, with a stern look on her face. She raised her hands as an invitation to stand. Once everyone was on their feet, she took a deep breath and smiled broadly. The choir smiled in response. Lillian nodded at her brother to begin. Pete played an introduction to the hymn, and then the combined choirs sang stanza one. Just the Glee Club sang stanza two; their sweet young voices made Lillian smile even more broadly. Pete sang stanza three as a solo; the adult choir stanza four; and everyone joined together for stanza five.

The soul that on Jesus still leans for repose,
I will not; I will not desert to its foes;
That soul, though all hell should endeavor to shake,
I'll never, no, never, no, never forsake.

Lillian turned and invited the entire congregation to join the choir in singing the last stanza again. The power of their voices rattled the stained glass windows. Everyone, including the district superintendent, enthusiastically applauded.

Once the choirs returned to their pews, Reverend Jones said, "Well, Miss Russell, that was one of the best reports I've heard in the entire district. Thank you. Now, what report is next?"

"Oh, I'm not done yet. Please allow me to finish." Everyone laughed, including Reverend Jones.

"Of course, continue."

"Blandford is a church that loves each other like a family. I have a rigorous schedule of visitation. Their pastor neglects no one. In the past quarter, I have made fifty home visits and twelve hospital visits. But in addition to my visitation schedule, we have organized groups to adopt a shut-in. These adoptions include visits, cards, and for those who have a phone, phone calls. In the past three months, I've made more than seventy-five contacts. Once a year, we organize and visit every member, including those who have become inactive, encouraging them to return to church. We made those visits in January. The love and fellowship of the entire congregation have grown broader and deeper."

Lillian turned to the next page of her typed report. "Once a year, Blandford Methodist Church has a revival, one of my favorite activities. As the pastor, I select a preacher well ahead of the revival week. As you know, publicity is critical to getting members and neighbors to come. We organize visits to all the inactive members and all those who live in the church's neighborhood. Last year we made more than one hundred visits. A twenty-four-hour prayer vigil was held the night before the first service. We planned covered dish suppers on three evenings to enhance fellowship time among the church members and extend the time to meet new people in the community. The revival we had last fall was the most successful one Blandford has ever had, with forty-nine people making a profession of faith in Jesus. I'm now discerning who our guest speaker will be and covet your prayers for my wisdom in this matter."

"I know you must be weary from this long report, Reverend Jones. I've just one more item to report." Lillian turned another page. "As every church member knows, the key event every summer is Vacation Bible School. I know not every pastor participates with VBS, but I'm one who does, from the beginning to the end. I start working on it in January, recruiting teachers and selecting curriculum. I select and lead the music. All of our children need to know "Jesus Loves Me," "This Little Light of Mine," and "Wise Men Build Their House Upon the Rock." I also love telling stories using flannel-backed Bible characters on a flannel board. Some of the parents stay just to hear me tell these stories to their children. Last year we had more than one hundred participants. Five new families joined the church as a result. I know some churches have decided to have VBS for only one week, but we will not follow that new trend. We will continue with a two-week program. If it were up to me, I'd have VBS all summer."

There was a groan from a few women in the congregation, and Lillian smiled. "Yes, it is exhausting for our faithful volunteers." Turning to Reverend Jones, she concluded, "Thank you for allowing me this time to report on the work God is doing at Blandford."

Lillian sat down, and the Quarterly Conference continued with other reports, concluding with a time of refreshments in the fellowship hall.

Lillian became famous in the Petersburg community for two areas of ministry— preaching and funerals. The same gifts that made her popular as an evangelist also make her famous as a preacher. One day, at a small restaurant in Petersburg, Mr. and Mrs. Robert Wicks, parishioners from Blandford Methodist Church, were having lunch with a couple from the local Baptist church. The Baptist husband asked, "We understand the Methodists at Blandford have a lady preacher. Isn't that a bit strange?"

Mr. Wicks spoke first. "Miss Russell's the best preacher we've ever had at Blandford Methodist Church, and we've had some outstanding preachers over the years. But nobody can hold a candle to Miss Russell."

"But can you hear her? A woman's voice can be so soft and quiet, and when they try to project, their voice becomes harsh."

"We've no trouble hearing her. Not even the older folks sitting in the back have any problems. And the tone of her voice is like that of a dove," Mr. Wicks said.

"What about sermon illustrations? Our preachers tell stories about sports, the military, politics, mechanics, things like that. What does your preacher talk about? Cooking, sewing, children?" asked the Baptist man.

Nevertheless, She Preached

Mrs. Wicks touched her husband's hand and nodded in an offer to speak to this question. "Be my guest," he said to his wife.

"Miss Russell tells stories to which everyone can relate. But it's more than volume and illustrations." Mrs. Wicks paused to consider how to say what was on her mind. "Her preaching is anointed. When she preaches, you feel like you're listening to Jesus. I remember her sermons, especially her stories. I could tell you right now about the sermon from last Sunday or even the Sunday before that. Two Sundays ago, she told the story of a mother who always wore white gloves. Her son didn't know why until after his mother died. It was then that he learned that when he was a baby, there was a house fire. His mother burned her own hands, rescuing him, leaving them scarred so severely that she always covered them with white gloves.

Miss Russell said, 'This is how our mothers love us. This is how God loves us. See the scars on His hands.' Of course, she told the story much better than I can. She's most remarkable—like I said, anointed. You really should come to Blandford Methodist and hear her preach. She preaches three times a week: Sunday morning, Sunday evening, and Wednesday night."

The Baptist couple never did hear Miss Russell preach at Blandford Methodist Church. They decided it was against their understanding of Scripture for a woman to speak in church or have authority over men. However, during Holy Week that year, they attended the community Maundy Thursday service at their pastor's encouragement. To their chagrin, the preacher was Miss Russell, who regularly preached at these community services. The competent reality of Reverend Lillian Russell forced more than one Baptist to change their perception of female clergy.

Lillian had been to many funerals before becoming a pastor and had witnessed firsthand what glorified God and what glorified people. She maintained a level of dignity at funerals that was above reproach. Before a funeral, she prepared everything with great care. Every word and motion were deliberate. She prayed she would invoke the Spirit of Christ in her very being.

She stayed with the family before the service, praying with them. Following the funeral, she stayed with the deceased's body from the funeral home to the graveside until the attendants replaced the sod.

But it was more than preparation and deliberateness. Lillian had a presence about her, a strength that conveyed the presence and power of Christ Himself. That power comforted the grieving and assured the doubting of the resurrection.

Even those who worked at the funeral home, and who generally sat in a side room during a funeral, stood in the back of the chapel to listen to Lillian speak. They would urge each other: "Miss Russell's doing this funeral. Let's go listen." These funeral home employees, who worked with death every day, needed a word of assurance and hope of the resurrection. They found it in Miss Russell. When there was a death in the community of someone who had no church home, the funeral director called Miss Russell. They knew she would take the responsibility seriously. She often co-officiated at funerals with local pastors, some Methodist as well as Baptist, Nazarene, and Episcopal. She was loved and much respected by her ecumenical colleagues in Petersburg.

Chapter Fifteen
The Call to Preach

When faced with opposition to her call to preach,
Bishop Leontine Turpeau Current Kelly
would challenge her opposer by saying,
"I know what Paul said, but Paul didn't call me – God did!"

$\mathcal{M}$ildred had been working at Dan Mills since 1935, eight years. At age twenty-nine, her appetite for the textile industry was satisfied, all her goals accomplished long ago. Now she was driven by a spiritual hunger she could not satisfy. She didn't just read her Bible every day; she studied and devoured it like a starving person. She was at church every time the doors opened. On her knees by her bed was her favorite spot to be. This hunger called to her like nothing she had ever experienced. Mildred had always been religious, but this was more, different.

She had taken the train to Biscoe for a weekend visit with her family.

Victoria's voice carried upstairs and into the bedroom. "Mildred, dinner's almost ready. Can you set the table?".

"In a minute, Mama. Let me finish what I'm working on."

For the past several weeks, she'd been studying Paul's letters to the early churches. Currently neck-deep in Romans, she didn't want to stop.

What seemed like a few minutes, but which must have been longer, Mildred heard her mother's footsteps coming up the stairs. "Mildred, what's going on?"

"Oh, I'm sorry, Mama. I got busy and lost track of time. I'll come right now."

"Never mind dinner. I'm more interested in what's going on with you." She sat down on the bed next to the desk where Mildred's Bible lay open. Mildred laid down her pencil and turned her chair to look at her mother. She noticed that her mother's hair was grayer than it had been at her last visit. She scolded herself for not visiting more often.

"I don't know what's going on with me, not really. God has stirred my Spirit in a mighty way, and I feel lost. No, not so much lost as desperate for a new direction. God's calling me to something, but I don't know what."

"Does it have to do with marriage and family? Is God calling you to get married and start a family before you're too old?"

"I don't think it has anything to do with marriage. I think it has to do with ministry. But I don't know what type of ministry. At Schoolfield Methodist, I've gotten involved in every ministry possible, thinking maybe it's missions, Bible study, or young people's program. But doing those things doesn't make the hunger go away."

"Does any one of those things feel more right than another?"

"That's a good question, Mama." Mildred looked down and thought for a minute. "What feels most right is Bible study and leading worship. I wonder what that might mean."

"I don't know, Mildred, but I do know you, and I trust that you'll sort this out."

Victoria's hazel eyes intently fixed on Mildred. Then she broke the stare, leaned back a little, and smiled. "I also know that the chicken's done and the potatoes need mashing. Can you come down and help me?"

"Sure, Mama. Sorry I've been so preoccupied."

"No apology necessary."

#   #   #

The next day Mildred returned to Danville in time to attend Sunday night worship at Schoolfield Methodist Church. Following the service during fellowship time, a middle-aged woman from the church approached Mildred. With stockings, heals, and a light blue satin dress, she was dressed better than any woman in the room.

"Mildred, I realize we might not know each other very well, but God has placed something on my heart to tell you."

Mildred had seen this woman regularly at Sunday morning worship services and several times at Mildred's weekly Bible study. Mildred knew she was married to a mill manager. Just then, the name came to her.

"I do remember you. Alice, right? You've attended several of my Bible studies."

"You've got a good memory for names. Can we sit down a minute and talk?"

"Yes, mam. Where do you want to sit?" asked Mildred.

"Can we go back into the sanctuary and sit in one of the pews? It'll be more private there."

"Yes, mam."

Mildred and Alice went to the sanctuary and sat in the back pew.

"Mildred, I've been given the gift of discernment. Sometimes God gives a message to me about another person. The message God's given me about you is the strongest I've ever experienced."

Mildred turned to face Alice more squarely. Simultaneously, she slid down the pew a few inches to create a bit more space between them. *This woman I barely know is coming on pretty strong.*

"I see a real gift in you, one historically held solely by men. It's the gift not only to preach but to serve a congregation as their pastor. I believe this so strongly that I've registered you for Columbia Bible College."

Mildred started to object, but Alice shook her head. "No arguments. The registration is already paid. You start the next term."

Mildred wasn't sure how to respond. She felt indignant that this stranger believed she could make decisions for her. Yet she had been praying for just this.

"But women don't preach."

"You need to expand your horizons, Mildred. There aren't many women preachers, but there are some."

"That's true. My worldly experience is pretty limited. But what about Scripture? It seems pretty clear."

Alice pointed her index finger to emphasize her point. "Don't you see God is about to do a new thing? Going to Columbia Bible College will help you see what Scripture truly says about this topic."

"I just can't believe you want to invest your money in me. I've so little experience in any of this. Why me?" Mildred started to cry. Soon she was sobbing, shoulders shaking and tears rolling.

"Forgive me, Alice, for my crying." Mildred snuffled. "Can we go to the altar rail?"

"Certainly," said Alice, and she gave Mildred her handkerchief.

Alice and Mildred walked down the center aisle of the sanctuary and knelt at the rail. After some silence, Mildred prayed out loud. "Forgive me, Father. I've been a stiff-necked follower. May it be with me according to your will."

Alice took Mildred's hand and prayed. "Heavenly Father, I give you thanks for your servant, Mildred. May she come to see the call you have placed upon her life and claim the gifts you have given her to fulfill that call faithfully."

After a few minutes of silent prayer, Mildred said, "Amen."

"Amen," repeated Alice.

They both stood and embraced each other.

Nevertheless, She Preached

Later that week, Mildred made an appointment to speak with her pastor. The walk from Hylton Hall to the church on this beautiful spring day helped to clear her head. Reverend Johnson had been pastor of Schoolfield Methodist Church for four years. Mildred knew they had mutual respect, and she was confident that he could help her sort things out. Reverend Johnson was outside, sitting on the side steps into his office. He was wearing a blue dress shirt and dress pants but no tie or jacket. As Mildred approached the church, he stood, smiled broadly, and invited her into his office.

Mildred had been in this office several times when planning Bible studies, young peoples' programs, and mission activities. It was a small, dreary room with only one window, heavy drapes, a wood floor, and every wall filled with bookshelves. Reverend Johnson communicated his love of study by the number of books. Every shelf was full of books, most vertically stacked but others horizontal. His desk was covered with folders and papers, some stacked, most scattered. Dust covered the typewriter's cover. Mildred liked Reverend Johnson and enjoyed working with him, but she did wish he would better organize his office.

"Please have a seat," said Reverend Johnson as he moved a magazine from a folding chair so Mildred could sit down. He sat in another folding chair on the opposite side of his small office.

"So what can I do for you today? Whatever it is, it sounded urgent."

"You know Alice, a middle-aged woman here at the church, wife of a mill manager?"

"Yes, of course. Nice woman."

"Well, she says she has the gift of discernment."

"I don't doubt that. She's a great listener, the key to discerning the movement of God."

"She told me she believes God is calling me to ministry."

"Mildred, that's not so much discernment as just describing your present reality. You're already in ministry." Reverend

Johnson smiled and crossed his legs. Mildred noticed his socks did not match.

"No, not that type of ministry, not lay ministry, but your type of ministry, ordained ministry."

"Now, that is discernment." Reverend Johnson uncrossed his legs so he could lean forward toward Mildred.

"But there's more." Mildred looked down at her lap and then up at Reverend Johnson. "She feels so strongly about it that she has registered me for the fall semester at Columbia Bible College in South Carolina, and she is going to pay for it, all of it."

"She's certainly invested in her discernment.," he said with a chuckle. "So what did you tell her?"

"I told her yes."

"Wonderful."

"Not exactly. Almost immediately after our conversation and prayer at the altar, I had second thoughts. I knew I had to talk to you. What do you think?"

Reverend Johnson leaned back and smiled. "Mildred, I'm not a bit surprised. For the past six months, you've been on fire with the Spirit. I knew something was going on."

"Thank you for that, but can I ask you about Scripture and women preachers?"

Reverend Johnson nodded yes.

Mildred continued. "Paul said women weren't to speak in church. You know the passage from I Timothy 2:12. *But I suffer not a woman to teach, nor to usurp authority over the man, but to be in silence.*"

"Yes, but remember Paul baptized Lydia, and she was the first Christian pastor in all of Europe. Also, Paul named women as leaders in the church, singling them out by name. Look at the end of Romans. I believe it's chapter 16."

Reverend Johnson picked up his Bible from a stack of papers on his desk and opened it to Romans 16. "Here it is. *Greet Priscilla and Aquila, my helpers in Christ Jesus: Who have for my life laid down their own necks: unto whom not only I give thanks, but also all the churches of the Gentiles. Likewise, greet the church that is in their house."*

"And Paul writes that there is no difference between Jew and Gentile, male or female, slave or free," Mildred added.

"Now you're getting it. You can't take one passage, but you must look at the entire message in context."

"Yes, yes, I know all about that."

"Mildred, something you may not be aware of is the Board of Ministerial Training reported at our Conference this year that the Methodists in Virginia, due to the war, need 75-80 students in college and seminary every year to meet the normal needs of supplying pastors to all the churches. With this demand for clergy. I believe the church is more open now than ever to women in the pulpit. Also, the women of the church are pushing for full clergy rights for women. Who knows what will happen at General Conference next year?" Reverend Johnson pulled his chair closer to Mildred.

"If you're interested, I can provide opportunities for you to lead, preach, and make pastoral calls with me. I'll try to get you in other pulpits as well, maybe for revivals."

He reached out, touched her arm, and lowered his voice. "Mildred, I encourage you to be obedient to the call you're hearing."

Mildred took the hand on her arm into her hand. "Will you pray for me, pastor?"

"Certainly." Reverend Johnson took Mildred's hands in his, bowed his head, and prayed. "God of Abraham and Sarah, Moses and Miriam, Joseph and Mary, speak to your servant, Mildred, with clarity. May she know your perfect will for her life. Amen."

"Amen,' said Mildred.

"Thank you for your time, and please keep praying for me."

"You know I will."

Mildred was more than willing to try out these new ministry opportunities. Over the summer, she preached as an evangelist in some area churches, continued to lead Bible study and worship, and accompanied Reverend Johnson on some of his pastoral calls. All these experiences allowed Mildred to try on the pastoral ministry robe. She had to admit; it felt good, even natural.

Mildred left Danville and Hylton Hall to go to school at Columbia Bible College in South Carolina in early fall. It had an excellent reputation, strong in Scripture. She wasn't yet devoted to becoming a Methodist preacher, but she was committed to finding out more about this call to ministry.

Mildred had graduated from Biscoe High School in 1932. It was now 1943. She was twenty-nine years old and out of the habits that academic rigors demanded. She went with the same determination that defined her transition to Danville.

Mildred studied at Columbia Bible College for five semesters. She was elected vice president of the student association and the college yearbook, *The Finial,* advertising manager. Also, as part of the Foreign Mission Fellowship Club, she served as a prayer group leader. But even with all the extracurricular activities, she received high marks.

Her Bible-heavy course work included introductory courses in the Old and New Testaments and more advanced work including the Gospel of John, Romans, Minor and Major Prophets, Matthew, and James. It was clear that her course work such as Story Telling, Sermon Preparation and Delivery, Hymnology, Essential Christian Doctrine, and Problems in Theology were preparing her to serve as a pastor in a local church. Each student at Columbia Bible College was to select a Bible verse that particularly spoke to them. Mildred chose Psalm 139:17 *How precious are thy thoughts unto me, O God!*

For the first three semesters, she had a full course load. But three of Mildred's brothers were now serving in the military. She needed to send more money home, so she registered for fewer courses, allowing her more time to earn money working at the college as an assistant to the Christian service director.

Nevertheless, She Preached

After two years of working for Columbia Bible College, the Mill invited Mildred to work as the assistant to the Director of Safety at Dan River Mills. Because of the war, the Mill was struggling to find workers. Given the financial needs of her family, she could not refuse this offer.

Mildred shared a room in a boarding house where she could live inexpensively. She tried to reconnect with friends at Hylton Hall, but everybody she had known there was gone. Her friendships at Schoolfield Methodist Church provided some continuity, but it just wasn't the same. With her education in the Bible, theology, and ministry practice, she felt caught somewhere between being a member of the church and being the pastor. She needed to move in one direction or the other.

All of the changes in the past five years confused Mildred. Her path to pastoral ministry was not a straight one, and the roadblocks were many. She sought clarity through a renewal of her call to pastoral ministry.

That renewal came when she preached revivals and assisted Reverend Johnson in starting Piney Forest Methodist Church, a new church in Danville. Her education at Columbia Bible College and her leadership experience in multiple capacities allowed Mildred to accomplish all these ministries with ease and confidence. She rapidly earned a reputation for being a great preacher with sound Methodist theology, practical application, and dramatic delivery.

One evening, Mildred received a phone call from Reverend Dr. H.P. Clark, Danville's district superintendent.

"Mildred, this is Dr. Clark, your district superintendent. I've got a request for you to consider."

Mildred had seen Reverend Clark many times at district conferences, quarterly conferences, and revivals. She thought he possibly wanted her to preach a revival for the district or lead a young people's event. So she wasn't surprised by his phone call.

"Mildred, I'd like you to serve as the pastor of Piney Forest. Their pastor is needed elsewhere in the Conference. Surprisingly enough, the congregation has requested you as their pastor.

Reverend Johnson also strongly recommended you for this appointment. So, what do you think?"

Mildred's brain froze. Yes, she had been preparing for this very thing for years, yet she didn't think it would happen so quickly. Maybe she should think about it, at least overnight, and then get back to him, but that is not what came out of her mouth.

"I'd be honored to serve as their pastor. I know the congregation well. It'll be a great match to have me as a new pastor at this new church. We'll learn together."

"Then it's settled. I'll call Bishop Peele in the morning."

Before Mildred could think of all the questions she should have asked, her district superintendent ended the call.

Bishop W.W. Peele supported this appointment to her first church. The fact that Bishop Peele had served as the pastor of the Aberdeen-Biscoe Charge in North Carolina some years earlier and knew the Long family personally provided some family background for this pioneering episcopal appointment. God had removed every barrier.

It was 1950, and Mildred, at age thirty-six, was employed as a Methodist pastor. Just like Lydia in the Bible, she had gone from weaver to pastor.

Chapter Sixteen
Ordained Elder

Let the elders that rule well be counted worthy of double honour,
especially they who labour in the word and doctrine.
For the scripture saith, Thou shalt not muzzle the ox that treadeth out
the corn.
And, The labourer is worthy of his reward.
Against an elder receive not an accusation, but before two or three
witnesses.
I Timothy 5:17-19

"*M*iss Russell, I want to be certain you understand how the Methodist Church works in terms of ordination," said Reverend Jones, Petersburg District Superintendent.

"I've been part of the Methodist church since my birth. I believe I understand ordination, but please review it again if you would like."

Lillian had prayed for patience and humility in this meeting with her district superintendent. It had been two years since her ordination as a deacon. Things were going well at Blandford; however, as soon as she stepped out of that setting to be with clergy, everything seemed to change. How many times did she have to prove herself to this man before he accepted her legitimate place among those called of God? She would not allow him to intimidate her, nor would she become defensive. She would be above reproach.

Usually, Lillian's father went with her, but she wanted to go alone this time. The wife of the district superintendent sat in the hallway, right outside the open door. It gave her the feeling of being monitored, and she didn't like it. It appeared either he couldn't be trusted, or she couldn't be trusted. But it was better than having her father accompany her. That made her feel like a child. Neither option was optimal.

Lillian sat on one side of a classroom table with her feet flat on the floor, knees together, and hands in her lap. She was wearing a white suit, one usually reserved for Sunday mornings. Reverend Jones sat on the other side of the table with his legs crossed, allowing a well-polished dress shoe to form a clear barrier between them. His considerable height, black suit, and red tie created a stark contrast to Lillian.

He cleared his throat and spoke as if he were a professor lecturing his students. "There are two orders in our church: deacon and elder," Reverend Jones made his point by tapping his index and middle fingers on the table. "As a deacon, you are authorized to conduct the Sacraments of baptism and holy communion in the church to which you are appointed. As an elder, you would be able to conduct the Sacraments anywhere in the world. The requirements for elder include completion of the Course of Study or graduation from seminary, as well as at least two years under appointment as a deacon."

Lillian nodded her head. She had read these sections of the *Book of Discipline*, so many times she had them memorized.

Reverend Jones raised the pitch of his voice slightly to give it an even more academic tone and lifted and turned his chin just a degree as if his chin were making the point. "Now, in addition to ordination, there is the clergy connection to his conference."

"His or her," corrected Lillian.

"Excuse me?"

"You said, 'his conference.' You should have said his or her Conference."

"Of course, his or her." He cleared his throat, shook his head, and went on. "These relationships are many and can change every four years at the whim of the General Conference. The Annual Conference has granted you a License to Preach, and you have served as a supply pastor. Now, as a deacon, you're a probationary member of the Conference, sometimes called "on trial." This status means you're not guaranteed an appointment by the bishop, and you need to appear before the Committee on Ministry every year to have your status renewed."

"I'm ready to do more than having my status renewed. I want to move to the next step. Today I declare my intent to seek ordination as an elder." Lillian straightened her posture and nodded her head.

"This is a big step. You were ordained a deacon just two years ago. Are you sure you want to do this so quickly?"

"I want to keep pace with the other pastors in the Conference. Those ordained deacons who have completed their seminary requirements and served two years as a deacon are applying. There's no reason for me not to do the same."

"True, but I thought as a woman, you might want to slow your process a bit, to allow time."

"Time for what? I've been an evangelist since age seventeen and have served Blandford since 1940. It's now 1949, so that's nine years of full-time local church experience. I've done everything the *Book of Disciple* has required. As far as I can tell, there's nothing to wait for."

"Well, if you're certain."

"I couldn't be more certain. God has called me, and I have been obedient. The question I have for you is, will you recommend me?"

"Allow me to review your records."

"Of course, but when you do, you'll find them impeccable. Blandford is a strong church, growing in every way. My service to them has been well received. Every year they ask for my return. I've completed all the requirements."

"Yes, Miss Russell. I cannot argue with that. Please allow me to be certain you understand that as a woman, you can receive ordination as an elder, but the Conference cannot receive you into full connection. The *Book of Discipline* does not allow women in that status. So you'd continue as a local preacher and need to appear before the committee every year to maintain your status. When you leave Blandford or when a male pastor needs that church, you might be without an appointment."

"As you know, Reverend Jones, there has been much discussion about the *Book of Discipline* changing in the matter of females in ministry. But, yes, I do understand that at this time in our history, ordination as an elder will not change my connection with the Conference."

"All right, with that in mind, I'll add your name to the list of clergy applying for elder orders. Surely you know you'll be the first woman elder in the history of Virginia Methodism."

"I'm more than aware. I look forward to meeting with the committee."

The 1948 *Book of Discipline* stated, "No person shall be elected to elder's orders except such as are of unquestionable moral character and genuine piety, sound in the fundamental doctrine of Christianity and faithful in the discharge of gospel duties."

Miss Russell had no concerns in these matters. Everyone who worked with her had the greatest respect for her faithfulness to Christ's Gospel and her many abilities to carry out her call to proclaim the Good News.

These years were a transitional time in the United States. With the war over, soldiers returned to their employment, forcing many women who had worked those same positions to return home and tend the fires there. Black soldiers, who had fought for freedom, returned home to Jim Crow and less than equal opportunities.

The news from Annual Conference in 1949 warned of mixed marriages between Roman Catholics and Anglicans. This issue was of particular interest to Methodists because their roots were in the Anglican Church. Annual Conference also reported that the Episcopal Churchwomen had declined seats offered to them at their governing meeting because those seats were without voice or vote. Randolph Macon College boasted of "twenty-eight sons of ministers registered at their college this season." Randolph Macon College, a Methodist, all-male school near Richmond, Virginia, was long considered the pipeline for successful clergymen in the Virginia Conference. The clergy alumni of Randolph Macon had become a tight-knit club in the Virginia Conference. Few made it to the Cabinet without having graduated from Randolph Macon College. Several of these "twenty-eight sons of ministers" were third and fourth-generation Methodist clergy.

The men were back in their "rightful" places. But change hung in the air, and it had the scent of women's perfume.

#   #   #

Lillian met with the Conference Committee on Ministry within two months of her meeting with Reverend Jones. That meeting went by the book, that is *The Discipline*. Several months after that recommendation, the 1949 Virginia Annual Conference met at the Mosque Auditorium in Richmond. The ordination service was held at Centenary Methodist Church in Richmond. The large, beautiful stone church served as the mother church in Richmond, giving birth to several other Methodist churches, including Highland Park. The sound of the pipe organ traveled down the center aisle, out the front door, down the steps, and into the street, calling everyone to this high, holy moment.

The candidates, all dressed in black suits, including Lillian, stood in a line before the hundreds of delegates seated in the sanctuary. She was the only one with a string of pearls around her neck.

The sanctuary's front doors stood open, allowing the fresh October evening breeze in, circulating the air around the packed pews, even up to the balcony. Lillian could see the trees outside, lining the city street. She thought *A new season is coming. Old ways are falling, making way for a season of a new birth. I hope I can make it through the winter to the spring of resurrection.*

The questions came from Bishop Peele, standing in the center aisle facing the candidates. "Do you believe in your heart that you are truly called according to the will of our Lord Jesus Christ, to the ministry of elders?" His voice filled the sanctuary.

"I do so believe," they all responded.

The men's broad shoulders on either side of her created a barrier, making it difficult for Lillian to see or be seen. The bishop paused and looked straight at Lillian. "Gentlemen, we have a lady in our midst on this historic day. I ask that you, who are on either side of her, take a step to the side."

The men looked back and forth to see where they stood in relation to Lillian, then sidestepped in the opposite direction from her.

"Now, Miss Russell, please take a step forward and assume your rightful place in history." Lillian took a step forward, then smiled and nodded at the bishop, who turned and faced the congregation.

"I now ask all of you, everyone in this sanctuary, to make room for her in ministry to this great Conference. She's going to need our wholehearted support. Today is a historic day, as we confer elder ordination to the first woman in our Conference."

From the back of the sanctuary, there came a solo but enthusiastic clap. Lillian glanced to where her family sat. Of course, it was Pete. He stood, a wide smile on his face, his big hands clapping as loud as they could. Immediately Polly joined in, followed by her entire family and then the people from Highland Park and Blandford who had come to witness this historic event. Soon nearly everyone in the sanctuary applauded, some with more enthusiasm than others.

This singular attention confused Lillian. She frowned. *There should be applause for God only.* But then she smiled in gracious appreciation for this affirmation. She lifted her hands to God and hoped people understood her gesture. The applause grew louder, and a few more people stood.

Once the applause ended and everyone sat down, the bishop smiled at Lillian, then continued the questions to the candidates. "Are you persuaded that the Holy Scriptures contain all truth required for eternal salvation through faith in Jesus Christ? And are you determined out of the same Holy Scriptures so to instruct the people committed to your charge that they may enter into eternal life?"

Lillian pictured the people of Blandford Methodist Church, her preaching, teaching, and study of Scripture. "I am so persuaded and determined by God's grace," she responded with the other candidates.

"Will you give faithful diligence duly to minister the doctrine of Christ, the Sacraments, and the discipline of the Church, and in the spirit of Christ to defend the Church against all doctrine contrary to God's word?" asked Bishop Peele.

Lillian considered the current tendency for Methodist churches to move away from the teachings of John Wesley and the *Book of Discipline* to a more Baptist theology and congregational polity. She always used the Methodist liturgy, considering Methodists a people of three books: Bible, *Book of Discipline*, and hymnal. Blandford Church, under her leadership, began each year with the Wesley Covenant Service. Her people would know nothing but Methodist doctrine and polity and strict adherence to the teachings of Scripture.

"I will so do, by the help of the Lord."

"Will you be diligent in prayer, in the reading of the Holy Scriptures, and in such studies as help to the knowledge of God and of his Kingdom?"

Lillian thought about the room behind her family home where she had her study. "I will, the Lord being my helper."

"Will you apply all your diligence to frame and fashion your own lives and the lives of your families according to the teachings of Christ?"

As a single woman, this question required a different understanding. Lillian thought, not of spouse and children, but her siblings, nieces, and nephews.

"I will, the Lord being my helper."

"Will you maintain and set forward, as much as lieth to you, quietness, peace, and love among all Christian people, and especially among them that shall be committed to your charge?"

Lillian remembered the conflict at Blandford when she first arrived, caused by the decline in membership and financial giving and the uncertainty of having a female preacher. All of that conflict was gone, replaced with a united excitement for the future. "I will so do, the Lord being my helper."

Finally, the bishop asked, "Will you reverently heed them to whom the charge over you is committed, following with a glad mind and will their godly admonitions?"

Lillian had known nothing but obedience her entire life, to her parents and pastors, district superintendents and bishops, but mostly to God, "I will so do."

At age thirty-five, with her biological and church families present, Miss Lillian Russell knelt before Bishop W.W. Peele. His hands caried the anointing of the Holy Spirit, beginning with Jesus himself, and passed down through the laying on of hands to all those who led His church through the ages leading to John Wesley, Thomas Coke, and Francis Asbury. Francis Asbury had actually preached in the church of her ordination. She was truly a part of history.

Lillian looked out toward the pews. Her family was standing, trying to see their little Lila receive the confirmation of the church. Their eyes were damp, and her mother held a hanky to her nose. Lillian knelt and bowed her head. The bishop placed his hands on her head and said the words of ordination.

"Lillian Phyllis Russell, the Lord pour upon thee the Holy Spirit for the office and work of an elder in the Church of God, now committed unto thee by the authority of the Church through the imposition of our hands. And be thou a faithful dispenser of the Word of God, and of his holy Sacraments; in the name of the Father, and of the Son, and of the Holy Spirit. Amen."

Chapter Seventeen
Piney Forest

For though I preach the gospel, I have nothing to glory of:
for necessity is laid upon me; yea, woe is unto me,
if I preach not the gospel!
I Corinthians 9:16 KJV

$\mathcal{P}$iney Forest Chapel was a new church, formed in 1949, by Reverend C.E. Johnson. Familiar with Mildred's abilities from his time as pastor of the Schoolfield Methodist Church, he asked her to assist him with organizing Piney Forest. They visited door to door, inviting people to become part of the new church. She also preached a revival for the Piney Forest community and led women's Bible studies.

When the Piney Forest congregation heard that Mildred was going to be appointed as their pastor, they recommended she be approved for a local preacher's license, which gave her the rights of ordination in the church where she was appointed. It was the only new license recommended in the Danville District that year. Mildred now had full authority to baptize, lead holy communion, preach, and officiate at weddings and funerals at the Piney Forest Chapel.

According to the *Danville Bee* of October 26, 1950, Mildred *became the second woman pastor of the Virginia Conference of the*

Methodist Church at the 168th annual meeting in Richmond. Miss Lillian Russell was the first, being appointed to her seventh year as pastor at Blandford Methodist Church near Petersburg.

The minimum annual salary for a preacher in the Virginia Conference in 1950 was $1,800 for full time accepted supply pastors who were single. According to the 1944 *Book of Discipline*, an accepted supply pastor was a man approved by the Committee on Accepted Supply Pastors and employed by a district superintendent to pastor a local church for no more than a year. This was an appointment made by a superintendent rather than a bishop and could be changed at any time. The minimum salaries approved by the Annual Conference were not applied to female pastors, few as they were. Mildred's annual salary was $1,500.

It didn't take long for Reverend Mildred Long and her congregation to appreciate each other. An article in the *Danville Bee* described her as the "most attractive minister in the Virginia Conference." But the article continued, "the congregation is prouder of the abilities of Miss Mildred Long."

The article continued: *The Piney Forest Chapel, which was organized during the gasoline rationing days of World War II, lists some 100 members and could reach about 300 through a good organizational job in a short length of time, according to its leaders. Believing that Miss Long is the person for the job, the congregation made requests of the conference – thus she has been assigned her first pastorate. Miss Long called on friends while passing through Danville today on route to the Eastern Shore to conduct evangelistic services through November 13. Her first service at her charge is set for Wednesday, November 15.*

Mildred witnessed daily the second-class status of women. She knew as a preacher that she had a unique opportunity to impact that, but she learned quickly that these attempts had to be subtle. In her preaching and teaching she spoke often about the important role of women in the Bible and in church history. She used illustrations of modern day women and their importance. In a newspaper article from the *Danville Bee*, May 21, 1951, a detailed description is given of a study taught at Mount Vernon's Church School by "Danville's only female pastor," Miss Mildred Long.

"Hezekiah's father had been a wicked ruler, but despite a bad father, he had a godly mother. As she began to teach him, to lead him in the right way, the prophet Isaiah began to use his influence for good. Today we stand in a chaotic condition. We know that our nation is in peril, that politics are rotten, that our statesmanship is at a low ebb. And not one of us can look Almighty God in the face, as did Isaiah and say: Here am I, Lord. Send me."

Mildred was a learned Bible teacher and gifted preacher, and her congregation loved her. But she had a lot to learn in administering the affairs of the local church. Columbia Bible College provided her a solid background in Bible, theology, and church history, but little in church administration. For that she turned to her employment and volunteer experiences at the Dan River Mills and the Schoolfield Methodist Church. At thirty-six years of age, she had a fair amount of life experience; she needed all of it.

The Methodist Church provided the Course of Study as a route to receiving necessary training even without a master's degree from a seminary. This program, offered on a seminary campus during the summer, included careful study of books such as *The Bible Speaks to Our Generation,* by Lankard; *The Christian Faith and Why,* by Rall; *Methodism Has A Message,* by Kern; and *A Young Man's View of the Ministry,* by Shoemaker.

The *Virginia Conference Annual* of 1950 included this report:

"In American Methodism, fifty percent of rural charges have supply pastors. Of these, thirty percent are ministerial students and fifteen percent are retired ministers. Fifty percent of these rural supplies are forty-five years of age or older. It is obvious, therefore, that our Methodism greatly needs and would be severely handicapped without our supply pastors. All these men need additional training, although some of them are rendering truly superior service. It is the desire of your board to do a great deal more for these men, but find ourselves limited by the financial resources."

Mildred attended the Course of Study at Duke Divinity School, even though she was not one of the "men" described in the report. In 1950, in an effort to better equip the sixty-six approved supply pastors, the Virginia Conference gave four student loans and seven scholarships to attend summer school sessions at Duke and Emory Universities.

The course of study was a program that did not provide a degree; it did, however, provide an education nearly equivalent to a seminary degree and allowed a person to progress to ordination as an elder and become a "traveling preacher" in the conference. This full connection assured full clergy rights, which meant guaranteed appointments. However, women were not eligible for that status.

Piney Forest was a rural church with limited opportunities for new members, but Reverend Long baptized babies and received many members into the church. The war had ended and people were returning to churches in droves. Piney Forest was located too far away from Danville to reflect the growth experienced by many town and city churches, but the membership grew by eight in 1950, by three more in 1951, and by an additional fourteen in 1952. Worship attendance was not recorded at that time, but the records indicate the Sunday School attendance grew as well.

Because Piney Forest was a new church, it had no parsonage. Mildred led the process of funding and building a parsonage. In 1951, Mrs. Charles Flora, a steward of Piney Forest, appeared before the Danville District Committee on Church Location and Building on behalf of the proposed parsonage for the church. A contract had been let to build a parsonage consisting of three bedrooms, a living room, dining space, kitchen, and bathroom with a floor furnace in a central hall for the sum of $7,600. The church already owned the lot and parsonage furniture. The loan of $6,500 would be paid off in monthly payments of $62.25. It was approved, and the parsonage was built at 710 Holbrook Street, Danville. This marked the first time Mildred lived in a home alone.

With her church experience, Mildred easily learned the weekly rhythm of a pastor. There was the "relentless coming of Sunday" with a sermon to write every week. At first, the task was daunting, but eventually she found the dependability of discovering a fresh word from God every week. Previously when she had studied the Bible, it was for her own edification, for class at Columbia Bible College, or, on occasion, for a sermon. Now, so much of her time in the Word was in preparation for the weekly sermon or for the Wednesday night Bible study. It was both life-giving and time-challenging; Mildred wanted to be in the homes and hospitals with her members, especially during their times of need.

Mildred knew the most valuable service she had to offer in times of personal need was faith. She made it a practice to recite Scripture, and to pray with her members. The time she spent in her car visiting members and traveling to meetings, she used to memorize Bible verses. Her goal was to memorize one verse every day.

Administrative work of the church included meetings of the Administrative Board, quarterly conferences, finance, trustees, evangelism, Women's Society, and much more. Mildred found the administrative duties more challenging and less fulfilling than preaching and pastoral care.

The Danville District had made it clear that their priorities were three: recruitment of qualified clergy, temperance, and evangelism. Mildred tried to make those an emphasis in her ministry as well. The temperance was natural for her, as she spoke often in many settings about abstinence from all forms of alcohol. Members of her own family had issues with alcohol, and she witnessed firsthand at Dan River Mills the value of abstinence. But carving out time to just sit and study the Word of God was not always easy. Mildred was often up early in the morning and late at night with her nose in the Bible and her pen in one of her Bible commentaries.

The clergy in the Danville District met monthly and she was expected to be present for those meetings. Time with all these clergymen reminded her of her times at the YMCA in Danville. She felt out of place and awkward. And few of the clergymen tried to make her feel at ease; most just ignored her. She had to spend extra time on her knees before those meetings.

Mildred shone in the areas of preaching and teaching, and she took diligent care of her flock. She also promoted the leadership of women. She had witnessed firsthand at Dan River Mills what women could do if simply given the opportunity. Mildred saw to it that about fifty percent of the Piney Forest delegates to district conferences were female, sometimes even more.

It took Mildred longer to get a handle on the paperwork. Piney Forest was listed more than once as not submitting reports for quarterly conference. Without other clergy to mentor her, Mildred sometimes found herself in the dark about things her male counterparts seemed to know. She had to work harder and ask more questions. She wished she had a colleague she could be comfortable with, to just be herself, and ask whatever she needed without fear of ridicule.

That special colleague came into her life when she met Reverend Lillian Russell. Lillian could be her mentor, but more than that, her friend.

Chapter Eighteen
A Home of Her Own

And the Lord God said, "It is not good that man should be alone;
I will make a help meet for him.
Genesis 2:18 KJV

"**D**addy, I need to talk to you about something," said Lillian
one morning at the breakfast table.

"Sure, what is it?"

"I've heard some discussion among the leaders at Blandford
about the possibility of building a parsonage. Some think it's time.
What do you think?"

E.W. put down the newspaper. "Well, the people who started
the church thought a parsonage would one day be a possibility.
That's why they purchased land right next door. Blandford has
been debt-free for some years and has been meeting all of its
financial obligations putting it financially in a situation to go to
the bank for a mortgage. And it certainly would help you. It
would be convenient and make you even more available to your
congregation. What do you think?"

"I don't want it to be about me. This decision needs to be about
what's best for the church."

"But Lila, you can't separate the two. What's best for you in this situation *is* what's best for the church. As far as I can tell, everybody wins. What are your reservations?"

"This is so out of my experience, Daddy. I know nothing about house design, construction, bank loans, and all the rest. How will I ever give leadership to this?"

"All you have to do is get the right people in leadership and they'll take care of the rest. You've got good men as your stewards. Allow them to do this work. Your responsibility is to support them and make sure they go through the proper channels with the city and the Petersburg District. Pastors aren't expected to know about these kinds of things. Don't feel inadequate because you're a woman. Most male pastors don't know much about construction either."

"Thanks, Daddy, I needed to hear that."

Her father poured himself more coffee. "But I do have a different concern about a parsonage. I don't like one bit the idea of you, a single woman, living alone. Being next door to the church doesn't provide you with security. You'll need a roommate, a godly woman, to live in the house with you."

"I'll keep that in mind. Having the right roommate would provide companionship to me as well."

Not long after this conversation, Lillian met with the stewards, who recommended a parsonage be built. The congregation and the district leadership discussed the possibilities and the options. It was agreed that with the growth in ministry, finances, and membership, Blandford Methodist Church was ready for a parsonage. It needed to be a home large enough not only for a single woman with a roommate, but also for a future married pastor with a family.

#   #   #

The construction of the parsonage was completed in six months. Church members were so excited that they took furniture from their own homes to put in the parsonage. Some pieces were in better condition than others, but Lillian was appreciative of all the donations from her church.

Lillian and her mother were in the kitchen finishing up the breakfast dishes. Lillian would work from home that day. She had a sermon to write, a Bible study to prepare, and a Quarterly Conference to organize.

"So far I have a bed, a dresser, kitchen table and chairs, a sofa, end tables, lamps, and a rocking chair. It will be so wonderful. I can hardly wait to see it all come together!"

"Your father and I have been talking about this," said Goldie, "and we would like to give something to the parsonage also. We're thinking about donating a dining room table and chairs. There's a very nice set down at the furniture store, on sale."

"Is it the one in the window display?" Lillian said as she laid down the dish towel and plate she was drying.

"That's the one. It's been there several weeks. The price has been reduced because one of the chairs has a crack in the seat, but your father can repair that. It'll be just like new."

"I swoon over that dining room set every time I walk past it. It's perfect! Are you sure you and Daddy can afford this?" Lillian finished drying a plate and put it in the cabinet.

"We've been setting aside money for months in anticipation of giving something to your new home. We can do this. But, Lila, what about a roommate? Do you have one yet? I don't want you in that house one night by yourself." Goldie untied her apron and hung it on a hook next to the sink.

"I've asked around Blandford and heard several suggestions. Some of the people I know, and some I set up appointments to meet. Frankly, Mama, none of them are right for this. I feel I'm David and I need my Benjamin."

"Or Mary and you need your Elizabeth."

"Or Ruth and I need my Naomi." They both laughed.

"Maybe you are looking in the wrong place. What if your Ruth is right here in our neighborhood?" said Goldie. "I was thinking about Mary Gills, the woman who accompanied you to Cumberland."

"Oh, my. She would be perfect," said Lillian. "Why didn't I

think of her? I'll go to her house this evening. Does she still work at Southern Bell?"

"I believe so," answered Goldie. "Do you want me to go with you? I could talk to her mother while you talk to her."

"Sure, that's a good idea. Right after supper."

That evening as soon as the dishes were done, Goldie and Lillian walked to the Gills' home. Lillian noticed it hadn't changed much in the previous five years. As they got closer, Lillian could see Mary and Mae sitting on the front porch. Both were reading and looked up as they heard footsteps on the sidewalk.

"Good evening, Mae. Good evening, Mary," said Goldie. "Oh, what a pleasant surprise," said Mae. "Mary, look who's here."

"May we visit for a spell?" asked Lillian. "I have something to ask you." Lillian was looking at Mary.

"Certainly, we would love to have you visit for a while. Let me get two chairs from the kitchen," said Mary.

Mary scurried inside and brought out two chairs and rearranged the other chairs to allow for better conversation. "Would you like a glass of water?"

"No, thank you," said Goldie. "We're fine."

"Yes, just fine, thank you," said Lillian. "But I do have a rather unusual situation. As you know, I'm a Methodist pastor, serving in Petersburg. In a few weeks, a brand new parsonage will be completed and ready for me to move in. Of course, as a single woman, it's not proper or safe for me to live alone in the church parsonage. I'm seeking a roommate. My mother suggested that you might be persuaded."

"This is an unusual request. Can I ask some questions?" said Mary.

"Certainly. Ask whatever you want. This is a big decision," said Lillian.

"First, can I keep my employment at Southern Bell?"

"I don't see why not. You still have your car, right?" Mary nodded her head. "So you can make that drive every day.," said

Lillian.

"Will there be room for my things, not furniture, but clothes and personal things?"

"Yes, the parsonage will be completely furnished including linens and dishes, but there will be plenty of space for all your things. You can park your car in the church parking lot. It will be safe there."

"That's good. My other big question is about mama. Will I be able to visit her here, maybe even spend nights here?" asked Mary.

"Yes, there will be times I will want to visit with my family in Richmond or will have meetings out of town. Those will be ideal times for you to visit your mother and spend the night. I believe we can work out a schedule," said Lillian.

"Please allow us some time to talk about this," Mary nodded to her mother. "And let us pray about it. Would it be all right for us to get back to you in a few days?"

"Yes, can you get back to me Sunday night? That should give both of us plenty of time. I appreciate you considering this. I so enjoyed the time we had together in Cumberland."

"I can't tell you how relieved I am," said Goldie. "I've been praying night and day for God to find Lila a suitable roommate. I believe you are the one, Mary."

Mary leaned toward Lillian, her voice earnest. "As I told you before, I want my life to count for something for the Kingdom. Helping you in any way at all, like driving you to your appointments would bring me so much happiness. While I don't much enjoy being a switchboard operator, even answering your phone would be a great honor."

"We could work together. Once I move from home, I will need somebody to talk to in the evening, a friend to share my day with," said Lillian.

"Are you sure you don't want a cold glass of water?" asked Mae.

"No, thank you, we need to be going," said Lillian. But before I go, we should pray. This is an important decision we are about to make, one that will affect all three of us. Can we kneel and pray?"

The women bowed their heads and folded their hands. Lillian prayed.

"Holy Father, throughout Scripture we read about how you created friendships. Just as you created Eve for Adam, a mate fit to live in the garden with him, so I am asking you to find a roommate fit for me, someone to live in the parsonage with me. If Miss Gills is the one you created for this purpose, please confirm that in our spirits. We trust your wisdom in this and in all decisions of life. Help us to listen intently. In your son's name, Jesus, we pray. Amen."

The next day Lillian walked around the parsonage construction site, seeking divine guidance. It came. She had a peace that Mary was the one, her roommate, her Ruth.

#   #   #

Construction of the parsonage was completed in 1951, and the mortgage paid off in 1952. Lillian had a roommate and a driver. E.W. and Goldie were relieved. Mary had a higher purpose.

Lillian missed the bus rides with her mother, but she loved living next door to the church. It was so convenient. She also missed her mother's cooking, and the fresh eggs from her chickens. She missed helping her father with typewriter repairs and sharing her study with the typewriter repair shop, including the smell of ink and oil. That little room her father had created for her many years ago had become a sacred space, a place where she wrote her sermons and Bible studies, a place where prayers led to discernment, and sometimes even miracles.

But it's time for me to move on. I'm thirty-seven years old. Living on my own is long overdue.

The building of the parsonage and the end of the war changed the transportation issues for Lillian. With fewer soldiers around, Goldie no longer felt she had to accompany Lillian on pastoral calls. Mary changed her schedule to work swing shift at Southern

Bell, allowing her the time to drive Lillian to district meetings, the funeral home, and other day time responsibilities. When Mary was not available, Mr. Robert Wicks, an active member at Blandford, served as a dependable driver. Mrs. Wicks routinely accompanied her husband. Lillian continued to walk to make home visits in the immediate neighborhood, but she was wearing out fewer shoes by living in Petersburg.

Having a parsonage, Lillian soon learned new skills and improved on others. Her family members, who often told her that she was a far better preacher than cook, noticed new recipes and adjustments to the old standbys she had learned from her mother. Her cakes in particular were outstanding. Before moving to the parsonage, Lillian had more time for pastoral responsibilities because her mother did most of the housework so Lillian wouldn't have to. Now she had to modify her schedule to share with Mary the housework, laundry, grocery shopping, and cooking. Lillian noticed a greater connection with the women in the church, and better understood their excuses for not being able to volunteer every time Lillian made a request.

The smallest of the three bedrooms became her study. It took time for it to assume the spiritual power of her former study space in the typewriter repair shop. Early mornings and late evenings on her knees created a sense of holiness in her new study in the parsonage.

Salary took on a different meaning for Lillian with her move from her family home. Initially, while living with her parents, Lillian felt it was wrong to receive any salary. It seemed such a privilege to serve, and the offerings, given sacrificially by the church members, were needed for other things. In fact, up until the time she moved into the parsonage, Lillian spent the majority of her salary on expenses at the church and helping families in need.

The church provided the parsonage furniture, carpets, window treatments, linens, pots and pans, and dishes. They also paid the heating bill for the parsonage, and Mary Gills provided a small amount toward household expenses. Lillian did not understand the other expenses of a household like groceries, water, and incidentals until she was responsible for the parsonage. Receiving the minimum salary was necessary; however, when offered more than the minimum established by the conference, she refused it. The budget funds to defray the expenses of travel for pastoral care and ministerial meetings, Lillian gave to Mary and to church members who provided her with transport. Not having a driver's license and being a single female had created some unusual circumstances, but Blandford and their pastor found solutions that worked well for all.

Following the completion of the parsonage, many other improvements came to Blandford Church in rapid succession. They purchased a Hammond Organ in 1953 and a new piano in 1957. As a musician, Mary Gills was thrilled with both of these purchases. Then new carpet, and a new lighting system with a rheostat were installed in 1957 and air conditioning in the men's Bible class in 1959. They supported a missionary in Africa in addition to supporting national and local missions.

Lillian described this amazing period in her report to the Petersburg District.

We have grown in every way, and I think we have done our best to feed the ninety-nine in the fold, and go out to seek the one gone astray, but though we have done these things, it is mostly the routine business of the Kingdom of God. During this pastorate, the salary has increased from $1,100 to $1,500 with $600 expense allowance. In 1945, the total amount reported to the Conference for all causes was $5,487. We have three choirs: the Junior-Intermediate, the M.Y.F. Glee Club, and the Adult Choir. Our Lay Leader at present was elected to succeed Mr. O'Kennon. He is Mr. Robert Wicks.

In the same report, Lillian also described the improvements to the parsonage such as painting, a new refrigerator, and a new fence. The new fence protected her beautiful rose garden. She was proud of the church newsletter called *Visitor* which went out monthly to every home. She also was proud of the system for adopting and connecting with the shut-ins. This system involved recruiting, training and deploying members of the church to visit the homes and nursing homes of the elderly members.

Chapter Nineteen
Mildred and Lillian Meet

And Ruth said, Intreat me not to leave thee, or to return from following
after thee:
for whither thou goest, I will go; and where thou lodgest, I will lodge:
thy people shall be my people, and thy God my God:
Where thou diest, will I die, and there will I be buried:
the LORD do so to me, and more also,
if ought but death part thee and me.
Ruth 1:16-17 KJV

"Good morning, Miss Long. Please come in." said Reverend Clark, Mildred's superintendent of the Danville District. Once a year, each pastor in the district met with the district superintendent to review their work and determine if the pastor would return to the same church for another year or move to a different one.

"I've asked Mrs. Clark to join us for our conversation. I hope that's all right with you."

This was Mildred's first time for an annual conversation, so she wasn't sure what to expect, but she was accustomed to having a chaperone when meeting with men.

"Certainly. Good morning, Mrs. Clark." Mildred had seen Mrs. Clark, the superintendent's wife, at the ministers and wives' meetings.

Everyone took a seat, Reverend Clark behind his desk, Mildred in a wing-back chair in front of the desk, and Mrs. Clark in a folding chair in the corner.

"I've been reviewing your last quarterly conference reports. Good things are happening at Piney Forest. Thank you for your hard work. I have to say that you are a quick learner. So many of my new pastors struggle with all the paperwork."

"Thank you for the compliment but, honestly, this is a struggle for me. Fortunately, my experiences at The Mill in Danville taught me a lot about paperwork."

Reverend Clark went back to reading the papers on his desk. "Your Bible knowledge and theology are also strong. These are other areas new pastors struggle with."

"I credit that to my course work at Columbia Bible College. It provided a good foundation for my work as a Methodist pastor."

Reverend Clark put his pen down and looked up from the files on his desk to Mildred.

"One thing I've noticed, Miss Long, is your attendance at the monthly ministers' meetings. You're always by yourself. It's supposed to be a time of fellowship for the men."

"That, sir, is the problem. It's a time of fellowship for the men, and for their wives, but not for me." Mildred wanted to say more but stopped before she got herself into trouble. Mrs. Clark turned in her chair toward Mildred. Ministers and wives' meetings were hosted by the district superintendent and his wife, so she had particular interest in this topic.

"Mildred, I have a thought," said Reverend Clark. "There is one other female pastor in the conference: Lillian Russell. She's over in the Petersburg District, and has been at her church for several years. Maybe you could write her a letter. Correspondence with her could prove beneficial to both of you. You might not feel so isolated."

"I've certainly heard of Lillian Russell but have not had the privilege of meeting her. Thank you for this suggestion. I'll definitely follow up."

#   #   #

The day of the visit with Lillian, Mildred decided to dress casually with a simple skirt and sweater. It was winter, but Mildred hated wearing a heavy coat while driving, so she threw her coat on the passenger's seat and prayed the car would warm up quickly.

Her verse for the day was Proverbs 19:24. She would have no trouble memorizing it on this three-hour drive. *A man that hath friends must shew himself friendly; and there is a friend that sticketh closer than a brother. KJV*

A few miles from her parsonage the car began to warm, and Mildred was comfortable enough to relax and let her mind wonder.

Why am I so nervous? It's just another clergywoman. Listen to me, like there are dozens of us. Will she be holier than thou or more earthy like me? I wonder how old she is. She said she would prepare lunch for us. Maybe I should have brought something—at least dessert. Please stop second guessing yourself, Mildred. Just drive and memorize that Bible verse.

Mildred followed Lillian's detailed directions to Blandford Church. As she pulled into the parking lot, even on this dreary winter day, the small brick church was appealing and well kept. Bushes were trimmed, parking lot and sidewalk swept, and door and window trim painted. Mildred spotted the front door under the steeple that led into the vestibule. As she drove around the church, she saw a door on the left side with a neatly painted sign that read "Pastor's Study."

She parked near that door, checked her reflection in the rearview mirror, applied more lipstick, and ran her fingers through her hair. She grabbed her coat and pocketbook and went to the door. She knocked and then heard a woman's heels walking on a wooden floor, making their way toward Mildred. The door opened and there stood a petite woman about Mildred's age. She was dressed in a black skirt, white blouse, and black cardigan sweater. Mildred noticed a watch pinned to her sweater and a string of pearls around her neck. The light coming down the hallway created a halo effect to the braid wrapped around the top of her head. *Am I looking at an angel?*

"Miss Russell? I'm Mildred Long," Mildred extended her hand with a broad smile.

Lillian shook Mildred's hand and said, "Please come in. I'm so glad to meet you. Let's go to the parlor where the furniture is more comfortable."

Lillian led the way to the parlor and invited Mildred to sit on one of the wing-backed chairs. Mildred couldn't help but notice how perfect Lillian looked. Every blonde hair in place, clothes crisp and neatly pressed, not a mark on her black shoes, just a tad of pink blush and lipstick. In comparison to Lillian's perfection, Mildred thought she must look a sight.

Lillian stopped at a table she had already prepared with a tea pot, two cups, sugar, spoons, napkins, and a plate of cookies. "May I pour you some tea, Miss Long?"

"Yes, that would be lovely but, please, call me Mildred. And may I call you Lillian?"

"Yes, Lillian is perfect." Lillian poured a cup of tea, slipped a cookie on the side of the saucer and gave it to Mildred. After pouring herself some tea, she sat on the sofa across from Mildred.

"So how was your trip to Petersburg?" asked Lillian.

"Uneventful. Thank you for asking. Lillian, have you ever been to Danville?"

"Yes, I'm familiar with Danville. When I was an evangelist I traveled to Danville often. It's a busy city with the mills. The people are lovely and hard-working."

Mildred noted Lillian's distinct Richmond accent. She had heard it at the mill. *Her voice is so deliberate, no southern drawl, perfect elocution, deep, yet feminine. My homiletics professor would love her.*

"They are. I worked at The Mill for several years. So you were an evangelist? I did some evangelism work myself."

"We have so much to learn about each other," said Lillian. "Where do you want to start?"

"Why don't you begin?" Mildred suggested. "Tell me about yourself and how you came into this crazy business called pastoral ministry."

"Then I'll start with my family, big and loud as it is." Both women leaned back in their chairs for what they suspected would be a long, wonderful conversation.

#   #   #

Trips to Blandford became a priority for Mildred. She kept a mental list of all the things in ministry that she wanted to ask Lillian about. Preaching, Bible study curriculum, managing time, and difficult parishioners were on that list. As often as her pastoral responsibilities allowed, Mildred made the three-hour, 150-mile trip from Danville to Petersburg to visit Lillian.

They soon discovered that while they were different in personality, they had many things in common. Lillian was a true perfectionist; Mildred's goal was to get it right, not perfect But they both came from big families. Lillian wadded in the water before slowly moving toward the deep water; Mildred put a toe in and then jumped in the deep end headfirst. But they both were disciplined and determined. Lillian managed her tongue well and it seldom got her into trouble; Mildred struggled and her tongue got her into trouble often. They both loved growing roses.

Mildred and Lillian talked often about what clothing to wear for various pastoral occasions, and even non-pastoral occasions, like grocery shopping and yard work.

"So, what do you wear on Sunday mornings?" asked Mildred.

"I almost always wear a white suit. I have two of them." Do you wear white in the winter too?" asked Mildred.

"Sometimes. Sometimes I wear my black suit."

"What about funerals?"

"Oh, I always wear black for funerals. What about you?" asked Lillian.

"I have several suits, white, black, navy, beige, and light blue. I switch them around depending on the season, but always black for funerals. What about accessories?" asked Mildred.

"Mama always said you can't go wrong with pearls, so that's what I wear. I have a beautiful string my grandmother left me when she died."

"I wear pearls also," said Mildred as she reached for her pocketbook and began to rummage through its contents. "I have brothers in the military so I pay particular attention to all things military. Just this week I was reading a magazine article about clothing for the WAVES, the group called Women Accepted for Volunteer Emergency Service. I brought the magazine with me because we're always talking about what to wear."

"I may have read about that, too. It's fascinating. Some argued the women should dress just like the men, and others argued they should be more feminine," said Lillian

"The uniform discussion got so detailed with questions about color, braids, piping, and pockets. In the end, after the women put in their two cents, the WAVES uniform was announced." Mildred opened the magazine to the turned-down page.

"See, here's a picture."

"The attention to detail is impressive," said Lillian as she studied the photos in the magazine.

"The article suggests there were too many cooks in the kitchen," said Mildred. "Decisions were conflicted until they asked the women themselves. Then the dress code was unanimous, decision announced, and uniforms made.

"No such clothing committee was formed for us. We've gotten no fashion guidance," said Lillian.

"None," agreed Mildred. "Lillian, do you attend the monthly ministers and wives' meetings in the Petersburg District?"

Lillian responded with a half-smile. "Yes, I do. They're one of the, shall we say, less satisfying duties for me."

"Me, too. What do you wear to those meetings?"

"I generally wear a black suit and sometimes even a black tie, just trying to blend in. But to tell you the truth, I don't know if wearing a black suit and tie makes me blend in or stand out. I just feel so out of place and odd no matter what I wear. What about you? What do you wear?"

"I wear a white or light-colored suit, or a nice skirt and blouse," Mildred said. "Sometimes I feel like I'm the one bright flower of color in a sea of black, but it doesn't make any difference. I'm still invisible."

"I'll never forget the ministers' meeting where I fainted," Lillian said. "I had felt sickly the day before and hadn't eaten. Those men basically ignored me even when I was lying on the floor. As I was coming around, I heard one of our brothers say, 'She should loosen her belt.' I'm not even sure what that means."

Mildred couldn't believe what she was hearing. "Oh, my. He certainly conveyed poor pastoral care skills." They both laughed.

Mildred said, "Do they invite the wives to your meetings on the Petersburg District?"

"They do. The wives and men meet together for worship, then the wives go to a separate room for their time together. The men stay and continue the meeting run by the district superintendent and the president of the district ministers."

"Do you feel like you don't really belong in either group? We're neither wives nor men," Mildred said. "More than one wife has invited me to their meeting. One of them said, and I quote, 'I think you will find our topic today more interesting than what the men are going to talk about.'"

"What was the topic?" asked Lillian.

"Decorating the home for Christmas with a special interest in making Santa Clauses out of bleach bottles."

"And what was the topic for the men?"

"Preaching during Advent and Christmas season. There was a professor from Duke to lead that discussion."

"And this woman thought you would rather make round-bellied bleach-bottle Santa Clauses than get help in preaching?" laughed Lillian.

"I guess so. It's hard to know what they think."

Lillian's smile disappeared. "It's the language and the looks that make me feel very out of place. Why can't they just say the 'wives' and the 'ministers' rather than the 'wives' and the 'men?'

And the looks some of the wives give me are very suspicious, as if I have designs on their husbands. It's most uncomfortable."

Mildred sat up in her seat. "It's more than uncomfortable. It's insulting to our character. Besides, I wouldn't want any of their husbands anyway." Mildred and Lillian both laughed.

"I like you, Mildred. You say what I think but am too afraid to say out loud," said Lillian. They both laughed again.

Their time together was like manna in the wilderness, and Mildred was grateful for this gift of a friend and colleague.

#   #   #

The Methodist Church at that time moved their preachers every two to four years. After two years, Mildred moved from Piney Forest. During her tenure, Mildred's compensation rose to an annual salary of $2,400, an increase of sixty percent, clear evidence she was not invisible to her congregation.

#   #   #

In 1953 tragedy came to the Russell family. At age seventy, the patriarch of the family, E.W., suffered a heart attack and within three days died. Most of the family was present at his bedside with one glaring absence—Lillian. She was attending Annual Conference and could not get home in time.

Lillian sought out her friend. "Mildred, did you hear? My father was taken very sick, his heart. He has passed." Lillian broke down in great sobs. "This is just too much to comprehend. My daddy gone."

After a few moments of holding her hand Mildred began to pray, "Holy Comforter, come in tender power to embrace this trembling spirit. May she be carried on your wings, those wings that rise with healing."

When Lillian had stopped weeping, Mildred asked her,

"Would you like for me to take you home?"

"Oh, would you? Conference isn't over. Dare we leave early?" Lillian was desperate to get to Richmond, but her perfectionism was stopping her.

"There is nothing of importance on the agenda. And even if there was, nothing is more important than uniting you with your family. We will go to our hotel room, pack up our belongings and start the trip right now. You'll be home today, my friend."

The large classroom used by E.W. for The Russell Men's Bible Study had been under renovation for some years. The goal was to convert it into a chapel. Following E.W.'s death that renovation continued and by 1960, seven years later, it was completed and dedicated. The former classroom now had solid African mahogany pews, organ, piano, stained glass windows, altar, artwork, carpet, and new lighting. It was named "Russell Memorial Chapel". E.W. had grown that class of young men and older men to over 100 students. Lives were changed in that Sunday School class. E.W. was iconic at Highland Park Methodist Church but in the larger church community he was Miss Lillian Russell's father.

His obituary in the Progress Index, Petersburg told of his death this way:

> E.W. Russell, father of Miss Lillian Russell, pastor of Blandford Methodist Church, died early today in Richmond. Miss Russsell was attending the Virginia Methodist Conference in Roanoke when notified of her father's death.

Chapter Twenty
And Two Became Three

A charge to keep I have,
A God to glorify;
A never-dying soul to save,
And fit it for the sky.
—lyrics by Charles Wesley, 1762

$\mathcal{R}$everend Carroll, the Lynchburg District Superintendent, stood with Mildred Long and Nancy White in the corner of the fellowship hall of Fort Hill Methodist Church. Nancy was about Mildred's height, slender with blonde, shoulder-length hair. Mildred estimated Nancy was a decade younger than her. She wondered if Nancy was nervous by the way she was shifting her weight from one foot to the other as she looked around the room. The district program on evangelism had just concluded and the crowd of about seventy-five people mingled, coffee cups and cookies in hand. Mildred and Nancy were strangers to each other, but that was about to change.

"Miss Long, this is Miss White," said Reverend Carroll. "She is being appointed to Trinity Methodist in Altavista in the Lynchburg District. Miss White, this is Miss Long. She is being appointed to four churches called the Bellevue Charge in the Lynchburg District. You will share the parsonage of the Bellevue Charge. Your churches have been notified of this arrangement. I believe you will find this amenable. Do you have any questions?"

Mildred and Nancy looked at each other and then their district superintendent.

"No sir, we do not," said Mildred.

However, both lady preachers had a million questions, and they read that in each other's eyes.

He went on. "As you well know, it is most unusual to have a lady preacher on any district in our grand Virginia Conference. To have two on the same district is unheard of. Most district superintendents will not take even one lady preacher on their district, but it's 1952, and I consider myself more forward thinking in this matter." Reverend Carroll straightened his tie and pulled his suit coat together at the buttons.

"Do not embarrass me in any way. I will be monitoring you closely. As you see, we are meeting in public for this conversation. It is not appropriate for me to meet with you alone. In the future my wife will accompany me when I meet with either one of you. We must adhere to a strict etiquette and be above reproach. I know you agree."

Mildred and Nancy both nodded their heads. The district superintendent turned and walked away.

Mildred and Nancy looked at each other and Mildred said, "We need to talk."

"Indeed we do," said Nancy.

Mildred followed Nancy as they walked down a hallway to a classroom where they could talk in private. Mildred noticed Nancy had a spring to her step and her natural curls bounced on her shoulders.

Nancy turned just slightly toward Mildred and said, "This is my first appointment, and I'm most uninformed about many things, including the parsonage."

Once in the room, they pulled two chairs from a table to a corner of the room and sat down facing each other.

Mildred said, "Well, basically, the church provides everything but personal belongings. They provide all the furniture, the linens including bedding and towels. They also provide dishes and silverware. You just need to bring clothes, books, and personal hygiene items."

"That's perfect for me. I'm only twenty-five years old and haven't accumulated much in the way of furniture or household items."

"I understand. At thirty-eight, I have accumulated a few more things than I had at twenty-five, but it all still fits in my car. Do you have a car? Do you drive? Can you fit everything in your car?"

"Yes, yes, and yes."

"Then I believe we can make this work."

"When is moving day?" asked Nancy.

"It's next Wednesday. We're to arrive no earlier than noon on that day." Mildred continued, "The pastor who is moving out is to have the house vacated of all personal belongings and to have it cleaned and in good order by noon." Mildred pointed to her fingers as if checking off items on a list. "I'm moving from my parsonage in Danville that same day and will have my belongings packed in the car. I'll have the parsonage cleaned before noon, in time to allow me to arrive at our parsonage around 1:00 P.M. That will give me time to unload the car and organize everything. There'll probably be food in the refrigerator, including dinner for the first night and breakfast for the next day. How will that work for you?"

"I'll make it work. I'm so excited and, can I confess to you, scared to death! Frankly, I'm looking forward to our living arrangements. You already have two years of experience. I have none. I've so much to learn from you. I mean, my 'library,'" Nancy curved her index and middle fingers to form a bracket, "is basically my Bible."

"I have commentaries required for the Course of Study," said Mildred. I also have my textbooks from Columbia Bible College. You're most welcome to use any of them."

"That would be wonderful. I'll need them for sermon and Bible study preparation. Do you think the churches will have a library we can use?"

"That's not likely. They're too small. Our study will be in our parsonage, so sharing resources should prove to be workable. Now, what else do you need to know?"

"Where to begin, hmmm. Actually, it's too late to have this conversation. Can we talk on the phone tomorrow evening?"

"That'll work fine. Just call my parsonage number. Let me write it down for you."

Mildred found a piece of paper in the classroom, took a pencil from her pocketbook, and wrote her phone number. As they walked to their cars, Mildred thanked God not only for a housemate, but hopefully a friend. Her friendship with Lillian was spiritually close but geographically distant. Lillian had Mary as a housemate. Now Mildred would have the same benefit.

The next evening, as soon as Mildred had finished her dishes, she heard the phone ring. It was Nancy.

"Good evening, preacher," said Nancy.

"Good evening, Nancy. It's good to talk to you."

"So give me the full scoop but start with the basics."

"Okay, the basics. Beginning next week, I'll have four churches: Nazareth, Mt. Carmel, Bethany, and Oakland. There isn't time on a Sunday morning for me to preach at all four churches, so I'll preach at two churches the first and third Sundays of the month and the other two churches the second and fourth Sundays of the month. When there is a fifth Sunday, I'll have a Sunday off from preaching. This schedule will allow me to write a sermon every other week rather than weekly. Because you have a station church, you will preach at that one church every Sunday, so you'll need to prepare a sermon weekly."

"If I had four churches, I'd be so confused, I'd probably end up going to the wrong church. I'm glad to have just the one church. But I'm nervous about having a fresh Word from God every Sunday. How do you do that?"

"I had the same concern when I was where you are now, but trust me, God provides. I was reluctant to use a good sermon illustration for fear I would need it for my sermon the next week, but I've learned that God provides all I need, even illustrations.

The commentaries have some illustrations, but primarily my life provides them."

"My life up to this point has been pretty boring. I don't think I have any good stories," said Nancy.

"Oh, they don't have to be amazing stories, just things you have experienced in everyday life," said Mildred. "For example, my mother and I were with my dear sister as she lay dying. She looked up to the ceiling of the room and stretched out her hand and said, 'God, Mama, God.' My sister actually saw God." Mildred raised her arms and opened her eyes wide. "I've told that story several times and it never loses its power. People need to be assured God is real, and that story brings it home. Don't worry about illustrations. Now, back to my preaching schedule, I'm counting on you to help keep me straight."

"I'll do that if you'll help me with everything else."

"Nancy, can I be honest with you?"

"Sure, say whatever you want."

"I know our so called 'forward thinking' district superintendent feels like he's doing us a favor, but I also know that he negotiated a lower salary for me. Right now, I'm being paid $2,000 annual salary at Piney Forest. With the adjustment in moving to the Bellevue Charge, I'll be paid $400 less than I'm receiving now. That's less than the minimum paid for single pastors. I guess the rules don't apply to lady preachers even with our so-called enlightened superintendent."

"Unbelievable! Do you report that to somebody?"

"No, I don't report it to anybody. I just ignore the unfairness of the conference and then work with my local church to get a salary increase. Once they know you love them and you prove your worth, they're open to considering more. That's our only path for a fair salary. The Cabinet isn't interested."

Moving day came and Mildred and Nancy moved into the parsonage at Rural Free Delivery, Goode, Virginia. The parishioners put food in the refrigerator and flowers on the table. Mildred and Nancy selected their own bedrooms and set up their studies, one in the third bedroom and the other in the dining room.

They were there only a few days when Mildred received a phone call from their district superintendent. Mildred yelled up the steps to Nancy, who was busy working on a sermon in her study. "Nancy, the district superintendent just called. He and his wife are coming by tomorrow at 1:00 PM to talk to us about continuing our education."

"Okay, I'll be here. I've been thinking about that anyway."

The next day the Reverend and Mrs. Carroll came to the parsonage. Nancy and Mildred met them at the door. After escorting them to the living room, they offered the couple tea and cookies.

"No, thank you, we just finished lunch," said Reverend Carroll.

"Please, have a seat on the sofa," said Mildred. Mrs. Carroll's silk dress swished as she sat down, the blue in her dress complimenting the blue in her eyes and the flower print of the sofa. Her ample derriere descending into the cushions lifted the smell of her perfume into the room. She removed her white gloves and adjusted a curl of gray hair at her temple, then reached for a napkin and cookie, and set them on her lap. She took a bite of the cookie and a sip of her tea.

Reverend Carroll sat next to his wife. He had on a dark suit, white shirt, and dark tie. When he crossed his long legs Mildred noticed his garters, just before he brushed his pant leg down to cover his bare leg. "Now, as you both know, the entire conference is emphasizing the education of all pastors. I'm directing you to continue and complete your college education as soon as possible," he said.

This was music to their ears. Mildred had nearly completed a Bachelor of Arts degree from Columbia Bible College and was eager for more schooling. Nancy had taken several courses at Ferrum College.

Mildred asked, "Will the district or conference be able to provide some financial support? I can pay some of the tuition but paying all of it will be a hardship."

"The conference has set aside money for pastors under appointment, but there are far more pastors in need than there are funds. You can fill out an application and see what happens. I will make no guarantees." Reverend Carroll was all business. Mrs. Carroll reached for another cookie.

"That's enough for now, dear," said Reverend Carroll, "as we have to be going. I've other appointments this afternoon. You're welcome to go with me, or I can drop you off at home before making the other visits."

"I think I'd like to go home and get an early start on supper," Mrs. Carroll said.

Reverend and Mrs. Carroll stood and said farewell to Mildred and Nancy and then walked outside. Mildred turned to Nancy and said, "There is someone you need to meet who will teach you things you will never learn in any classroom. Her name is Lillian Russell. I wouldn't have survived my two years at Piney Forest if it weren't for Lillian. I'll set up a time for both of us to meet with her."

Chapter Twenty-One
A Threefold Cord

And if one prevails against him, two shall withstand him;
and a threefold cord is not quickly broken.
Ecc. 4:12 KJV

" *M*ildred, I'm sort of nervous," said Nancy. Mildred
tapped the turn signal as she approached Route 460.
"You've talked about Lillian in such glowing terms, I feel
I'm going to visit the queen of England. Is there anything I
should know, you know, like any points for royal
etiquette?"

"Relax, Nancy." Mildred chuckled and checked the
review mirror. "You'll love her and she'll love you. She is a bit
formal but don't feel you have to be formal. Just be yourself."

"All right," said Nancy and slouched slightly in the
passenger's seat.

Within an hour, Mildred and Nancy were sitting in
Lillian's kitchen at the Blandford parsonage in Petersburg.
Fall had come to southside Virginia. The kitchen windows
stood open and the breeze ruffling the curtains smelled of
musky, damp leaves. Lillian had made cucumber and
tomato sandwiches for the three of them. The sandwiches,
a bowl of coleslaw, and a plate of cookies sat in the middle
of the table.

"This looks delicious," said Mildred, her eyes wide open taking in the food on the table. "I'm so hungry. Unpacking all those boxes and rearranging things to make room for my things has made me ravenous." She licked her lips.

"There's more where these came from," said Lillian. "My parishioners continue to drop off the last remnants of their gardens. Have I put enough mayonnaise on the bread to suite you?"

Mildred took a bite of her sandwich and said, "Everything is perfect, as always. You even cut the crusts from the bread."

"You're the one who drove all the way here from Lynchburg. It's the least I can do." Lillian turned to look at Nancy. "Nancy, are these sandwiches sufficient for you? You've been moving and unpacking boxes too," said Lillian.

"Yes, this is plenty," said Nancy. It's like high tea-time with the queen."

Mildred gave Nancy a quick glance and scowled. Nancy smoothed the napkin on her lap and took a deep breath. "Thank you so much for including me in this gathering. I'm so honored and excited to be here."

"No need for flattery. We're just two ordinary lady preachers," said Lillian and waved her hand toward Mildred. They all chuckled. "I understand you're brand new to ministry. Mildred and I welcome you to our secret society. Honesty and confidentiality are what we do here."

Then, to be honest, I'm hungry. So who's going to say grace so we can eat?" said Nancy with a big grin.

"I'll be glad to offer grace," said Lillian.

After a brief prayer and some light conversation about weather and pastoral assignments, Mildred got down to business. "Lillian, as I begin this new appointment, I want to pick your brain. I have the two years' experience at Piney Forest, but I want to know how you do ministry. You're so successful here at Blandford, growing the church in every way. And the people love you. So tell me everything you know. Can we begin with youth programs?" asked Mildred.

Lillian took a sip of tea, dabbed her mouth with her linen napkin, and said, "Youth ministry, was my first love, where I began church work. But what I have learned is that as the pastor, I don't work directly with the youth, but rather with the volunteer adult leaders. I train them and then provide support and direction as needed. It's delegation. And it seems to be working because the youth program is growing by leaps and bounds."

"What about confirmation and youth choir?" asked Nancy.

"I do conduct the confirmation classes each year and direct the youth choir. We call it the Glee Club. Music is one of the main reasons the youth program is growing so fast."

"Speaking of music, what about the adult choir, do you help with that? The choir at my church is dismal. I cringe every Sunday during the anthem." Nancy said with a wince.

"Ah, choirs can make or break a church. When I came to Blandford, the choir was very weak. I joined the choir and helped them select good music. I listened when the congregation sang hymns and identified good voices. Then I invited those people to join the choir. You know many people don't know if they can sing. Sometimes they need a little help from their pastor." Lillian winked.

"But the primary instrument that helped our choir was my brother, Pete. He has been a great addition both in vocal quality and volume. Plus, he brings so much spirit and fun to everything he does. The choir rehearses on Wednesday nights. Immediately following rehearsal we have Wednesday night prayer meeting. It wasn't well attended when I first came, but as the choir has grown, so has the prayer meeting attendance. Pete's a great asset to Blandford. I don't know what I'd do without him," said Lillian.

"I wish I had a Pete in my ministry." Mildred looked up to the ceiling and said with a smile, "God, send me a Pete." The three women laughed out loud.

"I want to know more about Pete," said Nancy. "Is he married?"

"Nancy," said Mildred with a smile, "Pete's spoken for. You'll have to look in another pasture for a beau."

"Okay, I'll look on the way home. We went past lots of pastures on our way here," said Nancy and smiled.

Turning to Lillian, Mildred said, "Now, tell us about pastoral care. How do you manage that? I love pastoral care, but it can also be overwhelming. There're so many needs, and I'm only one person."

Lillian slid the plate of cookies toward her guests. "Here, please take a cookie. I baked them this morning. The chocolate chips are still soft."

Mildred and Nancy each took a cookie. Nancy had a bite and said, "Great day in the morning, you weren't kidding about these cookies. Delicious! I think I'll have a second one."

Lillian smiled. "Please do. There are plenty." Turning toward Mildred, she said, "Mildred, I know what you mean about feeling overwhelmed. My parishioners call me 'Miss Russell.' I both love and cringe to hear my name called out. It often means dropping whatever I'm doing and then walking or taking the bus to visit someone. But let me tell you about something I started just this year. It's called 'adopt a shut-in.' We are asking every able-bodied member to adopt one of our older members. They can visit, write cards, or call their assigned person. Every shut-in gets special attention, and my workday is not interrupted as often."

"That's a wonderful idea. I'm going to do that as soon as I get permission from the Official Board at Bellevue," said Mildred.

"And may I add this? It's something I learned early in ministry: real ministry happens in the interruptions."

"That's so true," said Lillian. "I hadn't heard that phrase before, but it makes perfect sense. Real ministry *does* happen in the interruptions. Making emergency calls is vitally important, not an interruption at all."

Nancy said, "I don't even know how to make a pastoral call. What do I do?"

"Nancy, just remember what you learned at licensing school," said Mildred. "Be a good listener. Always include Scripture and prayer. And keep the visit short."

"Short. I like that part," said Nancy, and finished her second cookie.

"Allow me to mention another activity Blandford does in terms of pastoral care," said Lillian. "Once a year, we visit every member with special attention to those who have become inactive. That's made a tremendous difference. Seeing those faces back in the church is wonderful. I highly recommend doing that."

Mildred reached down to her pocketbook on the floor next to her chair. She searched around and then pulled out a pen and piece of paper. "I need to write these ideas down."

Suddenly the women heard a loud screeching from outside. They all turned to look out the kitchen window.

"Oh my, such a commotion," said Lillian. "The starlings have roosted in that tree. Let me close the window."

Lillian closed the window, and the room immediately became quiet with only the muted sounds of birds outside.

"Ladies, let me tell you about one of my favorite things about being a preacher," said Lillian. "Summer Vacation Bible School. I loved it as a child, and I now love it as an adult. I start working on it in January, recruiting teachers and selecting curriculum. VBS has grown to more than 100 participants. New families join the church as a result of VBS. Some years VBS is two weeks long. After one week, the teachers are exhausted. But let me tell you, after a two week VBS, even the children are exhausted." Lillian leaned back in her chair and laughed.

"What role do you play in VBS?" asked Nancy.

"This is complicated because the male pastors generally don't do anything for VBS. They just want it to happen and let the women of the church do it. But I teach Bible stories using flannel-backed characters on a board covered with flannel. I also lead the music. VBS music is so much fun. Don't you just love hearing children sing *The Wise Man Built His House Upon the Rock?*" said Lillian.

The three women smiled and nodded and then spontaneously began to sing with hand motions, "The wise man built his house upon a rock, and the rain came tumbling down. The rains came down, and the floods came up." Laughter filled the kitchen.

"This has been wonderful," Mildred said. "Thank you so much for hosting us, Lillian. Nancy and I need to get on the road back to Lynchburg and unpack more boxes. Can we do this again sometime, maybe next month?"

"I hope so. I've had a great time," said Nancy.

"Absolutely. Please do come back any time," said Lillian.

"But can I ask one more question, Lillian?" asked Mildred.

"Certainly. What is it?"

"At Piney Forest, I could never get the leaders of the church to truly follow me," said Mildred. "I had good ideas about what to do, but seldom were they interested. So, most of the time, I ended up doing my good ideas myself. But, Lillian, you have your people so involved. They follow your lead. How do you do that?"

"This is what I've learned," said Lillian. "Here's the secret: They don't care what you know until they know that you care. First, love them. When the members know that you genuinely love them, they will listen to what you know."

"They don't care what you know until they know that you care," repeated Nancy. "I'm going to put that to memory. But to tell you the truth, I'm not sure what it means."

"It means," Lillian said, "that you do pastoral care before you ask them to serve. Visit every member at home. Visit them in the hospital before and after surgery. When there's a death, be the first person there. Send birthday cards. Call them simply because you didn't see them in church last Sunday. Let them know you love them. Once they know you love them, they will do almost anything you ask them."

"Wow, that's powerful," Mildred said.

"Now, I get it," Nancy said.

The three women shared more stories of ministry as they washed dishes and cleaned up from lunch. Lillian packed the leftover sandwiches in an empty bread bag.

On the trip back to Lynchburg, Nancy continued to pick Mildred's brain. She was particularly interested in learning more about Lillian.

"Mildred, Lillian seems so perfect. From her hair to her shoes, *perfect*. And the way she talks—it's so formal. It was like visiting my high school English teacher or, like I mentioned, the Queen of England. If I have to be like that to make it in ministry, I won't last a year."

"Don't' try to be Lillian. She's one of a kind," said Mildred. "Her goal is to be above reproach in everything she does so no one will find any reason to criticize her. At first, I tried to use her as a role model, but it didn't work. I didn't come anywhere close to being like Lillian. Just be yourself, your best self, but yourself."

"Whew, that's a relief. I don't think I could ever live up to her standards," said Nancy.

Chapter Twenty-Two
Commitment to Education

The heart of the discerning acquires knowledge,
for the ears of the wise seek it out.
Proverbs 18:15

$\mathcal{T}$he next semester, both Mildred and Lillian attended Lynchburg College. In two semesters, Mildred took six courses,
including Ethics, Philosophy of Religions, the Teachings of Jesus,
The Hebrew Prophets, Essentials of Bible History, and The Psalms
and Wisdom Literature of the Bible. Together with her course
work at Columbia Bible College, those courses earned her a BA in
Religion, which she received on June 8, 1953. It wasn't easy to go
to class, study for exams, and write papers while serving four
churches, but she did it and was proud of her accomplishments.
Her family from Biscoe and members of the Bellevue Charge
traveled to the college to celebrate her graduation.

In addition to college classes, Mildred also participated in
the Conference Course of Study through Emory University,
Georgia. Eventually, she discontinued correspondence courses to

attend with Nancy the in-person Course of Study at Duke Divinity School. Held in the summer, Mildred and Nancy traveled to Durham, North Carolina, to participate. They were both grateful for their Lay Leaders and Sunday School Superintendents who preached for them the Sundays they had to be gone for classes.

While Nancy and Mildred thrived academically at Duke, they struggled socially as the only female divinity students in the Course of Study. Some of the professors were supportive of them, but others were critical, even questioning their presence. Taking classes at Duke was far more expensive than the two dollars per course Mildred had paid for the correspondence courses. Students in the correspondence courses could also borrow the required books for thirty days from any of the nine Methodist theological seminaries in the United States for only the postage. Buying books for their studies at Duke was far more expensive, but it did help grow their personal libraries. Mildred and Nancy managed their money well and reached their goal: to be equally well educated as many of their male counterparts and better educated than most.

A few years earlier, in 1949, the Virginia Board of Ministerial Training and Qualifications had reported a total of sixty-six accepted supply pastors serving some of the problematic charges. "Difficult" was code for small, rural, and low salaried, plus an often inferior parsonage and conflicted congregation. These were the kind of churches to which uneducated men and women preachers regardless of their education received appointments.

However, Bellevue Charge was a good appointment for Mildred. All four churches had Sunday School weekly, even though they held worship only every other week. With hymns, prayer, Scripture reading, and celebration of birthdays, the opening exercises provided a consistent form of weekly worship. Only Sunday School attendance was recorded regularly in the conference journals because it was the only program scheduled every Sunday. The four churches' combined membership on the Bellevue Charge hovered around 500 people, with combined Sunday School attendance averaging between 150 and 200.

Nevertheless, She Preached

It was a time of tremendous growth in churches across the United States. Lynchburg was no exception. Mildred received many people into church membership and baptized many babies.

With a large number of young families, the charge needed a children's choir with strong leaders. Mildred could sing, but music wasn't her gift; however, it was Nancy's, so Nancy, at Mildred's invitation, took the baton and directed a most successful charge children's choir.

One afternoon, following practice with the children's choir, Nancy said to Mildred, "I don't know how much longer I can do this."

"Do what?" Mildred asked.

"Go to your church every week and direct the choir."

"Oh, no, why not?" asked Mildred in a panic.

"Every week I'm mobbed with people telling me how wonderful you are and how much they love you. They tell me how easy you are to be with, how spiritual you are, how you visit everybody and bring the Spirit of Jesus with you," said Nancy, waving her arms in grand gestures. "And, oh, don't get me started on your preaching and teaching. You're the best they've ever had, the best in the Conference." Nancy tried to imitate their voices.

"That's so good to hear. I do love Jesus and love my people. But please, don't stop leading the children's choir. I sing like a cow." They hugged each other and laughed.

"I'm just joking with you," said Nancy. "Of course, I'll continue with your children's choir. They're so much fun. I just wanted you to know how beloved you are."

# # #

Sundays were their longest days of the week. They rose early to prepare for their multiple worship services, attended fellowship times, visited people at the hospitals, and then ended with the youth meeting. By Sunday evening, Mildred was exhausted, but her extroversion told her she needed to talk.

This particular Sunday evening, more than a year into their appointments, Mildred and Nancy lingered in the kitchen following a light supper. Both had been too tired to cook.

Mildred spoke in a voice Nancy recognized as a combination of exhaustion and frustration. "I need to make a lot of adjustments. I miss seeing my people every Sunday due to the every-other-Sunday schedule. And I miss being part of the Sunday School, visiting the classes, providing support and guidance to the teachers. One of my roles as the pastor is to serve as the resident theologian. I need to know that the children, youth, and adults are learning solid Methodist theology, not the Baptist theology so prevalent in these rural churches."

Nancy just listened and nodded. She'd learned listening was often all that Mildred needed.

Mildred went on, "The administrative tasks, which I thought I was gaining in ability, actually have become more challenging. I now have four reports to do every quarter, one for each church. I've more meetings to attend, four budgets to oversee, and four church buildings to manage."

Mildred paused long enough to take a breath. "Probably the most complicated challenge for me is that while I love all four churches equally, they don't necessarily share my affection for each other. They're even *fighting* over me." Mildred pointed to herself. "They ask if I'm spending as much time with Nazareth as I am with Oakland. Time seems to be the measuring stick of fairness."

Mildred got up and poured herself a glass of water. "Do you want some water?"

"No, I'm fine. Go on," said Nancy.

Mildred took a drink of her water, sat back down, and continued. "You know I'm diligent about dividing my time based on the needs, but that doesn't seem to make much difference to the critical voices. The four churches aren't all the same size, so their needs differ. Also, they pay the pastor's salary and housing needs based on the size of the church. Some churches contribute more than others. Every church wants to be sure they're receiving their fair share of the pastor's time. It's exhausting!"

Nancy let Mildred vent.

"And just when I think I have it figured out, Mt. Carmel is talking about closing. It's become so small that it's no longer financially viable. With three churches instead of four, the whole schedule changes, allowing me to preach at all three churches every Sunday morning. So I'll be back to writing a new sermon every week and no fifth Sundays off. Will the changes ever stop? I'm tired of figuring things out only to have to start all over again."

Nancy sensed that Mildred had exhausted her rant, so began her own. "While I love sharing a parsonage with you, the location of the parsonage isn't convenient. I have to drive an hour to get to Trinity in Altavista. It's all right on good days, but on snowy or icy days, it's almost impossible. If the Cabinet wanted us to share a parsonage, they should've appointed us to churches closer together."

Mildred responded with a laugh. "That's odd because I'm the one with the reputation for driving fast. I even heard a parishioner say that if my preaching didn't scare the 'bad place' out of you, my driving would."

Indeed, it was during this appointment that Mildred got the reputation for being a fast driver. To get to all three churches on time, she had to hit the gas hard in her two-door gray coupe named Barnabas. It wasn't unusual for Mildred to talk to her car. "Come on, Barnabas, get me safely and on time to my next worship service. "

One parishioner witnessed, "Every Sunday worship begins when Miss Long dashes in from the previous service, mounts the pulpit area and drops to her knees for what is a serious plea for God's presence."

#   #   #

One Sunday evening, Mildred called Lillian to update her. "Today, a married couple visited my church. They're members of another church in the area, but they told me that they came today to see a lady preacher. I felt like a two-headed calf. Can you believe it?"

"Oh, I believe it all right. When I first came to Blandford, that happened almost every Sunday. If the people were longtime members of another church in the area, usually one visit satisfied their curiosity. But if they were looking for a church, they almost always came back, and most have joined. I know it's uncomfortable to have people visit your services just to see a female preacher, but God can use it for good. Just remember Joseph, who said, 'Man intended it for evil, but God intended it for good.' You'll get used to it."

"I certainly hope so. If I'm not careful, the devil gets in me, and I want to make monkey sounds or sell tickets. God help me!"

"God, help us both," Lillian laughed.

#   #   #

This scrutiny of a female preacher made Lillian, Mildred, and Nancy very deliberate about their pulpit apparel. Mildred dressed professionally in suits and high necklines, with pearls or a simple cross necklace. The length of her skirt was always mid-calf. Her stockings had a seam that drew a line straight up the back of her leg. She wore plain pumps, black or white, to match her suit. She deliberately dressed so nothing about her appearance would distract from the gospel message, even wearing a dress, stockings, and pumps to play softball at the church picnic.

Mildred was also very professional in her relationships with her parishioners. She addressed them by their last name as "Miss" "Mrs." or "Mr." and asked them to call her "Miss Long." The obituaries named her as "Miss Long" rather than "Reverend Long," although obituaries named male pastors as "Reverend."

This greenhouse existence took a different view when the local paper decided to do a story on Mildred and Nancy. This story included nine large photos of Mildred and Nancy doing everything from drying dishes in their parsonage to preaching and visiting the homebound. For this rural community to have *two* lady preachers in the 1950s was indeed newsworthy.

Mildred knew the power of prayer. She encouraged everyone at her churches, including herself, to have prayer partners. She visited her prayer partner daily, if possible, and spent most of the visit on her knees in prayer. More than a program or a study, prayer was a lifeline for Mildred.

When issues arose at church, she called everyone to prayer. Her answer to financial matters was not a stewardship campaign or a series of sermons on giving, but rather to take the finance committee into the sanctuary, have them kneel at the communion rail, and pray. After some time on their knees, she invited them to sit in the front pews where she asked if all of them were tithers, giving ten percent of their income to God. If not, then Miss Long called them back to their knees to pray.

When issues with the church building arose, she took the custodian to the communion rail, knelt, and prayed with him. Prayer was her natural response to both the blessings and the challenges of ministry and life in general.

Mildred's prayer life became especially critical in 1952, just two years after she arrived at the Bellevue Charge. The sanctuary at Oakland Methodist Church needed renovation that necessitated taking out the "slave balcony." The balcony at Oakland had a long, conflicted history. Taking it out carried the potential of considerable controversy. Some members thought it was long overdue to remove the balcony, a symbol of segregation and bigotry. Others were concerned about where people of color would sit if they were to attend Oakland Methodist Church. Mildred had established relationships of trust and respect with the people at her church. Because of that, she was able to navigate the congregation through all the renovations without incident. Stained glass windows were added, providing everybody with a new view and a more "colorful" future.

#   #   #

World War II had opened doors not only for Black Americans but also for women. Having the ability to pursue careers otherwise closed to women, they did not willingly go back home. A strong movement made its way up the Methodist Church ranks to give full clergy rights to women. Lillian and Mildred learned as much as possible and then waited to hear from the General Conference meeting in Minneapolis in 1956. All across the country, there were other Methodist clergywomen, like Mildred and Lillian, who had been ordained deacon and elder but forbidden by the *Discipline* to move from the probationary position. The Women's Society for Christian Service and other forward-thinking lay and clergymen and women worked together and wrote more than 2000 memorials (similar to a legal abstract) on the subject.

Mildred was eager to know the outcome as soon as it was determined. So she asked the only female delegate to General Conference to call her immediately following the vote.

"Reverse the charges, if you want. This is important to me."

Mildred stayed by her phone in the parsonage all day on Friday, May 4, 1956. Finally, around 4:00 P.M. the phone rang. A breathless voice said, "Mildred, this is June Scott. They just took the vote, but before I tell you the outcome, let me tell you some of what happened. It has been quite a day here in Minneapolis."

Mildred was reasonably confident from the tone of June's voice that this was good news. "All right, I'll wait to hear the results but talk fast. I've been waiting a very long time for this."

"Well, some district superintendents on the subcommittee reported positively and others negatively about women serving as pastors.," June said. "Everyone agreed clergywomen must not act aggressively but humbly with gratitude."

"What?" exclaimed Mildred. "Not aggressively but humbly with gratitude? For heaven's sake. But go on."

"There were some hard pills to swallow, but we knew we'd have to pick our battles. All of this happened in the sub-committee addressing this issue. Following this morning's worship and announcements, Bishop Harrell asked for the report on women's clergy rights. That report was presented, and then came a barrage of majority and minority reports, amendments, amendments to the amendments, substitute motions, and amendments to the substitute motions. Some of the motions suggested only single women or widows would be eligible."

"What? Single women and widows?" exclaimed Mildred again. "What would happen if a woman got married after being accepted into full connection?"

"The argument was that they would then lose that status. I know, crazy, huh? But others argued it's an "administrative issue." Mildred, this phrase is code for local churches refusing to take a woman and district superintendents then having a problem on their hands."

"Why is that an issue? That's just district superintendents and congregations being bias and uncharitable against women," said Mildred.

"Exactly," June said. "Some argued women can be deaconesses and missionaries. 'Isn't that enough?' they said. 'Men can't be deaconesses, so why should women be elders in full connection?' That was the argument."

"I guess that was just another hard pill to swallow," Mildred said.

"It was, but we pressed on," June said. "Now, the General Conference rules allow two speakers in support and two opposed to address each of the reports, amendments, and substitutes. Little wonder the debate went into the afternoon session. Laymen, clergymen, and district superintendents spoke. A delegate from Bengal spoke in favor, telling humorous stories from his own culture while making his point clear. He was for full inclusion. Finally, late into the debate, two women spoke, of course, favoring full clergy rights for all women. One of the delegates challenged the show of hands vote, and the Bishop called for a count. It just went on and on. Many delegates were confused as to what we were voting on."

"Finally, by mid-afternoon, after voting to extend the time to finish all that was before us, we voted on this motion." Mildred could hear June unfold a piece of paper and then clear her throat.

"Paragraph 313 will now read, "Women are included in the foregoing provisions and may apply as candidates for the traveling ministry, as provided for in chapter III of the "Discipline" entitled 'traveling preacher,' paragraphs 321 to 356."

"This was the substitute of the amended substitute for the majority report. How crazy is that? Anyway, it was approved 389 to 297."

Mildred jumped up and down. "June, thank you so much for calling. You have made my day; no, you have made my year. As soon as our Bishop gets back from General Conference, I'm going to start the process. I'm on track to be ordained an elder, hopefully, next year. This news is so exciting. Thank you, thank you, thank you. Enjoy the rest of your time in Minneapolis."

#   #   #

The Oakland Church was not the only building in need of repair on the Bellevue Charge. The two-story white frame parsonage that Nancy and Mildred had called home for four years continued to provide maintenance challenges. Mildred and Nancy learned much about home repairs, especially plumbing. The church trustees from both charges made frequent visits to the parsonage to repair items. Finally, everybody agreed it was time to build a new parsonage.

Mildred worked with the Bellevue Charge's Trustees to design a new parsonage incorporating the standards provided by the Conference. But Mildred and Nancy never lived in this beautiful brick parsonage, as they moved to a new appointment the same year the house was completed, 1957. Mildred did give a name to the parsonage. She called it "Ebenezer" because, like the words to the song, "Here I raise my Ebenezer. Hither by thy help, I come," she had raised it by the help of God.

Just two years earlier, another pastor in the Conference had written this humorous song.

"Don't Take the Pictures off the Wall"
By Ernest K. Emurian, 1955
While Pastor of Elm Avenue Methodist Church, Portsmouth, Virginia

Verse 1

We heard that we were moving, and they said, "It's in the bag,"
and you'd better get to packing, Brother E."
But a day before Conf'rence my hopes began to sag,
and someone tried to make a fool of me.
We had gathered up the boxes and the barrels by the score,
and prepared to heed the Macedonian Call.
Margaret had the house all cleaned and even waxed the floor,
and taken down the pictures from the wall.

CHORUS

Don't take the pictures off the wall.
Even if the Sup'rintendents call.
If the Cabinet can't say "Yes,"
Brother, you're in a mess.
Don't take the pictures off the world. (Amen!)

Verse 2

They said, "Now up in Richmond is the very church for you,"
And they're saying, "You're the very man they need.
It's the number one appointment and the best that we can do;
they'll go to town with Ernest in the lead."
So we set our vision northward and packed with might and main,
while the boxes filled the study and the hall.
And the people said, "What is our loss is surely Broad Street's gain,"
and helped us take the pictures off the wall.

CHORUS

Verse 3

The children were elated as they put their stuff away,
and the baby sang and danced in merry glee.
And they said, "Let's all get going to the Promised Land today,"
but a roadblock stood right there in front of me.
A solemn, pious layman said, "We don't think that he will do.
As a pastor, he has nothing on the ball!"
So the Bishop, for the ninth time, read us out "Elm Avenue."
We're putting back the pictures on the wall.
CHORUS

Chapter Twenty-Three
Moving Forward

"For I know the plans I have for you," declares the LORD,
"plans to prosper you and not to harm you,
plans to give you hope and a future."
Jeremiah 29:11 KJV

*M*ildred called Lillian and spoke so fast, Lillian couldn't wedge a word into the conversation. "I just got a call from Dr. C .C. Bell, my District Superintendent here in Lynchburg. He reluctantly told me that a church actually asked for me. Can you believe it?"

Mildred switched the phone to the other ear without skipping a beat. "The Cabinet always tells us how fortunate we are even to have an appointment because most churches don't want a lady preacher, and the Cabinet isn't required to provide us employment. Well, Lillian, things are changing and changing fast. There's more than one way to skin this cat. They can tell us no church wants us, but this proves otherwise."

Mildred paused to gasp for air, so Lillian took the opportunity to speak. "This is wonderful on so many levels. It's music to my ears. But I have to ask: What church asked for you, and are you going?"

Mildred laughed. "Oh, I guess I forgot the details. I'm going to Hillcrest in Fredericksburg. It's a nice size station church in the Richmond District. I told you how I went directly to the

Bishop and how he responded positively to my situation. Hillcrest sent delegates from their church to my church here in Lynchburg to hear me preach, and they were impressed. They told Bishop Garber they'd love to have me as their pastor.

"Congratulations! They're one mighty blessed church to have you," said Lillian.

But Mildred wasn't done. "And I'll be close enough to go to Wesley Theological Seminary. The seminary recently moved from Westminster, Maryland, to Washington, DC, a much closer commute from Fredericksburg. I can take some classes not available through the Course of Study at Duke. It'll be marvelous!"

"It is marvelous! But what about Nancy? Is she moving too?" asked Lillian.

"That's a whole different story. So many things are happening all at once. Nancy can't stay in this district because she has no female pastor to live with, and they couldn't find her an appointment near Fredericksburg, so she is applying to Union Seminary in Richmond and plans to attend there full-time. I've invited her to live with me in the Hillcrest parsonage, and I think she's going to do that, at least temporarily."

"There are a lot of changes, but they all sound very positive," said Lillian.

"God is truly blessing me with opportunities to serve. I'm humbled and grateful," said Mildred.

"Indeed, you're blessed; we both are," said Lillian. "The other lady preachers are so few. There are the two of us, plus Nancy, of course. But other than that, women are appointed for a year or so and then either quit or aren't appointed again. Few seek anything beyond a license to preach."

"We are indeed blessed, pioneers, for sure. I wonder if there will be more women who will come after us."

"Surely there will be others. I think of myself as clearing a path for other women to follow. May God bless our journey and keep the path clear for those who come behind us," Lillian said.

"Speaking of clearing paths, this is a big year for me in another way. I will finally be ordained an elder. You were the first, Lillian, ten years ago," said Mildred.

Lillian interrupted, "Now you come behind me and claim your place in history as the second woman to be ordained an elder in our conference."

Lillian cocked the phone between her shoulder and ear, so both hands were free to clap. "Hip, hip horary, for you, Reverend Mildred Long," said Lillian into the phone.

"Hold the applause, please, until the big moment." Mildred laughed and then paused before saying in a more serious voice, "Someday, I hope also to receive full clergy rights in our Conference. I'm confident I've all the credentials to be approved. Do you think you'll apply for full connection, too? It would be wonderful to be received the same year as you," said Mildred.

"I've thought and prayed about it for a long time. It would make my life easier in some ways in that I wouldn't have to appear before the district every year to have my work reviewed. But I could be asked to move from Blandford and would have to go where the Bishop assigns me."

Lillian looked out the window to Mary's car parked next to Lillian's prized roses. "As it stands now, I feel very comfortable being able to stay at Blandford for a long time. Not being able to drive is a significant consideration. Blandford and I have worked out an excellent solution to that. Also, I don't know what Mary would do. We've both become so dependent upon each other; I don't know what I'd do without her, either."

"So, it sounds like you've decided not to seek full connection. I understand, but if you should change your mind, I'd love to do this together," said Mildred. "I'll see you at Annual Conference. It's a big one for me. My family is coming up from North Carolina, and members from the Bellevue Charge plan to be there too, all to celebrate my ordination," said Mildred.

The next week Mildred and Nancy drove to Roanoke to attend Annual Conference. Mildred's mother and brothers made the trip to witness her ordination. Two dozen members from her churches also came.

From the time they entered the Civic Center, they could feel the energy. The Virginia Conference was the largest in the Methodist Church and growing. Just in the previous year, there had been a gain of 9,918 members. There were 674 pastors appointed to churches, and 220 of them were moving that year. Mildred was excited to be part of what God was doing in Virginia.

Like it had been for Lillian, Mildred was the only woman in a long line of men in dark suits, one tremble voice in a chorus of tenors and basses. Also, like Lillian, she felt God's hand on her head at ordination and on her life as a pastor. No one or nothing could take that from her.

The next week Mildred and Nancy packed up their belongings and moved to Fredericksburg. At forty-three years old, Mildred had been a student, weaver, manager, evangelistic preacher, and had seven years-experience as a local pastor. She was feeling confident about herself and her abilities. She hit the ground running full stride.

The local Fredericksburg newspaper attempted to hold her to a more traditional role, but Mildred would have nothing to do with that. The newspaper reported: *When asked how she found time to fit homemaking duties into her busy minister's schedule, Miss Long compared herself to the bachelor preacher whose needs were ministered to by his thoughtful congregation. Disclaiming any culinary ability, Miss Long was gently contradicted by her fellow minister, the Reverend Miss Nancy White, who says that Miss Long's barbecued chicken is something special.*

Mildred attended the first official church board meeting within days of her arrival at Hillcrest Methodist Church. When called upon to speak, she said, "I will not likely make reference to this again but allow me to say this now. I recognize that there may be a need for adjustments in the people's minds about having a woman minister. Be assured my concerns and interests are for the spiritual welfare of my people. My ministry is one of God's calling. No matter where God sends me, my work is with the people present and those we might reach."

Mildred paused long enough to assure everyone was still listening and then continued. "I know from experience that when the spiritual life of a church deepens in Christ, there are no financial problems. We have one life to live. It is God's gift to us. All we can ever do is never enough. We are more than members of Hillcrest Methodist Church. We are representatives of Christ. I recommend that we, as a congregation, pray about all our issues. Through prayer, God will meet us, and our problems will be resolved."

At the next meeting of the Official Board, Mildred shared what a pastor does during the week. "I know this is of great confusion for many parishioners. Let me assure you that there is far more to my work than preaching on Sunday morning. During the past forty-nine days, I have made 115 pastoral calls, including visits to hospitals. I have attended five meetings, conducted four extra services outside of Sunday services, spent 125 hours in study, attended three district meetings, and spent an entire weekend with the youth of our church.."

Mildred paused and looked with affection upon the church leaders seated in the sanctuary before she continued. "Hillcrest is blessed not only with capable people but with devoted faithful people whose response to the many obligations laid upon you prove the desire to place the Lord and His church first in your lives. These faithful ones are found both in leadership and in the role of followers and supporters of the church. I am very grateful for the privilege of serving and working with you. It is my earnest prayer that as we work together with the Lord, we shall realize a spiritual quickening and an expanding of the Kingdom in our midst."

#   #   #

After just one year in Fredericksburg, Mildred determined the time had come to move forward with a significant challenge: to become a full member of the Conference. To do that, she had to enroll with Wesley Theological Seminary as a candidate for the Bachelor of Sacred Theology with eleven credit hours per semester for two semesters. After Mildred explained the situation to her Board, they assured her that she would have their support in this strenuous task.

Mildred was one of four women enrolled at Wesley that year. Her classes included Old Testament, Speech for Ministers, Pastoral Psychology, Worship, Parish Administration, Methodist History, and Pastoral Counseling. She earned high marks of A's and B's. Wesley's tuition in 1958-59 was $125 a semester plus a $10 fee, creating a financial hardship for Mildred. The rigorous demands of traveling back and forth on US route 1 the sixty miles between Fredericksburg and Washington, DC, and the study required to receive excellent marks required much time away from her people. She consistently thanked the members for helping with the responsibilities at church while she was at school. After two semesters and twenty-two credits at the seminary plus a Greek class at Mary Washington College, she had enough credits to be eligible to become a full member of the Conference.

Mildred was devoted, disciplined, dogged. In her quarterly report in November 1959, she included these in her description of pastoral work: systematic visiting of sick and shut-ins, visitation of inactive members and prospective members, visiting for counseling and planning the work of the church, weddings, funerals, teaching course on worship Sunday evenings, Sunday School teacher, Wednesday evening Bible study, conducting membership class for youth, presenting a program for WSCS, and participating in the Stanley Jones Mission and Training School. It was little wonder that the church leaders annually asked the District Superintendent to reassign Mildred to Hillcrest.

Nevertheless, She Preached

The issue of the parsonage raised its head again in Fredericksburg. Nancy White spoke to Mildred one evening in a bit of a panic as she dashed in for a quick bite of dinner. "Mildred, as you know, I have completed my work at Union Seminary and am being appointed as the associate pastor at Park View on the Lynchburg District. They do not have a parsonage for the associate pastor, so I may need some of my furniture back."

"Wow, that has been five years," replied Mildred.

"I think we marked everything. It's just the one-bedroom suite," remembered Nancy.

"Okay, I think we can manage that," said Mildred.

"But there's more. I also need to have it delivered to my house in Lynchburg."

"Anything else?" continued Mildred.

In a timid voice, Nancy responded, "Yes, dare I ask for more. Do you think your church could provide a small amount of remuneration for the use of that bedroom suite for the past five years? That would help me so much."

"All I can do is ask the church leaders. It seems reasonable to me, but I don't know what they'll think," says Mildred.

"Well, please bring it up and let me know what they decide. Do you mind doing the dishes tonight? I have so many things to do," Nancy said before running out the door to get in her car.

Hillcrest Methodist Church was quite familiar with and fond of Nancy White. Not only had she lived with Mildred in the parsonage, but she had been the guest speaker at a revival as well as guest speaker for the WSCS Bible study and Quiet Day. The Parsonage Committee delivered the bedroom furniture to Nancy's new residence in Lynchburg and purchased a new Hillcrest parsonage suite. They did not offer Nancy the remuneration for the use of the furniture.

Chapter Twenty-Four
History Is Written Again

I knew a man in Christ about fourteen years ago
(whether in the body I cannot tell or out of the body I cannot tell,
only God knoweth)
was caught up to the third heaven.
II Cor. 12:2 KJV

𝒫ete sat in his sister's parsonage kitchen in Petersburg. It was New Year's Day, 1961. Lillian's calendar was open on the table, and she was writing in the key events for the year.

"Let's see; Easter is April 2 this year. I have a revival in May and two weeks of Vacation Bible School in July."

Accustomed to his sister's practice of talking to herself, Pete continued reading the Richmond Times-Dispatch's sports page. But then she stopped and directed her full attention at him.

"Pete, I think this is going to be a big year for Blandford Methodist Church."

"I think it's going to be a big year for their pastor, Reverend Russell," said Pete. He kept the newspaper open but set it down in front of him and looked at her.

"Well, it could be a big year for both the church and for me. The leaders here are determined to write a complete history of the church. They've put together a committee, including some of our oldest members," said Lillian.

"Given the age of some of your members, they're smart to write this history now. Some of these folks don't have many years left," said Pete, with a smile.

"I'm afraid that's true." Lillian set her pencil down and spoke with a stern voice. "Pete, you've got to get the whole family here when this celebration happens in the fall. Mama hasn't been here much at all in the ten years since Daddy died. I understand her grief, but it's important to have her here. She's as much a part of Blandford's history as anybody. I couldn't have made it through those early years without her. Do you think you can get her here?"

"I'll mention something to her when the time gets closer. It's much too soon now to say anything. You know how she worries," said Pete.

"You're right. I'm just so anxious for her to be here and to be part of this celebration."

Lillian went back to her calendar and Pete back to his newspaper.

"Oh, my, I have a speaking engagement this month. With the Christmas activities, I forgot all about it. I'm supposed to preach to the women of the Petersburg Brotherhood." She tapped the eraser end of the pencil on the table and looked at her brother. "Pete, are you listening to me?" She was speaking in that stern voice again.

"Yes, preaching to women at a men's meeting or something like that." Pete stopped reading but didn't put down the newspaper. "I don't know why women can't have their own groups. Why are they always connected to some brotherhood? Anyway, you have preached so many times; you could do this in your sleep. Not to worry, little sister."

Mary came into the kitchen, refreshed Pete, Lillian's, and her own cup of coffee.

"Good morning, Mary," Pete said. "How are you?"

"I'm very well. Just grabbing the ladies' section of the newspaper, and then I'll be out of your hair."

"Come, join us," Lillian said and patted the chair next to her.

"No, I'll let you two banter a bit more," said Mary with a smile. She took the style section of the newspaper and walked into the dining room.

Lillian picked up the conversation with her brother. "I agree with you about the whole ladies-auxiliary-brotherhood thing. I've never been asked to preach at the Petersburg Brotherhood, just the ladies' group. But I don't agree one bit with you about not having to worry about what to preach that night. You know, I take every speaking engagement very seriously. God might use that very sermon to bring somebody to Christ. You just never know. And, by the way, I'm ten years older than you, remember? So I'm not your little sister."

"Yes, but you're ten inches shorter than me, remember?" Pete rolled up his newspaper and tapped his sister on top of her head.

Lillian decided to preach on love, particularly God's love. She felt good about the message but had no idea the impact it would have on the ladies of the brotherhood.

The night of the worship service, Lillian arrived her customary thirty minutes early at Ettrick Methodist Church, Petersburg. It was a bitterly cold January night in southside Virginia. As Mary dropped her off at the church door, Lillian said, "I doubt there'll be much of a crowd tonight, given this cold and wind."

"You know God will use your message to reach whoever it's supposed to reach," said Mary. As Mary parked the car, Lillian looked around and noticed a long line of car lights coming toward the church. *I better get inside and prepare myself. People are already arriving.*

By 6:50 P.M., there wasn't an empty spot in any of the main sanctuary pews nor the two wings into the main balcony. Ushers began to seat people in the east wing balcony and then the west wing balcony. People just kept coming, delaying the start of the service.

At 7:10 P.M., the ladies group president said to Lillian, "I think we can start in five minutes. All the possible parking spaces are taken. Once the guests who have parked are seated, we should be able to begin. I've been attending these for years, but I've never seen such a crowd. God must have something special in mind tonight." She scurried off to tend to the ushers' questions.

Indeed God did have something special planned. Lillian felt the presence of the Holy Spirit so powerfully that when she rose to preach, she felt as if her spirit left her body. She heard her voice but didn't feel in control of it. Her manuscript was on the pulpit in front of her, but she never turned a page. Her words had power beyond any amount of preparation.

Although the pews were groaning under the weight of the packed house and the wind was howling outside the stained glass windows, everything was eerily quiet in the sanctuary. Lillian could hear nothing but her own voice. As she looked out at the ladies in the pews, she knew their spirits were listening to God's Spirit speaking through her.

"My sisters, most of us have people who love us. In fact, most of us have many people who love us. We know the difference love makes, how it changes how we think, who we are. When I was an evangelist, I had a suiter who was truly tall, dark, and handsome." Lillian smiled, and the congregation of women laughed.

"He loved me; in fact, he asked me to marry him. His love made me feel as if I could fly. But I turned down that wedding proposal. Why? Why would I turn down a wedding proposal from a handsome man with a good career and impeccable character? I'll tell you why. Jesus came to me and asked me, just as He had asked Peter 2000 years ago along the Tiberias Sea, 'Do you love me?' I said to Christ, as Peter said to Him, 'You know that I love You.' Jesus said to me, 'My love is more than enough for you. It's all you need to feed My sheep.'"

For as long as she could remember, Lillian was a serious person. Most jokes she didn't get and the ones she did understand got only a chuckle from her. But she had learned the value of humor in preaching. Laughter has a way of opening up the soul. If a preacher could get the congregation laughing, she could get a congregation open to receive the message. It was a technique she carefully planned and practiced. These women were laughing, so now was the time to make her point.

Lillian left the pulpit and walked to the center of the chancel. She raised both arms. Her white robe made her look like an angel, and her braided hair wrapped around the top of her head provided the halo. She said, "Sisters, this is how our Jesus loves us. This is how He loves you. Right now, He is walking around this sanctuary, telling each one of you how much He loves you. I can see Him. Can you? He is telling you that even if nobody else loves you, His love is more than enough to fill your entire being with joy, great joy. He is inviting you to open your hearts and receive His love, to say 'yes' to His proposal."

One of the women in the room stood, raised her arms, and shouted, "I open my heart to You, O God. Come fill me with Your love."

The presence of God was palpable. Lillian could feel the power. She continued to see the Spirit of Jesus moving around the room. She felt His warmth.

More women stood, raised their hands, and shouted prayers to God. Other women bowed their heads and wept.

Lillian continued to preach the love of God until the women sat down, and the sanctuary was silent except for her voice.

"Let us pray. God of love, thank You for coming here tonight and sharing Your son Jesus with us. Our hearts are full, overflowing with Your love. We will never be the same, indeed never be the same. In the mighty name of Jesus, we pray. Amen."

A loud "amen" filled the sanctuary.

Lillian waited several days before calling Mildred. Lillian had had similar experiences as an evangelist, but that night was different from anything she had ever experienced. She needed to talk to her friend about it. Who else could possibly understand what had happened that night?

"Mildred, this is Lillian. Do you have some time to talk?" said Lillian on the phone.

"Sure, I always have time for you. But is everything okay? Is your mama all right?" asked Mildred.

"Yes, everybody's fine. But I do have something serious to talk to you about."

"I'm listening," said Mildred.

"I was a guest speaker at an event Sunday night. It was the ladies of the Petersburg Brotherhood."

"Ladies of Brotherhood? What?"

"I know it's non-sensical. But that isn't why I called. It's what happened that night."

"Keep talking," said Mildred.

"I had what seemed to be an out-of-body experience. I felt my spirit leave my body, and something else took over. I'm not sure. It's hard to explain. But God's Spirit was powerful in a way I hadn't experienced before." Lillian paused for a few seconds. Mildred waited for Lillian to find the words.

Lillian continued. "But, Mildred, it wasn't just me. It was as if a similar or the same thing was happening to the other women in the sanctuary, as if their spirits came alive and took over their bodies. It was like God's Spirit in me talking to their spirits. I could almost see, no, I could see Jesus walking or floating or both around the sanctuary, going from person to person, touching them with His love. My sermon was on God's love. Have you ever had anything like this happen to you? Am I crazy? Or was it the cold outside, or the heat inside?"

"Ah, Lillian. What a beautiful blessing for you and all who gathered Sunday night." Mildred's voice was gentle, deliberate. "You aren't crazy, not one bit. God just used you. God used your mouth and voice to convey His love to His people. You were a vessel of the Word. I've had out-of-body experiences several times, but for me, it happened when I was by myself praying. Those have been both a gift and a puzzle for me. But this, Lillian, for you, was public so God could use it to bless more than just you. Truly a beautiful gift."

"So you don't think I'm crazy? And you think I didn't imagine things? I'm relieved. Frankly, I wasn't sure about even calling you for fear you would think I needed to spend some time in a mental hospital."

"Oh, Lillian, not at all. You're far from ill. You're an instrument of the Word of God."

"Thank you, Mildred. Thank you for listening and for sharing your own experiences. I feel the confirmation of the Spirit, and it's a tremendous comfort."

This is how one local newspaper described the preaching event:

> "A near-capacity crowd heard Miss Lillian Russell last night as she addressed the annual ladies' night meeting of Petersburg Brotherhood at Ettrick Methodist Church. Blandford Methodist Church's dynamic pastor held her audience spellbound for twenty minutes as she proclaimed the "Love of God" for humankind here on earth. People of all denominations heard Miss Russell preach. She is reported to carry the spirit of Jesus in her. Witnesses testified that if you hear her preach, you will be changed."

#   #   #

All year people went through their attics, closets, and basements looking for historical information. They found old bulletins, newspaper clippings, and pictures and then organized everything. One group worked to compile a written history. Another group put together a display of photographs and other memorabilia.

October came, and the big week finally arrived. The District Superintendent accepted his invitation to preach the opening Sunday service. The Bishop was invited to speak the following Sunday, Homecoming Sunday, but declined the invitation. Lillian was disappointed, but her members told her not to worry, that she was a far better preacher than the Bishop anyway, and everybody knew it.

People from all around Petersburg, Richmond, and the entire southside came to Blandford at least once during that week. One evening was a hymn sing, a second evening a man dressed as a circuit rider rode in the church parking lot on a horse, another evening Mildred Long preached. One of the highlights of the week was when Pete both preached and sang.

The final Sunday was the largest attendance Blandford had ever had. Pews were packed. Church members set up extra chairs in the aisles. Everyone who didn't arrive twenty minutes early didn't find a place to park or sit.

After the worship service, a picnic on the grounds was held, complete with fried chicken, ham, potato salad, coleslaw, deviled eggs, collard greens, beans, ambrosia, and pies. A program followed the picnic. The church had rented and set up a loudspeaker for the day. The speakers began with the oldest and youngest members starting with the written greeting from Bishop Garber. Each household received one copy of the Blandford History. Arthur E. Duell, who compiled the book, was invited to share the highlights. A member of Blandford Methodist Church since 1894, he was considered the absolute authority on everything Blandford. As he stood and took the microphone, a hush fell on the crowd.

"Good afternoon, friends. It is my joy to have you here on this glorious day. Let's get started with our program. Please turn to the third page of the history." Mr. Duell held up a copy of the booklet. "You'll see there the list of all the pastors who have ever served this church. Notice this list includes the years they were at Blandford and the salary they made. Do you see that none of the pastors served more than five years? That's been the pattern. All across Virginia, most pastors serve two to four years. But that changed in 1944 when Miss Lillian Russell came to Blandford. She has served us faithfully for seventeen years, longer than any pastor has served any church in the Virginia Conference. She has made history here simply by her tenure."

Everyone applauded and continued until Lillian stood and thanked them. Then Mr. Duell continued, "Blandford has always been a small church with many struggles, including a fire that destroyed our building. Another hardship for our church was the damage to the buildings, community, and families of Petersburg during the Civil War. We survived with the financial assistance of our mother church, Washington Street Methodist."

More applause erupted, this time for the Washington Street congregation. Mr. Duell invited the members from Washington Street to stand so Blandford could properly thank them.

"When Washington Street discontinued its assistance in 1894, the Conference agreed to provide assistance until 1925," Mr. Duell went on. "But when the Great Depression hit in 1929, Blandford again sought assistance from the Conference Board of Missions. By 1933, we had gotten so small that many church leaders felt her days of service were coming to a close. The Conference extended assistance until 1938 when Blandford finally grew enough to be independent once more."

"This on-again-off-again financial independence did not put Blandford in good standing with the Conference. Many felt the resources would be better spent in other areas, other churches. But despite the hardships and sacrifices, Blandford Church weathered it all, even The Great Depression. The debt for the improvements to the facilities was paid off so that by 1937, a dedication service was held. We were finally free of encumbrances."

Mr. Duell took the microphone off the stand and moved as he continued to speak until he was standing behind the chair where Lillian was seated.

"But the real turning point in Blandford Methodist Church, as well as the entire community, came in the fall of 1944, when

Reverend Lillian Russell, the first woman licensed and ordained to preach in the Virginia Conference, was sent to this charge."

As the applause started again, Mr. Duell motioned for silence. "Please, allow me to finish." He waited for quiet again, then continued, "The question as to the ability of men over women as preachers has certainly been dispelled in this case, and at no time in the history of Methodism in Petersburg has any one person's work stood out more prominently than Miss Russell's at Blandford. When she came to the church in 1944, the total membership was 168. At present, it is 457. Every part of the church has shown growth beyond calculation, both materially and spiritually." Mr. Duell paused to clear his throat and then went on, "Basically, Blandford Methodist Church is known for two things: being the first building in our community to receive electricity in 1910, and Miss Lillian Russell. Now you can applaud," said Mr. Duell.

He set down his microphone and joined everyone in long, boisterous applause. The crowd was on its feet. Lillian could not hide her glow of gratitude and pride. She stood and spoke through her tears.

"Thank you so very much. To God be the glory. Great things He has done."

The applause just grew louder.

Finally, Lillian raised her arms to quiet everyone. Her voice cracking, she said, "I'm too overwhelmed with emotions to pray, but I think prayer is what we need right now. Would somebody please pray?"

After a period of silence with people looking at each other around the tables, Lillian's mother stood and said, "Let us pray."

Mr. Duell gave Goldie the microphone.

Lillian couldn't have been more surprised or pleased. Goldie had barely left the house since EW had passed, and now she was standing before this large crowd and leading in prayer.

"Heavenly Father, we thank You for Blandford Methodist Church and their pastor, Lillian Russell. From the time she was just a little girl, Your hand has been upon her. You kept her alive, and her daddy kept his promise to give her to Your service. She has served You faithfully all these years, first as an evangelist and now as a pastor. We give You thanks for what You have accomplished through her witness. We pray You will continue to give her strength and wisdom to lead Your people. In the name of Jesus, our Lord, we pray. Amen."

Everyone responded, "Amen."

"And now, let's have dessert!" shouted Mr. Duell. "I believe we have enough pie for everyone to have at least one piece. God is good, indeed."

Everyone laughed, and dessert was served.

Lillian lay in bed that night, exhausted from the day. *A good exhaustion,* she thought. *I was right when I predicted this would be a good year for Blandford, and Pete was right when he predicted this would be a good year for their pastor.* She smiled as sleep overcame her.

Chapter Twenty-Five
Full Clergy Rights

Verily I say unto you,
wheresoever this Gospel shall be preached in the whole world,
there shall also be this, which this woman hath done,
be told as a memorial of her.
Mt. 13:26 KJV

*M*ildred invited the church members to stay after the worship service for a brief announcement. The congregation buzzed with speculation.

"Is she moving this year? She completes her fourth year, so that's a possibility."

"I hope not."

"Does it have to do with the parsonage or maybe air conditioning the sanctuary?"

"Shhh. We're about to start."

The members of Hillcrest Methodist Church turned to face forward in their pews.

Mildred had removed her preaching robe and stood next to the lay leader, Richard, in the center of the chancel. Richard was a man in his fifties with a groomed mustache and dark-framed glasses,

"I have some very good news to tell you." Mildred paused and cleared her throat. The tension in the sanctuary heightened.

Mildred looked at the congregation and could see their concern. She smiled and said, "Relax, I said this is *good* news." Everybody laughed.

Mildred continued, "Methodists are methodical. That's how we got our name. The Methodist Church has two primary categories for clergy. One is the ordination category and includes both deacon and elder. The other category is the relationship to the Conference, which includes sub-categories such as licensing as a local pastor, supply pastor, part-time and full-time status, and associate membership, probationary membership, and full connection—sometimes called 'traveling preachers.'" Mildred used her index fingers to make her points. Everyone listened intently.

"Initially, I was licensed and appointed as a supply pastor. Then, in 1955, I was ordained a deacon and accepted on trial as a probationary member of our Conference. Both of those allowed me to administer the sacraments in the churches to which I was appointed. Women were not allowed to be traveling preachers in the Methodist Church, only men, meaning we could be ordained elders, but not received into full connection with the Conference. The primary benefit of full connection is generally referred to as guaranteed appointment. "

A young man, slight in build with a full head of curly hair, a professor at Mary Washington College, who had joined since Mildred had been their pastor interrupted her. "What does the guaranteed appointment mean?"

Mildred responded, "This means that once the Conference accepts you as a full member, they're required to provide you with a full-time appointment, guaranteed. Of course, it also means that a pastor must accept whatever appointment the Bishop gives him. The term 'traveling preacher' is often used to describe clergy in full connection because they itinerate, meaning they travel."

"It's a bit like tenure for a professor. But it seems quite unfair, even wrong. Is that rule about women still in effect?" asked the same young professor.

"No, I'm glad to tell you, it's not. In 1956, the General Conference changed the church law, and women are now allowed into full connection," Mildred said.

"I am somewhat familiar with the long-fought battle for equal rights for women in the clergy through the work of the women's group," said an attractive, red-headed middle-aged woman, who was president of the Women's Society at Hillcrest. "They petitioned General Conference three times before it passed. So where are you, Reverend Long, in all of this Methodist mish-mash?"

Richard broke into the conversation. He was a local business owner whom Mildred had been grooming for crucial leadership. He was in her Bible study and had been a member of the Pastor Parish Relations Committee and the Administrative Board before becoming the lay leader. "In 1959, Miss Long was ordained an elder, the highest order in the Methodist Church. Lillian Russell is the only other woman in Virginia to be ordained an elder to date. Her ordination as an elder was years ago, in 1949. You know her because she preached a big revival here. Her brother, Pete, sang that amazing new hymn 'How Great Thou Art.'" The nodding heads acknowledged that they all remembered Lillian and Pete.

The lay leader continued, "Now, Miss Long has applied for full connection."

"That's wonderful. But she's been eligible for five years," said a local banker, dressed in a three-piece suit complete with a pocket watch and chain, who was chair of the finance committee and was diligently tracking all the information. "Why didn't she apply before now?"

"I'll explain this one," Mildred said. "My previous District Superintendent wouldn't accept me into this process. So I went to Bishop Garber and requested to be moved at the 1957 Conference. When he learned I had finished college and completed the Conference Course of Study at Duke, he advised that I receive Elder's Orders at the 1957 Conference and present myself for conference membership. I was ordained an elder at the Conference in Roanoke, June 1957."

"That's the year you came here to Hillcrest!" exclaimed the president of the Methodist Men, an older, rotund, bald man.

"Yes, that's right. The Conference received me on trial the same month I moved to Hillcrest. Now I've applied to be brought into full connection and have been approved. I plan to be received into full connection at this year's Annual Conference in June at Virginia Beach. Nancy White—you all know her, as my roommate and she has preached here several times— will also be received into full connection."

Richard interrupted again and exclaimed, "But listen to this!" He walked down the steps of the chancel and looked the members at eye level. "Because the ministers are received in alphabetical order, and Long comes before White, Miss Long will be the first woman to reach this status in the history of Virginia Methodism. "

The group broke into applause. The youth coordinator asked, "Can we go? Nothing beats a road trip!"

Mildred smiled from ear to ear. "I'd be highly honored to have you present, all of you."

#   #   #

Mildred, and the twenty-five members of Hillcrest who accompanied her, heard the cry of the seagulls over a car radio blasting "Little Sister" by Elvis Presley as they walked from their cars to the Dome in Virginia Beach. Just a few blocks from the Atlantic Ocean, Mildred could smell the salt air. She took a deep breath, wanting to remember every detail of this Annual Conference.

As they entered the Dome, Mildred noted the women were fewer in number but stood out in their colorful shirtwaist dresses. She heard the click of their heels on the pavement and smelled their hairspray over the scent of men's cologne. The Dome, with its metallic round roof, looked like a flying saucer. The Russians had launched Sputnik just a few months earlier, but Virginia Beach with the Dome looked like it could take off next.

People do not always recognize history when it's happening. That would be true for the 1961 Annual Conference. Mildred and Nancy did their best to stand out, with Mildred wearing a bright pink suit and Nancy a pale green suit. Both of them wore pumps to gain a little stature in the line of tall men.

The Bishop invited all clergy to be received into full connection to come forward and stand before the Conference. Once again, it was a sea of dark suits and two petite splashes of color. All the candidates for elder ordination and full connection into the Conference stood before their colleagues for examination. Because Mildred was ordained an elder, these historic questions didn't apply to her. Nancy did respond to the questions, as she was to be ordained an elder that evening.

The questioning of the ordinands had been a solemn part of Methodist conferencing since John Wesley's days. A Bishop had asked every clergy in attendance these same historical questions. To hear them each year had become a self-examination of one's own call and spirit. The vote to approve clergy into the sacred fellowship of full connection was a right and a privilege.

Bishop Garber presided. Tall, slender, wire-frame glasses, commanding bass voice: he had the appearance and the sound of a bishop. "Now, please consider Minute Question 28, who are admitted into full connection."

This question marked the making of history. Mildred knew it would be short and did not want to miss it. *Will anyone object? Would the Bishop even allow such an interruption?* She clenched her fists in anticipation.

"If you approve these standing before you for full connection into the Virginia Conference, please signify by saying 'yes.' Remember, only those already in full connection are eligible to vote."

Hundreds of male voices responded with a resounding "yes." Mildred exhaled, relaxed her hands, and allowed herself to smile.

Bishop Garber continued, "Let us welcome our new brothers in ministry." The auditorium grew loud as everyone stood in enthusiastic applause. Mildred wanted to correct the bishop to include "sisters" in his welcome, but the applause overwhelmed any thought she had of language correction. She had worked a long time for this moment. Yet there was no explosion of a spaceship taking off and everyone looking toward the heavens. Mildred's historic acceptance into full connection was as simple as a vote. What happened today *may not seem like much to most people, but nobody can take this away from me. Thank you, God, we did it!* Nancy and Mildred found and hugged each other, creating a short splash of color.

Mildred, Nancy, Lillian, and a crowd of their families and congregations gathered around tables in the Dome's eating area. The acoustics and loud voices made it impossible to hear, but that did not dampen their celebrative mood. The youth coordinator from Hillcrest knelt next to Mildred's chair with a copy of the *Book of Reports* in his hand.

"What's all this that's coming up for discussion after lunch?"

"You mean the vote on the Negro church?" Mildred asked.

"Yes, we're all curious about this. Can we go someplace quiet to talk about this vote?"

"Sure. It's quieter in the auditorium than in here. Let's all meet at the back of the auditorium in fifteen minutes," Mildred suggested.

"That's perfect. I'll gather everybody together." He returned to his chair and finished his lunch.

The group moved back to the auditorium and pulled chairs together to form a circle. Everyone had their *Book of Reports* opened to the issue at hand.

Mildred started the tutorial. "Three major changes are on the agenda that will lead to significant changes in the Methodist Church. I expect the third to be quite controversial.

"The third proposal is about procedures by which Negro churches may join white annual conferences. Is that right?" asked Richard.

"Yes, the Methodists split around the slavery issue just before the Civil War into Methodist Episcopal and Methodist Episcopal South. Then, in 1939, we reunited. But the amendment proposed this year crosses more than geographic lines. It crosses racial lines. Let me warn you; emotions are high and false information is rampant. It sounds like we're about to reconvene. Let's get these chairs back in order."

Everybody got up and returned the chairs to neat rows. Nancy, Mildred, and Lillian moved closer to the stage and sat with the other clergy. Their families and congregations stayed in the back of the auditorium.

All the delegates and guests listened carefully as Dr. C. C. Bell of Lynchburg made a clarifying statement at the beginning of the discussion. A tall, imposing man, he stood on the stage, gazed out at the 1,500 people in attendance, and spoke into the microphone in a calm, authoritative voice. "This amendment has no reference to integrating white and Negro members in the same local churches. This subject is not discussed. The sole matter relates to a principle of administrative procedure, a democratic one. Suppose a local Negro church desires to join the white annual Conference in which geographically it resides. In that case, provision is made whereby this becomes possible if there is a two-thirds vote by the local church's quarterly Conference, by the local church membership, by the Negro membership, by the Negro annual conference to which the church belongs, and by the white annual Conference which it desires to join. Those are five votes that have to be taken."

Dr. Bell paused to clear his throat and take a sip of water, and then went on. "Assume that in time, a half-dozen Negro churches thus secured admission to the Virginia Annual Conference. It would mean that these churches would send their pastors and lay delegates to our annual sessions. The presiding bishop would presumably, in making the appointments, send

Negro pastors to Negro churches and white pastors to white churches. White church members would belong to white churches and Negro members to Negro churches. This whole amendment contemplates that all Negro churches will belong to white conferences in time, but this has no reference to integration within a given local church. It does not forbid it. It does not approve it. It does not refer to it whatever. There is nothing in the passage of this amendment to occasion concern."

Lillian, Nancy, and Mildred turned to look at each other after this painful explanation. Lillian said, "This sounds all too familiar, like churches with women. Sure, there's permission to ordain women elders, even receive them into full connection, but no local church has to worry about being *forced* to receive one as their pastor."

Mildred and Nancy shook their heads in grieved agreement. "All too familiar," Mildred said.

"The very same leaders who are opposed to including the races are also opposed to including women. But things are changing in our world, whether people in power want the change or not." Lillian's voice was adamant.

The three men sitting behind Mildred, Nancy, and Lillian leaned forward, pushing their fingers against their lips. "Shhh," they said. "We're trying to hear what the man is saying. What this man has to say is important."

Mildred balled up her fists and pushed them into her lap. "Like what the women have to say isn't important."

One of the preachers came to the microphone and said, "Bishop, I call for the vote. This subject has been discussed in board meetings and around kitchen tables throughout this Conference for years. It's time for us to make a decision."

"All right, Virginia Conference, what's your pleasure?" asked Bishop Garber. "If you're ready to end the discussion and take a vote, raise your hand."

The hands raised indicated the body was overwhelmingly ready to vote.

A lay delegate came to the microphone. "I call for a secret written ballot. I believe we'll get a more honest vote that way."

Nancy asked Lillian and Mildred, "So how should I vote on this one?"

Lillian replied first. "You can vote how you want, but I believe secret ballots are a bad idea. They take a terrific amount of time and create mistrust, hurting the fellowship of the body."

"I agree," said Mildred.

"So what is the pleasure of the body? Do you want a written ballot?" asked Bishop Garber.

A loud "no" came from the body.

"It appears we'll not take a written ballot," said the Bishop. "So let's move forward with the vote. If you are in favor of approving this amendment to abolish the Central Conference and have a unified church, please raise your hand."

The amendment passed by a wide margin, and a door opened to black churches receiving them into the Virginia Conference. No more segregation of conferences. The *Virginia Advocate*, the official publication of Virginia Methodists, noted only the color change with no mention of women being received into full connection.

However, the Fredericksburg newspaper reported on this Annual Conference in an article entitled "Hillcrest Pastor Ordained, Pioneer Woman-Minister." The article also mentioned Nancy White. *"The two women ministers are good friends, and when Miss Long first became pastor at Hillcrest, Miss White stayed here a week helping out. The two women and thirty male ministers were ordained at the Conference."*

This article was wrong because Mildred was not ordained at this 1961 Annual Conference but only received full connection. As she tried to explain to her congregation, she had been ordained an elder in 1957.

The controversy that gripped the 1961 Annual Conference and claimed the spotlight also came to the local churches. By then, Miss Long had gained the trust of her people, so when she proposed a resolution to the Official Board about seating everyone in their sanctuary regardless of race, it passed unanimously. The resolution read:

> "In the event that Negroes, or members of any race, come to attend the service of worship, the ushers will seat them where convenient with the same courtesy that would be shown our members."

Many churches in Virginia voted not to allow blacks into their churches and trained their ushers to escort them out. Even at Hillcrest, the decision was not without controversy.

"Lillian, have you had problems with the integration of Blandford?" asked Mildred.

"No, we just decided not to deal with it," said Lillian. "People here would rather not talk about it, so we don't."

"People here would rather not talk about it too, but I won't be silenced." Mildred's voice conveyed her commitment. "These are God's children. We are all one family, equal in the eyes of God. People may be shocked when they get to heaven and find us all in the same room, eating from the same communion table."

Lillian knew that when Mildred's voice conveyed this level of passion, it was best not to argue. "Have you gotten any push back from your members?"

"Of course, lots of it," said Mildred. "But you know me. No one will silence me about injustice. It seems the longer I am in ministry, the bolder I get. It gets me into trouble, but it's good trouble."

"Just be careful, Mildred," said Lillian. "People have become even violent over this issue."

"I am careful, well, at least somewhat. I check my tires every morning to be sure nobody has slashed them."

Mildred laughed, and Lillian followed suit.

"No doubt you can be fierce. I'll bail you out of jail, if need be," Lillian laughed again.

Another social issue for Methodists in the mid-century was alcohol. The Commission on Christian Social Concerns and the Women's Society of Christian Service often encouraged the church members to write their legislators on various alcohol distribution issues.

But alcohol wasn't the only hot topic Hillcrest addressed in the ten years Miss Long served as their pastor. They also openly discussed mental health, political affiliations, labor relationships, liberalism versus conservatism, church versus state, and the Federal Anti-Poverty Program. The resources provided for the Women's Society encouraged dialogue on all these topics, equipping the women of the church to be fully engaged. But many of the men in the church resisted. They refused to have those topics on the agenda of their monthly meetings, complained when mentioned during worship, and never signed the preprinted postcards provided by the Conference to elected leaders. However, Mildred's family's interest in politics, plus her time at Dan River Mills, had made her comfortable with topics avoided by so many other pastors.

Chapter Twenty-Six
Hillcrest

Guide me, O Thou Great Jehovah, pilgrim through this barren land.
I am weak, but thou art mighty, Hold me with thy powerful hand.
Bread of heaven, bread of heaven, feed me till I want no more.
William Williams, 1745

*M*ildred was not one to turn down an opportunity to speak the Gospel, so her calendar filled up with speaking engagements: the Women's Society for Christian Service (W.S.C.S.), district youth events, high school baccalaureates, and commencements, retreats at the Wesley Foundation of Mary Washington College, grade schools, week-long revivals, radio broadcasts, Holy Week community services, Baptist church special services, convalescent services, devotions for the local P.T.A., community Thanksgiving services, and much more. She accepted the invitation from Lillian to preach a one-week revival at Blandford Methodist Church. Pete provided the music, making it high-spirited for all involved. These speaking engagements took Mildred across Virginia and even back to her home church in Biscoe, North Carolina.

The 1960s were marked by tensions everywhere in the country: the Viet Nam War, women's movement, civil rights, the growing use of non-prescription drugs, the sexual revolution, and the war on poverty. These societal issues challenged every church's ability to unite their people on the basics of the Gospel.

But Mildred kept her eye on the prize. Years ago, she had memorized Philippian 3:14, which reads in the King James Version: *I press toward the mark for the prize of the high calling of God in Christ Jesus.* It had become part of her very spirit. She started a Boy Scout troop at the church, paid off and consecrated the church's new education building, and worked for years to cool the sanctuary, first with more insulation, then an exhaust fan, and finally air conditioning. The next year a sound system had to be installed, allowing people to hear the sermon over the air conditioning.

A lack of money dominated the church meetings at Hillcrest. Every penny was followed and accounted for. Even Miss Long's purchase of a chair for the Sunday School's primary department got reported in the minutes. The cost was $2.50. In minutes from another meeting, Mildred reported she had purchased a copy of an illustrated edition of the Book of Romans for every member. Sometimes the only way to get an expenditure approved was to pay for it herself.

One of the relationships that sustained Mildred during her ten years at Hillcrest was a most unlikely one: a Baptist church in the Fredericksburg area. She knew she could always find an uncomplicated welcome there and was called numerous times to hold special services for them. When the time came to call a new minister, they invited her to deliver the church's installation charge. Near the end of her decade at Hillcrest, a local newspaper captured her understanding of how God provides in life: "Across the years, many good things have helped strengthen my faith. And the graciousness of God in giving me more blessings has more than overruled the deep hurts that I received at the beginning of my undertaking."

The Hillcrest parsonage became an issue. It was located right next to the church and needed replacing. The Conference was encouraging churches to build parsonages a short distance from the church rather than immediately adjacent to the church to provide the pastors and their families more privacy. The trustees presented three options to the Official Board. Eventually, the church leaders voted to buy a lot, move the current parsonage to a different location, sell it, and then build a new parsonage on a new parcel of land.

This move was Mildred's third appointment and her third time to oversee the decision to build a new parsonage. She had learned enough to know her best option was to direct the process and allow the leaders to make the decisions. The new parsonage was a two-story structure with four bedrooms and three baths, meeting all the conference standards.

#   #   #

It was Sunday night, a time Mildred and Lillian often talked on the phone. Mildred called Lillian.

"I don't know how you stay at the same church so long. You've been at Blandford for twenty-three years, and me at Hillcrest for ten. These ten years seem like both the blink of an eye and like an eternity. So much has happened in this time: so many sermons preached, pastoral calls made, Bible studies prepared, weddings and funerals officiated, and don't even mention the meetings—they just never end. But I think it's time to move to what God has for me next."

Lillian said, "I've often wondered what it's like for the other clergy, especially this time of year when they're getting calls from their district superintendents. I wonder what it must be like to have your life uprooted. There's a sense of excitement, I guess, a sense of something new. But I always come back to staying at Blandford. After all this time, it would be like walking away from my family. I pray I never have to move from here."

Mildred moved that year. This move wasn't the congregation's desire but the wishes of the Bishop and his cabinet. Having witnessed and benefited from the fruits of their pastor's labors, the leaders of Hillcrest Methodist Church wrote to Bishop Paul N. Garber,

We, the Hillcrest Methodist Church members in the Richmond District of the Virginia Conference, request and urge Miss

233

Mildred V. Long's return as our pastor. We have been incredibly blessed during Miss Long's pastorate among us and trust that you will see fit to reappoint her to Hillcrest.

Mildred's last Sunday was June 11, 1967. In 1964 a new Methodist hymnal was issued, and Hillcrest gave their pastor a leather copy with her name engraved in gold on the front. The final hymn that Sunday was "Guide Me, O Thou Great Jehovah," perfect for the occasion. She had lived in the new parsonage less than a month before having to move again.

Various members were asked to share a memorable time at Hillcrest with Miss Long. James H. Gallahan, Sr. wrote this:

"The Revered Miss Mildred Long asked me if I would be one of the drivers to take the Methodist Youth Fellowship on a trip to Washington, D.C. to visit the museum, zoo, and the Washington Cathedral. We met at the church — myself, Mrs. Alice Pierce, and Miss Long. Mrs. Pierce and I were to follow Miss Long, with me bringing up the rear. We had quite a group with three carloads. We arrived in Washington, D.C. with Miss Long leading. Round and round we went and onto Florida Avenue. Miss Long decided to make a U-turn right in the middle of Florida Avenue. I looked for the police any minute, of course. The kids went wild.

"We continued on our way, and suddenly she stopped again to ask a sailor standing on the corner the directions to the Cathedral. 'Lady,' he said, 'you're on a one-way street.' Miss Long replied, 'But I'm only going one way,' and, of course, that was the wrong way. You can just imagine how the kids were acting at this time. I just knew we were going to wind up in jail. Someone had to be looking after us from above. On we went to the Cathedral.

"After a great day and lots of fun, Miss Long said it was time to head home and took off. Mrs. Pierce looked at me, and I said, 'Mrs. Pierce, follow me.' Miss Long had high fins on her car's rear fenders, and if it had wings, it would have taken off.

"When Mrs. Pierce and I arrived back at Hillcrest Church, Miss Long came out and asked, 'where have you all

been?' We all had a great big laugh, and the kids just jumped up and down. The kids said to Miss Long, 'If we ever go on another trip, we want you to do the driving because we never had so much fun.'"

Mildred always called her cars "Jonathan" because they were like Jonathan was to David, a devoted companion.

#   #   #

Following her graduation from Union Theological Seminary in 1959, where she was the first full-time female student, Nancy received an appointment to Heathsville Methodist Church. The unofficial "requirement" for clergywomen to have a female roommate in the parsonage became an unenforced "recommendation," allowing Nancy to live alone in the Heathsville parsonage. Over the years from the Bellevue Charge in Lynchburg to Hillcrest in Fredericksburg, Mildred and Nancy had grown as close as sisters. The drive from Heathsville to Fredericksburg was nearly two hours, so they often replaced their visits with phone calls. Three years later, the Bishop appointed Nancy to Park View Methodist Church in Lynchburg as the associate pastor. Mildred and Nancy's visits were even less frequent after that move.

Then, in 1966, Nancy withdrew from ministry to return to school in social work. [2]Once again, it was only Lillian and Mildred in the growing sea of clergymen.

---

[2] See appendix for Nancy White's obituary.

Chapter Twenty-Seven
Lynnhaven

Do thy friends despise, forsake thee?
Take it to the Lord in prayer;
In his arms, he'll take and shield thee.
Thou wilt find a solace there.
Joseph M. Scriven, 1855

"**How** did I ever accumulate so much stuff?" Mildred said to Helen, the president of the women's group. "I remember the day when I could fit everything I owned in my car. Now I have to have a pickup truck. And I'm not as spry as I used to be. At fifty-three years old, these boxes seem a lot heavier than they did at thirty-three. And this June heat isn't making it any easier. I hate to do it, but can we call on some of the men to help us with this?" Mildred stopped to wipe her brow on her sleeve.

"I'll give them a call as soon as I'm done packing up this box of books. Do all preachers have this many books?" Helen asked as she taped a box closed and wrote "books" on the top.

"I'm not sure. I've never been in any parsonage other than Lillian Russell's and my own," Mildred said. "Lillian doesn't have quite as many books as I do. I lose all sense of discipline when I'm in the Cokesbury Store."

Three men came with a pickup truck and moved Mildred and her belongings from Hillcrest Methodist Church in Fredericksburg 150 miles to Lynnhaven Methodist Church in Virginia Beach. Mildred was sad to leave Hillcrest but excited to go to Lynnhaven. It was a small but growing church with 150 members and sixty in their Sunday School. Her annual salary would be $4,000, a slight increase.

Mildred was well received at Lynnhaven, primarily because six of their members had traveled to Hillcrest to hear her preach. They reported her to be one of the best they had ever heard. Reverend Carl Sanders, District Superintendent, assured them they didn't have to receive her as their pastor if they didn't want to.

Even though I'm an ordained elder and in full connection, Mildred thought, *I'm still considered optional. But I'll prove to them they were right to have me come to their church.*

Shortly after her arrival, a local newspaper reporter, L.E. Holt, came to the church to interview Mildred. She was the first female Methodist minister to receive an appointment to the Norfolk District.

The door to Mildred's church office was open. Mr. Holt knocked on the door frame and poked his head inside. He was a tall, stocky man with lots of curly gray hair and a wide smile.

Mildred walked to the door with her hand extended. "Hello. I'm Reverend Mildred Long. You must be the reporter, Mr. Holt. Please, come in and have a seat."

Mr. Holt shook hands with Mildred and then sat down in one of the metal folding chairs. "Good morning, Reverend Long. Thank you for allowing me this interview." He took a pencil and paper from his double-breasted jacket and dabbed the tip of the pencil on the end of his tongue. "Tell me about yourself, particularly how you work with the men and women at the church. Do you treat them differently?"

Mildred responded, "I don't try to make a distinction between the abilities of men and women. I do, however, lean very heavily on the leadership of the men in the church."

When pressed about women's primary home duties, Mildred was ready with a response because, over the years, reporters asked this question many times. "I don't think that women should neglect any of their duties at home to provide a service elsewhere."

Mr. Holt, still digging for an edge to the story, asked her about the Bible's teachings on female leadership in the church. Again, due to years of Bible study and responding to such questions, Mildred was ready with a thoughtful response. "The argument against women holding higher positions in the church probably comes from the Biblical teachings of where the woman's place should be. However, today's open-minded people realize that the Bible didn't place women in any place in particular at all. Proverbs 31 describes one woman, not all women."

She went on to say, "I've been wonderfully received at each of my pastorates. Here at Lynnhaven, I received the most cordial and enthusiastic welcome."

This article would be one of several written about Mildred in the local papers.

#   #   #

Monday morning, Mildred stepped outside the church to get some fresh air. She had been working on the next year's budget and needed a break from the tedium. As she was about to round the church's corner, she overheard two church members talking. She thought they were talking about her, so she paused to listen.

"Has she even read what the Bible says about women in the church? It doesn't seem right to me. Maybe we should talk to somebody."

Mildred stomped toward them with long strides, hands balled up in fists. She couldn't believe it. One of the members in this conversation was Marvin, leader of their youth ministry.

"Just exactly what are you talking about?" Not allowing them to respond, Mildred went on. "I have two bachelor's degrees and have completed the Course of Study and even taken Greek. I was ordained a deacon and an elder and received into full connection in the Virginia Conference. I've preached more sermons, brought more people to Christ than any male preacher I know. How dare you question my abilities." By this time, her face was red, and she was wagging her finger at them.

"Miss Long. We're sorry, but you misunderstood." Marvin said. "We weren't talking about you. Please calm down." He spoke with a soft voice. Both men stood up and took one step toward her. "Please, don't be angry with us. We were just discussing a conversation in Sunday School yesterday about leadership in the early church. It has nothing to do with you."

The color drained from Mildred's face. Humiliated, she turned and walked around the corner, mumbling, "I misunderstood. I'm so sorry." She was mortified that she had lashed out about something totally unfounded.

Back in her office, she closed and locked the door and fell to her knees, sobbing. "God, help me. Please, help me. Why do I carry so much hurt and anger? It's like an active volcano ready to erupt at any moment. I've spent so much prayer time about this; my knees are calloused. I've fasted many times trying to have a change of heart. I don't know what to do. Help me, God, please."

Mildred went from kneeling to laying down on the floor, with heavy sobs into the area rug. When there were no more tears, she stood up, straightened her dress, and looked at her bookcase. There was a picture of Lillian. That's *what I'll do. That's what I always do, call Lillian. But first, I must apologize to those innocent victims of my wrath.*

Mildred went outside and found the two men. They were getting into their cars. "Excuse me, gentlemen. Can we talk for a minute?"

They stepped away from their cars and walked toward Mildred. "Certainly, Miss Long."

"I must apologize for my behavior this morning. I misunderstood your conversation and was totally out of line in my response. Can you ever forgive me?"

"You were pretty angry, and your comments were unfounded. But we're Christian men and can and do forgive you," Marvin said. Both men smiled and nodded.

That night, Mildred called Lillian. "I know we just talked last night, but I need to talk now. Is this a good time?"

"Certainly," Lillian said. "I'm just watching the news. What's so urgent?"

"Well, it's the same old issue," Mildred said. "These men, our so-called 'brothers in ministry,' can be so very cruel. And the leaders of the pack, the District Superintendents, apologize to the churches when they appoint us." Mildred lowered the pitch of her voice to mimic a district superintendent. "'Sorry to make this suggestion for your next pastor, but the *Discipline* has changed, and we are asked to appoint women as pastors of churches. However, don't feel like you have to take one. Just say the word, and I can send you a man.' "

Mildred was incredulous. "Then when I'm not totally ignored by these 'brothers in Christ' as if I'm invisible, there are all the ugly comments. Some of those comments I remember like they were yesterday. 'Haven't you read I Timothy 2 or I Corinthians?' Lillian, I have more education than the whole bunch of them combined. Well, not exactly, but certainly I demonstrate more education than all of them combined. Those words strike me deep, at my very core. Some of the brethren in our Methodist church dare to challenge my very call to ministry. They try to spout all these theological, biblical, and even sociological arguments. They criticize my appearance, my voice, challenge my right to attend their meetings. Sometimes the comments are directed at me, but mostly they don't even have the common courtesy to look at me. They're cowards, afraid of me." Mildred was waving her hand in the air as if Lillian could see her through the phone line.

Lillian knew Mildred's anguish as she had heard this rant many times; plus, she had experienced all of this herself. Fortunately, abuse toward Lillian had eased because she had stayed in the Petersburg District so many years that most preachers had gotten used to her. They simply ignored her, and she had come to accept it.

"I don't know how to get rid of the anger, the hurt, the resentment," Mildred went on. "It churns inside my soul and then gushes out at the least provocation. Just today, two members of Lynnhaven Church were sitting on the steps of the church talking. I overheard part of their conversation. It sounded to me like they were talking about me, questioning my legitimacy as an ordained pastor because I'm a woman. Before I could even think, I just lit into them. They were shocked, confused, even frightened by the intensity of my anger. Then it turns out they weren't even talking about me. I was mortified. All I could do was apologize. I don't know if I can ever mend what I've done."

"Oh, Mildred, I'm so sorry for that situation. You are fierce in your convictions and can have a short fuse around women's issues. There's no fault in having strong convictions, but you might have handled this particular one differently."

"Lillian, what do I do? I don't seem to be able to help myself. The ancient hurts have caused such scars on my heart and soul. How do I ever find healing? I don't want to hurt these precious lay servants of the church. They're dear people, and I love them. They're the last people I want to unleash my anger on about issues that are mine to resolve." Mildred's voice was cracking.

Lillian waited a few moments to respond, and then in her most gentle voice, she prayed, "God who has called us to preach Your Word and administer Your holy sacraments, bless my sister, Mildred, as she pours out her soul to You. Do for her what she is unable to do for herself. Heal her scars. Create beauty where others have left ashes. Remind her of Your sacred calling upon her life and that no man, woman, or child can ever take that from her. Keep her strong in her convictions but gentle when she speaks of them. May Your Holy Spirit move among the brethren that they might have a change of heart, a renewal of the Spirit, and a more enlightened mind. Most, Holy God, put a new and right spirit within Your church. In the precious name of Jesus, we pray. Amen."

Mildred spoke through her tears. "Thank you, Lillian. Please keep praying for me."

"You know I do. You know I will. Only God can create a new spirit within."

"Yes," Mildred said. "Create a new heart in me, O God. Put a new and right spirit in me."

Mildred had a successful six years at Lynnhaven United Methodist Church. The congregation had already learned that pastoral leadership could come in fresh expressions when Reverend Rodriguez, a Cuban man, was appointed to their church in 1964. The church members had been favorably influenced by watching Ricky Ricardo on "I Love Lucy." It made the acceptance of this charismatic Hispanic man smoother. Much of their growth had happened in the two years Reverend Rodriguez was there. In 1966, nine classrooms were added to the church to accommodate the growing education program. The church purchased a new organ and became a station church necessitating the building of a parsonage. Reverend Rodriguez never lived in that parsonage. Reverend Hastings came in 1966 to become the first pastor to live in the new parsonage, staying only one year and making room for Miss Long's appointment in 1967. Mildred assumed the parsonage and the responsibility for raising the money to pay for it and the nine classrooms.

The church was considered small by most standards, with 85 families, but the potential was considerable. The community around the church had grown rapidly. Every day Mildred walked the neighborhood praying for each house; the people who lived there would come to Christ and church.

Mildred knew what type of leadership was needed to keep the momentum going and the bills paid. *Too many churches are all about programs,* she thought. *It is nothing but filling up the calendar and keeping busy. But programs won't grow the church. Only growing deeper in love with God will.* Mildred taught the Bible with renewed zeal, and people loved her teaching.

One member of her Bible study said, "We're learning so much. It's so interesting. Miss Long is offering both a morning class and an evening class. We use no book but the Bible. You must come." Members invited other members, family, and neighbors.

Mildred held confirmation classes in the parsonage. *Joining the church is becoming part of a family. What better place to have preparatory classes than in my home?* She loved working with the youth. She encouraged them to follow God's claim upon their lives.

One of the youth, Theresa Meadows Keezel, became a United Methodist clergy. She later said, "seeing a woman in the pulpit made it possible to believe that could be a reality in my own life. I remember Miss Long as formal, stiff, almost manly. As a youth, I didn't understand Miss Long's demeanor, but I fully understood after becoming a pastor. This demeanor is necessary for a woman to establish her rightful place of authority in the church."

Over the years, Mildred had been a student of her behavior. She learned that if she wanted her congregation to follow her as a leader both in the pulpit and in the board room, she couldn't dress, talk, or act in a too feminine or overly masculine way. She never wore sleeveless blouses and always buttoned her dresses within two inches of her neck. She never called attention to her breasts or hips, and no one ever saw her undergarments through her clothing or a gap in her clothing. The pitch of her voice was intentionally lower than most women without being too low. Her goal was for people hearing just her voice to question if the speaker was male or female. She walked with good posture without pushing out her chest and with one foot in front of the other without swaying her hips. Her hand gestures were deliberate; too many distracted from her message and made her look emotionally out of control. When appropriate, she initiated handshakes with men and looked them in the eye when talking. By the time she had gotten to Lynnhaven, she had become a master of being androgynous yet still a woman. It was a tightrope she believed she had mastered.

Mildred also helped organize a Youth Lay Witness Weekend. Reaching the youth was an essential part of her legacy, and she made it a priority.

Jana, an eleven-year-old youth at Lynnhaven, had been taking piano lessons for several years. Miss Long asked her to play for the opening exercises at Sunday School, encouraging her to use her talent to glorify God. One evening at supper time, her family heard a knock on the door of their home. It was Miss Long.

"Jana, I need you to come to the church right now to play the piano. A young woman needs to get married, and we want this wedding to have music."

Jana turned and looked at her mother. Miss Long made eye contact with Jana's mother and nodded. Jana's mother said to her daughter, "Quick, wash your hands and face, brush your hair and go with Miss Long."

"But what will I play?" Jana asked.

Miss Long responded, "Hymns, just like you always do at church."

With that, Jana freshened up and went out the door, running to keep up with her pastor.

The bride was just sixteen-years-old and expecting a child. Mildred had responded to this family crisis with grace and generosity.

When Jana was age-thirteen, Mildred promoted her to the sanctuary piano, where she played for the entire worship service. She did that for four years through high school. She remembered Miss Long as dramatic in the pulpit. One Sunday, Miss Long lay down prostrate in front of the cross in silence for several minutes.

"You could have heard a pin drop," Jana recounted. "No one will ever forget that Sunday! Without a word, Miss Long preached, 'We're to lay our lives down at the foot of the cross.'"

When Jana's uncle got cancer, Miss Long cared for him with great compassion, visiting him daily for prayer and scripture reading. "Yet she was a force to be reckoned with," Jana later said. "Miss Long demanded respect and received it because she was the "real deal."

The building needs of a growing church with an old facility were endless. In 1969 a building committee worked on the parking lot, made improvements to the kitchen—allowing the Health Department to approve it—maintained the heating and A.C. units, and kept up with a historic cemetery.

Lynnhaven Church purchased a bus and organized a bus ministry that brought children from the neighborhood to Sunday School and worship. Sunday School teachers made home visits to every Sunday School family, encouraging parents also to attend. The United Methodist Women organized into three circles, expanding their size and capacity to accomplish international missions. Lynnhaven published its first pictorial directory. Behind all these efforts was Miss Long praying, attending meetings, planting seeds, encouraging, protecting, and raising money. The budget grew from $16,461 to $24,274 and membership from 85 families to 173 in the six years she was their pastor.

Chapter Twenty-Seven
Kenwood

Blessed are the undefiled in the way,
Who walk in the law of the LORD.
Blessed are they that keep His testimonies,
And that seek Him with the whole heart.
They also do no iniquity:
They walk in His ways.
Ps. 119:1-3 KJV

$\mathcal{M}$ildred had dialed the parsonage at Blandford, so many times over the years she knew Lillian's phone number better than her own. They usually talked on Sunday nights, but big news had to be shared regardless of the day of the week.

"Lillian, this is Mildred. Do you have a minute to talk? I've got some good news."

"Certainly," Lillian said, "I've always got time for you. And I could use some good news."

"It's too soon to know if it's truly good news, but I'm hopeful," Mildred said. "Today, I got a phone call from Reverend Backhus, my district superintendent. You know I've been talking to him about a move this year. He's been encouraging me to stay until I retire at Lynnhaven. If I retire at age sixty-five, that will give me six more years here. I could do that, but I feel it in my spirit that I should move this year."

"Did you tell Reverend Backhus that?" Lillian asked.

"I did, and he told me he has been talking to your district superintendent about a church on the Petersburg District. Lillian, that would be a dream come true to serve out my last years in ministry with you in the same district," Mildred said.

"That would be wonderful," Lillian agreed.

"We could make some shenanigans at the monthly clergy meetings," Mildred said, in a mischievous voice.

"I think we're too old for that—should've done that years ago." Lillian laughed. "Do you know which church he's thinking about for you?"

"He wouldn't tell me yet, hopefully, this week. My Staff Parish Relations Committee is on pins and needles. I've been honest and open with them from the beginning, so they know I have requested to move. As always, some are sad I'm leaving, and others are glad."

"I know that dynamic all too well," Lillian said. "Reverend Johnson has been a fair Superintendent for Petersburg. I think you would enjoy working under him."

"I think having you in his district for nearly thirty years has significantly helped my chances. You aren't just evidence that women can serve with excellence; you're absolute proof," Mildred said.

"Thank you. God has been good to Blandford and me these years, leaving little doubt women are equipped for this work. Let me know when you hear anything."

"You're the first person on my list to call. Talk to you soon, I hope," Mildred replied and hung up the phone.

Two days later, Mildred was packing boxes of Christmas decorations. It was too soon to pack her books, but she could box up seasonal items whether she moved or not. The phone rang.

"Miss Long, this is Reverend Backhus. I want to let you know you are projected to go to Kenwood in the Petersburg District. Reverend Johnson will be calling you soon to tell you more."

Mildred laid down the red Christmas bow and twirled around, the phone cord wrapping itself around her skirt. She paused her dance and spoke in her professional voice. "Thank you so much for calling. I look forward to hearing from Reverend Johnson."

"And, Miss Long," Reverend Backhus continued, "allow me to say that I was uncertain when I heard I was to have a woman on my district, but you've been very effective at Lynnhaven. I would consider a woman again. Thank you for your faithful work here."

"Thank you for the honor of serving," Mildred said and then twirled in the other direction to unwrap herself from the phone cord.

That afternoon Reverend Johnson called Mildred to tell her she was projected to go to Kenwood in Dinwiddie County. "Miss Long, you are the first female appointment I have made. I inherited Lillian Russell when I came to the Petersburg District. I'd seen her good work there, and it encouraged me to talk to the leaders at Kenwood. Your gifts and experiences are a good match for this church. The chairman of the Kenwood Pastor Parish Relations Committee knew of Miss Russell. He'd heard her preach at revivals and valued her homiletic abilities. He'd also met some members from Blandford and knew the people there love their pastor. So he called the other members of his committee. They called an emergency meeting and, after some discussion, they agreed to poll the congregation informally. Many of them had heard you speak at revivals in the area and thought you to be a powerful speaker. They agreed to accept you as their next pastor. Do you have any questions?"

"No, sir. I'm quite familiar with the process. Thank you for the phone call."

"Miss Long, one more thing. Petersburg will be the only district in the Conference with two lady preachers. Don't make me regret this appointment. There's a lot more to serving a church than preaching."

"I'm well aware of that, sir. If you had done your homework, you would know my record is impeccable." Even as she said it, Mildred thought *I should say this differently. Why do I pass on so much of my resentment: Think and then speak!*

No sooner had she hung up from this phone call than she called Lillian with the news. "Well, I'm going to Kenwood."

"Kenwood? That's a great church. I've preached a revival there. And we'll be so close. God is good!" Lillian said.

"But listen to this: the Staff-Parish Relations Committee polled the congregation! The District Superintendent would never allow a church to do that for the appointment of a man. As they remind us often, the United Methodist Church is part of a "sent" system, not a "called" system like the Baptists. I guess my appointment is to a Baptis-Metho church, whatever that is."

"Where do you come up with these words, Mildred? But it's so true. The rules still don't apply to us."

"I'm looking at the *Conference Journal* right now," Mildred said as she fingered the pages to the statistics in the back of the journal. "It reports Kenwood's membership around three hundred and average worship attendance of 110. Reverend Johnson said my salary would be $8,850. So, Lillian, this is the largest church and the biggest salary I've ever received."

"You will do so much good at Kenwood," Lillian said. "Look out, Petersburg District, mark June 1973, on your calendar. It's when there's going to be two lady preachers on your sacred, historical soil.

#   #   #

The people of Kenwood quickly learned the compassion, conviction, and abilities of their female pastor. They also learned their pastor believed the answer to almost every problem was Bible and prayer. At the church board's first meeting, Mildred recommended a mid-week Bible study and prayer session. Everyone agreed that was a grand idea. But then she asked her board to lead the congregation by attending the Bible study regularly. They clearly understood their pastor's philosophy was to lead by example.

Finance issues at Kenwood were constant, and so was their pastor's response: prayer. When the church checking account balance was $1,667, and the bills were $2,126, she invited the finance committee to begin every day with Scripture reading and prayer.

While Mildred could be frighteningly serious, she also had a streak of humor. At one of the church board meetings, she told the story of her experience that afternoon.

"Today, I went to the local post office to mail the church newsletters. The place was packed, not a legal parking space in sight. So I did what I had to—I parked in front of the fire hydrant. First of all, what are the chances of the post office catching on fire? And second, if I heard sirens, I would go outside and move my car. But when I'd completed the mailing and was going back out, I saw a police officer standing next to my car writing a ticket. I ran to my car just as he was putting the ticket under the wiper. I told him, 'I'm the pastor at Kenwood United Methodist Church, and I'm here on church business. You can't give me a ticket.'"

"Excuse me. First, how do I know you're a pastor? Can you prove it? And second, even if you are a preacher, I can give you a ticket. No one is above the law."

"I saw the name on his badge and said to him, 'Excuse me, Officer Timber, I do have a clergy sticker on my back window just for situations like this. But I don't mean to suggest I'm above the law. I simply meant to suggest that you and I are partners in this community. We work together to make Dinwiddie a safe, peaceful place to live. We're on the same team. I'm the one you call in the middle of the night to inform a family their loved one has died in a car accident.'"

"He said to me as he tore up the ticket, "Okay, partner, next time, don't park in front of the fire hydrant. Agreed? Let's be on the same team, the one that obeys the laws.'"

"'Agreed,' I said to him. And with that, I got in my car and pulled away before he could change his mind."

The whole church board laughed. Their pastor was creating quite a reputation for herself.

The members at Kenwood witnessed unusual spiritual experiences with their pastor. Often when she held their hands to pray, they experienced an anointing of the Holy Spirit. "There is an undeniable power in this woman of God," members testified. When Mildred shared with some of her congregants that she sometimes had out of body experiences, they believed her.

Part of Mildred's disciplined routine included a daily walk with an accountability partner. At Kenwood, that walking partner was the choir director, Nancy Rowland. Even though Mildred was a generation older than Nancy, walking together all those miles, Nancy and Mildred became good friends. Everybody in the neighborhood could set their clocks by when Miss Long and Nancy walked past their homes.

Mildred had long had the habit of using time in the car to memorize Scripture. With thousands of miles behind the wheel, she had much of the Bible memorized, allowing her to teach Bible studies without notes. When she was counseling or making a pastoral call, the verses came to her, precisely the verses needed for the situation. Psalm 119 was her favorite, and she encouraged everyone to memorize it. With 176 verses Psalm 119 is the longest of the 150 Psalms. Many members tried, but none met the challenge.

Even though Mildred was now in her sixties, she kept her focus on the young people. She told stories of children in her sermons so they would feel included; continued to make Vacation Bible School an emphasis, giving much personal time to the two-week-long summer event; and knew all the children by name, not timid about calling out their names during worship if they misbehaved.

Mildred had high standards, not only for children but for everyone. "How can we call ourselves followers of Jesus if we don't demand high standards for ourselves?" she would often ask. Her sternness surfaced when standards were not high. For example, on the day of the parsonage's sale, the paperwork was not complete. She was so irritated that she stomped out of the church, leaving everyone wondering what to do. About thirty minutes later, she returned and asked everyone to join her in the sanctuary for prayer at the communion rail. Prayer was the answer for every situation.

Mildred was always a decisive person, but she became more so with age. At a district meeting, another minister said something that she did not like. She directed the entire delegation from her church to get up and leave. The whole carload left, but they never knew what had set her off, and they were too afraid to ask.

Mildred had a notorious reputation behind the wheel of her car. Not only did she drive fast, avoiding tickets with her clergy status, but when she kept hitting the pole in the parsonage driveway, she cut it down. While Barnabas in the Bible was a trusted friend to Paul and an encourager to the apostles, many people felt Barnabas, the car, was a weapon.

In 1976, a Virginia State trooper was killed in the line of duty. The tragedy was reported in the local, state, and national news. Because he was a member of Kenwood, the family asked Mildred to officiate. There were 250 people present for this funeral, including the governor of Virginia. Her name and her small church were in newspapers across the country. Mildred had learned how to conduct a dignified funeral and, with her attention to detail and high standards, the whole event was flawless.

During one of their Sunday night phone calls, Mildred told Lillian, "The Bishop has asked me to serve on the Board of Ordained Ministry. I'm the first woman to be asked to serve in this capacity, quite an honor. As we know, they're the gatekeepers for all things ministerial, so their work is important, and it's not a pleasant experience to go through the ordination process without seeing a female face."

"So what did you tell him? Are you going to do it?" Lillian asked.

"I told him yes, but as I consider it more, I think one of the younger clergywomen should take this position. Most years we have one or two joining the Conference. It would be better for one of them to assume that post."

"Maybe you could suggest that to Bishop Goodson," Lillian said.

"I might do that," agreed Mildred.

#   #   #

Mildred served only one year as a member of the Board of Ordained Ministry but never attended a single meeting. She knew this was not a position she was to have. The next year, 1977, Bishop Goodson asked a newly ordained elder in the Conference, Margaret T. Kutz, to complete Mildred's four-year term. Marg became the first woman to actively serve on the Board of Ordained Ministry in the Virginia Conference. She served three years as the only woman on the board of thirty-six men and then another four years with two other clergywomen.[3]

---

[3] A fuller description of Marg's time on the Board of Ordained Ministry is included in the epilogue.

Chapter Twenty-Nine
Annual Conference, 1976

I returned and saw under the sun,
that the race is not to the swift, nor the battle to the strong,
neither yet bread to the wise, nor yet riches to men of understanding,
nor yet favour to men of skill;
but time and chance happeneth to them all.
Ecc. 9:11 KJV

*J*t was 1976, the Bicentennial of the Declaration of Independence. The whole country was celebrating, including the churches.
It was a time that called for the dramatic: music, poems, speeches,
and dramas that stir the soul of patriotism. Some clergy seemed
wired from birth for just this type of theatrical event. One of those
was Reverend Ernest Emurian. A United Methodist clergy in the
Virginia Conference, Ernest was famous for his humorous poems
set to melody, one he wrote in 1955, "Don't Take the Pictures Off
the Wall." In 1976 he was asked to write a drama that would
depict the twin histories of the United States and The United
Methodist Church. Both nation and church were born around
1776 and resembled each other in many ways.

In 1961, Reverend Emurian had come to know the Russell
family through the wedding of Lillian's niece, Phyllis P. Russell,
to Richard A. Hilliard, Jr., in Portsmouth, Virginia. Lillian's
demeanor and speech appealed to Ernest's cinematic ear. He knew
how he would conclude this bicentennial celebration.

Reverend Emurian's drama was allowed more than two hours over two nights of the Annual Conference in Hampton, Virginia. He included congregational singing and lay and clergy portraying famous Methodists and patriots from the past. The last person to appear was to tie the past to the present. Who could do that better than Reverend Lillian Russell? She was a present-day history-maker, a pioneer still actively serving Blandford Methodist Church. With her deliberate way of speaking and a manner of being that demanded respect, she was ideal. So with some direction from her colleague Reverend Emurian, Lillian prepared her speech, rehearsing it until she memorized it.

The stage crew dimmed the lights, making the coliseum dark except for the single spotlight revealing a small figure appearing from behind the curtains at the back of the platform. As Lillian stepped forward, the light outlined an angelic figure. Her hair stood out. Now completely gray and braids pulled up on the crown of her head, with the light shining through, it truly made her look like an angel with a halo. You could hear gasps, then applause. She glided like feet on clouds to the podium and looked around the room, pausing before she spoke.

Her voice was strong, conveying a message from the heavens. There was not a sound in the coliseum except the voice of this angel.

"As far back as 1851, 125 years ago, there was a woman named Lydia Sexton who made a reputation for herself as a pulpit preacher. And then, fifteen years later, in 1866, Margaret Newton Van Cott became the first licensed woman preacher in American Methodism. It wasn't until 1956 that the General Conference conferred upon the women preachers who were ordained full eldership. In the Discipline 1956 of the Methodist Church, paragraph 303, we were told that women were included in all the provisions of the Discipline referring to the ministry. In the 1972 Discipline of The United Methodist Church, there was made provision for associate membership in paragraphs 322, 323, and 324.

"Now as for myself, beloved, God has been so graciously good to me through these years in the call to preach, in the opportunities that He's given, in the doors that He's opened. Only He can ever know how truly thankful I am. And only He can know as I stand to state the facts that I've been asked to state that down in this heart of mine there is no spirit of boast. But there is such a sincere and abiding gratitude to my Lord and Savior, Jesus Christ, to whom I owe any good thing that I am, everything that I have, and all the opportunities that have come. He gave me a number of years to preach as an evangelist. Twenty-nine years ago, in 1947, I was ordained a deacon in the Virginia Conference of the Methodist Church. Two years later in 1949, I was ordained an elder by Bishop W.W. Peele, thus privileged to be the first woman ordained elder in the history of Virginia Methodism.

"I am told that tonight, as an associate member of this Conference, I represent all of the women preachers, not just in this Conference, but throughout worldwide Methodism, worldwide Christendom. It's a thought that humbles my heart anew. It's a privilege and a responsibility for which I will thank my Lord all the rest of my life."

With that, Lillian completed her speech, and applause erupted. The two-thousand United Methodists gathered in the coliseum came to their feet. Lillian's eyes scanned the room, taking in what was happening. *Indeed, God has been so very good to me,* she thought.

Mildred stood, applauding, and crying. She was so proud of her sister in ministry, so grateful for their friendship. *My cup runneth over.* She waved at Lillian, and Lillian nodded her head in recognition.

Finally, the applause ended, and people sat back down. Lillian stepped back from the podium. The narrator of the program stepped to the microphone.

She said, "Of the 780 pastorates in our Conference, Reverend Lillian Russell has been surpassed in tenure by only three others: John Sawyer, who is serving St. Paul's in Staunton, now for thirty-eight years, Otis Jasper, in Purcellville for thirty-eight years, and William E. Basom, at Beverly Hills in Alexandria, for forty-two years. Reverend Lillian Russell has served Blandford in Petersburg for thirty-three years."

Once again, the coliseum erupted in applause. Mildred stood, applauding and cheering while making her way to the platform. Lillian saw Mildred through her tears and motioned for her to join her on the stage. But Mildred shook her head "no" and then bowed with one hand extended to point to Lillian. This moment belonged to Lillian, and she deserved the spotlight.

Bishop Goodson shook Lillian's hand, and then a gentleman on the platform escorted Lillian down the steps off the platform. Mildred was waiting for her at the bottom of the steps. They held on to each other for a long time, tears of gratitude streaking their make-up.

Chapter Thirty
Retirement

In the bulb, there is a flower; in the seed, an apple tree;
In cocoons, a hidden promise: butterflies will soon be free!
From the past will come the future; what it holds, a mystery,
Natalie Sleeth, 1986

𝒯 he phone rang at the Kenwood parsonage. *Lordy, I hope this isn't a pastoral emergency. I'm beat. This ol' mare ain't what she used to be.* Mildred reached across her desk and answered the phone.

"Hello. Reverend Long speaking," Mildred said in the most cheerful voice she could muster.

Thankfully, the voice on the other end wasn't an emergency. "Mildred, how are you this evening?" Lillian said.

"I'm tired, but well. How about you," Mildred asked.

"No complaints," Lillian said. "Do you have a minute?"

"I always have time for you, dear friend. What's on your mind?"

"I've been thinking about retirement. Next year I'll be sixty-five. I know we can preach until the mandatory retirement age of seventy-two, but I don't think I'll do that. I'm seriously considering retiring next year. What about you?"

"Interesting, you should ask. I've been thinking about retirement, too. I've accomplished nearly all my goals here at

Kenwood, and I'm too old to start again at another church. Churches need young blood. I want to go out strong, not some old woman who has to sit down to preach." They both chuckled.

Lillian continued. "This is my thirty-fourth year at Blandford, and the church is doing well. But as I walked the neighborhood around the parsonage this evening, I was reminded this community is changing dramatically. All around us, people are moving out. Developers are tearing down homes to make room for commercial properties. Every church in our area is having the same conversation. Some have already made the decision and are in the process of finding a new location. It's probably time to relocate Blandford Church, but at my age, I don't think I can provide pastoral leadership for such a significant change. As you know, I have blood pressure problems. I don't want to have a heart attack in the pulpit." They both laughed. "I think it's best for the church and me if I retire next year. We've already lost some members over this issue of relocation. I don't want to be a barrier to the future of this church."

"Well, let's make a pact. Let's both agree to retire at the 1979 Annual Conference. We served together, so let's go out together. Besides, I can't imagine doing this without you. If you go, I'll go," Mildred said.

"This is starting to sound like Ruth and Naomi. 'Where you go, I will go. Where you lie, I will lie.'" They both laughed.

"Okay, Ruth and Naomi we are. I'll start getting my church ready for the transition. You should've started two years ago to get Blandford ready. They won't know what to do without you. In many ways, Blandford Methodist *is* Miss Lillian Russell," Mildred declared.

"Well, I don't know about that. But Blandford is my family, and I will miss them terribly. That's the hardest part about retiring. As you know, this is the main reason I chose not to itinerate. I couldn't bear the thought of leaving these wonderful people." Mildred could hear the tears in Lillian's voice.

"With my experience in saying goodbye to a congregation, I'll help you with this. Maybe you can still attend worship at

Blandford. Allow time and God's grace to guide you," Mildred suggested. "God will make a way."

#   #   #

Mildred started to prepare her congregation for her departure. With a sense of urgency, she tackled her top three priorities: the parsonage, spiritual growth, and the financial health of her church. She worked with the trustees on the issue of the parsonage. They recommended two options: remodel the current parsonage or build a new one. The church board voted to build a new parsonage. Mildred had constructed and or raised funds to finance a parsonage at all five of her appointments. She knew how to do this. But this time, she had an unusual request: she wanted to purchase the existing parsonage located across the street from the church.

The trustees communicated with the district superintendent, Reverend Jerry Fink. With his approval, the church moved forward with the construction of a new parsonage, just a block from the church, and the current parsonage's sale across the street from the church. The present parsonage was valued at $45,000, but the church agreed to sell it to their pastor for $35,000. This decision allowed Mildred some funds to complete the needed remodeling. The church leaders considered the parsonage furnishings and decided to give $300 to Mildred to purchase a lawnmower. Her walking partner, Nancy Rowland, had been mowing the parsonage yard using the mower owned by the church, and she would need another mower for Mildred's yard after retirement.

In 1977, the church leaders requested an increase in Mildred's salary of $500, bringing it up to the minimum salary. They also recommended an additional $50 per month as a bonus. However, in 1978, as the Finance Committee was preparing the budget for 1979, knowing of their pastor's retirement, they recommended an additional salary increase so the new pastor would receive $13,200, a salary above the minimum. Minimum salary would likely bring them a pastor directly out of seminary, and they wanted a pastor with some experience. Mildred understood the reasoning behind it, but it stung to know the incoming pastor would receive a higher salary than she. She mentioned that to the Pastor Parish Relations Committee but didn't push the subject. Compensation was a long-fought battle she was ready to abandon.

Spiritual growth was hard to measure, but Mildred felt a sense of satisfaction about the church's finances. The district's commitments were paid, there would be a new parsonage for the new pastor, and she had a lovely retirement home.

As she looked back over her life, gratitude filled her heart. In a multitude of ways and times, God's grace had provided for her. From Biscoe to Dan River Mills, from Piney Forest to Bellevue to Hillcrest to Lynnhaven to Kenwood, in every place, God was there. Mildred had set a high standard for herself but believed that, with God's help, she had completed the call placed upon her life. She was a pioneer, and she had made history.

Other women were coming into the Conference. Some of these women were single, some married to clergy, others married to laymen. Most were young, some mothers of young children. It was a whole new world for these women. The feminist movement of the 1960s had changed many things in society and the church. Mildred believed she had made a path for other women to follow. She prayed they would not face the difficulties she had met. She prayed the Conference would give opportunities to serve that they withheld from her. She knew God would be with them and provide all they needed just as God had done for her.

In 1978, Mildred received a letter from one new, young clergywomen, Margaret Kutz. The clergywomen would be gathering at Annual Conference for lunch and hoped Mildred would attend. Mildred called Lillian.

"Did you get a letter from Margaret Kutz about a lunch for women clergy at the Annual Conference?" she asked.

"Yes, I did."

"Have you responded?" Mildred inquired.

"No, I wanted to talk to you first," Lillian said.

"Same for me," Mildred said. "As much as I would love to meet these women, I know in my heart this is not what I should do. You know I still carry too much bitterness about how we have been treated over the years as second-class citizens. I don't want to convey that in any way. Surely their experiences will be different, better than ours. What do you think?"

"I agree with you," Lillian said. "This is a new day with new understandings. Will you write to Margaret on behalf of both of us that we'll not be attending? Be sure to mention we're very grateful for the invitation and will be praying for them."

"I'll do that this afternoon because the Annual Conference will be here before you know it. Time is moving so fast these days."

"Indeed it is. Too fast."

Margaret T. Kutz

Chapter Thirty-One
Passing the Mantle

Elisha said to Elijah, "I pray you, let me inherit a double share of your spirit."....And as they still went on and talked, behold, a chariot of fire and horses of fire separated the two of them. And Elijah went up by the whirlwind into heaven. And Elisha took up the mantel of Elijah that had fallen from him and went back and stood on the bank of the Jordan. Then he took the mantle of Elijah that had fallen from him and struck the water. The water was parted to the one side and to the other, and Elisha went over.
II Kings 2:9-14 KJV

$\mathcal{B}$ishop Kenneth Goodson presided over a very contentious 1979 Annual Conference held at the Coliseum in Roanoke, Virginia. The election of sixteen clergy delegates to the General Conference and sixteen more to the Jurisdictional Conference dominated the agenda. A small but strong vocal movement had organized to elect clergy delegates who were younger, female, and of color. That movement encountered a strong group opposed to electing new faces. Finally, on ballot number ten, the clergy elected the last three delegates to General Conference: James Turner, George Lightner, and Leontine Kelly. Reverend Kelly was the first clergywoman ever to be elected in Virginia Methodism to the General Conference. A vocal minority celebrated this historic event. The Conference also elected another clergywoman, Betty

Jane Clem, as a reserve delegate to Jurisdictional Conference. These two elections were not a significant victory for women in terms of numbers, but they marked a significant milestone. Both Mildred and Lillian had been watching carefully and were excited about the results. Only Mildred was able to vote, as Lillian was not in full connection.

On Thursday, June 14, 1979, with the Conference's business nearly complete, Mildred and Lillian greeted their families, who had traveled to Roanoke to be part of the retirement ceremony. Thirty-two clergy retired that year. They had 969 accumulated years of service, with the average years being 30.75 and the average age just over sixty-five years.

The retiring clergy and their wives walked up the steps of the platform in the coliseum. Mildred and Lillian walked up the steps, with Lillian going first and Mildred directly behind. They briefly held each other's hands at the top of the stairs and gave each other a reassuring smile and nod. Then they sat in the chairs assigned to them, alphabetical order. Once again, they were the two white suits in the sea of black suits, the odd ones right up to the very end.

One of the clergy, Reverend Dr. George Lightner, had been selected by Bishop Goodson to represent the retiring class. Another clergy, Reverend Peter Vaughn, had been chosen to represent the incoming class of ordained elders. Dr. Lightner had a long, illustrious history with the Virginia Conference, having served forty-four years, including two terms as a district superintendent. When he retired, he was serving as the executive secretary of Pensions and Ministerial Services. Peter Vaughn would also prove to have a successful ministry career, one that included an appointment on the conference staff as director of development. So clearly, a torch was passed that year.

But two other torches also passed, torches visible that night only to the Holy Spirit and revealed in time to those with eyes to see. Leontine Kelly, the last delegate elected by the clergy, was in 1984, by an act of the Holy Spirit, elected a bishop in The United Methodist Church. She was the first African American woman to be elected a bishop in any mainline denomination in the world's history—a truly historic event.

The second torch passed that night was one Mildred and Lillian eventually came to know. Thirty-eight-were ordained elders that year in Virginia. Of those thirty-eight, five were female. One of those five females, Cynthia Corley, in 1986, was appointed the first female district superintendent in the Virginia Conference.

Mildred and Lillian had no way of knowing on the day of their retirement about these other mantles. God had gathered up Mildred Long and Lillian Russell's faithful stoles and passed them to (Bishop) Leontine Kelly and Reverend Cynthia Corley. Their legacy of faithful service would continue, even a double share.

From the past will come the future; what it holds, a mystery,
Unrevealed until its season, something God alone can see.
Natalie Sleeth, 1986

Chapter Thirty-Two
Life in Retirement

I am no longer my own, but thine.
Put me to doing, put me to suffering.
Let me be employed by Thee or laid aside for Thee.
Exalted for Thee or brought low by Thee.
Let me be full, let me be empty.
Let me have all things, let me have nothing.
I freely and heartily yield all this
to Thy pleasure and disposal.
A Covenant Prayer in the Wesleyan Tradition

*M*ildred set to work, making the parsonage her home. For the first time in twenty-seven years, she could throw out any furniture she didn't want, and that's what she did. From sofas to window treatments and wallpaper, parsonages had a sad familiarity. Mildred often wondered if all parsonage committees used a secret catalog. The houses were so predictable, always twenty years behind in style. Always the low-end grade appliances.

Over the years living alone, Mildred had gained electrical, plumbing, and carpentry skills. The church had given her $10,000 for repairs, and she squeezed every penny's worth out of it until this "Ebenezer" became her pride and joy.

Lillian and Mary Gills found an apartment in Petersburg. They needed everything from sheets and dishes to sofas and beds.

Blandford Church gave Lillian a generous monetary retirement gift, and the members were all too happy to provide them with secondhand items. However, Lillian's real problem wasn't donated stained mattresses or lack of matching towels. Lillian was lost.

"Mildred, can I talk to you for a minute?" Mary phoned Mildred and spoke in a whisper. "I'm worried about Lillian."

"This sounds serious. Why don't you come to my house and we can talk privately? Do you want me to pick you up?"

"No, I can drive to your house. Besides, I'd love to see your most recent improvements," Mary said.

"That would be wonderful. I'm here all day today. What time do you want to come? I'll fix us some tea."

"How about 2 o'clock?" Mary asked.

"Two it is. I'll have the tea kettle on the stove," Mildred said.

A couple of minutes before 2 o'clock, Mildred heard tires on the gravel in her driveway. She looked out the kitchen window and saw Mary's car. Before stepping away from the window, she glanced around her yard, noticing how bare everything looked with the rose bushes cut back for the winter. Before Mary had time to ring the doorbell, Mildred had scurried to the front door and opened it.

"Mary, it's so good to see you. It's been far too long. Come in," Mildred said. She gave Mary a big hug. "You must see the mess I'm making in the hallway. I'm taking down the layers of wallpaper."

They walked through the living room to the hallway. Strips of bright flowered wallpaper hung at various angles from both sides. Buckets and tools cluttered the floor.

"I've tried scraping, steaming, vinegar, and anything else anybody mentions, but wallpaper is a bear to get down," Mildred said and put her hands on her hips.

"So what has worked?" Mary asked.

"Frankly, nothing and everything. I steam, then scrape, then spray a mixture of vinegar and water, then scrape, then steam, then scrape. You get the picture. The trick is not to gouge the sheetrock." Mildred shook her head. "But enough of this. Let's go into the kitchen, have some tea, and talk."

Mildred led the way into the kitchen, where she had already set out teacups and a plate of cookies still warm from the oven. She walked to the stove, got the tea kettle, and poured tea for both of them.

"So, what's going on with Lillian?" Mildred asked as she took a sip of tea.

"I'm worried about her. She doesn't know what to do with herself. She just mopes around that apartment all day. She's up by 5:30, like she's always done. I told her she can sleep in now that she's retired, but she said, 'This is my appointed time with God. I can't keep Him waiting.' By 6:30, she's making breakfast, and by 7:30, she's eaten and done the dishes. After that, nothing." Mary stirred sugar into her tea and watched the circles in her cup.

"I've noticed she doesn't call me, and when I call her, she doesn't have much to say." Mildred said. "Does she visit her family much?"

"Pete has moved so far away, but Polly comes by nearly every week. That's always a bright spot for Lillian."

"What about members of the church? Do they call her or stop by to visit?" Mildred asked.

"You know Lillian—everything strictly by the book. She told her members when she left that she was no longer their pastor and they weren't to contact her. I think they're grieving just as much as she is, but they don't call her. She does receive notes from people. Lillian lines them up on her dresser. I can't tell if they make her feel better or worse," Mary said.

"Isn't she still attending Blandford?" Mildred asked.

Mary laid the spoon down on her saucer. "Yes, she goes every Sunday. I drive her. We have to leave at precisely 10:42, so we arrive at precisely at 11:00 A.M. God forbid we hit a traffic light wrong. She wants to arrive just as the prelude is starting so no one will talk to her. We sit in the corner of the back row. Then at the end of the service, just as the pastor raises his hands for the benediction, we get up and leave. She never speaks to a soul. She almost seems worse after she's been to church."

"So what do you think we should do?" Mildred said.

"I don't know. That's why I wanted to talk to you."

Mildred got up from the table and looked out the window. When she turned back toward Mary, she had a bright smile on her face.

"Well, let's start planning some girls' days out. We can drive up into Richmond or even out to Nelson County to visit Pete," Mildred said.

"Oh, Mildred, I think that would be perfect." Mary clasped her hands together in a single clap. "Let's do that. Shall I tell her, or should you?"

Mildred sat down in her chair and put her elbows on the table. "It might be best if she doesn't know we had this conversation. She'd hate it if she knew we were talking about her. You know how she is." Mary nodded her head in agreement. "I'll give her a call in the morning. So what do you think we should do first? How about a trip to Thalhimers. That's every girl's dream," Mildred said.

"I would vote for that," Mary said. "Thank you so much, Mildred. A ten-pound weight has been lifted from my shoulders."

Mildred called Lillian the next day and arranged a trip to Thalhimers Department Store in Richmond. The following day they left Petersburg at 10:00 A.M., the perfect time for some shopping and then lunch. None of them bought a thing—Thalhimers was out of their price range. But they loved to browse, and the department store's dining area was the perfect way to top off their day. On the way home, Mildred initiated the planned conversation.

"Lillian, how are things in retirement? Have you found things to do?"

Lillian looked out the car window to the stores lining the streets of Richmond. "No, not really. I get invited to preach at a church on rare occasions, never a revival. Churches don't seem to have those anymore. When I do preach, I feel the old fire comes back. It ignites in me and rises quickly but seems to die as soon as I step out of the pulpit." Lillian turned her head slightly to look out the windshield. "Sometimes a women's circle asks me to give them a program, but never a Bible study. I tried a couple of new recipes, but with just Mary and me and no parishioners to share it with, it doesn't seem worth the time." Lillian looked at Mary sitting in the back seat. "No offense, Mary, just stating how I feel."

"No offense taken," Mary said.

"Maybe I shouldn't have retired. Maybe I should've just stayed until they rolled me out in a wheelchair." She attempted a laugh, but nothing came.

"Oh, Lillian, I'm so sorry," said Mildred. "I didn't realize you were in such a dark place. Let's try to do something about that."

"You can try, Mildred, but think about it. I've been doing pulpit work since I was seventeen years old. I don't know anything else. It's who I am. I'm truly lost without proclaiming God's grace." Lillian started to cry. She whispered the words of Paul, "Woe to me if I do not preach the gospel."

Mildred pulled the car into an empty spot along the curb and put the car in park. She unhooked her seat belt and leaned over to hug Lillian. Mary sat forward in her seat and put her hand on Lillian's shoulder. The three of them just sat there for several minutes until Lillian stopped crying and pulled back from her friends.

"Thank you, ladies. I'll be all right." Lillian said. Mildred and Mary leaned back into their seats. "Boots warned me when I was just a young woman that someday I might regret not having married and having a family. I think that reality has come home to roost. I see other women my age, and they seem so happy with grandchildren and such."

"But, Lillian, we've never been like other women," Mildred said. "We can't start now. You know Mary and I love you like a sister. You have so many people who love you, and you've lived a most remarkable life. God knows you have served only Him your whole life. Can't you just rest in that knowledge?" Mildred coaxed.

"I've been giving that considerable thought, and here's the question that haunts me." Lillian repositioned herself in her seat so she could look square at Mildred. "You know the story of Esther, right? We've taught it and preached it so many times, especially to women's groups. That whole thing about 'born for such a time as this.' Well, what if Esther sold out? What if she took the easy road, the one that made her a queen, and then she used the excuse of saving her people as the reason she made herself beautiful? Maybe she sold herself in order to be the heroine. Did I take the easy road? Did I sell out by not itinerating, by not knowing a man, by not bearing children? Was I faithful or fearful? Was all that sacrifice of God? Or was I just trying to make myself look good?" Lillian put her head in her hands and started to cry again.

"Lillian Phyllis Russell, look at me." Mildred's voice was warm but stern. Lillian raised her head and looked at Mildred. Mildred locked her eyes on Lillian's and said, "Nothing could be further from the truth. You aren't perfect, but you're as close to perfect as anybody I've ever met in my entire life. Our motivations are never pure. We just have to move forward in faith, trusting that grace will cover the rest. Believe the gospel you have preached all these years. Receive the good news of Christ and be set free from all this foolishness." Mildred softened the edges of her mouth and unlocked her gaze on Lillian with a wink. "Now, we're heading home, but not before we get some ice cream at that place right down the street."

Mildred turned off the engine.

"Mildred, you're not in a legal parking space," Mary said.

"We won't be long. Come on, let's go before we get a ticket. I seem to get one every time I come to Richmond." Mildred laughed.

Mildred, Mary, and Lillian got their ice cream before the police gave Mildred a ticket. They continued their road trips, but Lillian simply could not find her rudder.

Nevertheless, She Preached

Blandford Church continued the debate over relocation. People opposed to relocation wanted Lillian to take sides or at least express her opinion. They also talked about financial misconduct that involved both the treasurer and the pastor. Lillian grieved for her Blandford people but stayed out of the debates. Prayers for her church family, their leaders, and their pastor were the best she had to offer.

Two years after Lillian retired, Mary Gills learned she had cancer. Mildred, Lillian, and the Blandford Church gathered around her for support. Between visits, food, flowers, phone calls, and cards, Mary hardly had a minute to herself. Finally, on September 11, 1981, her heart gave out. Her funeral service was held at Blandford United Methodist Church and burial in Lynchburg next to her mother. Mary had been closer than a sister to Lillian from the days of revivals through the thirty-five years at Blandford. Lillian's spirit broke with grief.

Like many others in her family, Lillian suffered from heart problems. During one of those cardiac events, she was deprived of adequate oxygen to her brain and was never the same after that. Her sister Polly came to live with her. At Lillian's request, few visited her. It was hard for her to dress appropriately, have her long hair braided and wrapped, and make-up applied. Mildred was one of the few permitted entry into the apartment.

#   #   #

"Hello, old friend. How are you today? I've brought you some roses," Mildred said with her typical cheery smile. "This is a great year for them, and thankfully, the beetles seem to be feeding in someone else's rose garden."

Of course, this visit was scheduled, so Lillian was sitting up, well-groomed for her oldest friend. "I'm pretty good for an old preacher. But not near as good as you. You look better than ever. I think retirement has been good for you."

"It has been good. I have less stress and more time just to enjoy all that God has provided. I've even lost some weight."

Mildred twirled around. "I have several walking partners because I seem to wear them out!" They both laughed. "But you, my friend, are as beautiful as ever. Sometime you must let me come before your hair is done to brush it and braid it for you. That would give me such pleasure." Mildred smiled.

"I don't mean any offense, Mildred, but we tried that once and, if you remember, it didn't go well. One good wind and the bird's nest you created on the top of my head came undone, and my hair was down to my waist again. Sorry, friend, I'll continue to have Polly fix my hair." They both laughed.

Mildred and Lillian spent hours talking about the good old days of ministry. Over the months, Lillian's endurance got shorter and weaker. Sometimes she had trouble remembering the good old days. When that happened, Mildred told her stories, and they both laughed. Mildred had great stories to tell and was a remarkable storyteller. Most people would think Mildred was exaggerating at best, but Lillian knew from her own experience that they were mostly true, at least by preacher's standards.

Eventually, Lillian's care became more than Polly could manage. Polly's own health was declining due to colon cancer. In October of 1989, cancer took Polly's life, forcing Lillian to move to Snyder's Memorial Home for Ladies in Richmond, where she had round-the-clock nursing care. Per Lillian's instruction, no one but her family and pastor could see her; she said she could no longer make herself presentable to company. The district superintendent, Cynthia Corley, considered herself her pastor and visited her.

Mildred knew she was family and visited her regularly. She recited favorite Scripture to Lillian, and before she left, she took her hand, pressed it to her cheek, and prayed for her. "Holy Father, I hold in my hands the precious hands of a saint. I pray that You will grant the desires of her heart. Give to her a peace that the world cannot give or take away. Fill her with such joy and contentment that her heart is glad. I thank You, Lord, for the privilege of calling this woman my friend. In the name of our Lord and Savior, I pray. Amen."

Chapter Thirty-Three
Cynthia Corley: Another Glass Ceiling Broken

Forward through the ages, in unbroken line,
Move the faithful spirits at the call divine.
--Lyrics by Fredrick Lucian Hosmer, 1908

*J*n 1986 Annual Conference was held in June at Roanoke.
Cynthia Corley's appointment by Bishop Blackburn to the cabinet
highlighted a historic moment for the Virginia Conference. Not
only was she the first woman to be appointed to the cabinet
(comprised of all eighteen district superintendents and the bishop)
in the Virginia Conference, at age thirty-six, she was also the
second youngest person to be appointed. The youngest appointee
was twenty-seven years old, and that had happened in 1780.

Bishop Blackburn was a slender man in his sixties, hair still
brown. "Friends," the bishop said, "today I announce a most
historic appointment. For the first time in the history of our
Conference, a woman will be a member of the cabinet." The
bishop stood at the podium in the center of the platform in the
coliseum.

Cynthia, at five-feet five inches tall, naturally curly brown
hair, and glasses, stood off to one side. More than two thousand
people in attendance stood to applaud and cheer.

"Cynthia Corley, please address your conference family." He motioned with his hand for Cynthia to come to the podium.

Cynthia was sure her shoes were nailed to the floor. She pried them loose and made her way to the podium. The bishop lowered the microphone. Once the applause and cheering had stopped and people took their seats, Cynthia spoke.

"Thank you." She heard her tentative voice come out of her mouth, and then a much larger version of it come through the massive coliseum speakers. She pulled back, confused, and tried again. "Thank you for the honor of this appointment. I will try my very best, and with God's help, I will serve the Petersburg District to the best of my ability."

The timid voice she heard coming from her mouth, compared to the loud voice coming from the speakers, echoed how she felt about this whole situation. She was in way over her head, but it was done. Too late to turn back.

After more applause, Cynthia took a step back. One of the clergywomen presented her with a plaque; the bishop shook Cynthia's hand; camera lights flashed as pieces of another glass ceiling scattered over the Conference assembly.

The *Virginia Advocate* carried two poor quality pictures. Reverend Alvin Horton invited Margaret Kutz to write an article about Cynthia's appointment to the cabinet. Conference rumor had it that both Margaret and Cynthia had been considered for this appointment. These are some excerpts from that article.

> For many women across the Conference, this historic appointment comes at a significant time of the year. For me, this month marks ten years of ministry in the Virginia Conference. All of us celebrate the 30th anniversary of full ordination rites for women in the Methodist Church, as well as the 25th anniversary of granting full clergy rights to Mildred Long.

> This year over forty percent of the Wesley Theological Seminary graduating class are women, compared with only four percent ten years ago. Numbers from other seminaries indicate the same trend (30-50 percent). This year forty percent of those

ordained deacons and fifteen percent ordained elders in the Virginia conference were women. In 1976, there were none.

Today, approximately seventy women are serving under full-time appointment in the Virginia conference, compared with a handful ten years ago. Lee Sheaffer (senior clergy in Virginia) suggested, "Male clergy should prepare the way for female clergy. Females can't be fighting their own way in."

In the last decade, tremendous strides have been made. There is much to celebrate, but there is much yet to be done. Equitable salaries, representation on boards and agencies and at General Conference, leaves of absences, and sensitivities regarding the "preacher's (lay) husband": these are but a few of the many issues awaiting our future response.

#   #   #

One day, shortly after Cynthia began her time in the Petersburg District office, the secretary knocked on her door to tell her she had a visitor. Cynthia asked her to please have the person come in. An older woman walked into her office carrying a vase of roses and a bag of vegetables.

"Reverend Corley, I'm Reverend Mildred Long. I stopped by to welcome you to the Petersburg District."

"Mildred—may I call you Mildred?" Cynthia stood from her chair and moved around her large desk to greet her guest.

"Yes, please, do call me Mildred. May I call you Cynthia?"

"Yes, please. Have a seat," Cynthia said.

Mildred and Cynthia sat in one of the two upholstered chairs in the office arranged to capture the light from the two windows.

"May I put these beautiful roses on my desk? I'll have the secretary put the vegetables in the refrigerator here at the office. Did you grow all of these?"

"Yes, I love to garden and have become somewhat of an expert on roses."

"Well, I didn't know about the roses, but I've heard about you. You're famous around Petersburg. Truly one of the pioneers. Both you and Lillian Russell."

"Yes, especially Miss Russell. She wasn't able to come with me today, but she sends her greetings. Both of us want you to know what a celebration it is for us to have you as our district superintendent. We've worked long and hard for this moment. Please don't forget how you got here and who helped you get here."

"I'm very much aware of the path Lillian and you have made for me," said Cynthia, "and I am grateful. It's hard enough for women today. I can't imagine how difficult it must have been for you."

"I appreciate that, Cynthia," said Mildred. "If there is ever anything—we mean *anything*—we can do for you, please don't hesitate to call us. We'll be your biggest supporters. We know all too well the challenges of this life. You'll continue to be in our daily prayers." Mildred's voice turned more earnest. "May I pray with you?"

Cynthia nodded and accepted Mildred's gesture to hold her hands. After a pause, Mildred began, "Heavenly Father, we come to You now seeking Thy wisdom and strength. Send Thy presence upon this Thy servant, Cynthia. May she always know Thy abiding love and care. Grant her strength for the hard days, endurance for the long days, and joy for the good days. In the name of Thy precious Son, Jesus Christ, we pray. Amen."

Cynthia felt the presence of God in those hands. Like a mantel being passed, Cynthia claimed the succession of history of the Petersburg District. This district was the most historic in all of Virginia, going back to the beginning of Methodism in America. Francis Asbury, the first Methodist bishop, was a circuit rider in the 1700s and started churches in the Petersburg area. Lillian Russell and Mildred Long had served those churches as pastors, and now Cynthia Corley as the district superintendent.

#   #   #

"Lillian? Are you awake? It's me, Mildred." Lillian opened her eyes and raised her head.

"Oh, Mildred. It's so good to see you. I must have nodded off," said Lillian.

"I've just come from visiting our new district superintendent," said Mildred. "She's lovely, quite young, but I sensed a strong spirit in her."

"Tell me more. I want to know all about our new DS," Lillian said.

"I didn't stay long because I just wanted to introduce myself, so I didn't learn much, but I did pray with her. I also mentioned whose shoulders she stands on," Mildred said.

"My shoulders don't feel strong enough for a baby to stand on today," Lillian said. They both laughed.

"How do you think we can support her?" Lillian asked.

"I was thinking about that driving over here, and I think I'll continue to visit her some, maybe take her out to lunch," Mildred said.

"Those are excellent ideas. What about attending the ministers' meetings. You know how hard they were for us. I can't imagine how hard they will be for her as the district superintendent," Lillian said.

"That's a great idea. I'll go to the first meeting and sit in the back, more for moral support. I'll see how that goes and then decide how often to attend these meetings."

"I'm afraid I can't do much but pray for her, and I have been doing that daily," Lillian said.

"There's nothing of greater benefit than prayer. I'll join you in that. Maybe as charge conference season starts, I'll fast one day a week for her."

"The doctor won't allow me to totally fast, but I can give up sweets. Let's make a covenant to pray and fast for Cynthia. Agreed?" Lillian asked.

"Agreed," Mildred responded with a nod.

Mildred continued to visit Cynthia, especially that first year, bringing roses and fresh vegetables in season. Sometimes Cynthia discovered them early in the morning on the steps of the district office. Even without a note, she knew who had given them. On occasion, Cynthia looked out over the clergy group at the monthly ministers' meetings, spotted Mildred, and felt her strong, positive presence. Periodically, Mildred took Cynthia out to lunch. Mildred offered little advice, saying she didn't know much about the office of the superintendent. Her help came more in serving as a role model of a strong, confident clergywoman.

#   #   #

Cynthia drove to the Snyder Memorial Home for Women to visit Lillian Russell. Lillian had a private room, small but so clean it sparkled. She's *so tiny she barely makes a bump in the sheets. But my, my, my, look at that hair—every strand in place.* Cynthia smiled.

"Miss Russell? Lillian?" Cynthia touched Lillian's hand to see if she was really sleeping or just had her eyes closed. There was no sound, no movement. *She's sleeping.* Cynthia sat down on the chair next to the bed, opened her Bible, and began to read.

> *Fear not: for I have redeemed thee, I have called thee by thy name; thou art mine. When thou passest through the waters, I will be with thee; and through the rivers, they shall not overflow thee: when thou walkest through the fire, thou shalt not be burned; neither shall the flame kindle upon thee, for I am the LORD thy God, the Holy One of Israel, thy Saviour.*

"Reverend Corley, may I come in?" Mildred Long stood in the doorway of the room.

"Absolutely," Cynthia said and got up from the chair.

"How's Lillian doing?" Mildred's voice was a whisper.

"Sleeping right now. She sleeps most of the time. I've been reading Scripture to her. Do you want to come and offer prayer?"

"I'd love to do that." Mildred walked to the bed and took the hands of Cynthia and Lillian.

"Let us pray. Heavenly Father, we turn to You this morning because You have been our help and stay in all the times past, and we have come to trust Your wisdom, Your love, and Your power. Surround our sister, Lillian, with Your presence and all the benefits that it brings. May she know a peace that nothing in this world can take away. In the precious name of our Savior, we pray. Amen."

"Mildred, would you like to step out of the room and go to the lobby to talk?" asked Cynthia.

"I'd like that very much."

Cynthia and Mildred walked to the lobby of the nursing home in silence. Once in the lobby, they sat down.

"She's a dear, dear soul," Cynthia said. "Frankly, I've never met a minister, male or female, like her. She has a spiritual depth that forbids questioning. If she told me to do something, I believe I would do it regardless of what it was. She lives so close to God; you feel that when she speaks, it's straight from God's mouth. There's a fierce gentleness to her. I think of her as Mother Teresa. She speaks the truth in love."

"I know what you mean." Mildred nodded.

"I think of Lillian as Mother Teresa and you as the Apostle Paul," Cynthia said and smiled.

"I have raised some ruckus at times, just like Paul." Mildred slapped her knee and chuckled.

"I've tried to describe Lillian's voice to people who have not heard her speak," Cynthia said. "It's so distinctive; I don't know quite how to describe it."

Mildred picked up where Cynthia left off. "When I first met her, and I was still so new in ministry, I thought I might try to imitate her voice, but I couldn't. Her accent is definitely Rich-mond. The pitch is low yet feminine. It's deepened over the years that I've known her. Her cadence is not particularly fast or slow — more deliberate, like every word is so important, like you said, direct from God."

"Yes. When Lillian speaks, her presence and her voice say, 'Listen up, I have a word from God for you.' No wonder people flocked to hear her preach. One of a kind."

"Yes, one of a kind," Mildred said. "So many times over the years, I've come to her for direction, and she gave it. She is the dearest friend I've ever had. Her illness has left a huge void in my life. Cynthia, thank you for visiting her. So many in the Conference have simply ignored her all these years. And here she has been the first woman in Virginia to receive a license to preach, the first to receive an appointment, the first to be ordained a deacon, the first to be ordained an elder. She's a pioneer and a spiritual giant. The Conference should erect a statue to her."

"Sometimes I've felt the only real recognition we clergywomen receive is from those who think we're peculiar," Cynthia said. "I was invited once to speak at a church. The response was so good that the pastor told me, 'If I had a red-striped jacket, straw hat, and cane, I could sell tickets to your preaching.'"

Mildred nodded her head. "Lillian used to talk about the almost sideshow atmosphere she experienced as a young woman preaching revivals. It sounds like that hasn't gone away even now."

Both women remained silent, thinking, then Mildred continued. "We get some recognition from the laity, but not recognition from the leaders of our church. Having you as our district superintendent gives me hope that a new day is on the horizon. I don't want to think Lillian and I have walked this path in vain."

Chapter Thirty-Four
Death of the Saints

For all the saints, who from their labors rest,
who thee by faith before the world confessed,
thy name, O Jesus, be forever blest.
Alleluia!
William W. How, 1864

$\mathcal{T}$ he day Mildred fell down the steps appeared to be like any
other Sunday morning in southside Virginia. The clear blue sky
provided the perfect backdrop to the delicate white flowers on the
dogwood trees dancing in the wind. It would be two more months
before Mildred's roses bloomed, but the azaleas were showing off
their shades of pink. The people at Kenwood United Methodist
Church were in their favorite pews, singing their favorite hymns.
All was right with the world, or so they thought.

The doors to the sanctuary burst open, and in came a
breathless Nancy Rowland. Everyone turned to see her hurrying
down the church's center aisle toward the pastor, Reverend Wade
Creedle. Reverend Creedle's eyes grew large as Nancy whispered
in his ear. The pastor cleared his throat and focused his gaze on
his flock. "Nancy has come to tell us that Miss Long has fallen. She
fell down her basement steps this morning and appears to be

unconscious. The rescue squad is with her now and will be taking her to Southside Regional Hospital. Let's bow in prayer."

Reverend Creedle moved to the communion rail and knelt. "Gracious God, giver of life, healer of all, we turn to You now to lift up one who is very dear to us. Please surround Miss Long with Your healing power. Take away any pain she may have. Heal any broken bones. Restore her body to wholeness that she might continue to serve You. Give wisdom to the medical team treating her. Surround her family and friends with a peace that nothing in this world can take away. We pray this in the name of the One Miss Long has served so faithfully all her years, Jesus Christ. Amen."

He stood and faced the congregation. "If any of you want to go with Nancy to the hospital, please know you can do that." A few women picked up their purses and Bibles and followed Nancy out the door.

It was the first Sunday after Easter, and the choir had selected a rousing Gaither resurrection song, "The King is Coming."

The marketplace is empty.
No more traffic in the streets
All the builders' tools are silent.
No more time to harvest wheat
Busy housewives cease their labors.
In the courtroom, no debate.
Work on earth is all suspended,
As the King comes thro' the gate.

Refrain:
O, the King is coming.
The King is coming
I just heard the trumpets sounding.
And now His face I see.
O, the King is coming.
The King is coming

Nevertheless, She Preached

Praise God; He's coming for me.

Happy faces line the hallways.
Those whose lives have been redeemed
Broken homes that He has mended
Those from prison He has freed.
Little children and the aged
Hand in hand stand all aglow,
Who were crippled, broken, ruined
Clad in garments white as snow.

Refrain

I can hear the chariots rumble.
I can see the marching throng.
The flurry of God's trumpets
Spells the end of sin and wrong
Regal robes are now unfolding.
Heaven's grandstand's all in place.
Heaven's choir now assembled.
Start to sing "Amazing Grace."

Refrain
Praise God; He's coming for me.

In the parking lot, people spoke to each other in amazement. "Wasn't the anthem powerful?"

"Yes. I was so moved."

"It was like a prayer for Miss Long. I'll never forget it."

Reverend Creedle said, "I didn't see a dry eye in the sanctuary."

Nancy drove the car that carried three of the women from the church to the Southside Regional Medical Center, a fifteen-minute trip from Kenwood. They went straight to the receptionist at the emergency desk.

"Has Mildred Long been admitted yet?" Nancy asked. "She's a Methodist minister."

Another woman with permed hair, using her purse to make her way to the front of the group, said, "She fell down her basement steps this morning."

A third woman, donned with a flowered pink Easter bonnet and white gloves, using her ample hips, made her way to the front of the group. "She was unconscious. We're so worried."

"Ladies, ladies," the receptionist said, "I've no idea. The ambulance has just arrived. I'll let you know as soon as I know something. Is one of you a family member?"

Nancy responded with a commanding voice to indicate she was clearly in charge. "No, we are former parishioners and good friends. I called her brother before I drove here. He's on his way. I'm her best friend. Can't I go back to be with her? She would want that."

"I'm sorry. Hospital rules. Now, if one of you was a clergy, then maybe you could go back."

"No, she's the clergy. We're her members, or were her members," said Nancy. "Anyway, please, let us know as soon as you can about her condition."

"I'll do that. Please, find a seat over there in the waiting area. We've coffee and soft drinks available."

The four women walked to the waiting area and took a seat. They were silent for a moment, then Nancy said, "Can we join hands and pray? You know that is what Miss Long would expect us to do."

The women nodded and joined hands. After a long silence, Nancy said, "I guess one of us should pray."

After more silence, Nancy said, "Okay, I'll pray, but it won't be as good as one of Miss Long's prayers." She drew a deep breath. "Holy God, the Great Healer, we beg you to look favorably on your servant, Mildred Long. Please, please God, restore her to us. Bring her brother, Raymond, safely here."

Nancy paused and looked at the other women. "Did I miss anything?"

The lady wearing the hat and gloves said, "I think you covered everything. Just pray in Jesus' name."

"Of course, I know that," Nancy said in a disgusted voice. They all bowed their heads again. "We pray this in the most precious name of Jesus. Amen."

"Amen," the other women echoed.

Chit chat filled the hour or so until the receptionist called them over to her desk. "Your friend has been admitted and is in I.C.U. I'm sorry, but you'll not be allowed to visit her there unless you're family or clergy."

Just then, Reverend Creedle came into the emergency department. "Problem solved," exclaimed Nancy. "There's our pastor. He can visit, and then let us know."

Reverend Creedle heard the latest information about Mildred from the receptionist and the four women, including her room number. The women followed him in a single line, purses on their arms and heels clicking on the linoleum floors. They all got on the elevator and went to the floor with the I.C.U.

"Wait here," Reverend Creedle said. "Let me check on her and then I'll come back and report."

The women waited in silence for about fifteen minutes. As soon as the door opened and they saw their pastor, they stood up and rushed toward him. "So how is she?" they all asked in unison.

"She's still unconscious. They believe she had a cerebral hemorrhage. She may have gotten it when she fell, or she may have fallen because of it. I hate to tell you this, but it's pretty serious. The doctors don't think she'll regain consciousness. You might as well go home."

"I'm not going anywhere," said Nancy with a stomp of her foot and arms crossed. "I need to wait until her brother gets here."

"How will the rest of us get home?" asked the permed hair woman. "My family must be starving by now."

"I can take you home," Reverend Creedle said.

After a brief prayer led by the pastor, the three ladies and Reverend Creedle left.

It was nearly five o-clock when Raymond got to the hospital. Nancy filled him in on all she knew. He then went into the I.C.U. to visit his sister. When he came out, about twenty minutes later, Nancy saw his teary eyes and red nose.

She jumped to her feet and asked with wide eyes, "Is she still...alive?"

"Yes, but it's touch and go. There isn't much the doctors can do but wait. It's up to Mildred now."

With that, Raymond wrapped his arms around Nancy, broke down, and sobbed. "She's been like a mother to me. I don't know how I can go on without her. How can God let this happen? She's done nothing but serve Him all her life. She should live to be 100 years old."

Nancy held him and patted his back. She could feel his tears and nose running on her dress and could see a box of tissues on a table but was afraid to let go, confident he would fall if she weren't supporting him. So she just let him cry. Finally, he stopped crying and pulled away from Nancy, sniffling.

"I'm sorry," he said.

"No need to apologize," Nancy said as she went to the table and brought the whole box of tissues, pulling one out and handing it to him. Then she took one for herself. "I guess I've been doing my own share of crying. Your sister's the best friend I've ever had."

"I was only three years old when my father died. Mildred was fifteen. I don't remember much, but everybody said Mama was overwhelmed. Edith died just four years later, and Mildred managed nearly everything from laundry to helping us with our homework. Mama was working as the Postmaster then. It was a crazy time, but Mildred always made us believe everything would be all right."

"That's the way she was with everybody. Take charge and assure you everything will be okay," said Nancy.

"When I had my troubles, and my wife died, Mildred was right there to visit and call and do everything she could to help even though we lived in different states. I can never thank her enough for all she's done for me." Raymond started to cry again, and Nancy gave him another tissue.

The two of them sat down across from each other. They were silent for a while. Finally Raymond spoke. "So what happens now? Should I stay here or go to her house? Is it locked? Do you have a key?"

"Let's do this," Nancy said. "Let's both go downstairs and get something to eat. You can visit again after that. One of us can spend the night here so the other can get some sleep. Miss Long seldom locked her house, but I have a key. Are you expecting any other family to come?"

"I called everybody before I left. Frankly, there aren't many of us left, and those who are still living are scattered. You've been here most of the day. Let me spend the night, and then we'll go from there."

Throughout that day and night, there was no change in Mildred's condition. Nancy returned in the morning, but Raymond would not leave. At 5:21 P.M., Monday, April 23, 1990, Reverend Mildred Victoria Long claimed the promise of resurrection. The King had come for her.

Raymond made all the arrangements through J.T. Morris Funeral Home in Petersburg. Her remains were then transported to Phillips Funeral home in Biscoe, North Carolina. Mildred had told her family that she wanted a simple service, glorifying God and not herself.

The obituary in the Biscoe paper was short: *The Reverend Mildred Victoria Long, 76, of Petersburg, VA, died Monday in Petersburg. Graveside service will be at 1:00 P.M. Thursday at Biscoe Cemetery. A Biscoe native, she was a retired United Methodist minister. Surviving are brothers, Auley C. Long of Milford, Del., Herbert N. Long of Delton, Fla., Raymond L. Long of Biscoe. The family will be at Phillips Funeral Home from 11:00 A.M. to noon Thursday.*

Five members from Kenwood United Methodist Church traveled together to Biscoe to bid farewell to their beloved Miss Long. She was the reason they had no fear of death. Their faith in the resurrection was secure because of the teaching, preaching, and witness of Mildred.

"I remember when I was a young mother," said a woman in the backseat of the car traveling south on Route 85. "I think the baby was six months old. I was really down but didn't know why. I realize now; it was probably postpartum depression. And here is Miss Long, unmarried, no children of her own, who just listened intently, without comment or judgment in her words or body language. She took my hands and prayed for me. I don't remember what she said, but I'll never forget the power. It came through her hands like a life force. I was okay after that. I'll never forget that day."

Nancy Rowland, squeezed in the middle of the back seat, said, "She had a way of making everyone feel special. From little children to the elderly, from the beggar at the corner to the church's Lay Leader. She taught us that all are special to God. She showed us all are special to her."

The man driving wiped his hand over his bald head, around his thick neck, and placed it back on the steering wheel. "I remember her preaching voice. She spoke clearly, slowly, and without notes. She must have had the entire Bible put to memory. I carry my Bible under my arm. Miss Long seemed to carry it in her very person."

The woman in the front passenger seat shifted her body to be heard in the back. "But she could be so hilarious. Remember the way she drove? Her poor cars got quite a workout." Everyone laughed.

The driver spoke again. "And she had a bit of a temper. When things were not done properly, according to the book, she could get quite agitated." He chuckled. "No one wanted to tangle with Miss Long then."

"Do you know what we should do?" asked Nancy. "We should start a library at Kenwood and call it the Mildred Long Library. She has already given us many books and has asked the remainder of her books be given to the church as we have need."

Everyone agreed that would be an excellent beginning to a church library. "As soon as we get back," Nancy said, "I'll talk to the powers that be about finding a room and getting this started."

Reverend Duke Lackey, the young pastor assigned to Page Memorial United Methodist Church, her home church in Biscoe, officiated at the graveside service. He knew Reverend Long was a retired pastor from the Virginia Conference, but he had no idea of the amazing life he was celebrating. How could he know? How could anyone know? Maybe Lillian could have shed light on Mildred's life, but she was not well enough to travel.

Miss Mildred Long's remains were laid to rest in the Biscoe Cemetery next to her mother and father, and other family members. The tombstone read *Rev. Mildred Victoria Long, January 30, 1914-April 23, 1990.*

With the worldwide web has come the opportunity of placing "reverend" in front of a name. It's as easy as getting on the internet, completing a form, and paying a fee. People in the digital era may find it hard to comprehend Mildred's hardships to achieve "Rev." on her tombstone. After attending more than six schools beyond high school, driving thousands of miles, reading hundreds of books, preparing for dozens of interviews, attending hundreds of meetings; after insults hurled, doors closed, and doubts raised; after proving herself time and time again to people over her, under her, and beside her, Mildred was finally able to have the title "reverend" conferred and granted the same clergy rights as men. She had done what God had called her to do; had achieved what no other woman in Virginia Methodism had ever done before her. She had made a road for other women to follow.

Nevertheless, she preached.

#   #   #

Lillian was not always aware of her visitors, but they were faithful anyway. Her older sister Boots traveled from Falls Church to visit. Ernest Walter, Lillian's next youngest brother, regularly visited from his home in Portsmouth, Virginia. Sometimes he brought his wife, Sarah. Lillian had officiated at their wedding in 1972, just a few years before Lillian's retirement. Pete still lived in the Richmond area and often visited when Ernest was in the area to see their sister.

Pete acted as much a pastor as a brother to Lillian by singing hymns and reading Scripture. "Sis, remember the times our whole family went to nursing homes to conduct worship services? Now, here I am singing solo to you. I guess life has come full circle." He stroked her hair, which lay unbraided down her back. "I'm Reverend Pete now. Can you believe it? I'm a Baptist preacher. The Methodists wouldn't take me without more education, and I'm too old to go back to school."

Even when her body would no longer sit up but laid curled in the bed, her spirit heard the words of Scripture and the melody of music, and it soared. Lillian was in and out of awareness of the physical world but was keenly aware of the spirits in the next world. She often reached up to them and called out their names, "Mama, Daddy, Polly, Mary, Mildred."

Finally, on October 15, 1992, at age seventy-eight, Lillian drew her last breath. She had lived so close to God all those years that her journey was a short one. The angels who carried her were barely distinguishable from the one in their arms.

J.T. Morris Funeral Home in Petersburg, the place she had conducted funerals countless times, now received her body and prepared it for burial. Reverend James R. Maddox, the pastor at Blandford United Methodist Church, officiated. The funeral home chapel was packed with family, members of Blandford United Methodist Church, and community leaders, but few from the district or Conference came to celebrate this community icon and church saint's life.

At Lillian's request, a single orchid lay on the top of the closed casket, a symbol of hope. Lillian had made clear to her brother Ernest that she did not want her own life emphasized but rather the gospel of Christ lifted up. That was a relief to him because finding the words to describe his sister were not easy to come by. They sang some of her favorite hymns including "Great

Is Thy Faithfulness" and "Just A Closer Walk with Thee." Her nephews and several Blandford members served as pallbearers.

Lillian was never more distinguished than in the manner she conducted funerals. Given that fact, what happened between the funeral home and the cemetery was most unfortunate. The funeral procession was making its way north on Interstate 95 between Petersburg and Richmond, the hearse leading the way. A long line of cars followed behind, all with their lights on. Reverend Maddox rode in the front seat of the hearse with the funeral director traveling the 55-miles-per-hour speed limit, following a truck carrying a mattress and springs. Reverend Maddox mentioned to the funeral director, "That mattress is not tied down very well. It looks like it could come loose at any time."

And then it happened. The mattress blew off the back of the truck. It floated in the air like it had wings and landed on the hood of the hearse with a loud thud, then slid down the front of the car, and the hearse ran over it. The bumpy encounter tested the bolts holding the casket in place. The driver checked the casket's security in his review mirror, at the same time he put on his turn signal and pulled on to the shoulder of the road. The entire line of cars pulled off behind him. The driver got out of the hearse, signaled to the others to stay in their vehicles, and then examined the car's grille, radiator, and underside. There was damage to the grill, but the vehicle appeared to be drivable. He got back into the car, put on his turn signal, checked his side-view mirror, and slowly pulled back onto the interstate. Everyone followed in suit, grateful for a slow day on the highway.

The story of the mattress on interstate 95 became epic at J.T. Morris Funeral Home, repeated often, even told to new employees as an unofficial part of their orientation.

But Lillian had encountered many obstacles during her life. She was too young, too short, didn't drive; she was female. But none of these ever kept her from her destination. This mattress would not stop her from reaching her final resting place.

The remains of Lillian P. Russell were buried next to her parents in Oakwood Cemetery in Richmond. As per her directions, all of her sermons were destroyed upon her death. She didn't want any criticism of them.

Lillian Russell lived and preached the Gospel of Jesus Christ with every fiber of her being. Against incredible odds, this petite teenager traveled from church to church as a powerful evangelist. As the church pastor for thirty-five years, she studied late into the night and rose early in the morning for an hour in prayer. When the powers told her "no," she found another way, forging a path for other women to follow. When the voices of the world ridiculed and minimized her, closed doors, and questioned her fundamental right to be there, she did not doubt God's claim upon her life.

Nevertheless, she preached.

Thou wast their rock, their fortress, and their might;
Thou, Lord, their captain in the well-fought fight;
Thou, in the darkness drear, their one true light.
Alleluia! Alleluia!

Epilogue
My Story

Stoney the road we trod, bitter the chastening rod,
Felt in the days when hope unborn had died;
Yet with a steady beat, have not our weary feet
Come to the place for which our fathers (and mothers) sighed?
—Lyrics by James Weldon Johnson, 1921

*M*y husband, Bob, and I sat in the small lobby area of the
Arlington District Office in Alexandria, Virginia, waiting to be
interviewed by the District Committee on Ordained Ministry. The
two secretaries behind the half-wall were busy answering the
phones and directing people to offices. The calendar on the back
wall reminded me it was January 1974, and I would complete half
of the seminary requirements in May.

We sat on a small parson's bench just inside the main door
into the building. With the steady flow of people entering and
exiting, we were constantly moving our feet to let people get
by. "Excuse me," they repeated.

I was seeking ordination as a deacon and probationary
membership in the Virginia Conference. In the United Methodist
Church, ordination and conference membership are separate
categories. Both deacon and elder, in 1974, were clergy titles.
Generally, deacons were probationary members, and elders were
full members of the clergy. As a member of Mt. Olivet United

Methodist Church in Arlington, Virginia, I had been recommended for ordination by their Staff-Parish Relations Committee and Charge Conference. That process had gone very smoothly, according to the *Book of Discipline*, by people who knew and loved me.

It seemed strange to us that my husband would accompany me to this interview. What other fields of employment suggested such a practice? The traditional expectation in the Virginia Conference was that wives accompany their husbands to these interviews. Bob took a day off work so we could follow protocol.

In a few minutes, a young man came out of the District Superintendent's office. I assumed he was another ministerial candidate. A few steps behind him followed an older gentleman who invited us into the cramped office. A group of five men in dark suits greeted us with handshakes and introductions, then asked us to sit down on a loveseat. It was a 1960s vinyl sofa, low to the floor. Sitting on that sofa was even short for me at 5 feet, 3 inches, but for my husband at 6 feet, his knees leveled with his shoulders. The committee sat in folding chairs pushed up against the dark paneled walls. We were all nearly on top of each other, except the district superintendent, Reverend Dr. James Turner, who was one of the tallest, if not the tallest clergy in the Conference. He sat in his high-backed chair behind his executive desk.

Pleasantries ended as soon as everyone took their seats. "Tell us a little about yourself" immediately turned to "the itineracy." My husband worked for the federal government, so we needed to be close to the nation's capital, making the ability to itinerate anywhere in Virginia a challenge for us.

"Your situation is uniquely complicated. Frankly, we aren't sure what to do with you. Your husband's job takes precedence. After all, he is the primary breadwinner. You don't have any children yet, is that right?"

"Yes, no children yet," I said.

The interview stopped, and a discussion among the committee members started. They spoke in hushed tones as if we couldn't hear them, but, of course, in that small space, we could hear every word. I felt I had gone from a target to invisible.

"We assume they will have children, and when that happens, she may want to stay at home and tend to them, at least in the early years."

"Yes, but ministry takes precedence over all other vocations; after all, it is a calling. So, now we have a problem." Their voices got louder and took on a gravity.

"Men's careers come first. Ministry comes first. Gentlemen, we have not dealt with this issue before. Itineracy is a cornerstone of Methodism and cannot be ignored."

They slowly turned away from each other and back toward me. The interview continued. "What would you do if asked to move to Roanoke or Richmond or Tangier Island?"

"I would hope that with the many churches in Northern Virginia, you would find a place of service for me in this area," I responded.

"But that's not how it works. You go where the Bishop sends you. Have you thought about being a Director of Christian Education at a church? You would not have to itinerate," said Dr. Turner.

Another member chimed in, "Yes, that could be the perfect solution for you – Christian Educator."

"As I remember from reading your papers, you were a teacher, elementary, right?"

Heads were bobbing and faces smiling. The committee clearly believed they had solved the dilemma they themselves had created.

"Yes, I have a degree in education and taught elementary school for a few years. But I'm not called to be a D.C.E. I'm called to preach," I said.

"What makes you say that? Have you preached? How many lady preachers do you even know? How do you know this is what you want?" Questions from around the room bombarded me.

"Well, I've preached only once. My home church in Pennsylvania sent a woman into ordained ministry. I know her. And I've met several women at seminary who have student pastorates. I've talked to them about their experiences." My response sounded so weak against their cacophony of objections.

And so the "interview" went. No questions about my call, nothing about my theology or my gifts and graces for ministry— all those disciplinary questions I had prepared to answer were never asked. Finally, they told me to go, that they would have to discuss this further and get back to me. It did not look good.

Bob and I walked to our car. I could hardly contain the tears. My call to ministry was so compelling that I had given up a coveted full-time teaching position to attend seminary full-time. This could not be happening. Bob opened my car door. Once inside the safety of the car, I started to cry.

Bob said, "I'm sorry."

"Sorry? For what? You didn't do anything wrong. They just don't get us, a marriage of equals."

"What do you think will happen?" he asked.

"I have no idea," I said.

The next week I learned through a letter that they had sent my papers to the Conference Board of Ordained Ministry without a recommendation from the District Committee. The chairman of the Conference Board, Reverend Dr. Lee Sheafer, said that without the Arlington District's recommendation, the matter was not properly before them. So, at a meeting I was not invited to, the District Committee agreed that if I wrote a letter with the following conditions, they would recommend me to the conference board. First, I would itinerate as directed by the bishop. Second, if I could not or would not itinerate, I would surrender my credentials. I wrote the letter, and I received the recommendation from the district committee.

Because it was too late to be interviewed by the full Conference Board of Ordained Ministry, the board officers considered my application in an executive session the night before the Annual Conference in Hampton, Virginia. If approved, I was to be in Hampton by noon for an orientation session. Ordination was that same evening. Bob's mother and stepfather planned to travel from Pennsylvania and be present.

I stayed up late that night, hoping somebody from the Board of Ordained Ministry would call me. When no one called by midnight, I went to bed but not to sleep. Finally, by 5:30 A.M., when I had not heard anything, I decided I had no choice but to call Sue Sheaffer, wife of Lee Sheaffer. She gave me her husband's hotel number. A groggy voice answered in Hampton, "Hello."

"Reverend Sheaffer, this is Margaret Kutz. I'm sorry to call you so early. Your wife gave me your phone number. I need to know if you approved me for ordination."

"Yes, Margaret, we met last night. A little after midnight, we discussed your situation and approved you for ordination. You're to be here at noon today. Ordination is tonight at 7:00 P.M. Some of the grogginess had cleared, and he sounded more official.

"Thank you so much. I'll be there," I responded with a cheery voice, thinking the result was good, but the situation did not put me in a good light with this tired man of authority.

Bob and I called his parents, packed up, and set out by 9:00 A.M. to avoid rush hour traffic in the D.C. area, but still in time to get to Hampton before noon. Bob looked for a hotel room while I attended orientation.

That night Bishop Kenneth Goodson ordained me a deacon, received me into probationary membership, and granted me a license to preach in the Virginia Conference. It was a holy moment only slightly tarnished by the road I trod. Bob's mother and stepfather were also present to celebrate this accomplishment with us.

To the best of my knowledge, I was the first woman to enter the ordained ministry through the Arlington District. Reverend Raymond Wrenn, a long-time Methodist historian, told me there might have been a woman who received a license to preach on the Methodist Protestant Church's Alexandria District. I could not confirm that either way. Later the Alexandria District split to become two districts, Alexandria and Arlington.

I am one of the few who was approved by the Conference Board of Ordained Ministry sight unseen. To the best of my knowledge, I am the only candidate for ministry asked to write a letter pledging my allegiance to the itinerate system. However, itineracy was used against many married clergywomen for years, those, like myself, married to laymen and those married to clergymen. Seldom was it used against men, married to career lay women or clergywomen.

My First Appointment

"Fear not, I am with thee, O be not dismayed,
for I am thy God and will still give thee aid;
I'll strengthen and help thee, and cause thee to stand
Upheld by my righteous, omnipotent hand."
Lyrics "K" in Rippon's Selection of Hymns, 1787

*I*n the spring of 1976, I was in my final semester at Wesley Theological Seminary in Washington, D.C. Upon graduation, I would receive an episcopal appointment to a local church. The church the bishop projected was Graham Road United Methodist Church in Falls Church, Virginia, walking distance from our home. Itinerating was not an issue with this appointment. But there were other issues, even more fundamental than location. Because I was being asked to serve as the associate pastor, I met with the senior pastor, Reverend Moody Wooten, at the church study.

"Good morning, Margaret. Please come in and have a seat."

His study was a small, paneled room with a large single window. He rose from his office chair behind his desk to sit next to me in one of the two matching upholstered chairs.

Reverend Wooten was a stocky man in his early forties with a full head of dark, curly hair. He was wearing a blue clerical collar shirt, dress pants, and sports jacket.

"I understand you are a Wesley grad. I'm a Duke grad myself. What were some of the course work that you enjoyed most?"

"I especially enjoyed systematic theology and an independent study of process theology."

"Oh, so you are a more academic type."

"No, not really. I also liked the more practical courses like homiletics."

The conversation continued as he asked other questions about me, my family, and my ministry experience.

"Graham Road is a large church with more than 1,300 members and averages more than 200 in worship on Sundays," Reverend Moody said. "Tucked away in this young-professional neighborhood, it is surprising we are this strong. And we continue to grow, with new people visiting nearly every week." Reverend Wooten repositioned himself in his chair and crossed his legs. "What we need is somebody to do follow-up visits. Because most families are two-income households, these visits have to be made at night, when people are home from work. So in addition to assisting me with worship and pastoral care, I need an associate who can lead the ministry with our youth and visit our visitors."

Reverend Wooten paused and uncrossed his legs. "Let me be honest. I'm not sure about women preachers, but my wife thinks it's a good idea, and I'm willing to give it a try. However, if you're appointed here, you'll be part-time because it wouldn't be safe to have you out at night by yourself making home visits. Does that make sense to you?"

"No, not really. I'm out at night by myself regularly. I drove into Washington for night classes at the seminary. When I was working at Mt. Olivet, I went to night meetings in Arlington. Being out at night by myself is not an issue for me."

"Well, I don't want to be responsible for you if anything should happen. If we're both willing to take this appointment to the next step, then we'll meet with the Pastor-Parish Relations Committee. We'll see what they think, but I believe they will agree with me. So are you interested in continuing this conversation?"

"Yes, I would very much like to meet with your Pastor-Parish Relations Committee," I said.

I was disappointed but did not want to turn down my first appointment. Another offer might take me far away from the D.C. area. Yet listening to Reverend Wooten was like hearing someone from another culture, certainly a different period of history. I thought to myself, *so when the streetlights come on, the children and the associate pastor have to go inside.*

The meeting with the Staff-Parish Relations Committee was a night meeting, and ironically, I went alone. During the meeting, when discussing part-time vs full-time, every person around that table except one man agreed with Reverend Wooten. I spoke of calling; he spoke of what is rational. The man who voiced the minority opinion illustrated it with the fact that his wife regularly came to choir practice and women's meetings at night by herself. But the majority and "reason" ruled, and I was to go to Graham Road as their part-time associate pastor.

In my mind, there were many issues with this, but two surfaced as very practical. I had just completed ninety hours of seminary, including all the required and recommended courses that prepared me for pastoral ministry. Only one of those courses was in youth ministry—ironically, it was a night course. The other issue was that to be considered for elder orders and full connection in the Conference, I had to serve at least one year in a full-time appointment. My part-time status would not allow me to move forward.

So I called Dr. Turner about my concerns. I told him about Reverend Wooten's uncertainty about clergywomen and the issue of part-time status due to no nighttime work. Dr. Turner's response was, "Look, none of us are jumping up and down about getting one of you. If we do, we just have to make the best of it."

This conversation obviously was not going well. So, I talked to Reverend C.P. Minnich, the senior pastor of Mt. Olivet, where I had worked and was still a member. He was confused by Dr. Turner's behavior. C.P. and Dr. Turner were good friends and roommates during General Conference. He didn't know him to have this opinion about women. He encouraged me to try another strategy. I memorized the words C.P. gave me and made an appointment to see Dr. Turner.

As I entered Dr. Turner's office, he raised his gaze from papers on his large executive desk to scowl at me, clearly not in a good mood. I sat down on the low vinyl couch and pressed my sweaty hands against my skirt. Maybe this wasn't such a good idea, but it was too late now to change course. I took a deep breath, and in a rapid-word fire, repeated verbatim what C.P. had told me to say.

"Dr. Turner, I do not think you can represent me fairly on the cabinet. I would like to deal directly with the Bishop concerning my appointment."

There I said it. Now breathe.

Ever so slowly, Dr. Turner pushed himself away from his desk and started to rise out of his chair. He just kept standing, inch by inch, until he was leaning out over his desk, glaring down at me. By then, I had nearly slid in the crack in the baseboard. He shook his finger at me and said, "You just try it and see what happens."

I'm not sure, but I don't think I said another word, maybe a squeak, as I tip-toed out of his office. I never contacted the bishop. It appeared I was going to Graham Road as their day-time associate pastor.

I graduated from Wesley Theological Seminary on May 3, 1976, my twenty-eighth birthday. By this time, Bob and I were parents to a one-year old son, Robbie. To celebrate my graduation, I joined the end of Bob's business trip to California for three days. When I got home, I received a phone call from Dr. Turner.

"I've been trying to reach you for days. Where have you been?" he scolded me.

"I was in California with my husband," I said.

"This is appointment season. You should call me if you're going to be away. Honestly, you shouldn't go away."

"I'm sorry I didn't know." Truthfully, I didn't know there was an appointment season, let alone the rules for the season.

"You have an appointment," he continued.

I was standing in the kitchen using the wall phone, but I felt I was on the edge of my seat or maybe a cliff. *Was this Graham Road associate position official?*

"You've been appointed to Round Hill on the Winchester District. It's a station church, and you'll be their only pastor."

"Round Hill. Where's that?" I asked, having lived in Virginia only a few years, so not familiar with all the small towns.

"Look it up on a map. And one more thing." Dr. Turner cleared his throat. "I'm glad I'm going off the cabinet this year. I don't ever want to appoint a woman again." With that, he hung up.

I didn't even have time to be incredulous. Everything I knew about ministry—weekly preaching, pastoral care, Bible study, funerals, weddings, church finances—all passed in front of me like a speeding freight train. I felt my knees buckle, and I grabbed the counter to steady myself. But as I hung up the phone, I felt an assurance that it would be all right, that all of these things and more would come. But they would come one at a time. I could do this.

About six weeks later, Bob, Robbie, and I, surrounded by packed boxes, greeted four men from Round Hill United Methodist Church at our front door in Falls Church. A truck was in the driveway, and they were ready to help us move the fifty miles to the Round Hill parsonage. I would be their first female pastor, and they would be my first church.

Later, I learned the story behind the story: how I got from part-time at Graham Road to full-time at Round Hill. Lee Sheaffer became the Winchester District Superintendent in 1976, the same year I went to Round Hill. As an incoming D.S., he had been invited to sit in, even participate in the appointment-making process. As he tells the story, the cabinet had been meeting for days to get the right preachers in the right churches. Believing they had finally completed their task, they closed their notebooks. Then Reverend Esdras Gruver, outgoing District Superintendent of the Winchester District, said, "Bishop, I have one more church open, Round Hill."

They all groaned as they reopened their notebooks to see who they might be able to scare up. One D.S. suggested a retired minister. Then another D.S. mentioned a lay preacher. That's when Lee Sheaffer spoke up, "What about Margaret Kutz? I have had dealings with her through the Board of Ordained Ministry. She's assertive. I like that. I think she would do a good job there."

"Reverend Gruver spoke up, "Lee, I don't think Round Hill will take a lady preacher."

"Have you asked them?" Lee persisted.

"Well, no," said Reverend Gruver.

"Then let's ask them," came back Lee enthusiastically.

So, Lee called Mr. Cooley, President of Round Hill Community Bank and chairman of their Pastor-Parish Relations Committee. Given the other two options of a retired pastor or a lay preacher, Mr. Cooley thought it best to select the young, seminary-educated, female candidate. Still, he needed to check with others on the committee. Within a few hours, Mr. Cooley said the committee agreed. So, the cabinet wrote my name in their notebooks as the next pastor of Round Hill, and were free to go home.

Other Appointments

When through fiery trials thy pathways shall lie,
My grace, all-sufficient, shall be thy supply;
The flame shall not hurt thee; I only design
thy dross to consume, and thy gold to refine.
"K" in Rippon's "A Selection of Hymns," 1787

*R*ound Hill United Methodist Church was not an easy appointment. It hadn't been for the pastors before me nor for the ones to follow. Some of the people there became dear friends, but others were what are often called "preacher eaters" or "toxic." I was inexperienced, and they took advantage of that. They were critical and even hurtful. I remember coming home from a meeting one night, never going upstairs to sleep with my husband, opting to stay downstairs on the sofa and cry myself to sleep. I didn't want him to know my pain.

But then this little Volkswagen Bug would pull up in the parsonage yard, and out of the car came my favorite District Superintendent, Reverend Dr. Lee Sheaffer. I would pour out my heart to him, and he would assure me that it wasn't me, that it was the people at the church. I had so little understanding of myself and church life. It never occurred to me that we wouldn't do anything but simply love each other.

I tried harder and harder, working more and more hours, doing everything any member might suggest. But they were never content with my performance.

I would never have stayed in the ministry without the support of my district superintendent, Lee Sheaffer. Later research would prove that the single most crucial element in women staying in the ministry of the local church is the support of their district superintendent.

Many years later, Reverend Rita Callis recalled the contrasting experiences she had with district superintendents. Rita started ministry as a college student in 1976, serving part-time at the Northumberland Charge assisting the pastor. By the time she graduated from college and started at Wesley Theological Seminary, she was married. But that marriage did not last long. Her D.S. at that time was Reverend Dabney Walters. He supported Rita through this most challenging time. The bishop at that time, Robert Blackburn, was particularly concerned about clergy divorce and had established a process that was more punitive than redemptive. Reverend Walters tried to protect Rita from the hurt of that process. But when Rita moved from Reverend Walters' district to serve High Street United Methodist Church in the Petersburg District, she encountered a D.S. with a different understanding of how to deal with divorce.

At Annual Conference, her new district superintendent talked to her privately behind the platform. Sternly he said, "Reverend Walters told me of your gifts and graces for ministry. That is why I took you on my district. But he failed to tell me you are divorced. I don't want to hear a word about your salary." And with that, he walked away. Rita had been under appointment for seven years but was barely receiving the minimum salary of $14,200. Complaining would serve no purpose. That had been made abundantly clear.

While my acceptance at Round Hill United Methodist Church was mixed, my status in the larger church community was one of celebrity. Like the women who went before me, people came to worship just to see a lady preacher. Other churches invited me to speak at their men's groups, women's groups, and Wednesday night potlucks. When there was a community service at Thanksgiving or during Holy Week, I was the one they wanted to preach. It wasn't that I was a seasoned, gifted preacher like Lillian Russell or Mildred Long, but I was a novelty. Being invited to tell my story so often, I developed a standard speech of about 15 minutes, memorized it, and used it on many occasions.

One evening I was looking through the Cokesbury catalog, clergy apparel section, all male models. I needed a shirt with a clergy collar. I had had some trouble at the intensive care unit at the local hospitals. Only family and clergy were allowed to visit. The staff and volunteers standing guard at the door did not believe I was clergy. They wanted proof. A friend had taken my ordination certificate, made a reduced copy, credit card size, and laminated it. That made no difference to these folks. So I thought a clerical collar might help.

I yelled at my husband in the other room, "What does shirt size 14 ½ mean?"

He yelled back, "You know, it's your neck size."

My neck size? I had no idea what my neck size was. I knew my bust size, dress size, waist, and hip size, but not my neck size. So we measured my neck, 14 ½, and I ordered a white clerical shirt.

When it came in the mail, I immediately tried it on. It fit perfectly around the neck. But the rest of it was like a sack, long with no shape. I hemmed the bottom so it wouldn't hang below my skirts and shortened the sleeves to above the elbow. The collar did help at the hospitals.

One of the clergywomen told this story about clergy collars. "I was working nights at the hospital as a chaplain. I always wore my collar because it immediately identified me when called to a code blue. One morning I was getting on the crowded subway during rush hour. A man bumped into me, and his eyes fixed on my collar. He said, 'Excuse me, Father.'

"Then he took a step back and looked up and down my body, finally ending at my face with a confused look on his face, 'Mother?'" he queried.

The clergywomen loved to tell our stories when we gathered in Winchester at Shenandoah College for our occasional retreats. There were usually five or six of us present. Some were still in college or seminary. They came from all over Virginia. Most, like me, were the only clergywomen in their district and their community. We would drop everything to be together.

Reverend Lee Sheaffer made every effort to be inclusive of the lone clergywoman in his district. At district ministers' meetings, when the talk mentioned "the men and the wives," Lee would correct them to say, "the clergy and their spouses." It was awkward, as their D.S. was correcting them in front of their peers. After six months of this, I felt resentment from some of the clergymen, so I asked Lee not to correct them publicly. He didn't, and they began correcting each other.

By my second year in the Winchester District, Lee had appointed one more clergywoman to the district, Margie Turbyfill (part of a clergy couple). Lee was developing a reputation around the Conference for his support of clergywomen. He reported that at one meeting when he met with a Staff-Parish Relations Committee to talk about a change in pastors, the group said they didn't want a woman; in fact, they would rather have a black pastor than a woman. Lee picked up the phone in the room as if to call the Bishop and said, "That can be arranged." The group immediately changed their mind. Lee appointed the sternest clergyman he knew to straighten out that church about their biases.

Lee often said that all things being equal, if he had a choice between a male or female minister, he would take the woman every time. "They are always well prepared," he argued. Indeed, I found that to be considered as effective as my male colleagues, I had to be much better. So I was always well prepared.

The Pastor-Parish Relations Committee in 1978 recommend I move. Even people on the committee who supported me voted for me to move. They said it was for my own good — they hated to see me mistreated. Lee Sheaffer said he could recommend I stay or move, whatever I wanted. He knew it was hard for me. I still wasn't sure what to do. I prayed and prayed, but no answer came. Finally, Lee said because he was afraid Bob would hurt somebody, he moved me away from Round Hill. Just to clarify the record, I'm confident Bob would not have hurt anybody.

In 1978, after only two years at Round Hill, I went to Trinity United Methodist Church in McLean, Virginia, to serve as their associate pastor. I believe Lee must have talked to the senior pastor there, Reverend Al Stables, because Al welcomed me and treated me as if I had something valuable to offer. Al went through a challenging time my first year there and eventually left the ministry and his wife.

During that same time, Bob and I announced the anticipation of our second child. Chatter about that announcement abounded because of the timing and suspicion raised with the senior pastor's abrupt leaving. The day after Al Stables made his announcement about leaving the ministry, one of the elderly women in the church marched herself into his office and asked him directly, "Preacher, did you get that little girl pregnant?"

That same week I walked into the church kitchen where a group of church women was working, and I overheard their conversation about the same gossipy topic. When they saw me, they abruptly stopped talking and tried to brush it off with laughter.

I said indignantly, "This is not funny. It's insulting to Al and me both." And I stomped out of the kitchen.

As the months went on and I began to "show" even in my preaching robe, one parent of a teenager at the church said, "She should stay at home until after the baby is born. When she stands up there at the pulpit, you can tell that she *did* it. I don't want my children to see that."

During this same time, I received a phone call from a young woman, Susan, who attended worship at Trinity. She wanted me to visit both her and her husband at their home in McLean. We made an appointment, and I drove to their home one evening to visit with them. I didn't know the reason for the visit, only that she and her husband were lawyers.

McLean is one of the wealthiest communities in the country. Susan and her husband, Charles, lived in one of the older, modest homes. I pulled into their gravel driveway, and since it was after dark, I navigated the over-grown bushes and vines by the porchlight. Once inside, Susan got right to the point.

"I've just received an invitation from President Carter to serve as a federal judge."

"Oh my, such an honor. You must be thrilled," I said.

"Maybe I would be, but there's a complication: I am also expecting our first child."

"Then, double congratulations." I looked at both of them to measure their excitement. I knew not every couple was excited about a pregnancy. Charles seemed more thrilled than Susan.

"So, what's the issue?" I asked.

"It's not the invitation from the President or the pregnancy. It's the combination," said Susan. "The timing just seems wrong." She nodded at me. "You're a professional, public, pregnant woman. How do you handle all of that? Should I wait until after the baby is born, telling the President to wait a couple of years?" she asked.

"Why would you want to do that?" I asked.

"Well, just like you, I would wear a black robe, but as you know, it doesn't hide everything. Everyone in the courtroom will know. Will being pregnant make me look vulnerable and less in charge? Plus, I'll need some maternity leave. That will come just a few months after I start. That doesn't seem fair to the court system."

"For me, pregnancy is a power surge. I feel stronger and more in control than ever. This invitation is the opportunity of a lifetime. You can do both." I turned to Charles. "How do you feel about all of this?"

"Never in our wildest dreams did we think this invitation would ever happen to either of us. I'm 100% behind the baby and the assignment. I have no doubts." He smiled at his wife.

We talked some more, and I prayed for them. Susan was one of twenty-three women President Jimmy Carter appointed to the federal court in 1979, a history-making endeavor. She and her baby were seated in a male-dominated judicial bench, diapers and all.

The new senior pastor, Reverend Robert Regan, was terrific to work with. I learned much from him, working with him for three years. But the controversies around motherhood continued even after the birth of our daughter, Jennifer. She was a content baby, so easy to tend to, especially after our experience with our firstborn who had cholic for six very-long-months. So, just two weeks after I gave birth, I came back to work. I put a crib in my office, and when she was hungry, I closed the door to my office, turned my chair around, and breastfed her.

The Lay Leader at the church was the mother of five children who had interrupted her career to tend to her family. She did not like my maternity arrangements and began to express that concern. She asked staff and others if the baby was ever an issue. The church staff recalled one time I had to leave a staff meeting when Jenni started to cry.

The whole issue came to a head when the Staff-Parish Relations Committee invited me to their meeting. They laid out their concerns. Mostly they had to do with the lack of "a profess-ional appearance." A crib in my office and breastfeeding did not convey a professional status—clearly, professionalism defined by men.

I responded, "I have prayed about this, and this is where God has led me. Have you prayed about this?"

The chairman of the committee said, "No, we haven't. Frankly, it didn't occur to me. Don't you think prayer is limiting your resources?"

As if prayer could be a limitation of resources, another member of the committee responded to the chairman's statement,

"I do believe there's scriptural precedence for prayer."

There was more discussion, but I was not budging. The Lay Leader told me, "I had to choose between family and career, and so do you. You can't have both."

The back and forth did not last long. I stood up and said, "I believe the best we can do here is agree to disagree." With that, I walked out of the room and drove home.

The next morning I stood in front of Bob Regan's desk, wagging my finger at him, and said, "If you ever have an issue with me, take it to me first. I don't want to hear about your concerns at a Staff-Parish meeting." Walking out, I regretted the finger-wagging. He was a considerate person and did not deserve my scolding.

While this was 1979, following the influence of the feminist movement, changes were slow coming, especially in the church. It was not unusual for women in the church to work on their marriage, children, and career issues through their relationship with me, like the Lay Leader had done. It could be exhausting.

Wesley Theological Seminary, my alma mater, hired me to teach Field Education. It was a required two-semester course that met every week for three hours. The class was small, 12-15. All had employment in a church. It was my job to help them make the most of their experiences at these churches. Part of that strategy was to visit each one of the students on-site with their supervising pastor present. Those visits took me around Virginia, DC, Maryland, and even Pennsylvania.

I was not adequately prepared for this academic position, having worked as a church pastor for only four years. But Wesley had a growing number of female students, and they wanted at least one woman in this adjunct capacity. It pushed me to clarify and sharpen my awareness and skills. I worked that part-time job in addition to all the responsibilities at the church and home for three years.

After four years at Trinity, I was ready to have "my own church" again. Lee had told me that the appointment after Trinity was pivotal in my moving to a larger church. My goal was to find a healthy mid-size church. There were many of those in Northern Virginia at that time. I talked to my D.S., Reverend Kenneth Whetzel, about Ebenezer United Methodist in Stafford, Virginia. This appointment would be a long commute for Bob, but we had talked about it, and he believed he could make it work. Certainly, it was closer than Round Hill had been.

The D.S. was not familiar with the church, but I had heard that it had a bright future as it was in a rapidly growing area. So Ken Whetzel threw my hat in the ring. Initially, it appeared there would not be much competition. But as other district superintendents did their homework, they too realized the potential and nominated some of their young male rising stars.

When I learned that I was not the one selected to go to Ebenezer but instead was going to Sleepy Hollow in Falls Church, I asked my D.S. to reconsider my appointment. Reconsideration of an appointment was not done often—a bit of an act of treason. It didn't go well. Ken Whetzel reported to me later that Bishop Blackburn responded to my request to have my appointment reconsidered with some hostility. "Is Margaret willing to go anywhere in the conference?"

"I don't believe so, Bishop," Ken reportedly responded.

"Then Margaret's going to Sleepy Hollow!" declared the Bishop, as if Sleepy Hollow was my punishment for not playing by the rules.

And that was the final word. Sleepy Hollow was less than two miles from the house we bought while I was in seminary, and we were living there already as it was an easy commute to Trinity in McLean.

In many ways, it was an ideal appointment. The people there were kind and faithful to their church. It was here that I claimed a verse from Scripture as my mantra when being appointed to a "first appointment church."[4] The Scripture comes from a story in Genesis. After Joseph's brothers sold him into

---

[4] A first appointment church is one that is served by a pastor as their first appointment. My first four appointments were to first appointment churches.

slavery, which led to his imprisonment in Egypt, he was able to say to his brothers, "Man may have intended it for evil, but God intended it for good." In every appointment, God was present in the people, and I experienced resurrection life. Indeed, God intended it for good.

Board of Ordained Ministry

And he said unto me, "My grace is sufficient unto thee,
for my strength is made perfect in weakness."
II Corinthians 12:9 KJV

$\mathcal{I}$n June 1977, I received ordination as an elder and full connection in the Virginia Conference. The approval process had gone smoothly, writing the necessary papers and going through the required interviews with the Conference Board of Ordained Ministry. Because Bob's parents had attended my ordination as a deacon, the plan was to have my parents attend my ordination as an elder. Traveling from Pennsylvania on a Sunday morning, they got as far as Round Hill in time to attend worship. But after lunch, they said they had looked at the map and realized Roanoke, Virginia, was still several hours away. They needed to get back home. Dad had grass to mow.

I was angry and hurt but to no avail. My mother, father, and youngest brother stayed for lunch and a brief visit and then got in the car and drove back to Pennsylvania. I don't think they had any understanding of the significance of ordination in my life. Bob and I packed up our things and our two-year-old son and drove to Roanoke.

Bishop Goodson preferred married couples kneel together for ordination as a symbol of partners in ministry. Bob and I didn't realize this would be the arrangement until Bishop Goodson announced it just minutes before we were to go up on the stage. Both of us kneeling did not correctly reflect our relationship. Bob offered to kneel or not kneel, whatever I wanted. I opted for him to stand next to me with his hand on my hand. This posture symbolized support for me rather than ministry partners. The years in ministry and marriage proved this posture an accurate description of how we worked together.

Each ordinand was allowed to invite one other elder to participate in the ordination by laying on hands. I asked Reverend Betty Jane Clem, one of the very few younger clergywomen in the conference, to participate in my ordination. Bishop Goodson laid his hand on my head and leaned down to speak in my ear. "Is it Kuts or Koots?"

I said, "Neither, it's Kutz, like puts."

Bishop Goodson had a thick neck and several chins. They all jiggled as he shook his head and good naturally growled, "Grrr."

So with his hand on my head, Betty Jane's on my shoulder, and Bob's in my hand. I heard the words, "Margaret T. Kutz, take thou authority to preach the word, administer the sacraments, and order the life of the church. Amen."

There were two other women ordained elder that evening in Roanoke: Sara Hudson and Leontine Kelly. Ordination happened in alphabetical order. Leontine was ordained just before me. "Tinie" was African-American and a widow. Her brother, a United Methodist clergyman from California, stood next to her in support. At the time, I had no idea of the path God had ordained for this older, tiny, African American woman. We had been together several times, and she had shared her powerful story. Already she had become a mother and a power-house of the Holy Spirit in my life.

In July that same year, I received a letter from Bishop Goodson asking me to serve on the Board of Ordained Ministry. It would require two annual commitments of three to four days each plus preparation for those meetings. I called my district superin-tendent, Lee Sheaffer. He told me the drives to Blackstone would help clear my head, and I would be more effective at Round Hill because of this time away. He also conveyed the board needed women on it and that he had recommended me to the Bishop. So I called the Bishop's office and agreed to serve. My commitment was for three years because I was completing the four-year term of Mildred Long, who had not attended any meetings the one year she served. Years later, it became apparent that she changed her mind about serving on the Board when she decided to retire, hoping a younger woman would receive the honor, precisely what happened.

The meetings were held at a large assembly center in Blackstone, Virginia. Being the only woman on this board of thirty-seven people, I had my own bedroom. Clearly, the men were not accustomed to having a woman on their hall, some of them leaving their doors open regardless of their situation. I learned to walk down the hall with my eyes straight ahead, never looking to the right or the left, and because there were no locks on the doors, to wedge a chair under the doorknob to my room to be sure no one came into my room.

Initially, I was assigned to the committee considering theology. But after the first round of interviews, I asked to be switched to the committee on call. The interview teams for each committee were generally three people. One served as chair, but all participated fully. Many people were applying for ordination during those years. We often started interviews immediately following breakfast, stopping only for lunch and dinner, finally ending at 9:00 or 10:00 P.M., creating extremely long, tense days. There were many side conversations to which I was vaguely aware but not privy. There was so much I didn't understand. Primary among those uncertainties was who to trust. I knew not every man on the board welcomed my presence, but clergy have a warm, gracious smile that can be applied when needed.

During meals, if I was the first to sit at a table, I was often the only one to sit at that table. I learned to sit at a table with people already seated there. I also learned to ask for permission as the men often saved seats for each other. I mostly listened.

Some of the men were very courteous to me, including me in their conversations. Some treated me like a sibling. I remember

Reverend Gerald Fink particularly. He liked to sit down next to me, slap his hand on my knee and say, "Brother Klutz, how are you?" Or worse yet, "Brother Klutz, you're just one of the boys." Ministry had been a boys' club for a long time. They struggled to include me.

At our second meeting in 1979, there was a celebration of George Lightner's retirement. As a member of the Conference staff assigned to work with the Board of Ordained Ministry, George had been a vital part of the Board. His favorite celebrity was Dolly Parton. The men arranging the celebration asked if I would carry in the cake. My physical appearance has no resemblance to Dolly Parton, none. And I had no idea what the protocol was for any of this. With no time to consider and no one to talk to, I said yes.

They played one of Dolly's big hits while I brought in the cake and set it down in front of Reverend Lightner. The men around the table were laughing, applauding, hooting. After I set the cake down, I did something spontaneous, totally wrong. I pinched my blouse with my index finger and thumb of both hands and pulled it out to make myself better resemble Ms. Parton's most apparent attribute. There was no response, and I have always hoped that no one even noticed. After that, I didn't trust myself with the men during the informal times. I would go to my room and put the chair under the doorknob.

Our second child, Jennifer, was born in September 1979. By the time the Board met in January, I was still breastfeeding. My mother flew from Pittsburgh to Washington D.C. to go with me to Blackstone and take care of Jennifer. It was my mother's first time to be away from my father overnight except when she was hospitalized. If Jennifer wasn't sleeping, my mother had her in the area where the candidates waited between interviews. It was an excellent way to reduce their anxiety. When Jennifer was hungry, my mother would knock on my interview room door, and I would leave to feed her. I had gone through the Board without the presence of one woman and knew how difficult that was. I was determined to have every female candidate see a female face.

My years at Wesley Theological Seminary had taught me

well the importance of gender-inclusive language. When candidates used inclusive language in their papers, I commended them. Initially, the other members of my interview team would apologize for me. I assured them an apology wasn't necessary, that if a candidate had used inclusive language, they would gladly receive my commendation. Eventually, my team grew in their sensitivity around this issue to the point they would commend candidates for their use of gender-inclusive language. I was making progress.

After the initial three-year commitment, the Bishop asked me to serve another quadrennium, and I agreed. At the end of that second term, after I had been on the board for seven years, I motioned that gender-inclusive language be required in all papers. Reverend Edward Ridout, the board's chairperson, said he agreed with the motion but believed it would not pass. He suggested I change "required" to "recommended." I calculated that I had gained enough respect among the group to have the motion pass as required. So I made the motion that gender-inclusive language be required in all papers. It passed.

One of my biggest challenges with the Board of Ordained Ministry happened with a friend. Being the only woman on the board, I felt a strong sense of responsibility to make their process as fair as possible. A friend, Karen, was appearing for interviews. Ahead of each interview, a board member reported to the interview team that Karen had a delinquent car loan with the Conference Credit Union. Each of those interview teams then asked Karen about this. It threw Karen off to such a degree that the board did not recommend her for ordination.

The reporting of her delinquent loan was wrong on two accounts: 1) the information was confidential to Karen and the Credit Union, and 2) the information was incorrect as Karen's car loan was not delinquent. It was clear that Karen had not been approved because she was ambushed with false accusations creating her defensive stature.

When I raised concerns and was hushed, I raised them again more forcefully but was quieted again. I then objected a third time after dinner and was soundly silenced. There was a wall of protection ("clerical wall") around the people who had falsely accused Karen. They argued that she was not denied a recommendation because of her car loan but because of her defensive and angry attitude. I argued that these false accusations had set her up to be defensive and angry, but the male voices were loud and final.

I went to my room as soon as the evening meeting was over. I cried well into the night. I called Karen to apologize. She assured me that it wasn't my fault, but I knew I had failed her.

The next day I went immediately from the Board of Ordained Ministry meeting to a clergywomen's retreat. I tried to share my anguish with my sisters, but each time I tried, my throat swelled up to the point I could not speak, could barely breathe. I honestly had been silenced. I'm not a person given to this type of physical manifestations of mental trauma; to the best of my recollection, this is the only incident like this in my entire life.

#

I include this journal entry written many years after my time on the Board of Ordained Ministry, but the spirit behind it was born in that period of my life.

Dear Mary,

I look at the nativity scenes. They are everywhere—at home, church, stores and on cards and in books—everywhere. Most look very Caucasian; some represent a broader humanity, some caricatures, Disney-like. Some are glossy, most in color, some of wood, ceramic, plastic, corn husks.

But the one thing they all have in common is this: you are the only woman in the scene. Some have made the angels female, but that is not likely or accurate. When the Savior of the world was born, you were the only woman present.

Giving birth is never easy. Your first child's circumstances had to be especially difficult—away from home and family and the Nazareth mid-wife. There are still thousands of women who every day give birth in exceptionally difficult circumstances. Some things haven't changed much.

But, Mary, some things have changed, and that is what I want to tell you. There are other women at the manger now—you are not alone anymore! Sometimes we feel alone, but we are not. It is still hard to give birth to salvation, to be the carrier of the Good News. But I just want to let you know that you are not the only woman anymore.

And these women are of many nations, races, and ages. Some are married, and some single. Some have children; some do not. But we all hold the Redeemer in our care, and our souls magnify our God.

So, I just want to thank you, Mary, for being there with all those men, for holding your own, for holding a place for us. I just want to let you know you are not alone anymore.

Marg (Advent, 2011)

#   #   #

There is more to my story, so much more. I continued to pastor churches in the Virginia Conference as assigned by the various bishops. I did turn down an appointment three separate times. The first time was when asked to serve as the assistant to Reverend Beverly Watkins, district superintendent of the Alexandria District. He is the very person on the District Board of Ordained Ministry in 1974 who demanded that I write the letter promising to itinerate or surrender my credentials. At that time, my district superintendent told me that if I did not take this appointment with Reverend Watkins, I might not receive one at all. I decided that I would rather not have an appointment than work with him. I did not trust him. The bishop found another place for me to serve, and I did not have to surrender my credentials.

The other two times I did not accept an invitation to take an appointment was when invited to serve as a district superintendent. The first came from Bishop Stockton. With his invitation, the caveat was his insistence that my husband commute every day from Washington, D.C. to Harrisonburg, Virginia, or Ashland, Virginia. Bishop Stockton felt my husband needed to attend charge conferences with me. Both of these communities are hours away from D.C., even without traffic.

The second invitation to serve on the bishop's cabinet came from Bishop Charlene Kammerer. By this time, I was sixty years old, and I could think of no better way to complete my career than serving as a local church pastor. I felt confident and fulfilled in that role.

In 2001 I celebrated my 25th anniversary in ministry. The church I was serving at that time, Wellspring United Methodist Church in Williamsburg, Virginia, hosted a celebration. Reverend Rita Callis was present, as were laity from churches where I had served as their pastor. Again, the Virginia Advocate invited me to share my story. In terms of being a pioneer, I wrote,

> I never asked to be a pioneer. Sometimes I even resented it. People would worship with us just to see a woman pastor and hear a woman preach. On the way out, they would touch me (never touched one, either, I suppose) and tell me why they had come and then add some commentary like "You're not bad!"
>
> I felt like a monkey in the zoo. Like I told a more conservative member, "My earthly father determined my gender (you know, the Y chromosome thing), and my heavenly Father determined my call." She said she couldn't argue with that.
>
> The part of pioneering I chose, I love: leading the church differently. I love the challenge of breaking up the seats of power (finance, trustees, etc.), of creating a community of trust and prayerful discernment, of giving the church back to the ownership and control of God. Now, that is plowing new fields! I also love "thinking out of the box" about Bible and theology and presenting it to people in a way that makes sense. It's like planting seeds in great soil. Creating worship that makes people laugh, cry, and want to change is exhilarating, like watching crops grow where they have never grown before.
>
> Now, I genuinely do not see myself as a pioneer simply because I am female. I have lived on the frontier so long that it

surprises me when people are surprised that I'm not right out of seminary or "have my own church" rather than being an associate pastor.

God is faithful and sustains people, men and women, called to pioneer new territories for Jesus Christ.

When I retired in 2013 at the age of sixty-five, I had served as an elder in full connection under appointment to the local church longer than any other women in Virginia Methodism. Women of our generation were often called pioneers, and we were. But the scouts, the ones who traveled first in unexplored territory, were Lillian Russell and Mildred Long. I never met either one of them, a loss I didn't understand until I started the process of writing this book. It is in researching Reverends Russell and Long that I realized what all the clergywomen in Virginia missed. I would have been a better pastor and a better person had I known these two most incredible women who, against all odds, fulfilled their high calling in Christ.

The world is a better place because—*Nevertheless, They Preached.*

Appendix
Additional Information About
Lillian and Mildred

Lillian stayed close to her family even when she moved to the parsonage in Petersburg. They considered her their family pastor officiating at Pete's wedding to Iris Wallace in 1946 and brother Ernest to Sarah Dozier in 1972. She celebrated with her older sister "Boots" when Boots graduated from college, got married, and began teaching in Falls Church, Virginia, eventually becoming a school principal. She also maintained contact with Boots' husband, Fenner Hazlegrove, as he successfully pursued politics in Falls Church, becoming the mayor. She went to as many softball games as she could to see Pete and Polly play. Lillian celebrated with them when they were inducted into the Central Virginia American Softball Association Hall of Fame. Years ago, her parents had taken in and raised a nephew and niece, Shep and Anna. Of course, Lillian kept up with their activities as well. Then as her siblings married, along came another generation of nieces and nephews. Four of her siblings had children. The Russell family became well known in Richmond, Petersburg, Northern Virginia, and beyond. They sought further education and ways to use that education to better the world.

Lillian loved buying and wrapping Christmas presents for everyone. Because there were so many people to buy for, gifts were small. For years Lillian proudly purchased white handkerchiefs for everyone, sometimes doing needlework to make them more personal. But eventually, they told her the family secret: these lovely hankies were just stacking up in their drawers, never used.

Whatever she purchased or made for them, wrapping them was the best part. In earlier years, the dining room table, which had served as Revival Grand Central Station, was cleared to make room for wrapping. Lillian and her mother, Goldie, spent hours wrapping all the gifts. It was one of Lillian's favorite things in the whole year—it brought her such joy.

The male clergy of those decades, 1940 through 1970, described both Mildred and Lillian as oddities. The almost side-show element of the revival days with a young woman evangelist seemed to follow them. The majority of clergy didn't recollect any memories of the two women. Even those who served on the same districts didn't remember them. It was as if these women were invisible.

The few clergymen who took the time to get to know them had strikingly different memories. One minister, after witnessing her lead a funeral service, described Lillian as "dignified."

Mildred exhibited more defensiveness around her male colleagues. Several ministers described her as "stiff, formal, stand-offish." The laity in their churches, the ones who knew them best, described both of them as dedicated, loving, deeply spiritual, and great preachers.

Lillian loved words; she loved the power of words. She understood that the Bible is the Word of God, that Jesus is the Word. In all manner of speech, Lillian carefully selected her words. Not one for idle chatter, she valued the power of words to build up and tear down. This orator particularly appreciated poetry. She read it often and almost always included a poem in her sermons. Many preachers followed the sermon outline of three points, a poem, and a prayer. Sometimes Lillian used poetry from others, and sometimes she wrote her own. In 1961 Miss Russell wrote this poem for the funeral of a twenty-five-year-old woman.

> *She was so very young, we say, and surely that is true;*
> *Still, God needs the young in the homeland.*
> *He said to her, "I have need of you."*
> *She loved life, this we know, life boundless and free.*
> *In the Father's House of health and love*
> *She will live eternally.*
> *She loved beauty in all things, with quiet dignity.*

Those who knew best the things of God
Sing "How beautiful Heaven must be."
All things that to her were dear of life and peace
The Master now will daily provide
In measures that never cease.
She bore without complaint, her portion of joy and pain.
No suffering, hurt, disappointment, or harm will ever be here
again.
Since by death alone, our spirits are really set free.
There is a blessing to be found in death.
That is, this life could never be.
She was God's before she was ours – then surely we can say
"We give her back to Him who gave her in love.
And in love, hath called her away."

Lillian was not a political person, yet aware of the alliances other pastors made to position themselves for appointments at a higher salary. She knew having college and seminary degrees were generally rewarded with larger churches and sometimes a cabinet position. She had had conversations with her family about this but had no interest in climbing the ladder. Lillian felt so honored to be the pastor at Blandford Church and wanted nothing more than that. She participated in the correspondence course at Emory, giving her the education needed to be effective and maintain her status in the conference. Not having a driver's license limited her educational options, but the correspondence course was more than sufficient.

Sunday nights in the Russell family were full of Christian fun. Three Sunday nights a month, they loaded up the car and headed out to one of the area's nursing homes. But the fourth Sundays and the occasional fifth Sunday, the extended family gathered for the evening at E.W. and Goldie's home. Aunts, uncles, cousins, nieces, and nephews traveled from central, eastern, and northern Virginia, bringing food to share. Even without card playing or dancing, it was loud and wonderful.

When she was free from responsibilities at her church, it was the perfect ending to the week.

The majority of the Russell family were fun-loving folks, full of jokes and lots of laughter. Lillian tended to be more subdued. While she had a good sense of humor, she seldom made jokes or told funny stories, but she often chuckled at the stories others told. Some funny things happened in her week; religious life was not without its humor. But Lillian didn't feel at liberty to share stories of her flock. So she mostly listened, enjoying every moment of this wonderful time together.

Nancy Cleveland White
Obituary, News Advance, November 9, 2014

Nancy Cleveland White of Lynchburg died Tuesday, November 4, 2014, at her residence. She was born in Lynchburg on March 14, 1927, a daughter of the late Lemuel Wills White Sr. and Nannie Frazier White. Nancy was the youngest of their eight children and was the last one surviving.

Nancy studied at Ferrum College, Lynchburg College, and Duke University. She earned her divinity degree from Union Theological Seminary in Richmond, where she was the first full-time female student. Nancy became a Methodist minister and served a number of churches, often as their first woman pastor. She later earned her master's degree in social work from Richmond Professional Institute, now part of Virginia Commonwealth University. She was a local social worker for the City of Lynchburg and later for Virginia's Commonwealth, from where she retired. Nancy also taught sociology at Lynchburg College and established the social work degree program at Longwood University. After she retired from the state, Nancy returned to the ministry. She also conducted Bible study programs at numerous churches.

Nancy is survived by Mary Ellen Hylton, her companion of 44 years. Also, surviving are three nieces, three nephews, her church family, and many friends. The family wishes to express their appreciation for the loving care provided by hospice and Generation Solutions. A funeral service will be conducted at Tharp Funeral Home in Lynchburg on Monday, November 10, 2014, at 11 A.M. with Pastor Al Stewart officiating. Interment will follow at the Presbyterian Cemetery. Those wishing to make a memorial contribution may consider Forest Community Church or the American Cancer Society.

Cynthia Corley
The Rest of Her Story

Reverend Cynthia Corley heard the phone ring in her parsonage study. *I wonder who that could be. I need just a few more minutes, and I'll complete Sunday's sermon.* She glanced at Sunday's bulletin and noted the sermon title, "Wrong Signs." It was based on the lectionary reading for the day, Mark 13:1-8. Jesus was warning his disciples about signs that will not predict the end of the age. She enjoyed creating titles for her sermons, but she wasn't sure this was one of her best. Too late now; the bulletins were already printed.

As she got out of her chair, the phone rang a third time. She cleared her throat and picked up the receiver. "Hello, this is Pastor Cynthia at St. Paul's United Methodist Church. How can I help you?"

"Good morning, Miss Corley. This is Bishop Blackburn. How are you this morning?"

Cynthia's heart went from idle to overdrive. Why was the bishop calling her? Quickly recovering her composure, she said in a cheery voice, "Good morning, Bishop Blackburn. I'm very well. How are you?"

"I'm also well. I was wondering if you could come to my office next Monday morning. There's something I want to talk to you about. Is your calendar open?"

Cynthia had no idea what she had on her calendar Monday morning, but she knew she would be in the bishop's office regardless. "Yes, sir, I can."

Cynthia's mind spun even faster than the rhythm of her heartbeat. *What can this possibly be about? Has someone issued such a severe charge against me that it's gotten to the bishop's desk?* She searched the files in her mind, clicking through people who might be unhappy with her. Somebody always complained about something, but nothing that required the bishop's attention.

"And, Cynthia, except for your parents, let's keep this to ourselves. There's no need for alarm, but for right now, this is confidential. Understood?"

"Understood, absolutely, sir."

"Okay, I'll see you Monday morning around 10:00 A.M. Is that okay?" the bishop asked.

"Yes, 10:00 A.M. is fine. Thank you."

Cynthia heard the phone on the other end of the line click. *What in the world is this about? I'm just thirty-six years old and was ordained only six years ago. My career in ministry could be really short. The bishop said I couldn't talk to anybody but my parents about this. I think I'll start with my heavenly Father.* She bowed her head and, after several deep breaths, she prayed. "Heavenly Father, I have no idea what is going on, but You do. Help me. Calm my nerves and let me get through Sunday. Prepare me for what lies ahead. In Your Son's name, Jesus, I pray. Amen."

Cynthia then called her mother. "You'll never guess who just called me!" Before her mother had a chance to answer, Cynthia continued. "The bishop. He wants me to go to his office Monday morning of next week so we can talk. Mother, I'm scared to death. What in the world have I done?"

"Now, Cynthia, calm down. I'm sure everything is fine. He probably just wants to ask you to do something, maybe serve on some conference committee, something like that."

"Do you think so? But what if that isn't it? What if I've done something really wrong?"

"Well, can you think of anything? You've never mentioned anything to me that's out of the ordinary."

"You're probably right. Maybe the bishop just wants me to serve on a committee. I'm already on the Board of Ordained Ministry, but they're trying to get women on all the conference committees. "

"I'm sure that's it."

"Thanks, Mother. I'll call you Monday after I meet with the bishop."

Cynthia tried to stay busy to get her mind off the Monday appointment, but she couldn't get the uncertainty to go away. Just when she thought she was fine, it would grip her like a vice, and her mind entertained all kinds of possibilities. Not everybody at her church was happy with her. Maybe one of them made up something and reported it. That happened all the time in church life.

After the longest three days of her life, Cynthia found herself in the bishop's office's waiting area. The drab paneled walls and tan carpet offset green drapes on the windows. The bishop's secretary, Estelle Pruden, a pleasant young woman, greeted Cynthia from behind her neat, modest desk. "You must be Cynthia Corley. Please, have a seat. The bishop will be with you shortly. He's expecting you."

Growing up in a military family, Cynthia knew to be punctual, even early, and she was early for this appointment. But it wasn't long before the door to the bishop's office opened, and out stepped Bishop Blackburn. This slender man in his sixties, his hair still brown, greeted Cynthia with a smile, "Good morning, Cynthia. Please, come in."

Cynthia stood up, paused to check her legs' reliability, and followed the bishop into his office. The bishop's office repeated his secretary's office's color scheme with dark paneling, brown carpet, and green drapes. The only significant difference—the carpet was dark brown. The large executive desk and leather chair plus two wing chairs completed the earth-tone décor. Books filled the bookcases around the room. Once they were both seated, each in one of the wing chairs, the bishop spoke. "How was your drive here this morning? I know the traffic on Route 64 can be a real headache in rush hour."

"I allowed for traffic. Luckily, there was very little."

"That's good to hear. How's your work at St. Paul's? I hear many good things about your ministry there."

Cynthia was relieved to hear that but wondered all the more why she was there. "Thank you. I'm having a good time at St. Paul's. They're a good congregation with much promise."

"That's good to hear. The reason I asked you to come here today is I want you to consider the superintendency."

Surely my hearing has gone bad. What did the bishop just say?

I'd better not respond until I'm sure what he's saying.

"Several districts will require a new superintendent next year, and I'd like you to assume one of those positions."

Cynthia felt she was standing on a tennis court, holding a baseball bat, and somebody just threw a bowling ball at her. She never saw this coming and was in no way prepared to respond. Her next words just tumbled out. "But there are so many people with more experience than me. I don't think I'm ready for this."

"Cynthia, I can appreciate your reluctance, but I've been watching you, as have others on the cabinet. You'll get advice from all of us. We'll help you be successful." Bishop Blackburn's voice held a fatherly tone. Cynthia saw support in his eyes.

Cynthia remembered leading a Bible study at Annual Conference the previous year. *I guess that was part of my test. I don't know how to answer.* "Bishop, can I pray about this?"

"Certainly, I'd expect that. Take some time, then, within the next week, call me with your answer. If you have any questions, just give me a call. Estelle will be glad to put you through."

With that, Cynthia left and drove home, praying all the way. She prayed off and on the rest of the day. Her mind was telling her no; there would be plenty of time for her to serve as a superintendent. If she could wait another ten years she would be more experienced, more mature. She would tell the bishop she wanted to wait.

Sunday morning, Cynthia prayed, "Lord, I need Your wisdom. Please, God, tell me what to do." Then she turned on the radio in her bedroom. A preacher was reading from I Kings 3.

God said, "Ask what I shall give you." And Solomon said, "O Lord my God, thou hast made thy servant king in place of David, my father, although I am but a little child; I do not know how to go out or come in. And thy servant is in the midst of thy people whom thou hast chosen, a great people, that cannot be numbered or counted for multitude. Give thy servant, therefore, an understanding mind to govern thy people, that I may discern between good and evil; for who is able to govern this thy great people?" It pleased the Lord that Solomon had asked this. And God said, "I give you a wise and discerning mind." (KJV)

Cynthia nearly fell to her knees. God had asked both Solomon and Cynthia to lead. Both had prayed for wisdom. Through this radio broadcast, God had answered her prayer, given her wisdom to respond to the bishop. The next day she called Bishop Blackburn and told him she accepted his invitation. The bishop told her not to tell anyone except her parents for three months. At that point, the bishop himself would publicly-announce the news.

Bishop Blackburn instructed Cynthia to send a picture of herself to him to use in the *Virginia Advocate*. Cynthia sent a passport photo. After receiving it, he told her he wasn't pleased with it because she wasn't smiling and asked her to have another one taken. So she got her hair and makeup professionally done and had Caston Studios in Richmond take several pictures. She selected one and brought it to the bishop.

In March 1986, the *Virginia Advocate* carried the announcement of the first female district superintendent in the history of the Virginia Conference. Cynthia held that honor but missed the distinction of being the first in the jurisdiction. The bishop in North Carolina had announced the first woman in his conference three hours earlier.

All across the conference, preachers were calling and congratulating Cynthia. Before the official word was out, rumors were rampant. Some said to her, "Remember me when you come into your kingdom." They hoped that she would appoint them to a church with greater status and more salary when she held a position of power.

Not everyone was pleased with this appointment. Bishop Blackburn showed Cynthia a letter printed on blue paper, unsigned. "Cynthia, I want you to know that not everyone approves my appointment of you to the cabinet. This letter is from somebody, probably clergy, probably male, in our conference. He wrote that you're too young, that you haven't paid your dues, that there are others more deserving than you. He said you leap-frogged over others."

"So what happens now, Bishop?" Cynthia asked.

"Well, I could write something in the *Advocate* explaining my actions, but, frankly, Cynthia, it doesn't deserve a response. Progress always brings resistance. My spirit and my observations tell me that you're the right person at the right time."

Cynthia was relieved that her bishop had so much confidence in her. She came to remember that letter as "the blue letter."

Not long after Cynthia moved into the Petersburg District parsonage, she received a Mickey Mouse stuffed animal holding two helium balloons from Reverend Rhonda VanDyke-Colby. Rhonda knew that Cynthia was a big Disney fan. The clergywomen surrounded her with support. Every year at Annual Conference for the next five years, a clergywoman daily left a small gift at her designated chair. Some days it was balloons, other days cookies or flowers. She never knew who put them there. It was organized by the Clergywomen's Collective, a group formed to support clergywomen and work for justice in the Virginia Conference.

The summer went by without any significant issues. Emma Jean Nockengost, the district secretary, had seventeen years of experience in her position, and she used that experience to guide Cynthia through the transitions of her new duties. Emma Jean had a map of the district with all the churches marked. She walked Cynthia through the district committees' structure, the district finances, regular office hours for the superintendent, district politics, and race sensitivities in Southside Virginia.

One of the issues the secretary was less sure about was fashion. Cynthia sought advice on clothing appropriate for a member of the cabinet. She turned to Bishop Blackburn. He suggested she get a Joseph A. Banks catalog. There were a couple of pages in that catalog with women's clothing, enough to provide Cynthia some guidance.

The fall brought charge conference season. Cynthia held a

meeting at each of the fifty charges on the Petersburg District. Sunday through Thursday nights, she was out driving the country roads. Sometimes on Sundays, she had three charge conferences, two in the afternoon and one in the evening. Every charge conference began with a brief worship service of prayer, hymns, Scripture, and proclamation. Sunday mornings, she often visited churches where a local pastor required her evaluation of his or her effectiveness in preaching and leading worship. On other Sundays, she attended worship in churches where she had received complaints and wanted to assess the situation. Some Sundays, she just slept in, exhausted from the week.

#   #   #

"Bishop Blackburn, good morning." Cynthia was in the bishop's office in Richmond.

"Cynthia! So good to see you. Happy New Year. How are you?"

"Well, that's why I'm here. It's January, and I'm more than half done with my first year in this position. In my opinion, *it's* going all right, but *I'm* not doing all that well. I came to ask you if I can quit." Cynthia tried to calm the quiver in her voice.

"Please, have a seat, and let's see if we can work this out." He sat in the chair in front of his desk and motioned to Cynthia to sit in the chair next to him. Once they were both settled, Bishop Blackburn asked, "How did your charge conferences go?"

"Pretty well. As you know, I had fifty of them. Most went without a hitch, but a few were, let's say, interesting."

"Tell me more."

"Most of the pastors were well prepared, but, as you would guess, some were not. One pastor came in with a knapsack of papers. He dumped them on the table as if to say, 'Here are my reports.'"

"Oh my, what did you do?"

"I didn't want to embarrass him in front of his church people, so I suggested we begin with refreshments and fellowship. The pastor and I stayed in the sanctuary sorting the papers while everybody else went into the fellowship hall. We got his papers sorted enough to conduct the Charge Conference business."

"Did you say anything to him?"

"Oh, yes. I told him that he could never do this again. He had to have his reports organized, copied, and in order. I was firm with him."

"Good for you. You handled it perfectly. So, what else is going on? Did any of your charge conferences have conflict?"

"Yeah, for sure. At one church, there's a big rift between the older members and the younger ones. When we got to the Nominations Committee report, every name on the list was from the older group. I asked, as I always do, are there any other nominations from the floor. It turned out that the younger people had put together their own slate of officers, even made copies of it. So we voted for each position with a show of hands, and the younger people were elected with few exceptions. They had done their homework."

"Did it end there?"

"No, sir. It's still going on. I'm still getting letters complaining about how I handled the meeting, that I should never have allowed the second slate to be considered. But I pointed out to them the rules in our *Discipline*. You know, sometimes that book is more important at a charge conference than the Bible!"

"True, but let's not repeat that out of this office."

Cynthia and Bishop Blackburn both laughed.

"Are you feeling the support of the other ministers?"

"Definitely. One of them told me that a group of the pastors, I think it was Roy Creech, John Crawford, and Tom Dunkum, got together and committed to each other to support me publicly and privately in every way and speak out if they heard anything negative. Their support has been tremendous." Cynthia smiled broadly.

"I'm so glad to hear all of this. Then why are you even considering stepping off the cabinet?" Bishop Blackburn leaned forward toward Cynthia.

Cynthia looked out the window, then down at her hands folded in her lap. Her voice was quiet, and she spoke slowly. "I think it's because I'm so spiritually empty." She swallowed before continuing. "I miss the rhythm of weekly sermon preparation, that discipline of digging into Scripture to find a fresh word from God. I miss the rhythm of the liturgical year, moving through Advent to Epiphany to Lent and Easter. I think it became undeniable at Christmas. I love being in the church leading the Christmas Eve services with communion, candles, and carols." Cynthia paused, slumped her shoulders, and said, "My spirit is running on empty."

"Cynthia, you're so insightful. What you are describing is an issue for most pastors who take an appointment outside the local church. You're wise to recognize it, especially so early in your tenure."

Cynthia looked up from her hands to her bishop.

"I can tell you what I did," said Bishop Blackburn. "I tried to attend an Ash Wednesday service, Holy Week services, and Christmas Eve services at one of the larger churches where there are good preaching and music."

Bishop Blackburn spoke in a gentle voice. "Cynthia, you're doing fine. The first year is always difficult. Just get through Easter and, if you still want to leave, we can talk about it then. How does that sound?"

"All right, Bishop. I'll try to get through until then, but if I still feel the same way I do now, I may want to go back to the local church."

Cynthia took the bishop's advice and found it extremely helpful in her own spiritual life. By the time Easter came and went, she was committed to staying on the cabinet.

#   #   #

The cabinet of eighteen district superintendents and the bishop met regularly at the United Methodist Assembly Center in Blackstone, Virginia. The Assembly Center had been a girls' finishing school, but during World War II, the U.S. military established Fort Pickett in Blackstone, and the school closed. Parents did not want their girls dating men preparing to go off to war. The Methodists bought the school, one large brick building comprised of dorm rooms, classrooms, dining hall, kitchen, gymnasium, auditorium, and swimming pool. With some modifications, Methodists in Virginia converted the school into a conference center.

During breaks in their long meetings at the Assembly Center, the cabinet had become accustomed to using both the men's and women's restrooms. It simply expedited things. But with Cynthia in the mix, they had to develop a new practice. They waited until she walked out of the ladies' room, and then they used both restrooms dubbing the ladies' room "the laddies' room." Bishop Blackburn sometimes referred to the eighteen cabinet members as "Snow White and the Seventeen Dwarves."

"Good morning, Cynthia. How was your night?" David Balcom, superintendent of the Alexandria District, sat across from Cynthia at the breakfast table in the basement dining hall of the Blackstone Assembly Center.

"The bed was a bit lumpy, but other than that, I slept fine. How about you?"

"The guy next door kept me awake much of the night with his snoring, so I'm a little groggy this morning."

"I have a suite to myself; snoring is not an issue for me unless it's my own," Cynthia said with a chuckle. "One advantage of being the only female on the cabinet."

"Speaking of being the only woman, can I be of any assistance to you in terms of appointments? We start this morning. It can be brutal."

"Sure. I'm all ears, and I'll take any advice I can get. Shoot."

Nevertheless, She Preached

About a quarter of the fifty pastors in Cynthia's district would be asking to move to a different church, hopefully a larger church with a bigger salary. Some would stay in her district, but most would move to another district. This conversation with a seasoned member of the cabinet was an answer to many prayers.

"The bishop will start at the top of the master list, top salaries first. I don't think you have anybody on the first page. But that creates an advantage for you—gives you a chance to observe."

"Yeah, I don't have anybody until page three."

"Being brand new on the cabinet, you have both an advantage and disadvantage. Your advantage is that you don't owe anybody anything from last year. The disadvantage—"

Cynthia interrupted. "Nobody owes me anything from last year."

"Exactly. If you have somebody on your moving list who's known as effective, use that person as a bartering chip for somebody you want to bring on your district."

"Okay, I can think of two strong possibilities."

"Now, don't have this conversation in the cabinet meeting. That's a big no-no. Do this in the bathroom."

"Excuse me, the bathroom?"

"Oh, yeah, I forgot. We make most of our high-salary appointments and complicated appointments outside our meetings, generally in the men's room. You'll have to find another place. Anyway, let's say you want John Wesley from my district, and you have Charles Wesley in your district, both with recognized skills. So, you come to me and talk about Charles and how good he would be at Aldersgate Church in my district. I agree that's a good match. Then you mention that you're willing to do that if you can have John Wesley go to your district at Epworth Church. I agree with that. Now we have two gifted pastors nominated for two strong churches."

"Well, that sounds pretty simple. So, what happens in the cabinet meeting?"

"When Aldersgate comes up at the cabinet meeting, you nominate Charles and share all the gifts and graces he would bring to that church. The bishop will ask me what I think since Aldersgate Church is in my district. If I agree, then it's pretty much a done deal."

"I get it. When Epworth Church comes up for discussion, you nominate John, I agree, and deal made," Cynthia said.

"Made in heaven," David said.

"I already have some ideas, and I'm going to start my negotiations right now. Tom Coffman and Farmville District, here I come. Pray for me," Cynthia said to David and winked.

With that, Cynthia got up from her half-eaten breakfast and walked to the table where Tom Coffman was eating his breakfast. She pulled up a chair, and the negotiations began.

#   #   #

"Ouch, Samson, that hurt." Cynthia was at home, lying on her sofa. Her cat, Samson, had just walked across her chest. Cynthia touched the area that hurt and felt a small lump. Never one for doctors, Cynthia sought advice from friends and was advised to see a doctor. She did and learned from a needle biopsy that she had breast cancer. In May of 1990, at age 40, she had a lumpectomy and radiation for breast cancer. Being the only woman on the cabinet was never lonelier.

The cabinet supported Cynthia with cards, but most other typical gestures of support such as hugs, flowers, conversation, or food brought to the house just seemed inappropriate for a man to offer a woman. Some of the wives of the cabinet members did offer Cynthia what the men felt they could not.

Then, in August, she learned she had cervical cancer. At her age, with no special men in her life, she opted for a hysterectomy. She waited until November for this surgery, after charge conferences were complete. While Cynthia was in the hospital for surgery, Reverend Rita Callis brought her flowers, and the Clergywomen's Collective also had flowers delivered.

Nevertheless, She Preached

The prayers and gifts helped, but Cynthia lived those months in fear and loneliness. She longed for the support a congregation provides its pastor in times like this.   *It truly is lonely at the top*, she thought.

#   #   #

Cynthia continued as the Petersburg district superintendent for six years, the full extent of the time the Book of Discipline permitted her to hold this position. She wanted to extend her tenure but could not. In 1991, the bishop appointed Reverend Barbara Barrow to the cabinet. Cynthia was able to mentor Barbara, and the now "sixteen dwarves" were accustomed to not using both the men's and the women's restrooms during breaks from their meetings. Barbara and Cynthia made a couple of appointment deals in the women's restroom. Women had joined the cabinet and were there to stay.

Glossary of Methodist Terms
From the 1948 *Book of Discipline*
of The Methodist Church

Accepted supply pastor
A person holding a local preacher's license who has been recommended by the Annual Conference Committee on Accepted Supply Pastors and has been accepted by vote of the Annual Conference as eligible for an appointment during the ensuing year as the supply pastor of a charge.

Charge, pastoral
One or more churches organized under the Discipline with a single Quarterly Conference, and to which a minister has been duly appointed as the preacher in charge or pastor.

Circuit
Two or more local churches which are joined together for pastoral supervision, constituting one pastoral charge.

Conference, Annual
The basic administrative body in The Methodist Church, having supervision over the church's affairs in a specific territory, as established by the Jurisdictional or Central Conference. Also, the territory is administered by such a body.

Conference, District
As assembly which is held annually in each district where authorized by the Annual Conference. It includes lay and

ministerial representatives from each church and performs the duties assigned to it.

Conference, General

The legislative body for the entire church, meeting every four years, and having full legislative powers over all connectional matters. It is composed of elected representatives, ministerial and lay, from all the Annual Conferences.

Conference, Quarterly

The governing body of the pastoral charge

Credentials

The official documents certifying ministerial ordination.

Deacon

A person who has fulfilled the requirements for election to the order of deacon, as set forth in the Discipline, has been elected to that office by an Annual Conference, has taken the vows prescribed, and has been ordained by the laying on of the hands of a bishop.

Deacon, local

A local preacher who has been ordained a deacon but is not a member of the traveling ministry.

Discipline

The official and published statement of the Constitution and laws of The Methodist Church, its rules or organization and procedure, the description of administrative agencies and their foundation, and the Ritual.

District

The major administrative subdivision of an Annual Conference, established by the Annual Conference and formed by the bishop.

It comprises a number of pastoral charges and is under the supervision of a district superintendent.

District superintendent
A member of an Annual Conference in the effective relation appointed by the bishop to travel through his district to preach and oversee the church's spiritual and temporal affairs.

Elder
A person who, having fulfilled the requirements, has been elected to the order of elder and been duly ordained by the laying on of the hands of a bishop and other elders. This is the second and highest ministerial order in the church.

Elder, local
A local preacher who has been ordained elder but is not a member of the traveling ministry.

Minister
A person who has been ordained by a bishop and, ordinarily, is a member on trial or in full connection in an Annual Conference. The term is also applied to licensed, or licensed and ordained, a person serving as pastors of charges.

Minister on trial
A person who, after meeting the conditions prescribed in the Discipline, has been received by vote of an Annual Conference as a probationary member of that body.

Minister in full connection
A person who, having satisfactorily completed all the Disciplinary requirements, including the probationary period, has been elected to full membership by an Annual Conference.

Order, ministerial

The office or status of a person in the Christian ministry. In the Methodist Church ministerial orders are of two classes: deacon's and elder's.

Preacher, local

A layman who has been granted a license to preach, according to the law of the church. He continues to be a layman and member of the local church from or through which he receives his license or its renewal.

Preacher, traveling

A minister who has been admitted on trial or into full connection in an Annual Conference and who is serving under appointment by a bishop.

Station Church

A single church served by a pastor (as opposed to a multiple-point charge, which has more than one church served by a single pastor).

Supply pastor

A local preacher or a member of an Annual Conference who is employed by a district superintendent during the conference year to serve as the pastor of a charge.

About the Author

Margaret Kutz is a native of Western Pennsylvania and a graduate of Clarion University. She and her husband moved to Virginia in 1972 when they were married. For several years she taught elementary school. In 1976 she graduated from Wesley Theological Seminary with a Masters of Divinity. During her thirty-nine years of service in the Virginia Conference of the United Methodist Church, she served as pastor of Round Hill in Loudoun County, Trinity in McLean, Sleepy Hollow and St. Luke's in Falls Church, Wellspring in Williamsburg, and Chester in Chesterfield County, retiring from there in 2013.

Upon retirement she traveled with a friend to South Sudan to start a secondary school. They left three months later with the seeds of a school planted. Today that school has over 500 students. You can learn more at www.abukloi.org

In retirement Marg has been called back into service as an interim pastor at three churches (and counting). She also works as a pastoral coach. In her spare time she enjoys reading, painting, yardwork, and hiking.

Marg is married to Bob Kutz and lives in Chester, VA. They have two children and four grandchildren.

If you gather a group to read and discuss the book and would like to include the author in the discussion, contact her through the website. She will be delighted to join in! www.neverthelessshepreached.net

Made in the USA
Middletown, DE
05 June 2021